The Old Kingdom Ardänia

Volume 1:
Vermillion Skies

By Preston Robison

Copyright © 2013 by Preston Robison
Cover art copyright © 2013 by Michael Robison

Bison Publishing

ISBN-13: 978-0615750828
ISBN-10: 0615750826

bisonpublishing@gmail.com

www.facebook.com/bisonpublishing

www.facebook.com/vermillionskies1

Table of Contents

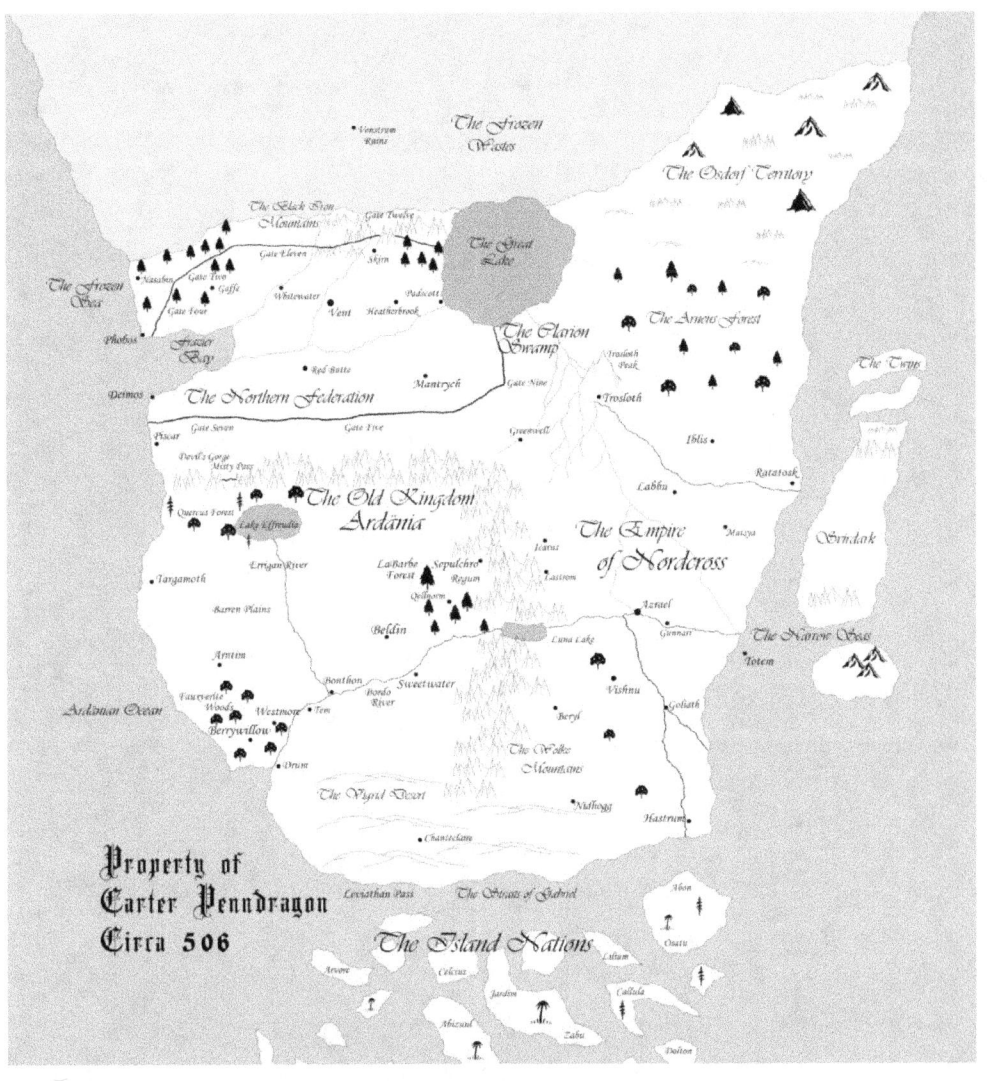

For more maps of Cygnus, visit Carter's Archives at
www.cartersarchives.tumblr.com

"Destiny is yours to control. Fate is not predetermined."

CHAPTER ONE: GENESIS

A young man emerged from the edge of a dark forest, his light skin covered in a veil of sweat and grime. In front of him, an immense expanse of tall grass stretched out into the darkness of the night. He looked to the sky and marveled at the myriad of stars spattered over the black backdrop.

He felt like he'd been running for days, but he couldn't remember why or where he was heading. He spared a quick glance over his shoulder and racked his brain, but he couldn't focus. Pulling his hand through his jet-black hair, he took a deep breath and let it out slowly. He tried to give himself a second to think, but everything was foggy, as if he'd been poisoned.

He looked over his shoulder again, sure that he was still being followed by something. All he saw was the wild underbrush of the forest…then something moved.

Without another thought, the young man bolted into the high grass, his slight frame easily weaving between the thick plants scattered throughout. Time and reason fell away as he focused only on his escape.

When the last of the grass gave way, the young man looked back to find that the forest had become little more than a small strip of dark green in the distance. He took a few timid steps, constantly scanning the wall of grass in front of him. There was a dreadful certainty in him that whatever was chasing him would break through the jade border at any moment, but nothing came.

As his mind calmed slightly, he smelled a familiar, grassy scent in the air and felt something slick underfoot. Thick moss covered the ground he walked on, and as his eyes searched, he came across roots buried under the soil. He followed them to a knoll, upon which a massive tree sat.

The fog blanketing his senses dissipated instantly, along with the rest of his fear, and he was immediately consumed by the tree's magnificence. His bright blue eyes traced the outline of the substantial trunk. Its bark was a deep maple color and had been gnarled with age, yet it was still untouched by moss.

The young man stared up into its infinite branches, each limb seeming to stretch on into the starry sky forever. He sat down under the comforting canopy of leaves as they danced in their flurry of countless hues of green and he leaned back on his palms.

He continued his gaze, attempting to make out the place where the leaves ended and the starry night sky began. In the distance, the three moons hovered just above the horizon—the smallest shone a deep maroon.

As he stared, he heard a soft, low hiss. A snake emerged only a few feet away from where he sat. Its thick, green and brown body blended in almost perfectly with the moss and the tree's many thick, tangled roots. If not for the noises, he would never have noticed it.

The serpent coiled its body in defense and the boy let out a small yelp. Two sleek heads stared back at him where there should only have been one. The young man sat, speechless and paralyzed, and his eyes never left the slithering fiend. The snake continued to stare at him with one head while the other searched for something.

He rubbed his hand across his chin, which was still smooth with youth—something his father had begun teasing him about since he'd turned fifteen the month before. As his father crossed his mind, he felt an urge to reach out and touch the serpent. Just as he shifted his weight, a small stone fell in front of him.

He quickly reached down to pick up the fallen rock and a dimpled smile spread across his face. He touched the pebble and rubbed his fingers over its smooth surface. Curious, the boy looked up, but whatever had dropped the stone was hidden by the leaves.

Another rock hit the ground with a tiny, muffled thump, this time closer to the snake, to which the limbless beast responded with a vicious hiss. A third stone fell, and as the young man watched it drop, he noticed a glimmer from a nearby gap in the bark of the ancient ash tree.

He stood and, hardly thinking, stepped over the forgotten snake and fallen pebbles to reach into the small hole. His hand found the small glittering item, its surface smooth and cool to the touch. He wrapped his fingers around the object and easily pried it from its hiding place.

When he opened his hand, a deep cerulean orb lay in his palm, and he marveled at his newfound treasure. The boy slowly turned the stone over, which glowed a dull purple as it reflected the light of the moons. He suddenly felt guilty for taking it and considered putting it back in the tree.

As he reached forward to act on his guilt, the thing began to vibrate and became uncomfortably warm. The young man reluctantly opened his hand, unsure what to do. Then a strangely familiar voice broke the silence.

"Meyral...the time is near. You are needed."

Meyral spun around, scanning the small hilltop, but he found nothing. He quickly brought his sights back to the branches of the tree, where he found a small, cinnamon-colored squirrel. The creature seemed oddly still, almost hypnotized, as it stared back at him. Relief washed over the young man as he gazed into the furry critter's black eyes. It was only then that he noticed a stone clutched in its tiny hands. His dimples returned as he smiled again.

The sounds of slithering and hissing returned, much louder than before, and the boy gripped the sapphire firmly. The stone continued to vibrate, but its solidity had a comforting effect.

He turned away from the squirrel and its tree, deciding he'd had enough. Halfway down the hill, a mind-shattering screech filled the air. The sapphire began to crack, sending out a thousand points of light that shone through the flesh of his hand. He tried desperately to drop the orb, but his body no longer responded to his commands.

His eyes watered and the sound became unbearable. He screamed as the sapphire shattered, tearing his hand to shreds and releasing a blinding light.

Then...

Nothing.

Meyral sat up, his eyes wide open as he gasped for air. His nose was filled with the same smell as before, but now he was surrounded by overgrown rosebushes. It took him a moment to realize that he was in front of his house.

How did I get here?

Gripped with a sudden dread, he looked down at his right hand, expecting to see a mass of torn flesh. Instead, soft, unbroken skin met his eyes, and he sighed with relief. He opened and closed his fist, just to make sure.

A dream?

He stood slowly and began to walk around his front yard. The sun was just setting behind the treetops, and he thought back to the moons from his dream.

It felt so real...

He turned to the small cottage that he'd spent his whole life in, becoming even more confused.

I don't remember going to sleep. And by the moons, why am I outside?

Meyral rubbed his hands over his face, trying to recall what he had been doing before the bizarre dream. The only thing that came to him was the sound of the babbling creek that ran behind Guillaume's mill. It would have been peaceful, if not for the cold fear that was slowly sinking into his stomach.

Why is it so quiet?

He raised his head over the thick, thorny border around his home. Beyond the rosebushes, the entire village, which had always felt alive even when the streets were empty, felt dark and deserted. The dirt road that made up the impossibly small town of Berrywillow was lined by modest wooden houses and a few storefronts that all looked like they'd been abandoned. A few doors stood ajar, and the only movement from the windows was the occasional wave of a curtain in the evening's breeze.

Meyral shook his head and let out a long yawn. He was more tired than he could remember and he quickly dismissed all thoughts of the village. He started to make his way back toward his house when a voice called to him. He froze, certain that it was the very same one from his dream. He was also certain that it came from inside his head.

"Meyral...the time is near. You are needed."

Then he felt something pulling him. He hesitated only a moment before giving in and following his impulse. He raced along a mossy path between his house and the Togrims' next door. The trail was overgrown with lilacs and blackberries, and the vines scraped at his face as he plowed haphazardly through them.

He stopped when he was standing in the thin stretch of clearing between the Fauxverite Woods and Berrywillow. In front of him was an ash tree that he couldn't remember seeing before, although it looked just like all the others that grew in that part of the forest. He had climbed them all often enough that he could recall every groove and curve of each branch with his eyes closed, but he couldn't remember anything about that particular ash.

Meyral could feel his heart beat faster and faster as he walked over and touched the rough bark of the trunk. Reality sank in—this was no dream. His palms began to sweat as he reached his hand into a hole, imagining for a split second that a snake was waiting for him inside. His surprise grew as he slowly wrapped his fingers around a long wooden pole.

An old walking staff emerged with a sapphire on its end—a brilliant blue orb with a strange warm glow. Aside from the carved symbols that ran down its shaft, the wood of the staff was smooth from years of handling. He examined the inscription, but it meant nothing to him. He spun the staff once and noticed that it was deceptively heavy, yet perfectly balanced. It felt oddly natural resting in his hands.

Aware that he was no longer alone, the young man whirled around to face the sound of approaching footsteps. Without thinking, he assumed the defensive stance that his father had taught him. The staff ran along his right arm, perpendicular to his body, and his left arm was raised in front as he waited for whatever was coming.

A man wearing a red leather breastplate burst into the clearing. His arms were muscular and his whole body was glistening with sweat.

"Thank the moons, Meyral, you're safe!" he exclaimed breathlessly as he slowed from a run to a walk.

The newcomer released his right hand, which had been gripping the thick hilt poking out from behind his shoulder. He ran his hands through his long, jet-black hair just as the young man had done moments before. Meyral relaxed his stance and lowered his weapon.

"Father, I'm fine," he said. "What's going on? Where is everyone?"

His father's face lost the look of relief and his eyes locked onto his son's newfound artifact. "Meyral…how did you find that?"

"I dreamt about it. And then I found it in there," Meyral answered as he pointed to the tree. It sounded like nonsense, even to him, but he always told the truth. His father demanded it. When his eyes returned to his father, he had resumed his air of rigor. "Did I do something wrong?"

He didn't answer. His eyes, which were the same shade of blue as Meyral's, never left the staff.

"What's happening?" Meyral tried changing the subject.

"We are being attacked," his father said slowly. "I told the villagers to flee north to Arntim. Hopefully it's still intact. Last I heard, it was one of the few places left in southern Ardänia that hasn't been demolished."

They had both seen the refugees from other towns trickling through Berrywillow recently. They came with stories of invading armies that pillaged nearby villages, and they sported the injuries to prove it. The rumors from the tavern were as varied as they were terrible, but they all agreed that the invaders were ruthless.

Father told me to prepare for the worst, but I never actually expected them to attack here.

His father's expression remained as unreadable as ever, while Meyral's betrayed a hint of fear.

"Are we the only ones left?" Meyral asked. "Aren't we going too?"

His father reached for his hilt again, his eyes still glued to the staff. Meyral had learned long ago that his father was most comfortable with a weapon in his hands.

He always knows what to do...why does Father seem so uncertain?

"What is this?" Meyral practically demanded, adjusting the staff and holding it out.

Meyral's father whispered to himself slowly and wiped a hand over his face. The spell seemed to break, and he finally looked at Meyral. He started to speak, but it sounded like he was waking up from a long dream.

"That is the last known remaining relic of the Old Kingdom. The Staff of Ardänia..." He paused, wondering how to continue. "Years ago, my grandfather used it to hold off the Tribes of the Monolith. It's supposed to hold enormous power."

"Is that why it was hidden?" he asked quickly.

His father looked past him, toward the ash tree, and he sighed. The look on his face was one he usually wore when Meyral would ask him too many questions about women.

"In time you will come to understand. Be wary of its power." Another pause. "There are people out there who would stop at nothing to possess it."

"What are you talking about?"

The man in front of Meyral closed his eyes and took a deep breath. "Son, I need you to do something for me. I want you to go to Mantrych, in the Northern Federation, and find someone by the name of Taryn. Can you do that?"

"Alone? Where will you be?" Meyral gripped the staff with fear.

6

"I'm staying behind. I have to make sure you make it out of here safely."

Meyral opened his mouth to argue, but his father's head snapped up. He seemed to be listening intently.

"I need you to leave now. I will send word when I make it to the North, and we'll meet up there. Now go!"

Meyral hesitated.

Father has never been wrong before, but this...this doesn't make any sense.

Meyral looked down at the staff, considering his next move, and a tree crashed to the ground in the distance. A flock of birds flew into the sky, sending a chill down his spine. His father pushed him forward, urging him to flee.

Meyral took a few steps before turning back. His father stared at the ash tree with his head still cocked to one side.

"Father...please, be careful."

The man turned and nodded to his son. "Go," he said. "I will send word."

After a moment's hesitation, Meyral slipped back between the houses, heading toward Berrywillow's main road.

Meyral quickly reached the shadows of the Fauxverite Woods on the opposite side of town. He ran around the outlying buildings to try to see his father one last time. In the village square, silhouetted against the light of the largest moon stood the man he'd looked up to his entire life, arrayed like one of the warriors of old he'd heard of in legends. Meyral stopped and glanced at the buildings beyond, somehow knowing for certain that he would never see them again.

He gasped as the bulking shadow of a man came into view only a few yards from him. He lugged a large sword behind him with both of his hands. Meyral turned back to warn his father, but he was already gone. The new man made no sound as he scanned the area methodically. Meyral ducked behind a fallen log to watch.

He was dressed in black from head to toe. The only part of his body that was exposed was his eyes. The man in black turned to where he was hiding and Meyral saw them—the man's eyes were solid black, and a ring of red encircled the enormous pupils.

Terror filled Meyral. He dipped down to hide himself completely, but as he reached his hand out, a twig snapped beneath him.

From a gap under the log, Meyral could see the man's dull black boots. He took a couple of silent steps toward Meyral's hiding place. Meyral's heart picked up its pace with each footfall and he turned away, his mind reaching full panic.

He looked to the woods for some semblance of an escape and he picked out a nearby tree to run to. As he readied himself to flee, he was stopped by a loud whistle that carried from the direction of his house, followed by a shout.

"I know you're out there!"

The large man was so close that Meyral could hear the low growl that escaped from his throat in response to his father's taunt. It was only after he heard the sound of the sword being dragged through the leaves that he dared to breathe, but he didn't move. He stayed behind the dead tree until the sound faded completely. After slowly raising his head to make sure he was alone, he bolted out from behind his cover.

He ran away from Berrywillow, away from his father, and away from that nightmare in black. Tears welled up in his blue eyes, but he didn't stop. He ran through the Fauxverite Woods, too terrified to look back. He ran until his lungs were burning and his breath came in ragged gasps.

Meyral slowed until he collapsed to his hands and knees, vomiting on the forest floor. While he caught his breath, fear transformed into panic. He had heard of Mantrych and knew it was somewhere in the Northern Federation, but he didn't know where or how to get there.

Then an idea struck him—there was a town to the northeast. It was a small hamlet of farmers where only a handful of families lived. There was a good chance that it hadn't been attacked yet. More than that, he had friends there. Friends who might be able to help him go north.

Meyral got back to his feet, stumbling as he tried to regain his balance. He put his hands on his knees and inhaled deeply, feeling determination swell inside of him. He looked ahead, straightened up, and ran on, ignoring the thick, black smoke that rose behind him.

CHAPTER TWO: DOXYLS

Eden could sense someone nearby. Her body was withered, but her mind was as sharp as it had ever been. She'd expected it for years, but she'd never told the kids. They wouldn't have believed her anyway.

A man clad in black armor silently opened her window and slipped in. The dark southern sky behind him transitioned to shades of emerald as the sun rose.

"I know what you want," she said.

The man held out his hand and stepped closer. She lay helplessly in bed as she watched sunlight glare off of the blade strapped along his forearm.

"It's not here," Eden said. "And I won't tell you where it is. Be sure to relay that back to whoever sent you."

He reached his arm out and held the blade against her neck. She looked up into his red and black eyes with as much malice as she could muster. He wasn't the first to try to find that staff.

Eden heard heavy footsteps coming down the hall. Her son was on his way to feed her breakfast, and all she could do was hope that the man would leave before Alberto found him.

* * *

Meyral's feet pounded the trail, his eyes red and swollen from tears and fatigue. He barely noticed that the dark and imposing forest had thinned, replaced by a weak, emerald canopy that matched the layers of varying green in the approaching dawn. He finally slowed to a stop, knowing that if he did he might not be able to start again. He stood for a moment in silence.

Meyral adjusted the staff from one hand to the other for seemingly the thousandth time and he took in his new surroundings. A thin mist blanketed the ground where about a hundred skinny trees poked through. He ran a hand through his hair and let out an exhausted sigh. Other than the unnatural sky, he recognized the lemon orchard in front of him. It had taken all night, but he had finally reached his destination—the hamlet of Westmore.

There was little chance of encountering someone there so early in the morning, but Meyral didn't want to risk it. The events of the previous night were still fresh in his mind, and he didn't have the nerve or strength to share them with strangers who would ask too many questions.

His father's words had been playing over and over in his head. Coupled with his odd dream and the memory of the monster with the giant sword, he had almost convinced himself that none of it had actually happened...that he hadn't truly left his father behind to fight an entire army alone. Then he looked down at the staff. It was his constant reminder that it had happened. All of it.

He retraced his steps into the woods and then circled around the orchards and small farmhouses. Soon he was at the eastern edge of the village, and in front of him, nestled between the last orchard and the village shrine, was the house he was looking for. It was little more than a stack of wood and small stones that looked like it might crumble in a strong wind, but in the early morning light, it was a sanctuary. Its lopsided walls were wrapped in ivy, and the tiny property was surrounded by the sweet smell of gardenias and juniper.

A lamp was already lit, casting the kitchen in a dim, orange glow. Through the window, Meyral could make out a woman with dark green hair and piercing lavender eyes standing by a stove, glaring at a pot of stew.

Across from the window was the arched doorway that led from the kitchen into the hallway, where the bedrooms were still shrouded in darkness. The interior looked as rundown as its exterior; there were no rugs on the worn hardwood floors, nor were there decorations on the cracked and flaking walls.

The woman had the look of a farmer who had fallen on hard times, not at all unusual in the southern parts of Ardänia. She wore a pair of black, faded shorts that Meyral knew had once been pants, and she wore a black blouse that, despite her thin frame, seemed too small for her. A thin ribbon of crimson was embroidered around the neck and sleeves in a complicated pattern of knots. It had been a gift from her mother, and she had maintained it meticulously.

Her hair was pulled back in its usual tight braid, and her face was set in its unbreakable frown. Meyral wouldn't call her unattractive, but he'd heard others talk about her at times. The other boys, along with some of the men, said that if she lightened up a bit, put on some makeup and showed a little skin like the other girls, she wouldn't be half bad. But in her worn, cotton apron, all she looked like to Meyral was someone's mother.

The thought made him grin. He knew Maxine fairly well, and she definitely wasn't one to wrap anybody in a tight hug or try to soothe them. She ran her home with all the care and emotion of an army general.

Meyral had heard whispers about how Maxine's father had abandoned his family when his children were barely old enough to understand why. While there were many theories about the reason for this, most people agreed that he had finally left to pursue his dream of becoming a master thief. To compound this misfortune, her mother fell ill when Maxine was thirteen, and she lost the ability to care for her children. Maxine was forced to take her place.

He didn't understand it at the time, but he had watched Maxine change from a young girl in pigtails to a woman capable of supporting a family over the course of a few months. It would have crushed most people, but Maxine soldiered on.

Meyral watched his friend as she continued to stir the stew. A single tear rolled down her small, pointed nose. For as long as Meyral could remember, Maxine had always been absurdly stiff and distant. She wouldn't giggle like the other girls when a boy walked by, wouldn't join in on conversations about clothes, and hardly ever smiled.

She never cries. What's going on?

Once Meyral had overheard someone tell his father that Maxine was "just hiding in her books, afraid to face the reality of the situation." It may have been true, but because of that there was no denying that Maxine was damned clever, and Meyral hoped that she would be able to help him.

He knocked tentatively on the window, hoping to get her attention, but not wanting to wake her mother. Alarmed, Maxine quickly turned around to find Meyral's bright blue eyes staring at her through the glass. She marched across the kitchen and threw open the back door.

"By the moons, Meyral, what are you doing out here? With all the recent raids you should be with your—have you been crying?" Maxine's anger dissipated instantly and she eyed the young man in front of her curiously.

"My village was invaded last night. My father stayed behind

but—"

"MEYRAL!"

Before either of them knew what was happening, Meyral was facedown on the dew-covered grass, the right side of his body feeling as though it'd been rammed by a buffalo. A man straddled his back and rubbed his head with a huge fist.

"Whoa, Alberto, c'mon! Get off, man!" Meyral said through a mouth full of grass.

He struggled to free himself from underneath Maxine's younger brother. Alberto was six years older than he was and twice his size in height and width, which rendered Meyral's struggles futile. Although they were so far apart in age, people said they had the same level of maturity.

"What? Oh, I get it," Alberto replied jokingly. His red hair stuck up in every direction like he'd just woken up. "You're here to sneak a little somethin' in with my sister, huh? Shame on you, Maxine, with our mom sick in bed like that! You could at least wait until she's had her stew. Not to mention the kid's barely half your age!"

Maxine acted as though she were at least ten years Alberto's senior, when in reality she was only two years older than her brother.

"Shove it, Bert," she said. "Let Meyral up before you smother him." Maxine crossed her arms and looked at her brother from the kitchen door, her eyes like daggers. She turned back to her stew, but she stopped when her gaze fell on the staff lying next to Meyral. "What is that?" Her eyes darkened slightly despite the rising sun as she pointed to the pole.

Alberto got off of Meyral and pulled him to his feet.

"Thanks, Bert," Meyral said ruefully as he picked up the staff. "I found it. Apparently it's some ancient relic or something," he explained as he brushed wet grass off the backs of his arms, "and it's been in my family for a while. I was trying to get more information about it from my dad, but…"

Meyral's eyes widened as he suddenly remembered why he had come.

"Maxine, my village was attacked! A-and my father told me to go to Mantrych, and I ran all night long and I…" He found it hard to think as the weight of the situation came crashing down on him. He stopped talking and closed his eyes. When he opened them, he continued more slowly. "I need to get to the Northern Federation, to a place called

Mantrych. I just thought that you two might be able to help."

Meyral looked up as Alberto and Maxine exchanged a nervous glance. He braced himself for the rejection that was more than evident on their faces.

"I know that if you're here without your dad, it must be serious," Maxine replied carefully.

"And as much as we want to help you, man, our mom..." Alberto added, but he couldn't find the words to finish.

"Bert," Maxine commanded coldly, "Take the stew to Mother. It's ready."

All humor left Alberto's face as he went into the house. Meyral followed close behind, almost hugging the staff as he went. When he entered the kitchen, Maxine took a deep breath and continued.

"Meyral, you know what it's like around here ever since our father..."

Maxine suddenly stopped. Meyral could feel the tension rising. He looked to Alberto, hoping he would tell a joke and make it all go away, but he had his back to them. The big redhead ladled the stew into a bowl and turned without looking up. He headed toward the bedrooms down the hall.

When he was out of sight, Maxine found her voice again. "Look, I'm sorry, Meyral. Ever since the raids started, Mother's condition has worsened. Now she can't even get out of bed without both of us helping her, so I can't even spare Alberto."

There was a short pause.

"I can tell you how to get where you're going though, and we might be able to get you a doxyl to take you up the river. Alberto made some extra money during the last harvest, so we might be able to spare you some coin. The moons know we owe your father at least that much. I really wish we could help more."

"Well, every little bit helps," Meyral said. He tried to sound upbeat.

Maxine's expression was impossible to read. "Meyral—"

A crash came from down the hall. They looked up as a man in black flew from the arched doorway into the den. He crashed into the far wall and came to rest upside down.

There was a sharp intake of air as Meyral realized that the man looked just like the one from the night before. The only difference he could see was that this one had strange blades strapped along his forearms instead of a sword.

Alberto barreled out of the hallway headfirst as the stranger gracefully launched himself off the ground. He spun in midair and delivered a kick to the side of Alberto's head that sent the big man skidding along the wooden floor toward the kitchen. Meyral dove out of the way and marveled at the power necessary to send a man Alberto's size flying like that.

"What's going on?" Maxine screamed as she rushed to her brother's side.

"I just found him in Mom's room! He slit her throat! I'll kill the bastard!" Alberto roared and jumped to his feet, huffing like an angry bull.

He rushed at the murderer, his face as red as his hair. He managed to duck under his enemy's slash and tackle him around the waist with surprising agility. As soon as they hit the ground, the intruder brought both legs up and launched Alberto into the ceiling. He came back to the floor with a loud grunt, bits of wood and plaster showering his back.

The man in black sprang to his feet, ready to strike again, and a small foot collided with his face. He spun around, seeming to forget the redhead lying on the floor in favor of his sister.

What Maxine lacked in size she made up for with speed. The killer slashed at her several times, but she was able to dodge them all and finally kick his legs out from under him. She delivered three more quick kicks to his face and stomach, causing blood to stain the black face-mask covering his mouth.

The man deflected Maxine's second round of kicks and spun on his back, using his legs to trip her. She landed hard, and he immediately climbed on top of her. He raised his arms and leveled his blades just above her neck.

Meyral watched all this while still standing in the kitchen. His father had trained them all in combat for as long as he could remember, but he had never actually been in a life-threatening situation before. He found himself paralyzed with fear.

Alberto regained consciousness and got to his feet. He grabbed his mother's killer by the neck and slammed him into the wall before he could decapitate Maxine. Alberto slammed him again and again, as if he were beating out a dusty rug. Finally he threw the man across the room and into the fireplace, showering the floor in bricks.

Alberto closed the distance between them quickly, eager to repay the demon that killed his mother and tried to kill his sister. The man leapt out of the small cloud of dust and slammed a fist into Alberto's stomach. He was about to slash Alberto's face when Maxine used a poker from the fireplace to bash him across his back.

The monster barely flinched, but he turned his attention away from her brother again, which was all Maxine wanted. She did three rapid back flips, narrowly avoiding the edges of the man's thick blades as he spun wildly. The distraction worked, and Alberto managed to drill his own fist into the dark man's ribs. The man in black flew headfirst into a corner, where a chunk of the wall collapsed.

Maxine held her brother back for a second, trying to contain his eagerness. The siblings slowly approached what looked like a pile of stones and rags. As Maxine bent over to check if he was dead, the killer sprang up from the rubble with a piece of broken timber. Using it like a club, he smacked Maxine and Alberto across their faces with a single swing. Alberto fell backward and Maxine was launched toward the demolished fireplace.

The man stood, dropped his makeshift club, and slowly turned toward Meyral. Those hideous black eyes with their rings of red were all Meyral could focus on as the murderer stepped over Alberto. Sure that he was watching his own death approach, Meyral braced himself for the inevitable, but it never came. Instead the man only held out his hand as he inched his way closer.

Why isn't he attacking me? What does he want?

Meyral's confusion cleared as he heard his dad's voice echoing in his head.

"There are people out there who would stop at nothing to possess it."

Something inside Meyral finally clicked and his paralysis broke. He swung the staff. The dark man dodged easily and slashed with his left forearm. Meyral anticipated it and went down to his knees. He used the momentum from his swing to spin as he dropped, and he hit the man in the ribs. Before he could recover, Meyral whipped the staff around, and it met the killer's hidden face with a soft crunch. He jabbed the staff deep into his attacker's gut, then used it to launch him into the air.

The man in black landed unceremoniously on a small table and broke it before rolling onto his stomach. Alberto lunged forward and stomped on the man's arms, embedding his deadly blades into the

15

wooden floor.

As he struggled to regain his freedom, Alberto reached down, put both hands on either side of the dark man's head, and then twisted. A loud crack echoed throughout the house.

Alberto slumped back so that he was sitting on the floor. He dropped his head between his legs. "Why…why Mom?" he cried. "Who the hell would want to murder a sick woman in her sleep?" He began simultaneously bawling and roaring, torn between rage and sorrow.

Maxine stumbled over, still feeling the effects of being clubbed in the face, and knelt down by the man's corpse.

Alberto cursed before getting up, still sobbing like a child. He made his way down the hallway toward his mother's room as a string of incoherent words left his mouth.

Maxine finished searching the dead man and pulled a bloody dagger out of the attacker's boot. Engraved in its hilt was a snapping turtle.

"The Nordcross Empire's insignia…? But what does Nordcross want with us?"

"There was one like him in my village before it was attacked," Meyral whispered as he stared at the body.

"By the moons!" Maxine drew a sharp breath. "They're probably scouts then. We need to leave now, before more come." Maxine looked up at Meyral, then back to the hallway. "Give me a second with Bert. We can't just leave like this."

Maxine headed down the hall after her brother, leaving Meyral alone with the dead man in the ruined den. He was terrified and fascinated at the same time, daring himself to look under the bloody rags that covered his face. Meyral's heart began hammering as he leaned over to pull at one of the strips of fabric. Something out of the corner of his eye grabbed his attention and his hand stopped. He looked up through a hole in the wall and saw smoke rising nearby.

They're not coming, they're already here!

Meyral sprinted down the hall to warn the others. He found Alberto cradling his mother's blood-soaked corpse in his arms, rocking back and forth. The big man was completely unaware that anyone else was in the room with him.

Maxine looked over at Meyral from her place by the window. She knew immediately that their time was running short. Without saying a word, she touched Alberto's cheek. He looked up, and a child's scared, green eyes met her gaze. He carefully laid his mother's lifeless body back down on the bed.

Alberto nodded and wiped his nose on his mother's blankets. Maxine cast a sideways glance at Meyral, and he got the hint. He left the siblings alone.

As he wandered down the hallway, he heard Maxine say something to Alberto in a hushed voice, and her little brother started bawling again.

She left the room with a sigh. "Meyral," she said as she stood nervously in the hallway, "we need oil from the kitchen and some flint."

"NO!" Alberto shouted from the bedroom. "No...we can't...it's not right!"

Maxine re-entered the room to console her brother, and Meyral finally understood. They didn't have time to properly bury the body, and they didn't want to just leave her. Their only option was to cremate her, right there in the bedroom.

* * *

The three of them watched the house as it burned, making quick work of a lifetime of memorabilia. Silent tears slid down both of the siblings' faces.

As the shouts of men and clanging of steel drew near, Maxine turned to her brother. "Bert, we have to go. There's nothing more we can do here." She spoke softly, trying to help him understand.

The wet trails that the liquid sorrow left on the big man's face shimmered bright orange by the firelight. Meyral waited anxiously in the shade of the Fauxverite Woods for the siblings, but Alberto refused to move.

In an act of desperation, Maxine slapped her brother in the face. "We will *all* die if we stay. Do you think Mom would want that?"

Alberto shook his head.

"Then we need to go now!"

Alberto tore himself away from the house and they ran into the woods, the embers from the house still burning. When the only sound they could hear was their own breathing, Maxine spoke again.

"We can take the Errigan River north." She saw the anxious look on Meyral's face and added, "We aren't swimming, don't worry. We'll be using doxyls for most of the trip."

17

Through the trees Meyral spotted a small trading post on the riverbank. As the trio emerged from the forest, Meyral's heart sank.

"No flag, and the doors to the storerooms are wide open," he announced solemnly. "There's no one here." Meyral imagined that the only way out of there was back the way they came or into the water, and he swam about as well as a rock.

"Those cowards just left without warning anyone!" Alberto yelled.

Maxine didn't break stride. "Look, there's still smoke coming from the chimneys," she muttered. "They must have left in a hurry. I'll bet they left something in the rush."

She threw back double doors, revealing what looked like a stable, then stood back with a sigh of relief. Of the half dozen stalls inside, the last few were occupied by four creatures that looked like hedgehogs with webbed feet.

"Doxyls," Maxine proclaimed, gesturing to the brightly colored beasts.

Every animal was a different fluorescent color and about the size of a pony. Alberto ran forward and pulled Maxine up into a hug.

"If you weren't my sister, I'd kiss you!" he joked.

"Put me down, Bert, we still need to get these guys harnessed so we can get out of here. Go find me a barge!"

Alberto put his sister down and ran toward the docks. Maxine quickly yet methodically attached harnesses and reins to the four animals. She threw the reins of one of the creatures to Meyral and nodded.

Outside, Alberto stood in the water up to his waist. He was steadying a flat, wide boat and grinning. Maxine led the doxyls to him and tied the harnesses to the barge.

"How are these little guys supposed to take us all the way up the river? I mean, Alberto is pretty heavy…" Meyral inquired skeptically as he inspected the spines on the back of the nearest doxyl.

"You'd be surprised at their speed, kiddo," Alberto explained. "And each one can typically tow somewhere between ten and twelve times its own weight. In the water, that is." He grunted as he helped his sister tie another one on. The sounds of snapping branches reached his ears and he glanced over his shoulder. "We need to speed this up, Sis," he added.

"Just one more second…" Maxine had her tongue out as she tied some sort of complicated knot. "Done!"

The three of them jumped onto the barge and Maxine snapped the reins. She yelled out a command, and immediately the doxyls dove underwater and began swimming. They accelerated more smoothly than Meyral expected, and before long they were speeding along the muddy banks of the Errigan River.

* * *

The panic subsided after a while, but despite Meyral losing whatever energy he'd had, he couldn't stop his mind from racing. When he realized he wouldn't be able to sleep, he resigned himself to staring at the shore as it sped by. Maxine kept herself busy by checking and rechecking the straps and knots, while her brother zoned out completely.

After a few hours of tedium, Meyral caught a glimpse of something strange in the distance. As they approached what Meyral first thought was a rock that had been mostly submerged in the river, he slowly realized that it was the top of a statue. Worn by years of weather and obscured by branches, he could just make out a man with his left arm holding a sword raised in victory.

"Guys, do you see this?" Meyral asked.

Alberto looked up and followed Meyral's line of sight. His frown disappeared and was replaced by an overly cheery smile. "What? You mean Good Ol' Pete?"

"This statue's got a name?"

"Sure!" The big man let out a hearty laugh. "That was made to pay homage to Prince Peter. He was a fierce warrior from the Dragon Age, the only one-armed knight in Ardänian history," he recited proudly.

Meyral stared openmouthed at his friend. Alberto's mood change seemed out of place given the circumstances, but it was the fact that Alberto knew anything about Ardänian history that really shocked him.

Maybe he knows something about the staff!

Maxine's raucous laughter interrupted Meyral's thoughts. "You've known Bert almost your whole life and you actually think he's some kind of closeted historian? You know, if both of you put your heads together, you would still be three sheep short of a flock!" She lowered her hands and let her awkward laughter fill the air.

"Hey! I know stuff!" Alberto replied defiantly. "Like all the Old Kingdom ruins that still stand along the river...I know where you can find it. Most of it, anyway."

"That's more than me," Meyral said. "I've never been this far north before. Maybe if you teach me we can keep our minds occupied so—" Meyral stopped midsentence and glanced at Alberto, sure that his friend would have reverted to his depressed state.

"Sure, you got it," Alberto answered happily. "It'd be a nice change to get my mind off Nordcross, those lemon-stealing whores!" Alberto shouted the last part so loudly that every bird for miles around took flight.

"And when he gets you lost, you have me," Maxine called from the front of the barge.

Alberto made a rude gesture at his sister's back. "So what do you wanna know, kiddo?"

CHAPTER THREE: TEM

Maxine sat at the back of the barge and watched as her brother and their young friend discussed the finer points of dressing a deer. It was her turn to nap, but her mind wouldn't stop whirling.

My father is gone, my mother is dead, and I was forced to burn my whole world to the ground.

They emerged from the woods just as the light from the setting sun reflected off the water, momentarily stabbing into her unadjusted eyes.

This is all I have left in this world...and a task.

Maxine loved a good task. She loved anything that kept her mind busy. A complicated journey to a place she had never been before...that was perfect by her standards.

She put her feelings aside as she filled her mind with all the facts she knew about the various towns along the Errigan River. As she named them one by one in her head, along with their respective distances from one another, one of the doxyls surfaced and made a low, mournful honk.

"Maxi, we need to give these guys a rest!" Alberto yelled over his shoulder. "We've been going at it for two days straight now!"

"I guess you're right," she muttered as she scanned the shoreline. "We should have put enough distance between us and them by now."

Alberto steered the barge onto a sandy beach and Maxine quickly jumped out. After tying their raft to a large stump, she started releasing the harnesses around the doxyls. Meyral stared at her apprehensively.

"Don't worry. They're well trained, they'll come back in the morning," she said matter-of-factly. "Now, let's set up camp."

"What camp?" her oaf of a brother whined. "We didn't pack anything other than a couple of loaves of bread, my hunting knife, his staff, and this fishing pole I took from the trading post." Alberto held up a long cane pole to emphasize his point.

Meyral rounded on the redhead. "You stole!?"

Maxine was amazed that it wasn't her scolding Alberto for once.

"Is that a problem?" Alberto waited for the punch line, but

Maxine knew that Meyral was outraged. The big man finally caught on and rolled his eyes. "What did we just sail on? A stolen barge pulled by four stolen doxyls! Would you rather have been killed by Nordcross?"

"Dad always said that there's no excuse for taking what's not yours," Meyral muttered sadly, his eyes fixed on a rock under his foot.

"With all due respect for the dead, your daddy isn't here!" Alberto shouted.

He may have been her brother, but for some reason he never learned to think before he spoke. Maxine rubbed a hand over her face and intervened. "Boys, stop it!"

Alberto had told her a thousand times that the looks she gave him sometimes seemed like they could melt stone, and she knew that was exactly the look she was giving. Little did he know, saying that only encouraged her to use them more.

"Alberto, that was a low blow and you know it," she continued. "Why do you always have to be such a dolt?"

Alberto kicked a rock and cursed under his breath. He looked back at Meyral, who had tears in his eyes. "Look, man…I didn't mean it. I'm sorry."

Meyral nodded and wiped his nose on his sleeve before responding quietly, "Just no more stealing, okay?"

"Deal. Now get over here and let's see if we can catch something."

Maxine nodded to herself as the two boys ran off into the shallows, giggling and splashing one another.

Life is a just a series of tasks…nothing more.

* * *

The three companions found themselves sitting in the cold and dark that night.

"This mushroom is delicious, Maxine," Alberto muttered.

"Oh, is it my fault neither of you managed to catch a single fish?" she asked with her usual air of superiority as she finished chewing.

"What good would catching anything be if we can't even build a fire and cook it?" he grumbled.

"Do you want Nordcross and everything else out there to know where we are?" his sister shot back. "You might as well sound the horns and play some drums."

"Maybe I would if you hadn't broken my trumpet four summers ago!" Alberto dropped a half-eaten mushroom and threw his hands in the air.

"You know that was an accident," Maxine said as she rolled her eyes.

Meyral had stopped paying attention to the siblings. He knew that this row, like all the others, would quickly devolve into a history of old offenses and name calling, and then finally culminate in several hours of silence.

While the quarrel continued, he ran his fingers along the inscription on the staff, wondering what the symbols could mean. His gaze rose to the top of the weapon, where it looked like the wood had naturally ensnared the fist-sized sapphire. He couldn't help but wonder in that moment how something so valuable could wind up hidden away in a place so remote and ordinary.

What made Berrywillow so special? Why was the Staff of Ardänia hidden in a tree in my own backyard? Was my father supposed to be guarding it? That almost makes sense, but he looked as surprised to see it as I was. Maybe someone else put it there, to hide it. And maybe I was meant to find it...

Meyral looked down and realized he was holding the staff so tightly that his knuckles had turned white.

That's ridiculous. But...I don't want it. So far it's been nothing but trouble. In less than three days, everything that I've ever known has been taken away. This whole thing is just unfair! I can't even blame anyone...except maybe myself...

"...coming up on a town in the next couple days anyway, so quit whining!"

Meyral's head snapped up at the mention of the word "town." Maxine crossed her arms as if the issue had been settled.

"Well, hopefully we can pick up some supplies there," Alberto grumbled. "I need meat. I can't live on mushrooms alone, ya know?"

"No fires, Bert! I keep trying to tell you, if Nordcross continues on the path they were going, they'll be heading this way as well. I just don't know if they've gotten this far yet."

"Oh, you think they're takin' their time then? Just out for a stroll?" Alberto snapped sarcastically. "Of course they've made it out here. Shit, they're probably just on the other side of the river, hiding in the shadows. And they've probably destroyed everything over there, too."

"Which is why we can't risk a fire!"

Alberto began grinding his teeth and closed his eyes for a moment. "You're always twisting my words and using them against me. I only want a small fire so we can cook."

"But you didn't catch any fish, so why…"

The argument started all over again. Meyral laid his head back and shut his eyes. He began to fall asleep amidst their bickering, and a small smile spread across his face. He'd never had a family, other than his father.

It's kind of nice to see what it would have been like…

* * *

"…I'm starvin'. What's for dinner, woman?"

It had been almost a whole day since Alberto had last spoken to his sister.

"Get it yourself, pig."

Alberto shrugged and rolled over onto his stomach. He poked his head over the side of the barge, watching the river glide by. In an instant his hand flashed in and out of the water, and a massive fish wriggled in his fist. Alberto flipped over onto his back, laughing for the first time since they had left Westmore.

"I always loved fishing!" he said loudly to himself. "Want some, Meyral? They're delicious raw!"

"Uh…no thanks. I'll stick with cooked food." Meyral cautiously pulled what was left of a loaf of bread from Maxine's small pack.

"How's about you Maxi, ya want some? I'll share, even if you're mean and don't cook for me."

"Shut up, Bert," she answered. "You know I don't eat meat. Besides, raw fish will make you sick, dummy." Maxine glared at Alberto, but he was too busy smashing the fish against the side of the barge to notice.

"Whatever, that just leaves more for me," her brother said with a grin.

Meyral took a bite of the bread. He chewed it slowly while he watched Alberto. "If you can do that, then why'd you need to steal the fishing pole from the trading post?" he asked with a mouthful of bread.

Alberto cursed loudly. "I thought we were past that!"

"I don't care about the stupid pole anymore. I was just wondering why we need it if you can catch fish with your bare hands."

"These are Ardänian Trout," the big man explained. "They're slow and stupid. But they're also delicious!"

He looked down at the fish lying in his hands and grinned. He raised the trout up to his mouth, took three large bites out of its stomach, then threw it overboard.

"There's no way...of knowing...what fish we might find...further north," Alberto continued, his mouth full of fish. "I plan on eating the entire way." He swallowed noisily and then nodded toward Maxine. "Of course, that's if someone will let us."

Maxine didn't react. She either didn't hear or didn't care.

Alberto turned back to Meyral. "You know, if you wanna grow up to be big and strong, like me, raw meat's the best way. Or eggs. When I was your age, I used to eat three raw eggs a morning, and look at me now!" the big man said as he flexed his muscles.

Meyral's face paled as he ran to the other side of the barge. He leaned over, and the piece of bread he'd just eaten came right back up and landed in the river.

"Huh, guess he couldn't handle my manliness." Alberto scratched his head.

"By the moons, Bert. You're as insensitive as you are stupid!" Although she sounded serious, a small smirk found its way to the corners of Maxine's mouth.

"At least I'm not some frail-ass veggie-terrarium like you!"

"It's pronounced 'vegetarian,' and you could at least cook the damned thing. You have no common sense, and now the kid's gonna be sick the rest of the trip..."

"Alright, alright, I'm sorry. Relax. You're always so uptight." Alberto propped himself up onto his elbows and bent his head back, looking at Meyral upside down. "You alright, kid? I didn't mean to gross you out."

Meyral gave a weak nod, but his face was still slightly green. "Sorry guys, I've never been on a boat before. I guess my stomach just isn't used to it," he apologized as he lay back down in between the two siblings.

"You know, you still haven't been on a real boat." Alberto pointed a finger at Meyral. "'Cause this giant piece o' crap is just a barge." He let out another hearty laugh.

Meyral couldn't help but smile. His happiness faded quickly as he looked up at the sky, which shone a ghastly emerald color.

"Hey, guys, do you have any idea why the sky changed? It makes me feel kind of...uneasy." Meyral thought back to the day that the sky turned green. It had once been a deep crimson, but a couple months earlier the heavens changed color.

"No idea," Alberto said, "but not long after the switch was when Mom got really sick." He stared into the river for a moment. "I guess she's in a better place now. I mean, that's what you always hear people say, right?"

Meyral looked at the big guy, trying to see what emotions he was putting out.

"They're in a better place now, sonny." Alberto wagged his finger and tried to mimic an old woman's voice.

Alberto had always had a knack for staying happy and never letting his troubles get to him, so long as those problems didn't deal with his stomach. Even in the worst of situations, the big man would always tell a joke and move on like nothing was wrong. Up until that moment, Meyral had always envied him, but now he understood that he was only avoiding reality, just like his sister. They were both masters at sweeping it under the rug. He wondered what would happen when it all became too much to bottle up.

"The news that Nordcross had begun invading Ardänia spread like wildfire around the same time," Alberto continued. "Do you think it's just a coincidence? Maybe those Nordcross bastards started using magic."

"Bert, that's ridiculous," Maxine interrupted. "Magic hasn't been used for centuries, since the Old Kingdom collapsed. Not to mention it'd be crazy to think that any magic would be powerful enough to alter something like the sky itself. If anything, it's the way the sunlight is hitting the atmosphere. Maybe Cygnus' orbit shifted slightly, or it's some sort of gaseous—"

"Aw jeez, Maxi, cut it out! You're makin' my head hurt! Why do you always have to act all smart?"

"I'm not acting, I'm just naturally curious about the world. It's not my fault I wasn't born half brain dead like you!"

Maxine tossed a piece of bread at Alberto, which he caught in his mouth. He chewed a few times and stuck out his tongue, showing his sister the half-eaten food. Meyral leaned over the side of the boat and retched for the second time.

Alberto swallowed and gave his sister a sheepish grin. "Sorry…again."

* * *

Meyral awoke from his nap and realized that they had stopped again. The barge was tied to a rock by a long bend in the river. He looked up at a pleasant meadow as he smelled something tangy in the air. Plants he had never seen before had settled between mounds of teal grass. Golden flowers with blossoms the size of his head mesmerized him as he stared.

The sun was setting behind the Wolke Mountains in the north, and the sky was splashed with bands of green and orange. Light, puffy clouds floated overhead, absorbing the colors and giving the landscape a dimmed and relaxing glow.

In the cattails along the riverbank, butterflies danced and dragonflies darted between the green blades. Meyral saw something like a cat, only instead of fur, its body was covered in black and white scales. It poked its head out of the marshes and shot out a long tongue. It caught a fat dragonfly and pulled it back to its mouth, where the bug made an audible pop as the creature crunched down on it. It swallowed and disappeared into the water as Meyral remembered Maxine telling him those were called scalekats.

It was almost as if he'd awoken in a new world, one devoid of fear.

"Wakey wakey, Meyral!" Alberto waved to him happily from a small campfire.

"Why did we stop?" Meyral asked groggily as he approached the warm glow of the flames.

Fat, black moths flitted around the fire. They danced with the tongues of the inferno in a deadly waltz that would only end in their delicate wings being scorched, sending them helplessly to the ground.

"Well, big smarty smart, Sis here thought it wouldn't be a good idea to enter Tem at night. But I did talk her into letting me start a fire."

"As long as you put it out before it gets too dark," Maxine added.

"Enter where?" Meyral asked as he used the staff to bat away a few moths.

"Sorry, kiddo, I forgot you don't know where you are. Just up the river about twenty minutes is the town of Tem. And as I was just saying, if it's still standing can we please, by the moons, stop to eat?" Alberto pouted. "I haven't had beef in almost a week...it's unhuman!"

"You mean inhumane," Maxine mumbled.

"Why don't we just catch a scalekat and eat that?" Meyral asked.

Alberto looked at him and laughed. "Even if we managed to catch one of those wily little critters, there'd barely be enough meat to feed a little kid. There's a reason nobody hunts them."

"Anyway, like I told you," Maxine said as she handed Meyral a plate of delicious-looking fruit, "there is plenty to eat here, and we have practically no gold."

"We had enough gold to buy you new shoes last winter!" Alberto exclaimed.

"That was last winter."

"What about the extra gold I made last harvest? I worked my ass off for that!"

"We need to make that last until we find Mantrych...in the North. It's a long journey!"

"It's my coin, don't I get a say in how it's spent?"

The two siblings started to squabble as Meyral bit into some sort of apple. He tried to distract himself by examining the strange, spiraling trees that grew where they sat. It was only a few seconds before he noticed something that made his heart sink.

He looked back at Maxine standing over her brother, pointing at him threateningly and saying, "...which is why they always called you 'Stubby!'"

"Guys...hey, guys!" Meyral shouted as he scrambled to his feet, spilling his fruit onto the ground.

"What!" they yelled in unison.

"There's smoke up ahead!" Meyral cried as he pointed at the thin, dark cloud obscuring the rising moons.

The other two looked at each other before they started laughing.

"Why are you laughing?" Meyral asked, a little disturbed.

"Tem is one of the oldest villages in the nation," Maxine explained. "It dates back to before the kingdom crumbled..."

"...and it's best known for its smoked fish!" Alberto finished. The redhead stood and did a small jig, saliva nearly pouring down his chin. "Maxi, please, I need meat, we have to stop."

"Fine, but only for food and supplies. Like I said, Tem is one of the oldest villages, so it's only natural that it would be home to the oldest profession, too. I'm not letting you two wander around on your own. Your father would kill me," she pointed to Meyral, "and then I'd gut *you!*" she added, redirecting her venom at Alberto.

The big man smiled shamelessly and dropped back onto his makeshift bed of grass, but Meyral didn't budge. He didn't understand what she meant.

"Really? Nothing? How can you be so…dense?" Maxine asked.

The look of surprise on his sister's face was so honest that Alberto roared with laughter. "She means whores!" Alberto shouted. "You know, harlots? Strumpets? Skanks, skags, ladies of the night? Chicks that do stuff, like sex stuff, for gold."

Meyral's face flushed a deep red, perfectly matching Alberto's hair. "People do that? …Maxine?" he stammered.

"Some do," she said. "Go to sleep. Forget I mentioned it." She scowled as Alberto continued to laugh.

* * *

When Meyral woke the next morning, Maxine and Alberto were already in bad moods.

"Now what's wrong with you two?" he asked grudgingly, annoyed by their constant mood swings.

"Look," Alberto said quietly, pointing at the clear morning sky.

"I don't see anything," Meyral responded with a sigh.

"Exactly," Maxine said as she hooked the doxyls up to the barge. "You don't see the blue smoke that always hangs around Tem."

As they rounded the last bend in the river, their fears became a reality. All that was left of the docks of Tem were a few charred pieces of timber sticking out of the water. Maxine tugged gently on the reins, slowing the doxyls to a crawl. Her brother stifled a slew of curses with the back of his hand.

Meyral stared sadly at the burnt remains of one of the oldest cities in Ardänia. Every building, even the temples, had been burnt to the ground. What wasn't charred black was stained maroon with dried blood.

"Is this what they've done to every village?" Meyral asked

timidly.

"Yea," Alberto answered. "I heard some traders talking about it when they came through Westmore, back when there was a Westmore. Guess their motto is 'Leave nothing in our wake.' I doubt there'll be anything left of Ardänia before yearend." He sat back down and stared at the barge, once again slipping into a troubled silence.

Meyral looked back at Maxine, whose face seemed to have lost all of its color. Her eyes were transfixed on something in the dark water. Meyral leaned over the edge to see what she was staring at.

Floating along with them, just beneath the surface, were hundreds of bloated, mutilated bodies. The trio's eyes finally lit on the severed limbs that littered the shores. For the third time, Meyral's stomach emptied itself into the river.

"They probably didn't even make sure they were dead before they tossed them in," Alberto muttered with a disgusted look on his face.

"Not a single Nordcross soldier is in here, either," Maxine said with a shaky sigh. "You'd think Tem would have fought back."

Meyral wiped his mouth, took a deep breath and steadied himself. He could hear his father in the back of his mind, telling him to face reality.

Maxine finally tugged on the reins and the raft started to pick up speed. "No reason to stay any longer than we have to. There's nothing left here," she stated coldly.

Is this what happened to my village? By the moons, what about Father?

"Where do you think they headed from here?" Alberto asked his sister.

"They'll probably head to Bonthon next. Then they could head east toward Qellnorm or west to the port of Targamoth. Either way, they'll keep heading north, but they'll stop before they reach the Northern Federation."

"Well, at least they won't attack Mantrych then. Father said it should be safe there." Meyral's own words should have comforted him, but for some reason he felt a trace of unease wind its way into his chest. He pulled the staff closer to his body.

"If they're only conquering Ardänia," Maxine continued, "the North will be safe. We have to make it to the border."

"By the moons, Maxi, do you analyze everything?" her brother whined.

"Would you rather I was more like you? You know…an imbecile?"

"You think too much, that's why…" Alberto started to squabble with his sister again.

As they passed the last of the decimated docks, Meyral's eyes flashed bright blue and he fell onto his back.

Where…where am I? …By the moons, I'm on the docks we just passed!

Except the docks he was standing on were no longer charred. They were practically brand new—moss hadn't even started to grow on them yet. He gasped out loud as he turned around and saw several large riverboats unloading their cargo. Men with wagons and buffalo hauled the goods away.

"Excuse me! Hey! You! Hello?" he shouted as he made his way through crowds of oblivious men and women.

Nobody seemed to notice he was even there. Meyral gave up on the dockworkers and turned to walk away. He stopped when he saw that, standing in front of him, untouched by war and bustling with people, was Tem.

Meyral gazed in wonder at the brick buildings draped in red-and-black banners. Each structure billowed blue smoke from their myriad of chimneys. He smelled the sweet aromas of smoked fish in the air, and he heard the muted rumbling of the fisheries that made it all happen.

How in the world…?

He reached a set of stairs leading to the top of the dyke that separated the city from the unpredictable waters of the Errigan. He reached out to grab one of the guard rails when he noticed that his hands were nothing more than a transparent kind of mist. His hands trailed down his body, but he couldn't feel himself.

What happened to me? Am I dead? I must have fallen in the river or something, and now I'm a ghost. Am I the only one? Where's Alberto? Maxine?

Meyral turned back to the shore to look for his friends, but he felt a strange pulling sensation, as if someone had attached a rope to his gut and was reeling him in toward the sky. He didn't even try to fight it. Before long, he was floating over the city toward some unknown destination.

The force pulled him until he was in front of a clock tower.

Below him he could see the entirety of Tem. The buildings were packed close together, each with a vaulted slate roof. Speckled around town were a few towers, like the one he was hovering by, that shot into the sky.

The blue smog from the smokehouses hung around in the alleys and backstreets, leaving the center of Tem free of smoke. This allowed Meyral to see the crowds of colorful people that bustled to and fro in the city.

Tem was one of the most spectacular things Meyral had ever seen, and he wanted desperately to get a closer look. No sooner had the thought occurred to him than he dropped from the tower back to the streets below. Colorful silks hung between two ornate buildings across the way, drawing Meyral's attention. Without hesitating, he went to investigate.

He slipped into the alleyway, and with every step he took he was drawn further into a different world. The smell of smoked fish was replaced by exotic fragrances and incense. The air itself seemed to taste something like honey. The colors and sounds all reminded Meyral of when his town had had its centennial celebration.

Something very important must be happening down here. Maybe...

A flash of green hair drew his attention to an open doorway on his left. Hoping that he had just found Maxine, he made his way toward the dimly lit shop. He found the woman standing just inside, but he noticed that her hair was too dark to be Maxine's. He continued to follow her anyway.

Meyral stepped out of a small hall and into a bright room. He let out an inaudible gasp. He stood in the middle of a large atrium, with mosaic-tiled floors and stained-glass windows set into the ceiling high above. There was a large mezzanine that encircled most of the room, and in the center was a circular bar where a large, middle-aged woman was selling drinks.

Everywhere he looked, women were either lounging or dancing in see-through robes and lacy garments. Some sat at the bar, but most lazily reclined on large cushions and smoked from elaborate pipes.

As he continued to watch, he saw a few men sitting among the women. Most were fat, ugly, hairy, or a disturbing mixture of the three...yet the girls were feeding them grapes and massaging their pasty backs.

These women must be blind!

One busy woman, whose silver eyes matched her hair, wore a pink, lacy robe. She led a young man with a boil problem toward a door of beads, behind which was a staircase leading to the upper level. When she pulled the beaded curtain back, she moved aside to let another woman exit the stairwell.

Meyral blushed full scarlet and looked away. The new girl was completely naked, and Meyral had been taught to look away if he came across a woman in that state. His adolescent curiosity got the better of him, though, and he risked a few glances before he remembered that he was a ghost. Then he gawked.

The woman looked different from anyone Meyral had met before. Her skin was tan with a hint of gold, and her eyelids were slanted, making it appear that she was walking around half asleep. There was a small birthmark near her navel that looked something like a star. She walked by Meyral, and he could see that her body was covered in sweat.

Her hair was silky black and, though she had it up in a braid that was frazzled and mostly undone, it still reached the top of her butt. The same butt that Meyral continued to watch as the woman walked toward the bar.

The large woman from behind the bar, who looked much more along the lines of what Meyral was accustomed to seeing, held out her hand. The older lady seemed jolly, and she had a cluster of rings on each of her fingers. She had a wispy bit of vibrant magenta hair on top of her head and she wore entirely too much makeup. Meyral snickered as he compared her to a clown he once saw at a gypsy carnival.

Whoever she was, she had to have been important, because the nude woman gave her a small bow before passing her a mound of gold. The lady split it into two piles and handed the smaller one back, along with a towel.

Realization finally dawned on him and he understood.

The oldest profession! So this is what they meant...

There was a violent pull from the invisible rope, and for an instant Meyral thought Maxine had caught him. Whatever force was driving him, it wanted him in the town square.

He followed the sensation and left back through the alleyway, but as soon as he reached the streets, he began to wander again. The first thing he came across was a cart run by a stringy-looking man who was shouting and holding up various items. He claimed to have furs and incense all the way from the Frozen Wastes, but nobody paid him much attention.

Another cart rolled by, led by an elderly woman who was selling vegetables. On the street corners, hairy men stood and shouted nonsense about damnation and salvation. Jugglers and bards wandered aimlessly, hoping for tips.

As Meyral marveled at the center of Tem, everything came to a halt. A hush came over the crowd and everyone knelt down. Excited whispers began as a large man walked through the center of the mass of people. Two small girls walked in his shadow, closely followed by two women. A little farther back, a handsome man finished what Meyral thought was a strange parade.

Meyral walked to the front of the crowd to get a better look. Normally he wouldn't do something so rude, but in his current ghostly state, he didn't care so much.

The man at the head of the procession wore a suit of black silk and a large, scarlet cape that flowed from his shoulders to his feet. On his head sat a simple crown of silver with five points; four were tipped with rubies, but the center prong was slightly taller and had a sapphire resting in it. From under this crown, thick, crimson hair flowed until it sat on the man's shoulders. He stopped in front of the clock tower, and he looked out at the adoring crowd with eyes that sparkled bright yellow.

Where have I seen him before? Wait...that's King Thessius! There was a portrait of him in Berrywillow's town hall. But he's been dead for centuries, since before the Old Kingdom collapsed.

Thessius lifted his right hand, and all the quiet whispering immediately stopped. Silence closed in on them as the other five people joined the king.

"As many of you know," Thessius' booming voice echoed throughout the streets with such authority that even Meyral felt compelled to pay attention, "seven years ago today, my brother's wife gave birth to the young lady that is to be your countess. Three days later, my wife also gave birth, to the girl who is to become your queen."

The girls that had been following the king stepped forward on either side of him. They were very young, and both had their bright blonde hair tied back in braids that trailed down their backs. On top of their heads sat circlets of flowers that matched their identical purple dresses. Meyral thought they each bore a striking resemblance to the king.

"Today, I bring these lovely girls out into this market to introduce them. My people, this beautiful young lady is my daughter, your future queen, Marie!"

Motioning to the girl on his left, he and the crowd began to clap. She curtsied before them as she blushed, clearly uncomfortable in such a public setting.

The king motioned to the girl on his right. "This is my brother Theron's daughter, Marguerite."

Meyral noticed a slight darkness come over the king's eyes, but it dissipated before he could give it any thought.

"I hope that as Marie's cousin, she will one day become not only a beloved countess, but a trusted friend and a worthy advisor to the throne."

The crowd clapped and cheered again and Marguerite curtsied. She was wearing an ear-to-ear grin, basking in the admiration.

"My king, where is Lord Theron?" a woman in the crowd shouted out.

"He sends his apologies, for he is currently bedridden with a slight fever. We expect him to make a full recovery and live many more good years."

Marguerite's grin vanished as quickly as it had appeared, replaced by a scowl.

"For the first time in Ardänian history," the king continued, "the descendants of the moons have bred with humans. My brother and I have fallen in love with women who, although they are extraordinary in every quality that a true lady should possess, are as normal as any one of you good citizens of Tem."

The king motioned, and the two women took their places next to their daughters. Both women were beautiful and well dressed. The one who Meyral assumed was the queen wore a tight, red corset that topped a billowing gown. Her hair was the color of corn silk, and her deep, scarlet eyes were set in a face that was perfectly round. She was pleasant to look at, and Meyral immediately got a rather motherly vibe from her.

He thought the woman on the king's other side was much prettier. She was shorter than the queen, but she had a much larger bust that was barely contained by her corset. Her hair was blonde as well, but lighter, more like the countess'. Her features were sharp and her eyes sparkled like emeralds.

"Our offspring are now the physical embodiment of the bridge that will forever span the gap between your world and that of my bloodline." Thessius pointed to the sky and the town raised their arms in unison.

"Klyntar, smallest of the moons, bless Ardänia!" the king shouted.

"Klyntar, smallest of the moons, bless Ardänia!" the crowd repeated.

As the royal family turned to make their exit, Meyral noticed that the other man hadn't been introduced. Most of him was obscured by a long, brown cloak that seemed so dull in comparison to his companions' eccentric outfits. He glanced over his shoulder at Meyral, something no one up to that point had done.

The strange man turned around and grinned, never breaking eye contact. His face was tan and smooth, and his honey-brown eyes were framed by a curtain of curly hair the color of maple. He wore a thin goatee and his wide smile was flawless.

"Hurry up, Shraka, or we'll leave you behind," the king called to the cloaked man.

"Yes, Your Highness, on my way," the man replied suavely. "Just lost myself in thought for a moment." His grin widened as he continued to stare at where Meyral's transparent body was. He finally spun around and walked away, leaning slightly on a long walking stick.

Meyral stepped forward in hopes of following the cloaked man, but his way was blocked by a large man in a bloody smock. Soon the town became too crowded to navigate through. Men, women, children, butchers, preachers, jugglers, and even the whores were filling his vision.

He lost track of the royal entourage as the new world began to spin. Everything became blurred until there were no longer people, only shapes and colors. Again a mind-shattering screech filled the air, until Meyral could no longer bear it.

His eyes opened as Alberto slapped him across the face.

"What was that for?" Meyral said as he rubbed his cheek.

Alberto allowed his friend to slowly push himself off of the floor of the barge. Meyral looked up as both siblings eyed him strangely.

"You passed out for a second and we didn't know what

happened. I was a little worried." Alberto scratched the back of his head.

"Only a second? It felt like hours!"

"What felt like hours?" Maxine's head tilted as she looked into his eyes.

Meyral reflected on what he saw and decided, for the moment, to keep it to himself. He didn't want them to start worrying about his sanity, because he was already doing that enough for all of them.

"Just a weird dream," he answered. "Haven't really gotten my water legs, right?" He chuckled feebly, but Maxine didn't look convinced.

"Give it a while, buddy, you'll be fine. Maxi, let's get on outta here already. I feel like if we stay too long those corpses are gonna come to life or something. Gives me the creeps!"

Maxine snapped the reins and they sped away. Meyral looked back and, for the briefest of moments, the burnt and desolate town was beautiful once again.

CHAPTER FOUR: BONTHON

"Did you say something, Meyral?" Alberto asked.

They had been on the barge for four days straight without any stops. Maxine had devised a plan where only two doxyls pulled at any time while the others rested. She and Alberto steered the barge in shifts and Meyral felt like deadweight.

"Me...? No." Meyral crawled to Alberto and sat next to him. "How are the doxyls holding up?"

"They're not happy, but they'll survive. I just hope we make it to Bonthon before Nordcross does or...well..."

"What about you?" Meyral interrupted.

"As long as we make it by dinner, I'm gonna be happier than a pig rollin' in shit!"

"Is it true that Bonthon is the capital? I heard some old-timers talking about it a while back..."

Alberto scoffed at Meyral's question. "Man, you *are* green. A capital implies that there's a government, but all we have is a few people from each town calling themselves councilmen."

Meyral shook his head with a confused look on his face.

"Basically, it's a bunch of people who have nothing better to do than stick their noses into other people's business, and...you know what? We don't have a real capital, let's put it that way."

"Would these representatives be able to help fight Nordcross?" A spark of hope ignited in Meyral's chest.

"Jeez kid, you're gonna make me spell it out? Okay, here's the issue. Ardänia doesn't have an army. I mean, did you ever see a soldier in your village? 'Cause I never saw one in mine! That means that outside each representative's little circle of power, nobody gives two squirts about what they have to say."

Alberto reached a cupped hand into the water and drank from his palm.

"And vice versa. They don't care about what they can't control, which leaves whole chunks of Ardänia in the dark."

He rapped his knuckles loudly on the front of the barge and

shouted a nasty word, rousing Maxine from her nap with a start. She practically rolled off the raft, which made Alberto laugh.

"Relax, Sis! We're just coming up on Bonthon."

Maxine rubbed her eyes and joined them at the front.

* * *

A couple of hours later, they were approaching the biggest city Meyral had ever seen. It was made out of thousands of mud-brick structures that looked like they were stacked on top of each other in no particular order. The whole thing was a jumbled mess, with buildings and streets all thrown together, but there was something warm and inviting within all the chaos.

As the barge pulled up to the first set of wooden docks, Maxine and Alberto untied the doxyls and pulled out two long oars.

"Doxyls don't like cities as a rule," the big man muttered to Meyral. "Closetphobic I guess."

"It's claustrophobic, Bert."

"What she said. Anyway, we'll let them go and they'll meet us on the other side," Alberto yelled from the back of the barge as he pushed them forward with his oar.

"How will they know where we'll be or when we'll need them again?" Meyral yelled back.

Alberto stopped for a few seconds, then shrugged and returned to his rowing. "I guess they've got magic powers or something."

"Bert!" Maxine shouted. "If you don't know, don't guess. He's asking a serious question!"

"Every question is a serious question to you."

Ignoring her brother, Maxine turned to Meyral. "Doxyls can smell underwater like a hound can smell on land, so they always know where we are as long as we are in the river."

Meyral nodded and raised his sights to the structures around him, some as high as five stories.

"Well, at least it's still here," Maxine said with a grimace as they passed by a tavern that was hanging halfway over the river. "The reason Bonthon unofficially claimed itself as Ardänia's capital is because it's the largest trading hub in the nation. If you need it, they've got it."

Meyral turned to Alberto, who stared at the city with wide, greedy eyes, and he understood the feeling. He wanted nothing more than to see all the wonders that the city held. As he thought about the things he'd seen in Tem, he noticed the look on his friend's face changing to confusion, and then to anger.

"Look at that shit!" The big man pointed to a few men in uniform putting up purple banners, complete with a golden snapping turtle embroidered in the flags' centers. "They're trading sides!"

"Well," Meyral said quietly, "at least we don't have to warn anyone. Looks like they already—"

"What the hell is going on here?" Alberto motioned to the people sitting on a nearby dock.

Their feet were hanging over the edge and their fishing poles were resting next to them. They were carrying on like it was time for vacation.

"They look like they don't even care that Nordcross is invading." Alberto stood and yelled as they passed, "Assholes!"

The dozen or so people on the dock turned toward the redhead.

Maxine grabbed Alberto's shirt and, with as much force as she could muster, pulled him back into his seat. "Sorry folks, he just hates fishing…won't happen again."

"But I love fishing." Alberto's face slipped back into confusion.

Maxine leaned toward Alberto until her face was only inches away from her brother's. "Listen," she scolded him through clenched teeth, "we need supplies, and you want a warm meal, right?"

Alberto nodded.

"Then we need to stop here and act polite enough that we don't get arrested or killed. Do you think you can manage that?" she asked soothingly.

Alberto nodded again, but Meyral could see that the anger was working its way back into his eyes. The big man caught Meyral's stare and spat before he stood up.

"Meyral, would you be so kind as to please help me tie off the barge?" Alberto asked in an overly polite voice.

"I would be honored." Meyral gave him a little bow in return.

They both chuckled as they pulled into the first empty spot they found. Before they could even unravel the rope, a man came out to greet them.

"That'll be nine pieces of gold per day," he said. "And how many days will you be staying, please?" The greedy little man held out his hand as his thick mustache quivered under his pudgy nose. In his other hand he held a leather-bound book and a quill.

"Nine? It used to be four!" Maxine argued.

"Yes, well that was before the war. Taxes have risen…how many days did you say?"

"Only one," Maxine said rudely, shoving a small pile of gold coins at him. "Taxes, huh? Sounds more like Bonthon is bribing Nordcross to me," she muttered.

The man counted the coins and gave Maxine a dirty look. He wrote something in his book and replied, "Be out by noon, or it's another nine pieces."

The short dockmaster turned and hobbled away. As Meyral stared at the back of the balding man's head, he no longer felt quite as eager to investigate the city. Alberto slapped Meyral on the back.

"I don't know about you, but I'm starving," the big man said. "As long as these traitors can feed me, I'll deal with them. Let's go find us some grub!"

"We have a problem, boys," Maxine announced as she finished tying the barge to a wooden pillar.

"Can't it wait, Maxi? I need food now!" Alberto's stomach growled as he spoke, as if to prove his point.

"We need supplies, like bedrolls, a pot to cook in, packs, maybe a change of clothes—"

"What's wrong with the clothes we got?" Alberto cut off his sister.

Meyral snickered at first, but then he took another look at his big friend. Alberto's red pants were patched in several places with blue and yellow polka-dotted fabric. His shirt, which had at one point been a black dress shirt, was missing more buttons than it had, and the sleeves had been torn off at the elbow.

Curious, Meyral looked down at himself and realized he wasn't much better off. His black pants and traditional Ardänian vest had been given to him nearly a year before, and he had grown about a foot since. His pants were wet up to his knees, and there were smudges of dirt on his vest.

There was no denying that Maxine had a good point, but neither he nor Alberto was going to acknowledge that.

"Fine, forget the clothes." Maxine sighed. "We still need supplies."

"So?"

"Alberto, we just used all of our gold!"

"You mean my gold!" Alberto shouted. "I thought you were the brains of this operation, so whaddaya want us to do about it?"

"It's not my fault Bonthon's taxes are so high!" she snapped back.

"Right, didn't you say something earlier about being polite? What was all that about taxes and bribes?"

Meyral was getting nervous. He'd never had to think about gold or anything like that before. In fact, he'd never even seen his father with gold. He always just managed to get whatever they needed.

"I guess we could always start stealing," the big man continued. "It would be alright, since this city is full of nothing but traitorous bastards. They're practically begging us to rob 'em."

Meyral jerked. "You promised!"

"Alberto, watch your tongue. And Meyral, relax! We're not going to steal. I'm sure there's a way for us to make some quick coin around here...maybe..."

Maxine waved the other two over to a dull, reddish yellow poster tacked to a pole. She slapped it with the back of her hand and a look of accomplishment dawned on her face. After a few seconds, her pride disappeared and her shoulders sagged a little.

"I forgot that you two never learned to read," she mumbled. "It says that there is a tournament held the third and twenty-third day of every month..."

The other two only stared.

"Today is the third. The winners of each match earn a prize. The prize is seventy pieces of gold, and the champion wins seven hundred—I figure Bert could win with his hands tied behind his back."

"A compliment?" Alberto asked. "You got it, Sis!" The big man started to flex obnoxiously, earning a few curious glances from passersby.

"That's enough of that!" Maxine hissed. "There's an address here. Let's go!"

* * *

They asked around and were finally directed to an old, rickety wooden bridge leading to the slaughterhouses. Maxine's face paled at the stench and she shook her head, but the other two led her across.

"You're never wrong Sis, remember? Now, let's just keep following those directions that the nice old lady with the black teeth gave us." Alberto grabbed her arm and dragged her to a small mud hut across the street from a cluster of warehouses.

An old man with a spiral pipe stood outside. "Whatcha need, kiddies?" he asked in a wheezy voice.

"The arena, for the comp—" Meyral started.

"What's with the walking staff, you some kinda cripple?" the man interrupted.

Meyral looked confused and almost said something stupid, but Maxine came to his rescue. "It was a farming accident two years ago," she said. "He doesn't like to talk about it. We were looking for the—"

"The Pit!" The toothless old man pointed to the nearest warehouse. "Right in there. People been comin' here all day. Good luck! You'll need it, by the looks of ya."

"Boy, he sure is a pretty one," Alberto muttered as they walked away. "By the way, sorry about your leg, Meyral."

"Shut up Alberto," he replied with a smirk. "That was quick, Maxine. Thanks."

"No problem," she said before lowering her voice. "Might help if you limp a bit, though."

"Are you sure about this?" Meyral asked.

"Of course, if you injured your leg you would—"

"Not the limp." Meyral shook his head. "That," he said as he pointed to the giant warehouse. Meyral didn't like the look of it, and he liked the smell even less. He could only imagine how Maxine felt at that moment.

"We need the gold, kiddo," Alberto interrupted solemnly. "I'll kick some ass and then we'll get back to civilization."

He nodded to two large men standing outside of a badly rusted door. Their arms were folded and scowls were permanently etched into their wrinkled faces. They barely acknowledged the three travelers as Maxine shoved her brother forward.

"We have an entry for the competition," she announced.

The guards eyed Alberto and grunted. They slid back the bolts holding the door closed and the trio stepped aside.

They walked down a corridor, and with every step they took, the smell of ale, blood, and piss became stronger. When they emerged into the arena, Meyral was almost certain that he'd just been dragged into

44

hell itself.

A pit of gravel stood before them, covered in blood. It was surrounded by a mob of sweaty, insufferable drunks that were all shouting at the same time.

"Quite the beauty, Sis. Good job with this one," Alberto muttered as Maxine shrugged.

A large man emerged from the crowd and made his way toward them. In his shadow was a short man with a thin mustache.

When the men reached the trio, the small man immediately started shouting in a high-pitched voice. "Who the hell let you in with a weapon?" he demanded.

"It's not a weapon. He's a gimp," Alberto said with much less tact than his sister.

"Well then, in that case," the man's whole attitude changed, "ladies and gents, welcome to The Pit!" He finished his introduction by tipping his top hat. "The cover charge is ten coins per person, and feel free to place your bets with any of my fine ladies."

The man waved a gloved hand toward the wall behind him, where a line of rough-looking women stood. They each wore patched top hats, much like the one the short man was wearing.

"We have an entry for the competition," Maxine repeated as she pushed her brother forward.

"Well then, it's thirty gold pieces per combatant and I'll waive your cover fees," the short man said. The large man held out his hand while his boss continued to chatter. "Now, don't be stingy. This is my place, so it's my rules…pay up!"

"There was no mention of a fee on the poster," Maxine said. She was almost a whole foot taller than the owner, and she looked down at him menacingly.

"You think I do this for my health? Of course there's a fee. I tell ya what!" He looked from Alberto to Meyral, and then his eyes stopped on Maxine. The look that spread across his face made Meyral sick to his stomach. "I'll let *you* fight for free. You seem…feisty enough." He winked and Meyral had to force himself to not vomit. "Although the only slot available at this late hour is a championship match—"

"I'll take it," Maxine responded.

The other two stared at her in amazement as she shook hands with the greasy man. He tipped his top hat again and walked away in the wake of his bodyguard. The drunken crowd parted for them as if the two were some kind of celebrities.

Alberto immediately rounded on his sister. "What the hell, Maxi? A championship match? This guy could be huge! Did you see the bouncer!?"

"Relax, it's just one guy. I could take down any one of these big, drunken goat lovers. Plus, I've got the element of surprise on my side." Maxine grinned and strolled off into the crowd to watch the next fight.

Alberto shook his head. "She's insane!" he yelled to no one in particular. "I must have been switched at birth. I should be a miller's son or some shit. It's the only explanation."

Meyral let out a nervous chuckle before heading after Maxine. When he finally rejoined her, two muscular men clad only in loincloths were walking into the arena.

The men circled the ring, each keeping an eye on the other. Alberto caught up, still fuming about parts of his family tree that might explain Maxine's behavior. He only stopped mumbling when the man with the top hat entered the arena and addressed the crowd.

The whole building went silent. The well-dressed man's voice could be heard all the way in the back, where Meyral and the siblings stood.

"This match is between the River Rat..."

The darker of the two men raised his arms and some of the crowd cheered.

"And the Alley Strangler!"

The second man raised his hands and a few more people clapped.

"Remember, there is only one rule in The Pit: he who dies first, loses!"

The entire crowd cheered as a bell rang out and the man ran through one of the doors. Alberto and Maxine exchanged horrified looks over Meyral's head.

"No. Oh, no," Maxine whispered. She backed up a step and stumbled into a toothless woman. "By the moons, no. Let's get out—"

The short man reappeared and Alberto immediately rounded on him. "I don't remember you telling us it was going to be a fight to the death!" he roared.

"I didn't tell you my name was Nancy either, but that's your problem now." As the man spoke, three goons approached them, each the size of a buffalo on its hind legs. The man named Nancy smiled, revealing several gold teeth.

"Come on, Bert, Meyral. Let's go," Maxine whispered.

"Don't even think about chickening out, girlie. This crowd is just as bloodthirsty as the combatants...I wouldn't want to see what they would do to you." His beady eyes scanned her body up and down. "All I know is that someone is going to die tonight, and I don't really care much who or how."

"Maxine..." Meyral pleaded.

"It'll be alright, kiddo." She knelt down and put a hand on his shoulder. "Don't watch." She bit her lip, battling with her words, and then turned away.

Alberto took her place. "Just wait here. If anything goes wrong, stick behind me." He turned to his sister and pulled her in close while Nancy eyed them impatiently. "Whatever happens, know that I love you, Sis. You're doing what you have to, just like D—"

Maxine's face changed so fast that Alberto thought someone had just punched her. Before he could say anything else, the crowd let out a groan followed by a roar, which meant that they had missed the whole fight.

"Your girlie is up, boys," Nancy said. "I suggest you go cheer her on—it might be the last thing you do for her." He twirled his mustache as he skipped off through the crowd, his bodyguards and Maxine in tow.

"You better remember the seven hundred gold pieces you owe us when we win, you little shit!" Alberto shouted after him, but Nancy made no indication that he heard him.

Moments later, Maxine was escorted into the ring. One of the burly men patted her down to check for weapons—Alberto and Maxine looked equally disgusted. The guy seemed to enjoy his job a little too much.

Laughs erupted from the crowd, and Maxine had had enough. She punched the man in the nose. The laughing turned into cheers and Nancy appeared at Maxine's side.

"Save it for the match, my dear...you're going to need it!"

Nancy snapped his fingers at the creepy man, who left the ring. Boos echoed throughout the arena until Nancy waved at the crowd.

"Tonight's final match is between the Fairy Princess," Nancy pointed to Maxine and the arena once again exploded in laughter, "and the Meat Grinder!"

A man about seven feet tall entered through the other door. His muscles alone were enough to stop someone dead in their tracks. Cheers erupted from the crowd and one woman even threw her shirt at him. The giant man raised his arms, and the cheering became a deafening roar.

Maxine pushed Nancy aside and sprinted for the Meat Grinder's back. The muscleman was still blowing kisses to the crowd and pumping his fists in glory.

The Meat Grinder turned quickly when Maxine was only a few feet away. He swung at her with a fist that could have killed one of their doxyls with ease. Maxine dodged it in a flash. She did the splits, and her own graceful fist shot right between his legs, into the weakest part of the Meat Grinder's body.

The audience let out a groan as the enormous man stood frozen where he was. His face turned blue and his mouth worked wordlessly.

Maxine ran up his body and wrapped her legs around his torso. The Meat Grinder raised his arms to pull her off his face, but Maxine slid behind him and put her arms around his jaw. When she had a decent grip, she twisted with everything she had.

The Meat Grinder's hands fell to his sides as an audible snap filled The Pit. She leapt off of his body as it fell to the ground, and she landed with the grace of a feline, staring at the audience with malice.

Someone near the back started chanting "Green Queen," and as she made her way to the exit, the chanting caught on and grew. The arena was full of cheers and clapping by the time Alberto and Meyral ran to greet her.

Maxine held her hands up. "Where's Nancy? I want my prize," she demanded. A look of fury dominated her face, and as she spoke, a shadow fell over her.

"Your prize?" a shrill voice asked. Nancy and his bodyguard had appeared behind them, as silent and creepy as always. "I would never pay a cheater, not in a million years!"

"Cheater? I was under the impression that there was only one rule, so how could I have cheated?" Maxine snapped.

"Damn straight," Alberto added, "so pay up, you little shit!"

Nancy cackled. "I never pay! Thirty pieces a combatant and nobody wins…it's the perfect game. Now, now, don't look so glum, my 'Green Queen.' After all, you're the new champion. As such, I will provide you with a high-end room, lavish food, all the drink you can handle, and any man—or woman, if you prefer—to satisfy your appetite." He said each perk slowly for impact. "As long as you keep winning, it'll be a veritable paradise. Hell, I'll even let your little friends stay, too." There was a large smile on Nancy's face as he twirled his mustache.

"And if we refuse?" Maxine watched as Nancy's two other goons, one of whom was sporting a broken nose, closed in on them.

"You don't get it. After that performance, I can't let you just leave, sugar-tits."

Alberto reached into his boot and pulled out his hunting knife. "Give us the damn gold, or we're going to maul you worse than anything you've ever seen in this arena."

Nancy ignored Alberto's threat and started throwing a small tantrum. "This bumpkin managed to slip a knife past you!?"

The little man continued to berate his goons when suddenly, in the middle of firing his men, he tried to slip behind them. Alberto grabbed him by the back of his collar and lifted him into the air so they were face to face.

"I don't think so, Nancy," he growled.

The airborne man squeaked. His bodyguard punched Alberto in the face and knocked his knife to the ground. The little man slipped out of his coat and scrambled away from the redhead.

"Get them, boys!" he yelled. "Don't let them escape!"

Maxine kicked the man with the broken nose, and Meyral thumped Nancy in the head with the staff. The little man's top hat flew off as he stumbled into a group of loud drunks. Nancy passed out in a puddle of spilled booze.

Meyral dropped down and donkey-kicked the other goon as a fight broke out amongst the crowd. In the confusion, Maxine dragged Meyral back, and Alberto caught up with them in the corridor. The trio barreled out of the warehouse before anybody noticed they were gone.

They ran nonstop until they reached a bright market, where people bustled to and fro. They slipped into an alley between a blacksmith's shop and a tavern to make sure no one was following them.

"Sis, that was amazing back there. I don't even care about the money!"

"Thanks, Bert. How's your eye?"

"It'll be fine." He waved her off. "Sure would have been nice to get some of that prize, though."

Maxine nodded as she picked up a longbow from a rack of

weapons along the wall behind them.

"Actually…" Meyral held out a sack of gold.

"Why, you little thief!" Alberto pulled him into a headlock and tossed the sack to his sister.

Maxine opened it. She looked at the mound of gold inside and let out a low whistle. She reached in and gave both boys a handful of gold. As she was about to lecture them, they ran into town without a second look back.

"I guess I'll just grab the essentials, you two, don't worry about me! And don't…"

She continued to yell after them, but Meyral was already in the middle of a throng of shoppers. He missed whatever she was shouting about drinking too much and philandering. He didn't know what that last word meant, but he didn't stop to find out.

He continued on until he found what he wanted—a leather shop. Inside there were whole sections dedicated to hats, pants, jackets, boots, and anything else that could be made out of leather.

An elderly woman with long, grey hair shuffled forward from behind a counter. "Can I help you, dear?"

"I need something to hold this." Meyral held out the staff that he'd been carrying in his hands since he'd left Berrywillow.

"A sheath, then? Ah, yes, anything you desire can be custom made, just for you. That's Marla's motto, anyway." She smiled her crooked smile and studied the staff. "I might actually have something in stock just this size."

She returned moments later with four sheaths, two black and two brown, all of different lengths and widths. She made to grab the staff from Meyral, but he held it just out of her reach.

"Fine, test them yourself," the old woman huffed and threw the sheaths at him.

She stalked away as Meyral held each sheath up to the staff, one by one. Immediately he noticed that only one looked like it might work. He stuck the staff into the longer of the black sheaths. He felt a tiny click as it slipped snugly in.

"This one, ma'am."

"Twelve gold pieces, boy," she demanded.

Her kind, old-lady demeanor had disappeared, and he had the strange feeling that she was ripping him off. Regardless, he handed the money over and slung the newly filled sheath over his shoulder.

He made his way back to the alley to wait for the others. Maxine was the next to return.

"Did you find everything we need?" Meyral asked.

He expected bags and satchels, but Maxine wasn't carrying anything.

"Sure did," she said with a slight smirk. "It's in the place we're staying at tonight. I got a pretty decent deal. Where's that lump of a brother of mine?"

"Hey, cuties..." Alberto hiccupped as he stumbled out of a nearby door that led into the pub. "Any chance one'a you's...did I...did I ever tell you 'bout the time..."

Maxine stopped her brother from running into a wall and grabbed him by the shoulders. "Bert, did you really spend it all on booze?"

It was more of an accusation than a question. Alberto hiccupped three times and stared at her with glassy eyes before he answered.

"Now, that...would be stupid. First I went out and..." He stared at Meyral, trying to focus through his black eye and his drunken stupor. "I bought a steak the size of your head..." He pointed lazily at his friend. "I spent the rest of the gold on..." He tried to poke Maxine, but he missed and stumbled into the wall. "The best ale this kingdom's got!"

He let out a large belch that reeked of digesting meat and Maxine shook her head. She put one of Alberto's meaty arms over her shoulders and led him to the inn without saying a word. Meyral followed behind the two of them, laughing quietly to himself.

* * *

The next morning, Meyral was woken by Alberto retching just outside their door.

"That's gross," Meyral said as he fought back a snicker.

"Stop yelling at me," Alberto muttered with his head in a bush.

"He's not yelling, Bert," Maxine said. "You have a hangover, which is nature's way of telling you that you're an idiot. Now pack your stuff, it's almost noon and we need to get out of here. And as much as you don't deserve it, I bought you a new hunting knife."

She tossed a blade about the size of her forearm at Alberto, who didn't even try to catch it.

"Thanks, Maxi." Alberto gingerly touched the swollen flesh

around his eye. "What happened to my face?"

Meyral was reminded of his purchase and he pulled the sheath out from under his bed. He slid the staff in it and slung it over his shoulder for the hundredth time, a grin forming on his face.

"Hurry up, you brute. I'm sure Nancy's already looking for us, and I don't want to be here when he decides to check the inns." Maxine glanced out of the window anxiously.

"That's right!" Alberto stood quickly, but he immediately dunked his head back into the bushes. "That's what happened to my eye…"

The big man chuckled weakly and stood again. He balled one hand into a fist and mimed punching himself in the face.

An hour later they were walking down the road toward their barge when Alberto shoved the others into a side street. Maxine opened her mouth to ask Alberto why, but he stopped her with a finger to his lips. He dragged the finger away and pointed to where their barge was, and standing on their dock was Nancy. His head was wrapped up with gauze, rather than the usual top hat, and he was talking to the old miser that had rented them the space.

"There's at least ten men with him. We need to take another street." Maxine noticed the looks on the others' faces and followed their gazes to the dead end behind her. "Or not."

"Let's just kick their asses!" Alberto said as he cracked his knuckles. His face paled and he turned away from the others to vomit.

"Or make a run for it." Meyral poked his head out of the alley and looked for an opportunity to slip past them. "We've caused enough trouble, don't you think?"

"We need to hurry this up before Nancy pays that man to cut our rope and lose us our barge," Maxine added.

"That's fine!" Alberto said as he wiped his face with the back of his hand. "We can just buy a new boat. That barge sucked anyway."

"You want to row that boat, brother? The doxyls only recognize the barge's scent." Maxine bit her lip and pulled the rest of the gold out. "I have an idea…"

As the three of them marched down the street, Nancy reached down to cut the rope with Alberto's old knife.

"I wouldn't do that if I were you, shit-stain!" Alberto shouted.

Nancy looked up to see Meyral holding the sack of gold he stole from him. "Why, you thieving little—"

Before Nancy could finish his insult, Meyral flung the bag into the air and let the coins shower the ground. People from every dock began to mob them, trying to get their share. A high-pitched squeal let them know that Nancy was helpless, and they slipped through the crowd. They each jumped onto the barge and Alberto cut the rope with his new knife.

The short dock manager chased after them, yelling about them owing another day's worth of gold. Meyral laughed and pointed to the coins littering the ground as the siblings pushed the barge through the slow currents.

They rounded a bend that took them past the last of the city's buildings, where their doxyls reappeared. Maxine quickly attached the harnesses, and before long they were sailing away from Bonthon.

CHAPTER FIVE: TRAUMA

It took a few days to reach the last of the trading posts as they continued upriver and entered the Barren Plains. If it hadn't been for the fact that they were trying to outrun an army, it would have been a rather pleasant journey.

At each mark of civilization, they stopped and warned the people that Nordcross was coming. Most were skeptical, but some actually took their advice and began packing, readying themselves for evacuation.

Two days after they reached the Barren Plains, the smallest moon was in the skies over the Old Kingdom, and the trio reached the end of the river.

Meyral gazed at the dense Quercus Forest beyond the shores of the Errigan. He knew its name because his father would tell him stories about the forest that used to blanket the entire kingdom, and at the tavern the old-timers would tell other stories of the ghastly creatures that still lived there. He'd heard about gnomes, imps, sirens, man-sized lizards, trolls, and even shape-shifting demons that could steal your soul.

Meyral looked out at the forest, and he was slightly disheartened to think that it had shrunk to something so small and insignificant. However, his sorrow was immediately forgotten as he laid eyes on the vastness of the lake.

"This thing is huge!"

"If I had a piece of gold for every—hey!" Alberto held his hand up to his ear where Maxine had just smacked him.

"It's called Lake Effreudia, after the pagan goddess of water." Maxine droned on and drowned out her brother's whining.

Alberto crossed his eyes, held his hands up and mimed caressing a woman's chest. Meyral had to cover his mouth to keep himself from laughing out loud.

"…its main source of water comes from the melted snow of the Wolke Mountains."

"Huh?" Meyral asked.

"I got this one, Sis." Alberto put an arm around Meyral, and he pulled him in close as he spoke. "These mountains are born from the sea itself. They begin as large boulders that jut out of the surf, battling the ferocious waves. As they come inland, they quickly grow into an impassible mountain range filled with high cliffs, deep valleys, and death waiting for you around every corner."

As he talked, he pantomimed mountains growing and waves crashing. Meyral watched intently as Alberto even added ridiculous sound effects.

"The Wolke Mountains extend east, way past this lake, and then south, becoming a natural border between Ardänia and Nordcross, cutting off those filthy dogs."

"If that's true, then who burned Tem to the ground?" Meyral asked innocently. He couldn't see Maxine, but he was sure there was a smile on her face as her brother tried to come up with an explanation.

"Okay, I got it. Underground tunnels left by mole-people centuries ago—hey, again with the hitting!"

"How many times do I need to tell you? If you don't know, don't make something up," Maxine huffed. "Meyral, the Wolke Mountains are not some impenetrable wall. After all, we have to cross them if we want to make it to the Northern Federation. But there are only three breaks that I know of.

"There's a pass just northwest of here. Then there's supposed to be a lake in a small passage in the east, but my bet is that Nordcross is coming in through the desert. The whole southeast of Ardänia is a wasteland, and unfortunately for us, it goes straight into Nordcross, so they have access…albeit an unpleasant route."

Something in the distance had caught his eye, and Meyral was only half listening by the time Maxine finished her geography lesson. He could just make out a crumbling parapet resting on its side, long forgotten by its creator.

A splash of water brought him back. Alberto had jumped into the shallows of the lake with his fishing pole, undoubtedly already looking for dinner. Maxine sighed and handed Meyral some supplies to take to the shore.

"The ride ends here. We're going to have to finish our trip on foot," Maxine said as she looked up to the sky. "We'll have to go through the forest, but I don't think we're going to be able to navigate in the dead of night." She looked to the others for their input.

"Sounds good to me, I'm beat," her brother said. "I need me a good dinner and some rest if you expect me to do any work anyway."

Alberto dove under the surface and re-emerged, then shook his head and splashed Maxine.

"You're lazy *and* annoying," she said. "You know that?"

"But that's why you love me, right Sis? I'm just irresistibly adorable!"

"No, I don't have a choice. I'm stuck with you. It's called 'unconditional love,' moron." Despite her cynical response, a smirk found its way to her lips.

"Hey! Is that a smile? Are you smiling? Meyral! Check it out! The ice queen is melting!"

"Shut up and make yourself useful! Go get our camp started. By the moons, you're ridiculous."

Meyral sat on the barge, laughing at the siblings' banter. He plopped into the lake and made his way toward the shore, followed closely by Maxine.

* * *

The night came fast, and two moons rose to replace the one that was setting. The three companions found themselves around a high, crackling fire that gave the rubble-strewn landscape a sickeningly beautiful glow.

"That smells delicious, Alberto!" Meyral inhaled deeply. "I didn't know you could hunt *and* cook!"

Alberto was roasting boar steaks on large stones Meyral had found around the lake. Somehow they had convinced Maxine to help make a snare out of some sticks and Alberto's knife. It amazed everyone equally when it actually worked.

"Just some of my hidden talents, man. I'm full of surprises!" He patted his chest with pride.

"If you could spell 'surprise,' then I'd be impressed." Maxine laughed at her own joke and Meyral chuckled a little.

"Don't take her side! C'mon! No teamin' up, that's not fair!"

"Get over it, Bert. You're bigger than both of us combined, so it's plenty fair," his sister said with a smirk.

When Maxine finished her dinner of berries and mushrooms, she started pouring sand on the fire to put it out.

"Hey, what're you doin'? We need that to see!" Alberto threw a bone at her. "You suck, y'know that?"

"Stuff it," she said. "I don't want to risk getting found because we left a huge cloud of smoke. The Nordcross army could be near."

"By the moons, Maxi, you've gotta learn to relax. You're gonna give yourself a heart attack some day!"

"Alright boys, go to bed. We've got a lot of distance to cover tomorrow."

Despite his grumbling, Alberto's eyes shut and he snored merrily as soon as his head hit his bedroll.

* * *

Hours later, Meyral was still wide awake. He made his way toward the sandy shore and sat down. The thick forest bordered the vast, black lake, which reflected the night sky so flawlessly that it was nearly impossible to tell which way was up. Meyral gazed at the starry heavens as his mind wandered to his father.

I left him. The man who always told me to be brave...is that what I'm doing? Did I make the right choice, listening to him?

Then a flash of the man in black, with his red-ringed eyes and that mighty sword, stalked into his mind.

There's no way that thing was human. Maybe one of the old codgers could tell me what it was. Of course, they're all probably dead now...no! I can't think like that. What would Father say? I know he's alive. They all escaped because my father saved them, and now he's waiting for me in Mantrych. I mean, he said he would be...

Meyral nodded to himself as he made up his mind. Believing that was the only thing he could do to keep himself from giving up. He looked back at camp, where the staff was safe in its sheath.

He said my great-grandfather used the staff. That was the first time I've ever heard anyone mention him. I've heard plenty about heat waves, floods, bountiful harvests, and prize-winning goats from as far back as great-great-grandfathers...but I've never heard anything about the Staff of Ardänia.

Is that thing valuable? It can't be powerful, that doesn't make sense. It just feels old to me. Wouldn't somebody have noticed it, or mentioned that an important artifact was missing?

My great-grandfather drove out an entire army by himself...well, with the staff. I shouldn't have taken it from Father! He probably needed it!

But he said he tried to use it but couldn't. My father is the strongest man I know...if he couldn't use it, what makes him think I could? Maybe I'm *the reason it doesn't seem so great...*

The only answer he got was Alberto's powerful snoring.

"Beautiful, isn't it, Meyral?" Maxine asked as she sat next to him.

Meyral jumped a little, not expecting anyone else to be up with him.

"The lake, I mean. The stars, the mountains, the moons...even the reflection."

Meyral sat silently. He had never heard Maxine talk like that before. He had no idea how to respond.

She turned to him with a strange look on her face. "Do you really think I'm so broken that I can't appreciate beauty? Just because I don't babble on all day about how I feel doesn't mean I'm dead inside, you know," she whispered.

Meyral recognized the look on her face. It was the same as he was feeling inside—hurt, alone, afraid. He didn't know what he could say to help her when he couldn't even help himself. He opted to sit in silence and hope that she would say something.

"I'm sorry, Meyral. I don't even know where that came from. I guess with everything that happened..." She paused awkwardly. "I'm sorry," she finished with a little nod.

They both sat until the crickets started their nightly symphony.

"You know the Wolke Mountains are the highest and longest mountain range on this whole continent? Nobody has seen the tops of most of the peaks, because clouds always surround them. Some people used to believe that the mountains held up the sky itself."

"...Maxine?"

"Yes, Meyral?"

"Do you think my father is alright?"

There was a slight pause. Meyral got the feeling that she was deciding if she should lie or tell him the truth.

"I honestly have no idea."

Meyral sighed disappointedly and stared at his feet.

"But if anyone could hold off an entire army, it would be your father." Maxine put an arm around his shoulders, and Meyral slowly looked into her violet eyes. "I've heard some stories about him that I would think were impossible if they'd been about anyone else."

"So *are* the stories true?"

"They must be. There were people in Berrywillow and Westmore that had witnessed some of them. You know, you come from a long line of warriors, and your father is certainly no exception."

Maxine rose to her feet and offered Meyral a hand. He nodded and allowed Maxine to lead him back to the bedrolls.

"Did you know my mother?" he asked.

"Yes. Not very well, though. But that's a discussion for another night."

Meyral had no interest in sleep, so he pushed a little more. "My father never talks about her, and I never knew her. I always wondered what it would be like to have a mother."

"How about this?" She smiled crookedly at him. "I'll take care of you. I'll yell at you, worry about you, nag at you nonstop. I'll even tell you what to wear. I can't be your mother, but—"

"I'd like that. Thanks, Maxine."

"Now get some sleep."

"Yes ma'am."

Meyral yawned and closed his eyes. Sleep found him quickly that night.

* * *

The sky was just getting lighter when Meyral woke. Dawn was coming, and he could just make out the charred remains of the previous night's fire. The sound of snoring told him that Alberto was still asleep, but Maxine's bedroll was cold and empty. He scrambled to his feet and spun around, but there was no sign of her. He looked down and found three pairs of footprints. One led directly from the lake to his bedroll and then seemed to disappear, as if the person who made them had floated away. The other tracks were much more chaotic, like someone searching for something. Then he saw the unmistakable ruts left from a person being dragged away. Meyral followed the ruts until they disappeared into the forest.

She's gone. Someone took her. By the moons, we have to find her!

"Alberto! ALBERTO!" Meyral yelled as he ran back to camp, but the big man didn't move. "Wake up, you lazy piece of armadillo dung! Maxine's gone! Alberto, someone took your sister!" he shouted as he shook the big man.

Alberto rolled over and let out a grunt before slowly sitting up. Meyral continued to yell and shake him.

"Who's what? Huh?" He looked up at Meyral.

Meyral grabbed each cheek and yelled directly into his face, "Maxine is gone! Someone took her! We need to go!"

Alberto's eyes widened and he jumped to his feet, his heart pounding. Meyral led him to the trail that ran through the foliage, where they found dark smudges on a cluster of leaves.

"Look, there's blood on—" Meyral was thrown aside by Alberto before he could finish his thought.

The big man tore through the forest, crushing bushes and knocking aside thick branches, clearing a path that a blind man could easily follow. They didn't have to go far before they found Maxine, unconscious and lying next to a bunch of shrubs.

Alberto knelt down beside her and looked her over. "She's fine…nothing serious. Let's get her back to the camp."

Moments later, Alberto laid his sister down on her bedroll and began tending to her wounds.

"There's a small cut on the back of her head. Other than that, she only has some scratches and bruises. She's gonna be okay." He looked at Meyral with large, tear-filled eyes. "Thanks, Meyral. It'll be a while before she can move. If you want to go back to sleep I'm…I'm going to stay up with her."

Meyral nodded and headed back to his bedroll, his mind restless but his body exhausted.

* * *

His slumber was interrupted by disturbing and jumbled images of blood-colored moons and talking corpses. Soon Meyral found himself running from something, something vile, but no matter how fast or how far he ran, he always seemed to be in the same desolate, grey expanse of rocky terrain.

Why can't I get away?

He saw a blue light off in the distance and followed it. The light was so warm and comforting that all he wanted to do was touch it, to be in it, but he could never quite reach it. It was almost as if it was leading him somewhere.

61

Where are you taking me?

The dream shifted. He found himself on a small knoll covered in frosted grass that crunched with every step. In front of him was a huge tree whose leaves had all turned a deep rust color. Something was protecting him here, something he couldn't quite explain, and he felt at peace. He looked up toward the top of the tree, and a red squirrel looked back from one of the branches. He felt some sort of déjà vu and warmth spread in his chest.

I've been here before. This tree...

He turned around to see what he had been running from and his thoughts were interrupted by a new wave of dread. He could still sense it out there...something disastrous. Its two heads were searching for him, trying to rid the tree of this new parasite.

He couldn't stand it anymore. He forced himself to wake up, to escape the dreadful beast's clutches.

Meyral opened one eye, relieved to find that he was back in reality, devoid of any two-headed monsters trying to purge him.

"Come on Maxi, tell me what happened," Alberto was saying. "Who took you?"

Maxine stayed silent for a moment, then spoke. "There were two of them. They dragged me into the forest, and one of them sneezed. I...I took a chance and attacked. I fought them off, and I killed the one who didn't sneeze, I think. The other one caught me from behind. He hit me with something and knocked me out. I guess he left me for dead...thank the moons you two found me."

Two? I could have sworn there were three sets of tracks...

Meyral stared at Alberto, who sat silently. From the screwed up look on his face, Meyral knew Alberto's mind was trying to process everything at once.

"So the Nordcross army is following us?" Alberto finally asked.

"I don't know," Maxine replied. "They could have just been slavers or lonely perverts."

"Or man-sized lizards?"

"Yes, Bert. Or man-sized lizards."

"So," Meyral said, drawing the siblings' attention, "the guy that knocked you out must have taken his friend's body back to their camp. That means he's probably not that far away—"

"And now they know we're here!" Alberto's face exploded with realization. "Shit! We have to leave!" He jumped up and started haphazardly tossing things into their bags. "What are you waiting for? Get your stuff together and let's go!"

Meyral rolled up his bedroll and shoved it into his pack, along with the pot and pan that had been used the night before. Maxine tried to stand, but her legs were still too shaky.

"Get on my back," Alberto said softly. "You're light, you won't slow me down."

She looked up gratefully and climbed onto her younger brother's back.

"You ready, Maxi? Let's get out of here. Mantrych is waiting."

Meyral smiled up at the both of them, overjoyed that his friends were still with him.

As they entered the forest, Maxine let out a sigh, and within moments she slipped back to sleep. Alberto started to hum a tune that Meyral vaguely remembered from his childhood, earning a sleepy smile from Maxine that only Meyral could see. The party forged on into the forest as a flock of birds took flight into the dim green sky.

* * *

It was hard to tell, but Meyral guessed that they had been walking for two days under the dense canopy of Quercus. Barely any light penetrated the leafy ceiling, and they were shrouded in darkness. Since Maxine's legs weren't in use, it seemed that all of her energy was redirected to her mouth.

"Woman, aren't you better yet? I know I'm always telling you to get off my back, but this might be the first time I actually mean it." Alberto almost tripped over a root jutting out from a nearby tree as Maxine rattled off the history of the Effreudian occult.

"Oh yea, I was going to tell you earlier this morning, but I was just so comfort—" Her next words were cut off as Alberto dropped her and she landed on her tailbone. "WHAT WAS THAT FOR!?"

"COMFORTABLE? By the moons, do you realize how exhausting it is to carry you through all this shrubbery? Next time you need a ride, get Meyral to carry you."

He took his pack from Meyral, who was more than relieved to give up some of his burden. He'd been carrying all of the supplies since they left Lake Effreudia.

Alberto slung the pack over his shoulder and grunted, but he didn't move. Neither did Meyral, despite Maxine's urgings for one of them to help her up.

"Are you seeing what I'm seeing, Bert?" Meyral stepped away from Maxine, still pouting in the dirt. His eyes were wide with hunger.

Neither of the boys noticed Maxine pulling herself up from the ground.

"Only if you see a campsite full of food!" Alberto exclaimed, his mouth agape.

Maxine crossed her arms and pursed her lips. "We don't even know who the camp belongs to! It could be the enemy, or—"

"Or generous farmers with more food than they can handle!" Alberto interrupted.

Before she could stop them, Alberto hurtled through the woods with Meyral charging right behind him.

They entered the campsite, where a few tents were set up around a fire. A pot of stew bubbled and frothed on top of the open flame. An aroma like spiced beef filled the site, but nobody was around and there were no footprints in the soft dirt.

"Anybody there?" Maxine whispered from behind them.

Alberto shook his head, but his eyes never left the stew.

"I don't know." Meyral stuck his head into one of the tents. "Looks like everyone left."

"Give me a spoon, or so help me I'm shoving my face into that," Alberto said as his mouth filled with saliva.

"I think we should leave." There was fear in Maxine's voice, but neither her brother nor Meyral paid her any attention.

The smell of meat and pungent spice slowly changed into something like honeysuckle and cinnamon. Meyral gave a great yawn as a sudden fatigue overtook him. Maxine leaned against a tree and her eyelids drooped like weighted fishing lures. Meyral dropped to his knees and pulled a few leaves together to make a pillow. Alberto seemed to be the only one unaffected.

The big man was gripping a ladle in his left fist, and he scooped the broth into it. He blew on the soup and poured it into his mouth. As Meyral closed his eyes, the last thing he saw was Alberto dropping the ladle and collapsing onto his back.

The next thing Meyral knew, he was awake with the terrible sensation of pure disorientation.

Feels like I've been asleep for ages…why is the world spinning so fast?

Meyral grabbed both of his ears. Before long, the world stopped and he was able to turn his head from side to side without feeling like he had to vomit. The only thing he found was his staff—the tents, the fire, even Maxine and Alberto were gone.

Why is that out of its sheath? Where are my friends? Aw, not this again!

He was reminded of his episode in Tem and he was slightly relieved.

Why does this keep happening? Am I a ghost again?

He pinched his arm to check, but his body was solid this time. He pulled the staff next to him and watched as the tip glowed a dim blue.

It's never done that before…

A twig snapped behind him. He immediately jumped into a defensive position, waiting for an attack. Instead, Meyral found himself facing a gorgeous woman, who was using her wide hips to help her hold a basket of fruit.

She was a whole head taller than Meyral, and her eyes, which were mostly hidden under her lids, shone an intense yellow. At the outer end of each of her eyebrows were exotic piercings that seemed to hook outward. As he stared, her face seemed to blur. He blinked a few times and his sight trailed down her body. Two thin strips of white silk strained to contain her voluptuous chest, and his attention was caught by a silver ring that ran through her navel. Just below that was a small birthmark in the shape of a star.

Meyral blushed as she walked toward him—he felt like a fire had been lit inside of him. When she finally spoke, he found her voice soothing and pleasant, like the sound rain makes on a tin roof.

"Now what do we have here? A lost traveler perhaps?" She set the basket down and put a hand on Meyral's cheek.

"Thank the moons, you can see me!"

His solid body and the fact that she could see him meant he definitely wasn't doing whatever he did in Tem. At that moment, Meyral's mind went fuzzy and he forgot that it meant that the siblings were missing.

"I was traveling with…"

"Are you not tired, Meyral?"

"Tired? No…I…" he tried to remember if he knew her, but he couldn't think straight.

"Would you care for some fruit?"

Meyral looked at the basket. Inside was a mix of raspberries, blackberries, and apricots. Those were the fruits that his dad would always bring him in the spring.

"Wait…what season…? How long was I asleep?"

"Perhaps you would like…something else?"

She knelt down in front of him, her head level with his belt buckle. Meyral stared down at her in awe, until the staff distracted him. The sapphire in its tip glowed bright enough to draw his eyes away. He shook his head, trying to break himself out of the stupor that had overtaken him.

"Where am I? Who in Klyntar's name *are* you? Where are my friends?" As Meyral spoke, his mind cleared. He pulled back from the woman and clutched the staff tightly in his right hand.

A bit of anger tainted the corners of the woman's full lips as she snarled. "Why don't you put down your weapon? You can't possibly mean to attack me, after all I've done for you!"

Suddenly Meyral smelled something wild, something like a rabbit's den after the summer season had passed. He took another step back and tripped over something. He looked at his feet and saw Maxine lying under a thin layer of leaves. Her face looked ashen. Her green hair was matted against her skin and her eyes were open in a glassy stare.

"I don't know what your game is, lady, but we're leaving."

Meyral looked back up and the enchantress' illusion faded. In her place was a rotting corpse—dry, greenish brown, and riddled with holes where the worms had feasted. The specter glared at him with dark pits that had once been eyes.

"You have chosen a cold and lonely death. You could have died in pure bliss, fool!"

The corpse lurched forward as Meyral took a fighting stance, the sapphire tip set next to his temple.

"You think your mortal weapon will affect me?"

The evil spirit tittered for a moment and then charged with inhuman speed. Just as it was about to close its rotting fingers around his neck, Meyral swept its legs out from under it with an upward motion of the staff. The monster fell to the ground with a hollow thud and Meyral jumped back toward the trees.

The campsite rippled out of focus for a moment as the corpse roared with rage. Vines dropped from the trees and wrapped themselves around Meyral's throat, choking him and pulling him upward. The undead beast cackled and raised its arms, commanding the flora to kill him.

Meyral swung at the vines with the staff desperately. In a flash of bright blue, he dropped to the ground. Brown, deadened vines fell next to him.

The campsite vibrated once again as the specter shrieked. Tents covered in slime and rust replaced the neat scene from before.

"What manner of magic is this?" the monster yelled, pointing to the staff.

Meyral didn't bother responding. He jabbed at the creature's face and twisted. Blue flames erupted from the staff, then enveloped the decaying pile of flesh. After a moment, it burst into a shower of ash. A smell like rotten eggs rose around Meyral.

He pulled the layer of leaves back and gently shook Maxine. As she slowly came out of her daze, her incoherent mumblings began to take form.

"I don't want fruit...stop...tickles. You're a w—"

"Hey, we got tricked. You okay?"

Meyral smacked her softly with the back of his hand. Her eyes slowly regained life.

"What is this place?" she asked sleepily. When she finally recognized Meyral, her eyes grew and scarlet started to rise from her neck.

"I don't know, but something strange is going on."

With a hand from Meyral, Maxine picked herself up off the forest floor. She began to brush the dead leaves off of her shirt. A look of disgust grew on her face as her grogginess dissipated and the truth of what happened must have sunk in.

"Where's my...? Alberto!" she yelled.

"I haven't seen him since—"

The sapphire on the staff shone bright enough to reach the trees and turn everything around them blue. When the light receded, the camp was gone. Large stones with odd carvings engraved on them jutted out of the ground and a thin veil of mist covered their feet.

They were standing in a graveyard.

"How did you—" Maxine's words caught in her throat as her eyes landed on her brother. "By the moons!"

Meyral turned to where Maxine was running. Between two dead and blackened trees, Alberto was hanging by his ankles. A dark grey slug seemed to be slowly devouring him, and it had already reached his chest. Meyral watched as it continued to pulse and work its way up his body.

"Alberto!" Maxine yelled again.

She pulled Alberto's hunting knife out of his boot and cut into the disgusting creature. A torrent of yellowish slime that smelled like decayed flesh poured out onto the ground as the slug split open. Maxine gagged, but she managed to catch Alberto as he dropped from the branches above. Between Maxine and Meyral, they were able to drag the big man to some soft dirt on the far side of the graveyard.

"Is he alive?" Meyral asked.

Maxine checked for a pulse. "Yea…but barely. We need to get out of here." She looked anxiously from side to side, trying to determine the best route.

"That woman must have been a diversion…" Meyral shuddered as he remembered the exotic beauty caressing his cheek.

"What did you say?" Maxine turned on him almost viciously.

"I dreamt…uh…forget it." Meyral shook his head.

Maxine seemed to relax until she turned back to her brother. "Help me wipe the slime off of him, it could be dangerous," she said as she pulled handfuls of goop from her brother's face. "Grab that arm and let's move him."

They managed to carry Alberto's still unconscious body, although they had to stop every few feet. Before long, fatigue set in. Maxine fell to her knees, breathing heavily. Meyral set Alberto's arm down, and as he reached for Maxine, he collapsed onto his side. He heard an animal rustling through the underbrush nearby as his vision faded to black.

* * *

Meyral woke with a start and he heard the faint sound of running water. He was on his bedroll, but he couldn't remember when he'd gotten there. He looked around and saw that someone had set up camp in a little meadow alongside a creek. There was a fire burning near him, and Meyral could just see the shapes of Maxine and Alberto nearby. He lay back down and sighed, thankful to be out from under the shadows of the forest.

He dragged himself out of bed and checked on Alberto, then headed down to the water. A black-and-white scalekat watched him intently, sitting on a rock that was half submerged in the water. Its bright, orange-and-black eyes stared back at Meyral as he reached into the stream, but even after he splashed the scalekat, it didn't flee. He washed his face and headed back to camp, and when he turned around, the scalekat was still sitting on its rock. After a minute, the small creature dove into the water.

That night, Meyral kept a constant vigil over Alberto, not daring to break the silence.

* * *

"Meyral?"

As soon as he heard his name, his eyes shot open. Fragments of an already fading dream skirted around his waking mind.

"Sorry," he said groggily, "must have fallen asleep." He recognized the worried look on Maxine's face as she hovered over him. "What is it? Is he alright?"

Maxine shook her head. "He's breathing, but he doesn't seem to be getting any better or worse."

"Well," Meyral said, "he'll probably be fine on his own for a bit. We should go wash in the river. We'll also need some water for later..."

Maxine continued to stare at her brother without a word. Meyral grabbed her elbow and gently pulled her toward the water's edge.

Once they reached a bend in the stream, Meyral stripped right in front of Maxine without much thought. He jumped into the deepest part of the creek and sighed with relief. The crisp water was cold and it washed away the filth. In the light of day, Meyral also let it wash away his fear.

Maxine looked around, then walked behind a large bush close to the water's edge. As she disrobed, the scalekat from before climbed out of the water and sauntered over to Alberto. It sniffed the big man, then scampered off into the forest.

"What are you staring at?" Maxine asked as she floated back

toward Meyral.

"A scalekat," Meyral answered. "It went straight to Alberto when we got in, then ran into the woods."

"Don't worry. They're harmless," she said as she dipped below the surface.

* * *

Meyral and Maxine lay on the rocky shore of the creek, letting the sun dry them and their clothes.

"What did you see?" Meyral asked. The question had been gnawing at him since they'd left the cemetery.

"What do you mean, 'What did you see?'" Maxine asked.

"In the camp...were you asleep the whole time?"

"Yes."

"Well...I don't think that slug thing was what set that trap," Meyral continued. "When I woke up, I saw a woman. She...uh..." He could feel his cheeks flush and he looked everywhere but at Maxine.

"Boy, you've got a long way to go," she said with a smirk, but Meyral was just happy she wasn't angry.

"So you didn't wake up at all?"

"I woke with you standing over me. Why?"

"No reason." He could feel Maxine staring at him. "I'm going to check on Alberto."

Just as Meyral got up to leave, a man emerged from the opposite side of the clearing. Maxine laid a hand on Meyral's shoulder as he jerked in the direction of his bedroll, where he had stashed the staff. The man noticed the movement immediately and reached Meyral's bed in a few strides. He pulled the blanket aside and crouched down, revealing a plum tunic underneath his heavy cloak. Meyral tensed as he recognized Nordcross' colors and he sprinted toward the man.

The stranger paid him no attention and removed his left glove, then extended his bare hand. He paused for a moment and twiddled his fingers anxiously before grabbing the staff. There was a flash and he dropped it with a curse. He waved his hand in front of his face and blew on it. Meyral stopped a few feet away with a curious look on his face.

"It still hasn't forgiven me," the man said quietly.

"Who are you?" Meyral demanded as the man straightened up.

"I'm the fool who saved your lives," he shot back as he slipped his hand into his glove. "Who do you think dragged you all here and started the fire?" He threw a log onto the dying embers and set a kettle over it. "Why do you think your big friend is still alive?"

"You're a liar," Maxine spat. "You work with Nordcross."

"Well now, that's unfair," he said, cocking his head to one side. "You've left me with no way to argue against your accusation."

"Huh?" Meyral asked.

"If I were to say I was not a liar, you would simply say that it was a lie. But if I say I am a liar, then I must be lying about lying; so I tell the truth. But how could I be telling the truth if I can only tell it through a lie?"

"That doesn't explain why you're here, or why you're wearing Nordcross colors," Maxine continued without acknowledging Meyral's questioning look.

"I wear blue in the north, I wear plum in the east, I wear black on ships and I curse the loser of every battle. I travel in the manner that allows me to pass freely without suspicion."

"You didn't answer the question," Maxine said as she circled around him toward her bow.

"No, I didn't." The man removed his cowl and ran a hand through his shaggy, salt-and-pepper hair. "Would it speed things up if I told you I was sent by your father?"

"My father?" Maxine gasped.

The stranger laughed loudly. "Not *your* father. His," he said, pointing to Meyral.

"What? Is he alright?" Meyral asked. "When did you see him?"

"I didn't." The man shrugged. "He used a dead drop. The letter wasn't as specific as I'd hoped, hence my late arrival..."

Meyral stared at him, uncertain if he could be trusted. The stranger was almost as tall as Alberto, but lean. His skin was worn and naturally tan. He had a light layer of scruff on his face, but his upper lip was bare. As Meyral opened his mouth, he noticed the man's eyes. They were surrounded by bushy eyebrows and thick lashes, but there was no mistaking that orange-on-black pattern.

"You've been watching us, haven't you?"

"You are your father's son," he said with a laugh. "I wanted to wait until you were away from your weapons and wouldn't immediately attack me." The kettle started to whine and the man pulled it from the fire.

"What's that for?" Meyral asked as he picked up his staff.

"This tea is what's keeping your friend alive." The man knelt by Alberto with a mug in his gloved hand.

"His name is Alberto," Maxine said. "He's my brother. I'm Maxine, and this is Meyral. Now this is the part where you introduce yourself."

"Call me Reaver." He tilted Alberto's head back and slowly poured the tea into his mouth. Alberto immediately swallowed, but he didn't wake. "A couple more days and he should be fine." Reaver finished the dregs himself and grinned. "What's for breakfast?"

* * *

By the second day after their encounter with the phantom, Alberto hadn't made any progress. Reaver insisted it was a good sign, but Maxine stayed skeptical. She insisted that someone keep an eye on Alberto until he woke, so they watched him in shifts.

When Maxine took over the watch, Meyral would follow Reaver into the woods. At first the tightlipped man kept to himself and refused to answer any of Meyral's questions, but eventually he gave in. He told him how to tell which direction he was going based on where the moss grew on the trees, which mushrooms made a tasty soup and which ones would kill a man, and how to trick a bear into thinking he was a rock. Reaver even showed him plants that could keep cuts from becoming infected, a certain kind of tree bark that could cure a fever if boiled in water, and moontear. It used to grow all over Berrywillow, although Meyral had always heard that it was a weed. Reaver, however, claimed he'd seen it used once to stop a man's severed arm from bleeding.

"It's been three days and Alberto hasn't changed. What gives?" Meyral asked as he followed Reaver along a game trail.

"The tea keeps him alive. The rest of his recovery depends on him."

"How do you know?"

"Well," Reaver grinned, "I've been around. I learned a few tricks here and there."

Meyral looked around and lowered his voice. "Like how to turn into a scalekat?" he asked. "Can I learn how to do that?"

Reaver chuckled. "No, I don't think your father would be very happy about that."

"Why's that?" Meyral kicked a stone.

"Because to gain the skills of the shadows, one must first join the Thieves' Guild," Reaver said as he fixed Meyral with a serious stare.

"You're a thief?"

"A master thief, thank you very much," he boasted.

"Then why did my father send you? How did you even meet him?" Meyral asked with narrowed eyes. He stopped walking, and it took a few seconds for Reaver to notice and double back for him. "Tell me why you're here."

"This story begins as they all do: a long time ago." Reaver grinned. "At the time, I was only an apprentice thief. I stopped in on this hamlet in the southern part of Ardänia following up on a rumor. There I found a woman whose husband was away. I wooed her with empty promises and careless whispers while I gathered information."

Meyral waited for Reaver to continue. The thief looked toward the sky with a wide smile and his eyes glazed over, as if he was reliving a particularly satisfying memory.

"I was surprised to find that she was holding on to something valuable. She had this old stick with a fat jewel on its tip. I didn't even have to steal it—she practically gave it to me...and that's when I met your father.

"He hunted me down three times in the next year: the first time in Bonthon, the second at Beryl in Nordcross, and the third in Gaffe, right near the edge of the Frozen Wastes. He finally got the staff from me just as I was about to sell it to an aristocrat with more money than he knew what to do with.

"I managed to tail your father for the entire length of the continent, until he got on a boat to the Island Nations. Somewhere in the Straits of Gabriel, my ship was overtaken by pirates—"

"Aren't they thieves too?" Meyral interrupted.

"Pirates and thieves are *not* the same," the thief growled. "Pirates plunder and waste, drink and whore. They use their profits frivolously. Thieves steal to prove their worth. Without honor, a thief is not a thief. He's a rat."

Meyral waited quietly. Reaver took a breath and rubbed a hand dramatically over his face.

"So the pirates took me back to their island. They were going to sell me to a ruler of some rock as his personal pincushion," Reaver grimaced. "But your father saved me. Ever since then, two things changed: I can no longer touch the staff without it burning me, and whenever your father needs my help, I come running."

Meyral looked back to camp for a second and then turned back to Reaver, who reached up and pulled a pear from a tree. He handed it to Meyral.

"Take this to Maxine, I'll be there to brew the tea in a few minutes."

* * *

"Where do we go if Alberto gets worse?" Meyral asked on the fourth night as Maxine pointed out constellations.

Maxine paused with her finger pointing straight up. She sighed and looked at Meyral, then back to the sky.

"If he doesn't wake up soon, then…I guess we'll have to find a Healer." She dropped her arm. "I'm sure he'll wake up soon enough. Probably say some sort of quip and then go right back to sleeping or whining about food."

"But if he doesn't, where would we find a Healer?"

"Well, there's no way we're going backward. That means all we can do is keep going north and hope we find someone along the way."

"How are we supposed to do that?" Meyral glanced over at Alberto's bedroll.

"I guess the simple answer is that we keep heading for Misty Pass," Reaver said as he slipped out from the dark woods with a full satchel. "Why you decided to cut through this cursed forest is beyond me. I guess you'll need my guidance more than I thought. It's too bad I missed you at Bonthon. By the time I got there, your coin riot was already the stuff of legend. The fools in charge welcomed Nordcross with open arms right as I was leaving."

"Misty Pass is the only way through the mountains, and this is the quickest path," Maxine said emphatically. "Quercus was our only option."

"The Wolke Mountains are not some impenetrable barrier," Reaver said as he set his satchel on a bedroll. "You really think that pass is the only way through? You just...have to know where to look, where to step."

Maxine chewed her lip, but she didn't respond. When he caught the confused look on Meyral's face, Reaver laughed and put a hand on his shoulder.

"You don't know much outside of your little village, do you?"

"I saw a map once, but I just...I have no frame of reference..." Meyral muttered as he skipped a rock over the water of the creek.

"Come here," Reaver said as he walked toward the shore. He picked up a stick and knelt in the wet sand. "It goes like this."

As he spoke, he dragged the stick through the wet sand. In the light of the moons, it was surprisingly easy to see.

"Ardänia has three main natural defenses. The west is bordered by the ocean. It's big, wet, and salty. To the south is the desert, and, like the ocean, it's big, dry, and sandy."

"That just looks like a big L."

"I'm not done yet, Meyral. If you pay attention, you might learn something that could save your life. Now, over here..." In the east he drew a crescent and then added a line that extended from the top of the crescent to the western shore. "...would be the Wolke Mountains."

Maxine took over, adding a few touches to Reaver's representation of Ardänia's borders. "This is Lake Effreudia." Near the middle of northern Ardänia, she added a sizeable circle. She drew a thin line running south from the circle to the lower left edge of the continent. "And this would be the Errigan River."

She drew another line that connected the center of the Errigan River to the mountains in the east. "This is the Bordo River. We saw its west end in Bonthon, where the two rivers meet. The Bordo flows out of..." Maxine added another big circle at the end of the river that cut through the Wolke Mountains. "The east. There's a lake that splits the mountain range. It's a sacred place..."

Maxine stared at her map for a second silently. Meyral got the feeling that, for once in her life, she had forgotten the name of something. Reaver took the lead again.

"Obviously, anywhere east of there is now Nordcross territory. We're here," he said as he made a little mark to the left of Lake Effreudia and circled it, "and we want to go here." He added an X north of the mountains. "So now we need to head through Misty Pass." Reaver stabbed the stick into the northern mountain range and left it there.

"I've heard from the old-timers that there used to be a big fort or trading post of some sort there, but I'm guessing there's nothing there now," Maxine added.

"Hell, some guy told me that there was a highway that used to connect the capitals of Ardänia and the Northern Federation at one point!" a fourth voice spoke out, joining their conversation.

They turned to find Alberto propped up on one elbow and scratching his chin.

"Come to think of it, that guy was really drunk when he said that..."

"Thank the moons!" Maxine ran over and hugged her little brother, nearly falling into the fire in the process. "What the hell happened?"

"I'll tell you in the morning," Alberto answered as he shrugged lazily. He lay back down with a yawn. "Right now, I need some more rest. And before I explain anything, you need to explain *him,*" he pointed to Reaver. "He's clearly not an artist, his drawing skills suck."

"Sure thing, you do look a little flushed." Maxine spoke softly as she fluffed the top of his bedroll. "Anything I can get you?" she asked.

"I could use some breakfast in the morning."

"Sure, anything. You just rest."

Meyral giggled a bit.

"What are you smiling at?" Reaver asked out of the corner of his mouth.

"Your drawing does suck." Meyral walked over and laid out on his bedroll. "Goodnight."

"My drawing doesn't suck," he muttered to nobody in particular as he sat on his own bed. "Besides, I didn't even make the whole thing..."

CHAPTER SIX: CONVICTION

The sun's early light poured in through the trees as Meyral rose, preparing to practice the staff techniques his father had shown him. As he assumed his first stance, his mind began to wander.

I'm glad Father sent Reaver. After all, we have him to thank for Alberto waking up. Although it still seems like he's less concerned with our safety than what happens to the staff...

Meyral jumped and spun. He kicked his foot out and bounced off of a stump before landing with a graceful tumble.

Sure, he saved Alberto and says he's "guiding" us, but how do we know we can trust him? He's a thief. He can't touch the staff without it burning him, which he even admitted was due to his own mistake...but that doesn't stop him from staring at it every chance he gets. What's the point? What use is something that you can't even touch?

He struck out with the staff and dove to the side. When he hit the ground, he rolled to his knees. He spun his weapon over his head and finished with a vertical slash.

The staff is magical, I'm sure of it. Maxine even saw it glow. I don't know how I did it or if I even did it, but I'm sure that it was the staff's power that saved us from that thing in the woods. If that's what it's for...I can't wait to meet this Taryn person. If I can learn how to use this staff, maybe I could...

Meyral's thoughts stopped in the middle of a jumping backslash. When he landed, he shook his head. He'd already forgotten what he was thinking, but it had left a bad aftertaste.

"He's up!" Maxine shouted. Her voice broke the still silence of the morning.

Meyral walked back to camp, the staff held loosely in his hand and almost forgotten. Alberto slowly sat up, and Maxine handed him a plate with various roots, berries, and mushrooms that she had spent all morning gathering for him.

"Oh…thanks Maxi," he grumbled, but he didn't reject the gift. "What happened? One moment I was chugging that soup, which didn't taste all that great, come to think of it," Alberto shuddered and stuck his tongue out, "and then I fell asleep."

The big man held his plate up and tilted it into his mouth. He got a mouthful of berries and started to chew obnoxiously. Meyral and Maxine exchanged looks, and Meyral got the feeling that Maxine wanted to change subjects.

"Wha's goin' on? Where are we?" He swallowed hard. "And where's that other guy?"

"We're in a clearing in the Quercus Forest. You've been out for the last five days."

Alberto spit out the root he had just been chewing on. "You're kidding. Really?" The big man gawked and looked to Meyral.

"It's true," Meyral said as he slung the staff over his shoulder, the pole once again secured in its sheath.

"So what happened?" Alberto asked again before shoving a large mushroom in his mouth. The redhead folded his arms and looked at the sky, chewing slowly.

"How about I start off?" Meyral said. "And Maxine," she twitched noticeably, but Meyral was sure Alberto didn't see, "you can fill in anything I miss."

"I just want to know what happened to us! Is that so wrong?" There was a mocking tone to the big man's request, and Meyral smiled a bit.

"Well, my dad used to tell me about creatures that lived in Quercus. Some would set traps to catch travelers and then steal their souls. Obviously, we walked into such a trap."

"Obviously," Alberto interrupted.

Meyral continued to tell the story of the demon, the slug, and the illusions. When he was done, Alberto had finished his plate and was rubbing his hand over the short beard that had started since they'd left Westmore.

"So let me get this straight. The demon used our desires against us to try to trap us?"

Meyral nodded.

"And the slug that was trying to eat me was either working with the monster or trying to steal from it?"

Meyral nodded again.

"And you pummeled the evil she-lich, and then that staff started glowing and saved us all?"

Meyral nodded again.

"Got any more to add about the hot chick?" He held up his hands, pretending like he was grabbing a woman's chest.

Meyral shook his head. Alberto turned to Maxine, who looked like she was trying to do her best not to be noticed.

"What about you Sis, were you visited by a hot demon chick too?"

The stupid look on Alberto's face told Meyral that he was joking, but Maxine didn't find it very funny.

She rose to her feet with fire in her eyes. "Just because you're so easy to capture you didn't need any convincing doesn't give you the right to question us like we did something wrong!"

"Whoa, Sis, why so defensive?" Alberto's eyes went wide and honest surprise dawned on his face.

"All that matters is that we got out alive, right?" Meyral tried to move the subject along to avoid any further damage.

"So where does that guy come into all this?" Alberto asked.

"The name's Reaver, big guy," Reaver said as he strolled out from the thick of the woods. He had a bow and a quiver over his shoulder, a pack on his back with the neck of a mandolin sticking out, and two bags of nuts and berries. "I'm glad you're finally awake."

"He fed you a special tea while you were out," Maxine explained. "He kept you alive so—"

"Ew!" Alberto smacked loudly and grimaced. "That must be that gross cherry taste I haven't been able to get rid of."

"You ungrateful twit!" Maxine grabbed the fishing pole and threw it at her brother. "I've seen some fish in the stream. If you want meat before we reach the Northern Federation, that's probably your best bet. I don't want to hear *any* more complaints. We'll leave at noon." She stomped off toward the bend in the creek.

Alberto looked to Meyral for some sort of explanation, but all he got was a shrug.

* * *

They followed the stream for the rest of the day, until it started to curve east. The four of them reluctantly left the sheltered banks to head into the forest again. After a few hours, Meyral saw something that took his breath away. He climbed out of the shallow ravine they were in and pointed excitedly.

"Hey, Bert, I think we found that highway of yours!"

A pile of stone rubble was strewn throughout the trees in front of him, but it quickly turned into a solid road as his eyes followed it northwest. It was ancient and crumbling, missing blocks and entire sections, but it was a road nonetheless.

When the others caught up, Meyral slapped Alberto on the back.

"Of course I knew this was here. The Grand Highway, they called it." The big man scratched the back of his head as Maxine scoffed.

"Look at that," Reaver said. He pointed to a fifty-yard section where the road was perfectly intact. It was so wide that carts could go both directions without getting in each other's way. In the center of this strip of highway was a thick groove, which was probably once a drainage system, and along it at ten-yard increments were pillars of stone where torches once burned.

On the closest pillar, Alberto saw a carving of an X inside of a circle and he let out a low whistle. "Who made this?"

"I don't know," Maxine said softly, "but I bet it goes straight into Misty Pass."

* * *

That night, they slept in a stone structure at the base of the Wolke Mountains, glad to have found shelter, even if it lacked a roof. The next morning, as the three moons set, the four of them resumed their trek.

"It's gonna be a good day," Alberto mused in the weak light of dawn.

"What makes you say that?" Meyral asked. He rolled off of his bedroll and slung the staff over his shoulder.

"This highway thing keeps going up the side of the mountain, so we'll have an easy go at it."

Meyral looked up at the piles of stones along the mountainside.

"It certainly lacks the grandeur of the stretch we saw in the forest, doesn't it?" Reaver asked, taking the words right out of Meyral's mouth. "People have been taking the stones for their own use for decades. And then they turn around and say thievery is no way to live, the hypocrites."

"Well, we haven't seen or heard anything from Nordcross, and my head isn't in a slug's belly…I'm telling you guys, things are turning around for us," Alberto said with a laugh.

As Maxine closed her pack, Meyral noticed she wasn't quite as chipper as her brother.

They traveled into the pass as the highway slowly rose up into the mountains. The pillars stopped, but the X's showed up on the side of the mountains. When they came around a bend in the road, they had a clear view of a long stretch of Ardänia. Not far to the southeast, a large column of black smoke rose into the sky.

"Guess the Nordcross dogs aren't done yet," Reaver said.

Alberto kicked a sizeable rock off the side of the mountain and listened for its echo.

"Let's keep going," Maxine muttered as she passed her brother.

"So much for that good day of mine." Alberto rolled his eyes and continued walking.

* * *

By late afternoon, they reached the top of the pass, where they were surprised to find a crumbling stone wall blocking their way. Where the stonework had failed, someone had used wood and mud to fill in the gaps. In the center of this gate was a massive X, painted in blood with a circle around it.

"What do you think, Sis?"

Maxine hesitated. She looked at her brother and only found honest curiosity. "There aren't any banners or flags or armed men, so I don't think we need to worry about Nordcross." She shrugged. "What about you, Reaver?"

The trio looked around, but their guide seemed to have disappeared.

"Where'd he go?" Maxine asked, startled.

"Don't worry, he'll be back." Meyral said with a shrug. "Let's check it out." He ran to the gate to study the dried blood. "This is the same insignia from the road."

"The rest were carved out of stone, but this one is painted on. It might be newer than the others we saw, like a copy…" Maxine trailed off, still glancing around nervously.

Alberto only grunted as he passed her. He gently moved Meyral out of the way and started to push on the gates, but they wouldn't budge.

The big man pounded on the gate, each hit getting progressively louder. A black-and-white magpie warbled as it shot out from the shadows and flew to the top of the mountains. Six heads poked over the fence to investigate the commotion.

A man on the left with long, grey hair was the first to start talking. "What the hell do you all want?" he shouted.

All of the faces looked haggard and malnourished. Meyral stepped forward, afraid that Alberto might start a fight, but Maxine was quicker than both of them.

"We require passage to the Northern Federation," she announced.

The grey-haired man opened his mouth to answer as an arrow embedded itself in the ground near Alberto's foot.

"What the hell!?" Alberto and the old man yelled together.

A young boy slipped backward off the wall and his bow clattered to the ground with him.

"Sorry! Sorry Dad, it slipped," a faint voice carried over the fence.

"Is anyone hurt?" The grey-haired man looked shaken as he glanced back and forth between his son and his visitors. "No? Good. Then it'll be a hundred pieces of gold to pass."

"A hundred!" Alberto shouted. "Even after you just about shot me in the foot!?"

"We apologize for that. But it'll still cost you a hundred gold pieces. Besides, no one was hurt," the old man replied delicately.

"But…I mean…a hundred! For what, exactly?"

Alberto was terrible at haggling, and Meyral looked to Maxine with a silent cry for help.

"Oi, you used our roads, mate!" a man with black, stringy hair shouted at them impatiently.

"That pile of rocks?" Alberto pointed behind him with a look of disgust. "There's no way that was worth a hundred pieces!"

"Look, if you don't want to pay the bloody hundred, find some other way over these mountains, eh!"

"Howler, cut it out!" the old man said in an attempt to regain control of the situation. "Look, it's Guild rules. If you want to pass, there's going to be a toll."

"The Guild still operates?" Maxine asked with shock.

"You're damn right it does," the man named Howler yelled.

"Sir, we don't have that kind of money with us." Maxine finally regained her focus. "Is there anything else we could do?"

"Food!" responded a wiry man with brown hair and sleek glasses.

"Yes, do you have any food?" the old man asked without hesitation.

"We have fish," Meyral responded.

"No..." Alberto muttered so only Meyral and his sister could hear.

"All of it! We want all your fish, eh!" Howler yelled as he flipped his hair out of his face.

Alberto gasped at the large scar on Howler's forehead. Looking around, he saw similar marks on every forehead facing them.

"What's with the scars?" Alberto blurted out as he clutched his bag of fish close to him.

Several sighs erupted from the wall and the child finally climbed back to the top. "What did I miss?"

Meyral noticed that even the kid's forehead had been branded, just like the others'. "The Ancroas," he said as his eyes widened. "Father told me Nordcross marks its criminals with those brands!"

"Three shafts of barley," Maxine recited. "One broken, one withered, and one rotten to the quick..."

"Blimey, what's with the history lesson?" Howler reached into his coat as he spoke.

"These are Nordcross markings, yes, and we are escapees from death row," the man with glasses explained. "But that doesn't change the fact that we are now in charge of this fort. If you want to pass, you will pay the toll and hand over your fish." The speech sounded like it had been used before.

Maxine snatched the bag from Alberto and handed it up to the leader.

"I appreciate it, really," the grey-haired man said. He pulled the bag up and opened it. "My name is—"

"I thought we talked about this!" one of them yelled from the far right. "No names!" Blue hair encircled the convict's soft face, and Meyral had a hard time telling whether it was a man or a woman.

"But they're just kids, what harm can they do?" the man retorted calmly.

83

"You never know," the blue-haired person whispered suspiciously.

"Relax, Cathari," the man with glasses said. "We're the Guild now. Besides, we can't hide forever."

"In any case," the old man waved his hand and continued before Cathari could restart the argument, "my name is Xander. I'm the unofficial Guildmaster, and this is my son, Jake. He really didn't mean to shoot at you."

The blond kid waved shyly.

"Forget it," Alberto mumbled.

The wooden gate swung open, splitting the bloody X right down the middle. The trio walked through, and they were immediately accosted by Cathari and Howler. The bespectacled man stood by the gate as he tried to explain their situation.

"We don't have the ability to take unnecessary risks at this point. So, while you're guests here at Misty Pass, we ask that you relinquish your weapons. When you leave you can have them back."

Cathari reached for Alberto's knife, and the big man swung. His victim easily dodged his fist and took Alberto to the ground, a surprising feat for someone so small.

"Hey!" Alberto shouted as he continued to struggle. When he felt the cold metal of his own blade against his neck, he finally gave up.

"No funny business, now," Cathari responded.

"Take it easy on him," the man with glasses pleaded.

Howler patted down Maxine and seemed to take a lot of joy in it. Despite the twinkle in his eyes, his hands never strayed where they shouldn't have.

The wiry-haired man looked at Cathari, and then at Howler before continuing. "The north and south gates will be sealed as long as you are here. We can't just have you wandering around, unless you get permission from the Guildmaster. We'll be watching you."

Cathari helped Alberto to his feet while nodding vigorously. The big man twisted and pulled away, but the convict's dark purple eyes stayed on the siblings. Howler moved on to Meyral and lazily patted him down.

"Now that those unpleasant formalities are done, my name's Arthur. This, as you already know, is Cathari."

Arthur straightened up after taking inventory of their weapons, which consisted of Alberto's knife and Maxine's bow and arrows. He passed them to Howler, presumably for safe keeping.

"We'll escort you to your lodgings for the night," Arthur explained.

"T'anks for da feesh!" an old man with thick spectacles shouted in Meyral's face as he turned, causing him to jump back and nearly trip over Alberto's foot.

Xander grabbed the old guy's shoulder and led him toward one of the many large buildings built into the side of the mountain.

"That was Gary," Arthur explained rather apologetically. "He's...well, he had an accident a while back and he lost his hearing. Hasn't been the same since, I'm afraid."

He and Cathari flanked the trio and led them to a large temple that seemed to extend well into the mountain.

"Just for curiosity's sake, what business do you have up north?" Cathari asked. "Usually the trade goes in the other direction, if at all."

"Just passing through," Alberto mumbled. The two members of the Guild gave him a piercing look and he retracted his statement. "Trying to escape the war, actually. Nordcross is ruthless."

"Trust me, we know." Arthur chuckled darkly.

Cathari continued to stare at the travelers, but Meyral stopped caring. He was busy taking in the most bizarre town he had seen so far. The old fort was built right out of the mountain itself. There were remains of a blacksmith's forge, something that looked like it used to be a mead hall, and a whole string of two- and three-story buildings that looked like they had been filled with dirt. The place was a ghost town. It was no wonder they were so desperate for food.

"When you're all settled in, come meet us in the mead hall. We'll feed you." Arthur motioned to the crumbling building across the way as he unlocked the door to the temple.

The building looked as abandoned as the rest of the fort, but it still had some shattered remains of its stained-glass windows.

"Relax, we only come across as mean and tough—"

"Because it's necessary for our survival," Cathari finished for Arthur. The blue, worn breastplate Cathari wore gave a rough look, matching the convict's snide tone.

"If you need anything, we'll be in that building next to Xander's." Arthur pointed to the only building that didn't have a second story, and the two convicts left.

"Do you think Arthur and Cathari are—?" Alberto asked.

"It's none of our business what they do in the privacy of their bedchamber," Maxine interrupted.

The big man busied himself with unpacking for a moment, but he couldn't hold back for long. He rounded on his sister as his stomach grumbled. "All my fish? Really, Maxine, all of it?" he cried.

"This place isn't all that bad." Maxine ignored her brother and looked around the large room. "I'm guessing it isn't equipped with a bathroom—"

"I think a bathroom is the least of our worries!" Alberto cut through his sister's musings. "We just gave up all my fish!"

"Little brother," Maxine said with a false sense of care, "shut the hell up."

"What!?" Alberto shouted as he bounded forward and hopped up and down.

Meyral noticed the same magpie perched in one of the broken windows and he stopped listening.

"…and why does Meyral always get to keep his weapon while I'm over here getting tackled by three guys just for my knife? All they had to do was ask!"

"It was only one, and they did ask."

"That's not the way I remember it. At least, that's not the way I'm going to tell it…"

Alberto mumbled the last part, but Maxine wasn't paying attention to him. She was eyeing Meyral thoughtfully, and it was starting to make him feel weird.

"My brother, no matter how brain dead he may be, does bring up an interesting point. Earlier it was easy to mistake the staff for a walking stick, but in that sheath, there's no question that it's a weapon. Why *did* you get to keep it?"

"I don't know. That Howler person walked up to me, and I was going to give him the staff, but he patted me down and walked away."

"I'm telling you, it's magic!" Alberto said a little louder than was necessary.

"Please, Bert, it's not magic. There are plenty of—"

"Meyral said it lit up in Quercus! It lit up a whole damned forest, Maxi. How do you explain that?"

"Simple, it didn't happen like that," Maxine said. Alberto opened his mouth, but Maxine continued on, talking over her little brother as usual. "We were all drugged, and the two people with brains in their heads had vivid hallucinations. Whatever we think we saw was a result of the poison or a trick of the light."

Alberto stared wide eyed at his sister for a long second before he yelled, "Buffalo dung!"

As the siblings bickered, Meyral toured around the temple. He wondered to himself how Maxine would explain a man being able to turn into an animal at will. His thoughts were interrupted as shards of glass broke under his feet. The temple was mostly bare, aside from a large wardrobe and an altar just next to it on a small stage. It looked as if the place had been robbed of anything of value long ago.

The wardrobe had an inscription written in silver paint along its base. Meyral studied the symbols for a moment, and then he pulled out the staff. A few of the characters that had been carved into his weapon were the same as on the wardrobe.

Sparing a quick glance over his shoulder, he placed the relic back in its sheath and put it gingerly inside the dresser. Something about it felt right, and he took a step back. He knew deep down he wouldn't have let the convicts take the staff from him, no matter how badly they threatened him.

Meyral made his way over to the altar and looked up. Above him was a window that was still partially intact. He could only see the lower left portion of it clearly, but it looked as if it depicted a journey of some sort. There were little wagons with turtles pulling them, and just below the image was a string of those same strange symbols.

He lowered his sights back to the altar and ran his hand through the thick layer of dust resting on the surface. Toward the back was a small dish with a pile of blue sand in it. Curious, he reached forward, but the magpie warbled and Meyral's hand stopped a foot from the bowl. The sand began to glow the same color as the sapphire on the staff, but Meyral didn't notice.

"Meyral," Maxine called as Alberto continued to grumble behind her, "can you go ask Arthur where we can find a place to wash?"

"Yea, sure."

Meyral looked back up to the window and paused as his mind cleared. He cast one last glance at the strange furniture before leaving the siblings to unpack for the night.

When he reached the house that Cathari had pointed out, he knocked and waited. Nobody answered, so he threw the door open and entered anyway, humming to himself. He heard the unmistakable clang of metal from deeper in the building, so he headed toward the sound.

The house didn't seem to be very large from the front, but it extended deep into the mountain. Soon Meyral was lost in a maze of halls and rooms, and the light that reached him was minimal at best. Panic started to creep in and he picked up his pace. He finally found sunlight and he ran through a door, thankful to be out of that labyrinth of dirt-filled tunnels.

Meyral stopped dead in his tracks—he wasn't outside. There were no windows in the room, and yet sunlight still filled the entire chamber. Pots and containers hung from the ceiling and sat on tables, each one holding a different plant.

Meyral's eyes danced across the myriad of leaves in all manner of color, until he fixed on a person standing in the center of this unique space. Cathari was bathed in the bright light, surrounded by neatly trimmed bonsai, completely nude. The breastplate was on the ground, which explained the sound he'd heard when he first entered. The armor was partially covered by the rest of her clothes.

A pot with a small cherry sapling hung from the ceiling in front of her face. The sapling split in three different directions and twisted upward. It took several seconds for Meyral to realize that Cathari was drawing water from a spigot and filling a tub.

When she finally turned around, Meyral was transfixed by a pair of perky breasts staring him in the face.

"Really, can't a woman change in peace around this place?" she huffed as she covered herself with a towel and turned away from Meyral. She glanced over her shoulder after a moment, and he was still staring at her. "You're as bad as Howler! Shoo!"

"You're a woman?" Meyral asked.

"Wow, a pervert and an idiot. My lucky day," she responded.

"What's that?" he asked as he pointed to her back.

Her smooth, white skin was broken by black lines that extended all the way from her shoulders to the bottom of her buttocks. It was as if wings had been outlined in ink on her skin.

She faced him again with fury in her eyes. "Gods, you're dense! Yes, I'm a woman. Haven't you ever seen one before?" she asked rather harshly. "Why are you still here?"

"Well…you have armor, and your hair is so short!" he blurted out.

"Hair and clothes aren't what makes a woman. Maybe when you're older, that lady friend of yours will explain it all." She made a shooing gesture and he took his cue to leave.

Meyral stopped at the doorway as he remembered why he had come in the first place. "By the way, do you know where I can find a bathroom?"

"Get out!" she yelled as she tossed her breastplate at him.

When he returned to the temple, he found it empty. It took him a moment to realize that the others had left for the mead hall without him.

He entered the large chamber and found Xander pulling his pants back up.

"…which is why I hate dogs," the Guildmaster was saying.

"Meyral!" Alberto shouted. "Glad you could make it. Find that bathroom?"

He shook his head and looked around. Meyral spied a few doves and a magpie perched on the rafters high above the table.

The plates were set out and the cups were filled with some kind of rank-smelling tea. The scent of fried fish met his nose, and judging by the voices coming from the kitchen, he guessed that Arthur, Jake, and Howler were doing the cooking.

"Please, sit. We were just telling your friends here…we apologize for being so harsh earlier." Xander motioned to the seat across from him and Gary.

Meyral sat down just as Cathari entered behind him in a purple dress. This time it would have been impossible to mistake her for anything other than a woman. She ignored him as she sat at the end of the long table. Alberto's jaw dropped, and he looked at his sister with surprise. Meyral was happy to know that he wasn't the only one who had mistaken her for a man.

Jake ran in from the kitchen holding two large platters. He slid them down the table. "Food!" he shouted as he hopped up and down.

Arthur and Howler walked in behind Jake, each carrying a bowl. Howler raised his free hand and brushed his hair back. His long, black coat swept the stone floor as he strolled across the room. He set the large bowl of vegetables down next to Maxine, and as he was leaning over the table, he whispered into her ear.

"My apologies for earlier, love. I didn't mean to be so rude to such an exquisite woman. See, I'm a man of action. When passion comes my way, I pounce on the opportunity to act on it. In any case, I don't believe we were ever properly introduced."

Maxine blushed noticeably. The conversation around the table died down as the suave ex-con straightened up.

"My name is Robert—"

Alberto coughed loudly and held up his fork. He aimed his instrument threateningly at Howler's throat.

The failed flirt turned away with a strained chuckle. "Well, people call me Howler."

When he finally took his seat next to Meyral, Alberto put his fork back down. Arthur sat next to Cathari and shoved another bowl, this one full of bread, toward the platters of fish.

"I love da feesh! I'm so t'ankful dat you all shared wid us!" Gary shouted.

Maxine cringed, but Alberto was eating it up. He mouthed words to Gary, mostly nonsense, and Gary cupped an ear.

"Say again? I can't hear you, young man!"

Alberto roared with laughter and slapped his knee as Maxine smacked him in the back of his head. This time it was Howler's turn to laugh—it sounded like a hyena being tortured, and Meyral suddenly understood his nickname.

"Damn, Arthur, you really are somethin' special. Where in the bloody hell did you learn to grow such scrumptious veggies?" Howler asked when he stopped laughing. "I didn't even know it was possible to grow anything in this barren place." He lifted his small bowl of vegetables and sniffed it.

"I…well…" Arthur was taken aback by the compliment.

"He's just got a green thumb. Always has," Xander answered. "It's a gift. You've seen those bonsais he keeps."

Meyral choked on a piece of bread.

"Everyone has a hobby." Arthur blushed, obviously not used to the attention.

"So, you're all ex-convicts?" Maxine asked.

Xander nodded solemnly.

"And you all escaped death row?"

Again Xander nodded.

"I can't imagine that was a simple task," she continued.

"Maxi, really, it's time to eat," Alberto whined. "Can we not talk about something seriously depressing for once?" He flicked a pea at her.

"Actually, it's not depressing," Arthur responded. "It was practically a miracle. I'm still not even sure to this day how it happened." He looked to Cathari, who nodded.

"Most of us were at separate high-security prisons," Cathari continued for Arthur, "and somehow we all eventually ended up on the same train. We were being transferred—"

"Train? What's a train?" Meyral interrupted. He looked to Maxine, but for once she also wore a genuine a look of confusion.

"A train?" Howler barked a round of laughter. "Blimey. It's...how to put it...like a metal box that goes really fast. You can get in it and it'll make a day's trip on horseback seem like nothing." He grinned and took a large swig of the ale he brought out with him.

"Ahem," Cathari's face was set and her eyes were cold, "if you're all finished...like I was saying, we were all being transferred at once when the train took a detour. Let us out right at the border, and here we are today."

"Actually, we never meant to revive the Guild. We just found this place and set up camp, away from everything." Arthur took a sip of his wine. "Then one day, an old merchant passed through and paid us a toll without us even asking. Said it was 'Guild law.' Right then, we realized we might be able to live again."

"What's the Guild?" Meyral asked.

"You do ask a lot of questions, don't you?" Arthur sipped more of his wine before he continued.

"In a bygone era, this was the busiest overland trade route in all the nations. Goods went back and forth between Ardänia and Venstrum, nowadays known as the Northern Federation, all under the watchful eye of the Guild. It was a large organization of merchants that kept trade routes open and safe between the various governments. Misty Pass was their crowning achievement at the height of their success. This fort was manned year round. It kept the bandits away and served as a safe haven from the snows of winter.

"All this paled in comparison to the bridge, though. That was the thing the Guild was most proud of. It spanned one thousand feet across Devil's Gorge, and although there are places where the gap is smaller, the Guild wanted to make a bridge that would impress all travelers who used it. So they did." Arthur downed the last of his wine.

Meyral desperately wanted to ask where Devil's Gorge was, but since everyone else seemed to know, he let it rest.

"Oi, you do tell a good story, mate. Did I ever tell you that?" There were more barks of laughter from Howler, and Jake joined in.

"Yes, well, it seemed that our only option with these brands was to fall back on a business that was long dead." Xander motioned to his forehead. "Nobody will ever hire us. We'd be arrested immediately if we entered the borders of any nation, no matter where we went…"

Xander closed his eyes and sighed.

"So we live here, outside the jurisdiction of all of the nations. Hell, until a few months ago, when the damned sky turned green, we had people living and working here because they actually wanted to. But trade has slowed to a crawl with Nordcross invading and causing all this trouble. That's why we're so desperate now."

Silence followed. Arthur adjusted his glasses as Cathari speared a chunk of fish with her knife. Howler pushed his plate to the side. Gary and Jake looked at each other, then stared at their meals. Xander kept his eyes shut.

"Wow, Sis, way to liven up the party. Look guys, I apologize, she has no tact." Maxine's jaw dropped as Alberto criticized her social skills. "In any case, let's eat this friggin' grub, yea? Oh, and if you're not doing anything later, Cathari, how 'bout you and I make the beast with two backs?"

"*I* have no tact!?" Maxine screamed as Cathari spit the chunk of fish she was chewing back onto her plate.

She and Arthur had identical looks of disgust on their faces, but Xander, Howler and Jake all started to laugh. Even Gary, after looking around the table, joined in with a wizened chuckle.

"Meyral," Maxine said as Howler told Alberto a crude joke, "where did Reaver go, and why didn't he take us?"

Before he could answer, Howler made a rude gesture and shouted, "Reaver? Tall, left handed, leathery skin and a stupid half beard?"

Maxine nodded.

"That conniving charlatan better not show his face around here, unless he's plannin' on handing over the gold he owes me."

Meyral wasn't surprised to find that a hall full of criminals would know a master thief.

"He beat you fair and square," Arthur chortled.

"He did not!" Howler shouted. "I was drunk and he told me he had no idea how to play Reds and Whites. He took all my coin! I had half a mind to break my cue stick over that bastard's head…"

"The con beat our con," Xander said with a smile. "This is how it works."

"He's a bloody coward, nothing more." Howler crossed his arms and a bird in the rafters pooped on his shoulder. The hall exploded with laughter.

Meyral turned to Maxine with a curious look on his face. "Maxine, do all girls have wings on their backs?" he asked.

Cathari choked on her drink. Arthur's fork was suspended in midair, an unreadable expression on his face.

"Pardon me?" Maxine asked with a sideways glance toward Cathari.

"Well, Cathari has wings on her back, and I asked about 'em, and then she asked me if I'd ever seen a woman before—"

Alberto and Howler interrupted him with bouts of immature snickering. The big man leaned over and rubbed Meyral's head. He said something that was muffled beyond comprehension by the chewed up fish in his mouth.

Cathari chuckled and continued eating while Arthur stared at her.

"No, Meyral, it's called a tattoo. Cathari's wings are…she's one of a kind," Maxine answered slowly. She fixed the blue-haired woman with a cold glare, but Cathari only shrugged.

"Oi, Catty, I wanna see!" Howler shouted, and once again the room was full of laughter.

The fish feast continued into the late hours of the night, and it didn't stop until Xander had to carry an intoxicated Howler out of the hall.

"I think that's our cue to get to bed. C'mon, Maxi…" Alberto stood and swayed a little, but Maxine's eyes were glossed over and she looked right through him. "Maxi?"

"You…you're just a big goofy kid. Y'know that?" she mumbled under her breath. Maxine made as if to get up, but she fell backward and laughed herself into hysterics on the ground. "Big…goofy…kid!"

"I never thought I'd see the day…" Alberto's eyes widened. "You're more drunk than I am!" He grabbed her by the arms and slung her over his shoulders. "Time for bed, Sis. C'mon."

Meyral followed Alberto out into the fort and shouted his thanks to Xander and Gary behind him. When they entered the temple, Alberto began speaking, but Meyral couldn't understand him. It sounded like his voice was coming from deep underwater, and his vision became cloudy.

He stumbled over to his bedroll and fell to his knees. Distorted laughing came from where he assumed Alberto was as his eyes flashed blue. He passed out facedown on his pillow.

He felt shivers through his body, and it was several moments before Meyral realized he was floating above Misty Pass. He was surprised to see that the fort was filled with people, and its buildings were immaculate.

He felt that familiar pulling sensation and his body was dragged down to the ground, in front of the temple he'd passed out in. The temple was now, however, whole and beautiful. Long panes of stained glass looked out onto the huge crowd that had gathered in front of it, and a booming voice rang out from its doors.

"People of the Guild!" shouted a large, well-muscled man with skin the color of ink. "Today marks the completion of a new stronghold, another station dedicated to the wellbeing of every nation. It is our mission to aid those in need! No longer will the impoverished be subject to the whims of monarchies, despots, and tyrants! No longer will the citizens of these many nations suffer because of others' greed and selfishness!"

Cheers rose up around Meyral and he was impressed. The crowd was as large as the one in Tem that had praised Thessius. Meyral turned back to the man, but he found him looking toward the temple. Meyral followed his gaze.

He couldn't see what was so important, but when he looked back, the dark man was staring right at him. The shock of being noticed made the vision fade for a moment, but it quickly returned.

A short man in a white robe stood next to who Meyral assumed was the Guildmaster. "Lawrence," the robed man whispered fervently while holding a sapling, "it's not too late to abandon this foolishness and stay out of the war. Protecting the weak, it's righteous, but getting in the way of Venstrum…it's suicide!"

Lawrence shook his head and took the sapling from the man. He placed it in a small hole in the middle of the fort and turned back to the crowd.

The priest walked over to Lawrence and pulled a pouch from inside his robes. "With the blessing of Klyntar," the robed man raised the pouch above his head, "I christen this fort..."

He opened the bag and grabbed a handful of its contents, sprinkling them on the new tree. The blue glow coming from the scattered sand was the same that Meyral had seen in the bowl inside the temple.

"Misty Pass!"

* * *

Meyral woke up to the sound of a magpie's warble. He saw the bird perched on the wardrobe just before it flew out of the temple. Sunlight poured in through the wall-length windows that gave them a panoramic view of the fort. He got to his feet and roused Alberto, and together it took them half an hour to get Maxine out of bed.

"By the moons, my head feels like it's splitting down the middle...how can you do this to yourself all the time, Bert?" she asked as she lifted herself onto her feet. "Maybe we can stay just one more night?"

"Maxi, we can't stay."

She squinted up at her brother as she turned to face the sunlight.

"They can't even feed themselves," Alberto continued. "We'd be killing them if we stayed any longer than we need to."

Maxine nodded and rolled up her bedroll. Meyral turned away, becoming very interested in the empty cabinet from where he'd just retrieved the staff. When the three of them were all packed, they headed out of the door to find the Guild waiting for them at the northern gate.

"We figured you'd head out early," Howler said, "so we wanted to make sure we were here to say goodbye." He stepped forward and handed Alberto his knife. "I wish you a safe trip, mate."

Alberto took his weapon back with a smile. "Maybe I'll see you again. You owe me a big beer, got it?"

The two of them laughed and clapped each other on the back.

"We appreciate the lodgings and the feast. Really." Maxine's eyes were half closed, but the sincerity in her voice was undeniable.

Xander smiled and returned her bow and arrows. She gently slung them over her shoulder as she knelt down by Jake and whispered,

"Even when you get older, don't drink. It's bad for you. Promise me?"

"Okay lady," Jake said as he looked up at her with wide, curious eyes.

His blond hair was just beginning to reach the stage of unruly, and Maxine ruffled it with her hand.

"Alright, ladykiller," Arthur told Meyral. "Be a little more careful in the next town. I don't wanna hear that you're off sneakin' peeks at naked women again." He gave Meyral a stern look, but his cheery voice told a different story. "Some girls aren't as forgiving as Cathari. She acts tough, but she's a softie at heart."

"Stop telling the kid lies, Arthur," Cathari muttered. She wore her blue breastplate again, but this time she had a purple cape attached to the back. "I'm not a nice woman. I just don't hurt children."

Meyral couldn't tell if she was joking or not.

"Goodbye, travelers," Xander called to them. "May your days be plenty and your happiness boundless. Should you ever need anything from us, feel free to ask." He bowed as the trio exited the fort.

They turned back for one last look and saw each Guildsman waving enthusiastically.

"BYE!" Gary shouted.

"They sure are a pleasant lot," Alberto mused as they rounded a curve. "For criminals, anyway."

"Did I hear you say something about criminals?" Reaver said as he stepped out of the shadow of the mountain.

"By the moons," Alberto said with a jolt, "where the hell did you come from?"

"From a land far away. Now, what were you saying?" he asked with a twinkle in his eye.

"I said they aren't all bad," Alberto answered.

"You noticed that, did you?" Reaver asked.

"Imagine that—the big oaf caught something important," Maxine said. "They were very...normal."

"Makes you wonder about them," Reaver added. "What did they do to get sentenced to death? Could they have been wrongfully imprisoned?"

Maxine stopped and looked into Reaver's face. "You know, that is exactly what I was thinking. I don't think they stole anything from us, and I don't get the feeling that we're walking into a trap. Just what is their deal?" Maxine paused. "Or are work camps really that effective in treating criminals?"

"Maxine," Meyral interrupted, "maybe Alberto's right. Maybe you do analyze things too much." He winked and dodged as she tried to slap him.

As they rounded a corner, a breathtaking sight met them. A stone bridge spanned a giant fissure in the mountain. Unlike the highway and the fort that were falling apart, the bridge was fully intact. Four stone towers reached into the sky, two on each side of the gorge.

Ropes as thick as Maxine were anchored into the mountain, then draped across to the opposite towers. From these two mighty cords, hundreds of smaller ropes extended downward, each attached to great timbers that lay on their sides that were as long as the highway was wide.

"Did they...did those ex-cons do this? All by themselves?" Alberto asked nobody in particular as he whistled. He stepped onto the bridge and looked over the edge. "I can't see the bottom of this thing."

Meyral tossed a rock in and they waited, but it never made a sound.

"This thing is amazing!" Alberto looked back toward the mountain, and even though the fort was out of view, he saluted and a look of respect filled his face.

"Worth all your fish?" Meyral asked. He sprinted away as Alberto chased him across the bridge. Excitement welled up inside him as he imagined the highway leading directly to his father, wherever he may be.

CHAPTER SEVEN: CABBAGES

As soon as they reached level ground, the road beneath them disappeared into an ocean of knee-high, light red grass. The sun had just peeked out from over the Wolke Mountains, and its warmth covered them like a blanket as the grass waved in the light breeze.

"Only a half-day's walk until we reach the border," Reaver announced. "Though I'm not entirely sure where to get in…"

"Oh good, a guide who doesn't know where we're going," Alberto grumbled. "That's about as useful as tits on a bull."

"A guide who isn't sure is worlds apart from a guide who doesn't know," the thief replied with a grin. "I can get us in, I just don't know the best way to do so. Yet."

"The border is supposed to be an impenetrable stone wall," Maxine said.

"Nothing is impossible." Reaver shrugged. "There's a way."

"If you say so." Alberto took a deep breath and stretched his arms out, soaking up the new sunlight.

"And then we can finally take baths!" Maxine sighed.

"Sis," Alberto shook his head, "I've said it a million times. You chicks are worried about the dumbest things! I mean, a bath…who cares? What we need is a damn good hot meal."

"From the smell of you, I'm not surprised that you've never worried about a shower!" Maxine waved a hand in front of her face, making Reaver laugh.

"And didn't we just have a hot meal at Misty Pass?" Meyral asked. He smiled at Alberto, who merely shrugged his shoulders and laughed.

"Now that you mention it," Alberto turned around to glare at Meyral, "without the fish all we'll have are nuts and berries until we find a town."

"You're welcome," Reaver said pointedly. "I didn't really expect to have to feed three others."

"Why couldn't you have brought some jerky?" Alberto whined.

"You are *so* ungrateful, Bert," Maxine said through clenched teeth. "Besides, nuts and berries are good for you."

"That stuff is what food eats, Maxi—and then we eat that food. Delicious, scrumptious, meaty food. You can't go skipping steps in the chain of life. It just doesn't make any sense." He stopped in his tracks, his mind wandering into the realm of mutton, beef, and pork.

Reaver laughed as they continued on, leaving Alberto drooling in the high grass.

By midday, they found a dirt road that cut through the land like a long, brown snake. Ruts ran through the trail, each deep enough to hold a small pool of water even in the hot sun.

"Looks like we should follow this." Alberto bent down and touched the ground lightly. "Traders..." He squinted his eyes and nodded. "No doubt, these are wagon tracks. See Meyral, I'm like a puma, with my amazing sense of smell and ability to hunt down any prey." He began crawling along the ruts, sniffing the air obnoxiously.

"My friend," Meyral said with a grin, "whose size is only matched by his brainpower."

Despite Meyral's jab, Alberto stood up and puffed his chest out with pride.

Maxine marched past her little brother with her nose in the air. "Grow up, Bert. You need to take this trip more seriously."

"What?" Alberto asked. "Are *you* serious right now? Lighten up, you prudish—"

"Finish that sentence, I dare you!" she snarled as she spun around and grabbed the collar of his shirt.

Alberto's eyes widened and he shut his mouth.

"That's what I thought," Maxine finished as she let go. With a scoff, she twirled around and continued down the trail.

Meyral tapped on Reaver's shoulder. Reaver looked toward Alberto with worry, but Alberto only rolled his eyes and shrugged.

As evening came and the sun hit the horizon, they found themselves on a high hill with the Northern Wall resting in front of them. The massive, alabaster border extended on either side of them for as far as their eyes could see.

It snaked its way over the land, hugging every curve along the countryside. Meyral sprinted to it once the shock dissipated. The barrier was made of brilliantly white stones, each perfectly square. Meyral stretched out his fingers and touched the edges of one of the massive cubes. It was stacked ten blocks high, and as Meyral ran his hand along its surface, he was even more in awe of its texture.

"It's so smooth!" Meyral exclaimed. He looked up at a large banner as his friends caught up to him.

The blue was complemented by a symbol embroidered in silver. A raven was perched on the bottom of a crescent moon, which stood in front of a second, larger crescent moon. The two satellites were aligned with another larger moon, outlined with bright gold.

"That's the official seal of the Northern Federation," Maxine stated, answering the question before it was even asked.

"Look at that. There must be a million of them." Alberto pointed off into the distance, where a number of blue dots trailed their way east.

"And look over there!" Meyral pointed to a man in blue armor. He stood on top of a small divot in the wall between two of the banners. "Is there a guard between every one?"

Maxine slowly nodded her head. "The old men in the tavern always talked about the border to the Northern Federation being well defended, but…"

"Right," Alberto waved his hands and used his old lady voice, "enduring centuries of war without its citizens ever having to face turmoil." He dropped his hands and muttered under his breath, "At least that's what they used to say. There's got to be a way in, though."

"Of course there is," Reaver said. "And Mantrych is northeast from here."

"We'll keep heading east, then," Maxine said. "If this is a wagon trail like my brother seems to think, then it has to go somewhere."

Meyral looked over at Alberto, who had screwed up his face like he was trying to figure out whether he was just complimented or insulted. As they walked back down the hill, Meyral ran his hand over his sheath. His father's words echoed in his head.

"There are people out there who would stop at nothing to possess it."

Slightly east of them, just to the south of the Wall, was a string of trees that stretched on along the hillsides. Meyral pointed to the trees and nodded.

"Like I said, just like your father." Reaver smiled. "We didn't come this far to get caught by Nordcross agents. We should take cover until we get to a gate."

As they walked, the hills gave way and the ground smoothed out completely. The Wall acted as a new, higher horizon, and all sunlight disappeared long before it should have, casting them in darkness as they pushed through the foliage.

* * *

Alberto was hungry, tired, and cold. When he pulled on his shirt earlier that day, his last few buttons had given out. He had been walking with his belly fully exposed to the night air, and he looked down grudgingly.

I think I'm losing weight...by the moons, I'm wasting away on this stupid journey. I should have just—

"Shh! I hear something!" Meyral shouted.

He had stopped and was waving so enthusiastically that Alberto thought he might take off like a little bird. Alberto laughed, but Reaver clapped a gloved hand over his mouth and took him to the ground.

Why that little...who does he think he is?

Alberto was about to break one of Reaver's fingers when the scent of roasting meat reached his nose.

That's pork! Or maybe it's mutton. Or beef. Whatever it is, it's gonna be in my belly soon!

Alberto sampled the air again as Meyral and Maxine squatted behind them. Saliva filled Alberto's mouth while Meyral carefully poked his head over a bush that was hiding them.

He pulled his head back and his eyes were wide. "Three carriages," Meyral announced. "They're camped around a fire, and they're cooking."

"I know." Alberto inhaled deeply, savoring the scent of the spices mixed in with the meat. "I can smell it...oh yea, baby."

Maxine and Meyral shifted noticeably, even in the dark, and Alberto noticed that they were both staring at him.

"What, is this about my self-control again?" he whispered angrily.

Meyral looked ashamed and turned back to the caravan, but Maxine was still watching him.

"I'm not just going to charge past you guys and pull a chair up to their fire. I have a little more smarts than that. For Klyntar's sake, we don't even know whose side they're on!"

His sister nodded unapologetically. "I'm glad you learned *something* in Quercus Forest."

"Wait, where'd Reaver go?" Meyral asked, but the others weren't listening.

Maxine had joined Meyral, peering through the bushes. Alberto found a spot of his own, and, after getting tangled up in a spider's web for a second, he squinted at the camp with the others.

"See the emblem on the side of those wagons?" Maxine pointed to the nearest vehicle. "They're Northerners."

Grudgingly, Alberto admitted to himself that his sister's know-it-all-ness was actually useful. Regardless, he was relieved to find out that the food was in allies' hands.

"So we're safe?" Meyral asked.

Alberto smiled down at his friend. "Of course you're safe, you're with me!" He pointed to himself for emphasis.

Meyral giggled a bit, but the ice queen didn't find her brother's joke funny at all.

"I wonder if they'd be willing to give us a ride." She waited a second and then turned to Alberto. "You should go ask them."

That was the straw that broke the doxyl's back.

"Again with your free rides!" Alberto grumbled. "If anything, I'm going to ask them for dinner."

"Do you ever think with your brain, or is it always some other part of your body?" his sister snapped back.

"Maybe you should do less thinking and try some work on your own, you lazy old bag!"

Women always hate it when you bring up their age. Look at her face! She's turning so red! I'm winning this one for sure.

"Oh, that's rich. I never asked you to carry me, you hero-wannabe. Now shut up and let's get going!"

Maxine reached for Meyral's arm, but all she got was a fistful of leaves. Alberto looked over at where his little buddy had just been, but his spot was empty, save for a pile of ants crawling out from under the bush. It only took Alberto about three seconds to find him—his tiny, shadowy arm waved at the traders, already halfway to the campfire.

"I guess he got tired of waiting," Alberto said with a grin.

* * *

"Excuse me!" Meyral yelled.

Eleven heads turned in the direction of his voice. A twelfth head, this one belonging to a scalekat, poked out of the shadow of a wagon wheel to watch him.

"We're heading up north," he continued. "Can you help us?"

"North? North, you say?" The closest white-haired man stood and stared at him. "Not a refugee, are we, hmm?" he mused.

The firelight reached the old man's face and Meyral recognized him immediately. He'd spent several summers working at his mill, grinding wheat into flour.

"Guillaume! You survived!"

"Meyral, is that really you?"

Alberto and Maxine finally made their way to the campsite as the old man hugged Meyral.

"Who are your friends, hmm?" Guillaume asked.

"This is Alberto and his sister Maxine. They're from Westmore."

Guillaume's face darkened. "I take it you know there is no longer a Westmore to go back to, hmm?"

The three of them nodded and Guillaume closed his eyes. His eyebrows were so long and thick that he looked like a blind monster with his eyes closed. "You have my sympathy, friends. I too no longer have a home."

"I thought Father sent everyone to Arntim?" Meyral asked.

"Aye, he did." Guillaume nodded vigorously. "And so we went." The old man motioned to everyone around the fire, but Meyral didn't recognize any of them. "I'm sorry, where are my manners, hmm? Introductions are in order.

"These are the Bartleins: Mary, Thomas and their kids." He pointed to the five people on the other side of the fire. "This is their caravan. Those are the Rowans: Sue, Sam and their daughter." He pointed to the people directly on his left.

Sue started to cry openly and her husband tried to console her.

"They were our landlords back in Westmore," Maxine whispered into Meyral's ear.

Sam tried to exchange some sort of pleasantries with his former tenants, but he couldn't bring himself to speak.

Maxine gave them a simple nod before returning to Meyral's ear. "They used to have two sons as well…I think they were a little younger than Alberto."

"And last are these two," Guillaume pointed to the other old men on his right, "the brothers Kurt and Willis. They are actually from Arntim."

The two old men smiled and waved in greeting before returning to their private discussion.

"They're a little eccentric, but rich!" Guillaume whispered in Meyral's other ear.

"Why did you leave? Did Norcross attack Arntim too?" Meyral's concern quickly turned to panic.

"No, no…well, maybe. When we got there, the place was flooded with refugees. Scuffles were breaking out all over for things like water and food. Hell, I saw a man kill another man just to have a place to sleep."

He cleared his throat and spat something in a handkerchief from his pocket. He looked at it, then put the cloth back into his pocket.

"I found the brothers here in a bar. They had just been kicked out of their own home by a large family from Sweetwater. We all decided to go north!" The geezer wheezed his old man laugh.

"So you don't know what happened to the others?" Meyral asked.

Guillaume shook his head.

"And you don't know what happened to my father?"

Guillaume shook his head again, more slowly this time. "Son, if I'd been thirty years younger, maybe I would have stayed and fought. Hell, I definitely would have. But an old man like me would have been of no use to a man like your father."

Guillaume looked up to the sky.

"I've heard stories about him, you know. Your father was one hell of a swordsman. But I've also heard stories about Nordcross." He fixed his sights on Meyral's watering blue eyes. "And your father is only one man."

He patted the young man on the shoulder and sighed.

"What he did was beyond honorable. You should be proud to have had a father of such merit."

"What's so special about the North?" Alberto interrupted, pointing to the Wall.

Maxine elbowed him in the ribs.

"We started out on a ship and got as far as Frazier Bay," Guillaume continued, "but when we tried to enter, the Northern Navy turned us back. Come to find out they've closed the borders since Nordcross began its invasion.

"When the ship came back south, they dropped us off this side of the Wall in a small fishing village that I never got the name of. We found the Rowans almost immediately. They had been dropped off the day before us. And on we went until we found this here trade caravan, and now we're all heading for the Clarion Swamp." He chuckled and pulled his handkerchief back out to repeat his disturbing ritual.

"Where?" Meyral asked with a sigh.

"It's neutral territory, technically," Maxine explained. "It's between the Northern Federation and Nordcross, right in the center of the continent. None of the nations have claimed it, since it's essentially a useless bog. I've heard there's supposed to be a handful of towns that exist out there that basically associate with whichever nation they want."

"Correct, young lady," Guillaume said as Maxine beamed with pride. "Except for the useless bog part."

Maxine's face fell. Guillaume continued with a large grin.

"There are some parts where there is money to be made, let me tell you. All you have to do is seize the opportunity and know how to get there!" He said the last part at just above a whisper, then winked at Meyral.

Nobody spoke for a moment. Even the other campers stared at Guillaume with exasperation.

"In any case, since you can't get through the border, feel free to come with us. We have plenty of food, and I'm sure youngsters like you can walk as fast as we older gentlemen can ride."

Meyral shook his head, but Alberto nodded vigorously while inching closer to the fire. He reached out a hand to try to grab a hunk of meat roasting on a spit, but was interrupted by a sharp jab to the ribs from his sister.

"My father said he'd meet me in Ma…the North, so that's where I'm going," Meyral said with determination.

"The North, hmm?" Guillaume repeated as he stared curiously at Meyral. He opened his mouth a few times, and on the third try he finally spoke. "If he said he'll meet you, then that's what he'll do. He is truly a man of his word. You can count on that."

Guillaume shut his mouth and nodded, but the look in his eyes was desperate, as if he were trying to convince himself of what he had just said. He raised his wrinkled face and saw Alberto once again inching toward the fire, while his sister watched with a sour look on her face.

"Boy, if you're hungry, have at it. We have plenty. We're traders now, after all." Guillaume gestured to the fire and Thomas nodded silently in agreement.

"Oh thank the moons, I'm starving!" Alberto pulled out a bowl and dashed toward the meat.

The trio finally sat and was soon enjoying the rich food the traders had prepared. Yet even with Guillaume's enthusiastic storytelling, the mood around the fire was somber.

When Meyral finished his second bowl of food, a sound like pots and pans banging together came from one of the carriages. Mary and Thomas immediately got up to investigate, but Meyral figured they wouldn't find anything. He'd seen a scalekat disappear into the shrubbery with something hanging from its mouth just after the clatter.

Thomas came back and handed Kurt a length of rope that was frayed at one end. "Best rope in Arntim?" he accused.

"Is anything broken?" Kurt asked with a raspy voice. He pulled the thin cigar he had been smoking from his lips and handed the rope back to his brother, who in turn threw it into the fire.

"No," Thomas shook his head. "We haven't gone through the whole mess though."

Guillaume looked at Meyral and smiled. "When I was young, they used to make a rope that was so strong…"

As the old man lost himself in yet another story of his youth, Meyral turned to Maxine. "If the borders are closed, how are we going to get in?"

"We'll find a way. Trust me." She tried to smile, but it faltered.

Alberto stared at Maxine. He shook his head and lowered his spoon. "Don't worry, Meyral. We'll get in. I'm sure Reaver will find us some kind of disguise, or—"

"Or we hijack the next carriage, set it on fire and ram it into the gates. In the confusion we can steal some Northern uniforms. After that, it's a cakewalk into the Federation." By the end of her plan, Maxine's eyes were wild.

Everyone around the fire stared at her.

"…what? I can't make a joke?" She sighed.

* * *

As the traders pulled out their bedrolls, Meyral bid Guillaume a hasty goodbye. He may have been an old friend, but that didn't stop Meyral from feeling a certain degree of resentment toward him for fleeing Berrywillow. The brothers from Arntim also kept staring at Meyral's sheath, and they refused to make eye contact with him. Eccentric or not, they freaked him out.

Alberto wanted to stay and rest, but Maxine insisted that they travel under the cover of night. When the light from the campfire was a dot in the distance, they found Reaver. The thief sat against the Wall with his mandolin in his arms. His legs were crossed and he was smoking a thin cigar. When they got near enough, he stopped playing and took a long drag. He threw the cigar to the ground and crushed it with his boot.

"What was that song you were playing?" Meyral asked.

"Can't remember," Reaver said and waved his hand. "Heard it a long time ago."

"That sounded a lot like the lullaby Mom used to sing to us," Maxine said quietly.

"Oh?" Reaver looked mildly surprised. He put the mandolin in his heavy pack. "What did she call it?"

"The Four Kings of Men," Alberto said with closed eyes. He shook his head and looked back at Reaver. "Those old guys had plenty of food. Why didn't you join us?"

"I find that the fewer people who know who I am or where I am, the better off I am."

Alberto scratched his head and stared.

Reaver pulled a piece of parchment from the bag at his hip and handed it to Alberto. "I found this map," he said. "You'll see that the nearest entrance is through Gate Five. It's only a few hours' trek to the east of here."

Alberto gave the map back to Reaver and the four of them set off.

* * *

"Looks like the old guy wasn't lying after all," Alberto said as he pointed toward two towers that jutted from the Wall and extended high into the sky.

Reaver smacked the back of Alberto's head as he passed him. Twelve men, six on each side, guarded the huge steel gates. They were clad in blue and gold armor, and each of them wielded a shield and a short sword.

The gates themselves were shut, and it didn't seem like they would be able to sneak past the soldiers, even with the help of a flaming caravan. As Meyral gazed up at the two towers, it was only too easy for him to imagine archers searching the landscape.

"This looks impossible, Maxine," Meyral whispered. "Why the hell are we even here?"

"I'm with Meyral, what's the point of watching an impassable gate?" Alberto murmured.

"Look," Reaver said, pointing to a lone, ox-driven cart heading toward the guards.

Several of the soldiers walked out to meet it. After some discussion, the gate opened and the cart passed.

"That's great, but we don't have a cart," Maxine grumbled as she started to walk away.

"We'll get one." The finality in their guide's voice stopped her in her tracks. "Now let's find a nice, big bush."

Meyral followed without asking for an explanation. The four of them sneaked back and found a cluster of trees not far from their destination. They hid in the bushes, like Reaver instructed them, and he laid out his plan while they waited.

They didn't have to wait long before another cart rolled into sight. Reaver started giving orders, but Meyral didn't pay any attention. His eyes were transfixed on the massive animal drawing the cart slowly forward.

A huge tortoise stomped across the land, pulling the cart by reins. Its harness was attached to it by tarnished screws fixed into the sides of its shell. Its head was a dull pink and its shell was black, broken up by lines of scarlet that formed thousands of pentagons and hexagons.

"Meyral? Did you get that?" Maxine asked as she waved a hand in his face.

"No," he replied, not taking his eyes off the creature.

"Here we go again..." Alberto rolled his eyes as Reaver restarted.

* * *

"Help! Help!"

A large man ran out into the middle of the road, and the driver of the cart narrowly avoided running him down.

"What in blazes are you running around like a maniac for?" the rider asked.

"It's my wife! Help!" the large man shouted. "She's givin' birth but...but there's somethin' wrong, there's blood everywhere! Please, you've gotta help me!"

"Where is she? Is she close?"

"She's right on the other side of those bushes. Quick, follow me!"

He glanced apprehensively back toward his cart and followed the man into the shrubbery. He fought his way through vines and brambles, but when he got to the clearing, he didn't see anybody.

"What the...?"

Too late, the driver realized his folly. He sprinted back as fast as his legs would take him. As he emerged from the wall of leaves, he noticed a young man feeding his tortoise and a woman inspecting his cargo. He opened his mouth to shout at the thieves, but he was interrupted before he had the chance.

"Sorry about this," a deep voice said from just over his right shoulder.

A gloved hand clamped over his mouth and a metallic taste hit his tongue. Within seconds, his vision faded and all he saw was blackness.

* * *

"Is he dead?" Alberto asked as he stuffed the man in the back of his own cart.

"What kind of villain do you take me for? I am a thief, not a murderer. He's only sleeping," Reaver explained with a slight frown. "Now strip off his jacket and hand it to your sister."

"Me?" Maxine asked with wide eyes.

110

"Yes, you. We'll hide in the cabbages," Reaver said.

Meyral and Alberto did as they were told. They crawled under the produce, then covered themselves and the driver.

When they were fully hidden, Alberto noticed Reaver was missing again. "Do we wait for him?" he asked.

Meyral saw a magpie fly over the Wall and he shook his head. "No, I think he'll find his own way in."

"Why the hell are we the ones who get stuck under the cabbages, Sis?"

"First, because that's the plan," she said as she put on the driver's jacket, "and second, you can't fit into the coat." She combed her hair and shifted her clothing. "Third, nobody suspects a woman."

Maxine jabbed a fist into the cabbages and immediately found Alberto's large head.

"Hey! Why are you hitting me?" her brother shouted.

"Lastly, shut up. Cabbages don't talk."

Meyral started to laugh, but Alberto shut him up with a hard pinch. "They don't laugh, either!"

* * *

As they approached the gate, Meyral shifted a few of the cabbages so he could watch through a hole in the side of the cart. A soldier with a cape attached at his shoulders and a tall spike on his helmet walked toward Maxine. The telltale Raven and Moons was embroidered with gold thread on the back of his cape, and he asked to see Maxine's travel documents. His eyes were glued to the beast pulling the cart.

"Never seen a giant land turtle before?" Maxine asked as she reached into several pockets and pulled their contents out.

She found a bottle of whiskey, a small bag of gold, some beef jerky, what looked like a snot rag, and some leather-bound papers that she hoped were the driver's documents.

"Oh, there they are. Aren't I just a silly woman, Mister...?" Maxine batted her eyes at the man.

"Captain Dallas, ma'am," he said monotonously as he reached for the leather fold.

"A captain!" She caressed his forearm lightly. "And so strong, too."

As Dallas started to look over the paperwork, Maxine slipped her shoes off and ran a hand slowly up her leg.

"My legs are killing me," she whispered seductively.

The captain stopped looking at the documents and stared at Maxine's newly exposed skin.

"Everything looks in order here." His tone hadn't changed, but he was still staring as he handed her back the fold. "Where did you say you were headed?"

"Right here. For the whole week, in fact…maybe you should come find me some night." She winked and gave him a coy smile before driving the cart on.

Moments later, they passed the steel gates of the outer wall and found themselves in the middle of a Northern fort. They hardly breathed for the next two minutes as they slowly rode to the other side and passed the far gates.

Once they were out of the fort, Maxine let out a long sigh. They were finally in the Northern Federation. Alberto and Meyral didn't waste any time climbing out from under the cabbages.

"Good thing his paperwork was in his coat, or we would have been busted," Meyral said as he sat next to Maxine.

"Yea, pure luck," Alberto jeered from the back as he finished the man's whiskey. "Hey, Sis, what was all that talk about how strong that guard looked? He was skinnier than Meyral."

Maxine turned red and coughed.

"I think she was flirting," Meyral said with a grin.

"That explains all the blinking. I thought you had something in your eye." Alberto yawned and stretched his arms out. "You sure are a bad flirt, Sis. I wouldn't have watched that if I'd been warned."

Maxine's red became a deep scarlet as she bit her cheek.

"This is the North?" Meyral asked, trying to change the subject.

"I believe they would call this a Gate City…so yes," Maxine explained.

Alberto rolled his eyes at his sister, but Meyral didn't mind her longwinded explanations as much as he did.

"You see, each Gate has a fort in charge of it. The soldiers there are paid well, but they are expected to stay out there for five years at a time. Before the North expanded, it was a three-day ride to any of the central cities. Because of this, small farming towns developed around the forts. But young soldiers, with more money and time than they know what to do with, tend to want more than food, so the farming towns eventually developed into trading communities.

"Some aspiring people moved in later and opened places to gamble, drink, sleep, and buy a woman for the night. These new towns had everything you could want—except any kind of law, which suited the soldiers just fine.

"It didn't take long for these places to become hotbeds for drunks, whores, land pirates, hustlers, assassins, bounty hunters, and anyone else that the civilized world would no longer tolerate." Maxine frowned as she thought about the scum that walked the same streets that they were currently riding through.

"The way I heard it, these towns are considered throwaways, so they don't even get proper names," Alberto interrupted. "They were numbered as they were founded." He smiled in triumph as he finished his sister's story.

The trio had found their way into what was known simply as Gate Five. The smell was intense, a strong mix of garbage and piss. The place was blanketed in a black fume that seemed to come from nowhere and hung in the air, making it a chore to breathe.

Most of the buildings were made of little more than mud and sticks, and the taller structures had started to tilt or sag. In some places the buildings actually leaned against one another, creating archways over the alleys. The streets were deserted, except for a few stray pigs and one dirty goat that approached the cart. It watched the travelers with eyes that seemed to point in opposite directions.

The goat's face was slightly skewed so that its features weren't quite symmetric. The left side of its face seemed to sag, and a sickly patch of hair hung from its chin. When it bleated, its voice was so broken and full of sorrow that Alberto's eyes actually began to water. He tried to reach out to the miserable creature, but they moved past the goat too quickly for him to comfort it.

Maxine directed the shelled beast into a dark alleyway behind a pub. The tortoise retreated into its shell and made a couple knocking noises. They put the rider back in his seat, with the now empty bottle of whiskey in his lap and the last of Maxine's share of the gold pieces added to his purse.

"That sure was nice of you," Reaver said from the shadows.

"We owe him for the use of his cart, at least," Maxine answered.

"Some would say sparing his life is payment enough," the thief added.

"They would be wrong, then," Meyral cut in. He stepped forward and stared at Reaver, who continued to grin.

"Are you sure you aren't your father?" Reaver walked around Meyral and looked at his back. "Maybe a puppet? No, I don't see strings!" He waved his hands around Meyral's head.

"I am not a puppet!" Meyral slapped Reaver's hands away. "Besides, shouldn't you be disappearing about now? Someone might see you."

"Weren't you listening?" Reaver asked. "Here I don't have to worry about being seen, even in Nordcross colors. The North is fairly peaceful, they don't care who's affiliated with which country."

"So a town full of scum is the only place where you can openly walk the streets?" Maxine asked.

"Ah, the young maiden wounds me with her words." Reaver made a slight bow. "Whatever have I done to deserve such scorn?"

Maxine rolled her eyes.

"By the moons…" Alberto mumbled.

"Right," Reaver said as he nodded to the building they parked behind. "This pub is where we're going. We need information, and the best way to get it is by lips loosened by booze."

Maxine and Reaver approached the tavern door. Meyral felt Alberto breathing on his neck. He looked up and saw the big man examining his back.

"I don't have strings!" Meyral shouted as he caught up with the others.

Light shone through the tavern windows, which were too grimy to see through. The sound of music reached Meyral's ears and he was slightly relieved. It'd been so long since he'd heard any. He reached for the door with renewed hope, but he was thrown against the building as a drunk nearly flew headfirst out of the bar. Reaver caught him by the collar and set him upright on his feet.

"No fighting, Karloff! You hear me? Now get outta here, ya good fer nothin'!" The bartender continued to yell at the inebriated man, completely oblivious to his new customers. The man named Karloff stumbled down the street as the four travelers made their way inside.

The pub was much cleaner on the inside. They descended a few steps into a room with vaulted ceilings. The walls were dark green with wooden paneling wrapped around the bottom half. Near the back was a group of round tables, where a few men played cards. To their left, a staircase led to a balcony overlooking the tavern—four doors led off the veranda, probably serving as the bartender's room and a few for rent. To their right was a small stage. The bar itself stretched from the bottom of the staircase, along the back wall, past the gambling tables, and ended just before the empty stage on their right.

As they stood in the doorway, the bartender walked back through the double doors. He bumped into Alberto and shuffled around them with a hard look on his face, mumbling some kind of apology.

"Never a bad time to earn some coin," Reaver said with a wink. "Meyral, keep your morals to yourself. Spreading the good word in here could get you killed." Reaver caught up with the bartender, and after a quick conversation he hopped onto the stage. He pulled out his mandolin and started to play a jaunty tune.

"Alright, it's best if we split up," Maxine said. "Bert, take the bar. Meyral, take the tables. I'm going to scour the booths. If you see someone who doesn't look too shady or like they're in a position of authority, try seeing if they know how to get to Mantrych. Meet back here in an hour, okay?"

"I got the bar? No worries. You can count on me!" Alberto chuckled to himself and bounded away.

Meyral turned to Maxine with a confused look. "Why would you purposely send him to the bar?"

"It's simple." She smirked as she watched her brother traipse toward a stool. "You know how he gets around strangers, babbling and telling bad jokes? He'd blow our cover, and then everyone would know where we were going. This way he'll just drink at the bar and stay out of harm's way." With that, she turned and left for the first booth.

Meyral scanned the saloon until he saw a card game he recognized. He walked over and awkwardly hovered for a few moments before interrupting.

"Excuse—excuse me, do any of..."

Every head at the table turned his way, each face wearing a scowl.

"This ain't no place for kids." A man with an eye patch stabbed a dagger threateningly into the table. "I suggest you scat, unless you wanna place a bet."

Meyral reached into his pocket and pulled out the gold he had left over from Bonthon. He sighed and held it out. "I've got three coins.

Is that enough?"

"Sure, kid. That'll work just fine," a fat, greasy man said. He snorted and raised his hand, gesturing to the one-eyed man. Meyral opened his mouth to give his name, but the fat man interrupted him like he'd read his mind. "We don't do names here."

A skinny man with glasses and long, blue hair that hung in his face dealt the cards so fast that Meyral was surprised they didn't catch fire.

"You know poker, kid?" the fat man asked with a hand on Meyral's shoulder.

"Sure. My dad showed me once."

The gambling men all grunted and tried to conceal grins.

The dealer slid Meyral some cards and pushed the hair out of his acne-pocked face. "We ain't gonna tell you twice. Place yer bet."

Meyral tossed a coin onto the table and picked up his cards. The skinny man folded instantly. The man with the eye patch cursed and threw his cards at the table.

"Looks like it's you and me kid," the fat man announced with a chuckle. "Tell you what, let's make this quick. I raise you two." He tossed two more coins on the table with a sneer.

Meyral looked at his cards before placing the rest of his gold on the table.

"You have to raise or call," the skinny man prompted impatiently.

"Oh sorry, I call."

The fat man laughed as he turned over his cards. "Can you beat a pair of kings?"

"Sure can." Meyral placed his cards on the table.

The fat man lost his smile. The dealer started to laugh or hyperventilate—it was hard to tell.

"Aces beat kings," the skinny man managed to say between breaths.

"Shut up and deal the cards. Beginner's luck, we all know it," the fat man muttered.

* * *

Maxine approached the first booth. There was an old man hunched over, crying into a glass of what looked like green milk. She immediately regretted her assignments.

I hate talking to drunk people, and I can smell this guy from here.

She took another step and gagged a little.

I can't do it, I can't...who's next?

In the next booth, a man and a woman appeared to be wrestling over the same cushion. She took a few steps closer, intending to help the poor girl, when she noticed that the man had his hand halfway up her dress. Rage boiled up inside Maxine and she opened her mouth, but when she looked at the girl, the only emotion she saw was boredom. Maxine stepped back and sighed.

Drunks, philanderers, prostitutes...this place is a pigsty.

Her eyes made their way to the stage, where Reaver was singing and playing. Someone walked by and tossed him two coins, earning a nod and a smile from Reaver. Maxine looked at the couple again and blushed slightly.

Cute dress...for a whore.

The next booth was deserted, save for some empty glasses lying on the table. Maxine sat down with a huff.

Thank the moons. It's about time I relax without Meyral and Alberto constantly jabbering away at me. Okay, get it together Maxine. You have a task, you must get information, and these people are the only way to get that information...you have a task, you must get—

"Can I get you anything, hun?"

Maxine jolted and looked up at the waitress.

The woman had red, silky hair that framed her heart-shaped face and flowed down her back. She wore a black, low-cut dress that left her breasts jiggling even when she stopped moving. The lines at the corners of her eyes and mouth showed her age, but there was no denying she was gorgeous.

"Can I have some water?" Maxine asked with a relieved smile. She waited patiently until the waitress returned. As she set the glass on the table and turned away, Maxine caught her attention. "I was just wondering if you knew how to get to Mantrych..."

The waitress smiled sadly and shook her head. "I've never been outside of Gate Five. Sorry."

As she sauntered away to another table, Maxine had the sneaking suspicion that the woman was lying. She sighed and sipped on her water as she continued to scan the tavern.

* * *

Alberto reached the bar, but before he could yell out his order, he noticed a woman sitting alone. His voice caught in his throat.

Her straight, dark purple hair was tied up in a ponytail that reached the small of her back. She wore a brassiere made from the bone of some animal, which was decorated with what was most probably the same animal's hide. She had a silk sash, the same color as her hair, tied around her waist. It draped down her right hip and over a black, leather skirt that barely reached mid thigh. The massive, double-sided axe she had slung over her shoulder was what made Alberto really sweat with excitement.

She turned and glared at him. Alberto scratched the back of his head and waved, his face turning the same color as his hair. He tried to walk over to her, but he wound up stumbling over a stool. He recovered quickly and managed to plop down next to her.

She smelled like juniper, and it reminded him of the garden his mom used to keep before she got sick. His tongue twisted itself in knots, and his throat became as dry as a bone.

"I…you…uh…hi," he managed to spit out as a goofy smile spread across his face.

Her glare softened a bit and she turned back to her drink. Alberto continued to take in her every detail.

Her skin was smooth, and it reminded him of freshly tilled dirt. Her eyes were light green and flecked with beautiful streaks of molten gold like he'd never seen before.

She finished off her drink in a vicious gulp before she turned back to face him. Alberto had just enough time as she turned to notice the thick piercings in her ear.

By the moons, she's a goddess!

* * *

After a few minutes, Maxine regained her nerve. She got back up to try the rest of the booths. Sitting at the table just next to hers was a man all by himself. He had a placid smile on his face and a brightly colored plaid coat on. He was definitely a weird one, but he smelled fine and didn't seem unfriendly.

"Do you mind if I sit here?" she asked softly.

The man nodded and his smile grew as he scooted over to make room. She hesitated for only a second before she sat down.

"So…I'm new here, and I was wondering if you knew the way to Mantrych."

Maxine leaned forward hopefully as the man nodded again. She waited, but he didn't say anything.

"See, I'm supposed to meet my mother there, but I got lost. I was hoping you could give me directions…"

The man continued to smile and his eyes watched her intently.

"Uh…hello?"

His expressions, or lack thereof, made her uneasy. She must have given something away, because the man's smile dropped and he suddenly became serious. His eyes never left her face, but she tried one more time.

"What are you drinking?"

The man nodded and the smile returned. He finally opened his mouth to speak. "Musha rai dama doo dama dah."

For a moment, Maxine simply stared. The man took a sip of his drink and giggled madly.

"Musha rai dama doo dama dah!" he said with more force this time.

When Maxine didn't answer, he just continued to stare. She decided it was time to go, and she slowly backed away. The man reached into his pocket, pulled out a few pieces of gold, and shouted his strange nonsense at her again, almost pleadingly.

Without responding, she slipped into the next booth, not even caring who she would sit by. Sitting around the table under a thin plume of smoke were two couples with a hookah between them.

"Hi there!" one of the men greeted her happily.

He had skin the color of mud, but she wasn't sure if that was natural or if he was just dirty. The woman next to him had long, blonde hair so matted with dirt and leaves that Maxine wondered if she'd even heard of a bath. The smell of burnt incense clung strongly to the dirty couple.

"At least you use Commonspeak…" Maxine muttered.

"Pardon?" the other man asked.

He looked normal enough, but the girl next to him was fast asleep. Maxine gave her a worried look.

"Don't mind her," the second man waved his hand, "she just

likes to be comfortable. I'm Will, by the way."

"Pleased," Maxine said as she took his hand. "I'm Janice. And you two?"

The dirty couple glanced at each other before laughing haughtily.

"Gaia," the female said. "We have no use for names, but if you must address us, do so with the name of the spirit of life that dwells within all of us." The woman smiled happily and took a drag off the mouthpiece she held firmly in her dirty fist.

"I was wondering about maybe getting a map? I'm new here…"

The male Gaia sat up and grunted. He held up his right hand as he took a deep drag on his hose with his left. He let the smoke out of his mouth slowly, then fixed Maxine with a serious stare.

"We don't have maps here, man. Maps are a product of greed. In fact," the female Gaia nodded along enthusiastically as Will put his arm around the sleeping girl, "every document you find lying around is never an accident. The senate is planting information everywhere to brainwash us all. They're really giant lizards, man, and they want to feed on us."

"Great," Maxine said as she slowly slid toward the edge of the bench.

Somehow I ended up in my brother's head…giant lizards! What's next, mole-people?

"Could you tell me how to get to Mantrych?"

"Mantrych?" the woman asked. "You can't be serious!"

The sleeping girl finally woke up. She leaned forward groggily, took a hit from the hose Will was holding, and resumed her slumber.

"I just need directions," Maxine muttered.

"Mantrych is where the senate secretly hides. They have an underground factory where they keep the corpses of the citizens they kidnap. Nobody knows their true form, but…"

Maxine didn't even care about being rude at that point. She got up and walked away, knowing full well she would never get an intelligent answer out of them.

* * *

Meyral had accumulated three tall stacks of coins in front of him. The fat man was beginning to sweat profusely, something that didn't go unnoticed by Meyral.

His father wasn't a gambler, and he didn't teach Meyral poker so he could rob strangers. No, he used the game to practice reading expressions, to demonstrate the virtues of staying calm, and how to keep face in stressful situations. As a result, Meyral had the best poker face the fat man had ever seen.

The skinny man let out a long whistle. "That's a large pile of gold, little man."

"Shut up. I raise you ten." The fat man threw more coins on the pile with a slight gleam in his eyes.

"I see your bet and raise you..." Meyral surveyed the table and compared their piles. "We're about even, wouldn't you say?"

The fat man nodded slowly, careful not to let anything show through his face.

"Alright, I'm all in." Meyral pushed his pile forward.

* * *

In the last booth were three well-dressed gentlemen. Maxine approached them hopefully.

"Good evening, sirs, I was wondering—"

"Look boys, it's a new girl!" the man on her right shouted.

A thin layer of scruff covered his face, and his ears were pierced with some kind of animal's tooth that dangled at his shoulders.

"Tell me darling, what are your *rates*?" the short man in the middle asked with a nervous chuckle.

"Rates...? There must be a misunderstanding, I'm not—" Maxine started, but the first man cut her off.

"What? You're too good for us?"

"She's definitely too good for you, but how 'bout me? I only got twenty though— can I get handy?" The leftmost man wore a fedora, and he looked like he didn't have many teeth left.

"I just need information, I'm not a—" she tried again.

"Can we get a group rate?" The short man giggled again as his face reddened. "I got thirty, so that's fifty we got together...how's about it?"

"Oh, how much for the three of us at once?" the scruffy man asked eagerly.

"I wouldn't touch any of you for even a thousand pieces of gold!" she yelled furiously.

"That's pricey! How about thirty each, but we get to watch while we wait," the toothless man continued.

Maxine had had enough. She turned to walk away and she heard disappointed groans behind her. She made a rude gesture back at them without looking.

Like you pigs really expected anything else?

Maxine found her way back to the empty booth, trying to calm herself down.

If I tell Bert, he'll cause a scene. That won't do.

She chewed on her fingernails, turning them one by one into tiny crescent moons.

Just relax, they're drunk. They're stupid. They're...they're men.

She sighed and sat back against the cushion of the booth. In the next alcove of seats, she heard the unmistakable sound of an unsatisfied woman leaving.

Well, now that his whore's gone, maybe he'll be able to answer my questions.

She scooted around the booth until she was right behind the man who had been violating the woman in the dress. She cleared her throat and poked her head over the divider. "Excuse me, sir?" Maxine tapped him on the shoulder and his head flopped backward.

When it circled around, finally coming to rest on his chest, she realized he'd either drunk himself into a stupor or he'd been drugged. Either way, he obviously got what he wanted...for a price. All of his pockets were turned out and he was snoring merrily.

* * *

The fat man peered at Meyral over his hand. Beads of sweat formed on his greasy forehead. He was an excellent poker player, the best Gate Five had ever seen, and he'd be damned if some kid was going to march on in and beat him.

"You've been havin' pretty good luck all night, but I think it's runnin' out!"

Meyral didn't say anything. He hardly even moved. The man across from him was practically panting through his half-opened mouth.

"What do you have, three eights? A full house? No, knowing you, you have a straight flush!"

"Well, are you going to see his bet? Or do you fold?"

"Shut up, you pock-marked goat lover. This is between me and the kid." He continued to stare at Meyral, who waited patiently.

Suddenly the fat man let out a slew of curses as he slammed his cards down onto the table. "Shit, I fold."

Meyral gathered his winnings and dumped the coins into his rucksack. He slung it over his shoulder without the sheath and grinned. The fat man reached forward and grabbed Meyral's cards.

"Hey, you ain't s'posed to do that!" the dealer yelled, but it was too late.

"You had nothing! You sneaking, vile, lying son of a bitch! You had nothing and I had three fives!" he roared as he lunged across the table.

"Don't they have a term for that?" Meyral asked snidely, dancing just out of reach.

"I believe they call it bluffing," the skinny dealer said, not even trying to conceal his grin anymore.

"I thought I told you to shut your blasted mouth!" he screamed. "I call that cheating! You know what I'm gonna do to you, pipsqueak?" He cracked his knuckles menacingly. "I'm gonna turn your sorry ass in for that bounty, you Ardänian piece of trash!"

"Sit down and shut up, asshole," the man with the eye patch finally spoke, something he hadn't done since Meyral had joined them. "Take your winnings and go, boy, you hear me? Get the hell out of here and don't look back." He turned back to the fat man, who looked torn between rage at Meyral and fear of the one-eyed man. "If you get the authorities involved here, I won't hesitate to cut you to ribbons. Got it?"

The fat man's face reddened and Meyral felt a hand on his shoulder. He looked up into Reaver's lined face and the thief nodded to the door. Meyral got the hint and slipped away from the table without another word.

* * *

The angelic woman surveyed Alberto like a cat watching a mouse.

"Do you want something?"

"I…uh…was just wondering…what's in your ears?" The words fell out of his mouth, along with his dignity.

"Gorilla knuckle bones from the island of Callula. Why?"

So many questions spun around in Alberto's head as he stared at her intimidating earrings. She downed her last shot and waited a few seconds for a response that wasn't coming.

"Well…if you don't mind, I ought to be going. I have things to do. Perhaps I'll see you later."

"What's your name?" Alberto blurted out as she got up to leave.

"Aldomein," she replied with an alluring grin.

Before Alberto could manage to form any coherent syllables, she left the pub. He shook his head, trying to release himself from her spell. He looked at the shot he'd ordered, which had been neglected in Aldomein's presence, but it was Reaver who raised it to his lips and gulped it down.

"Bert, we need to leave," he said with a sigh. "Now."

Meyral appeared at Alberto's side without him even noticing, still dumbstruck by the purple-haired huntress. Alberto followed the others silently as Meyral waved frantically at Maxine. The trio exited the pub and followed Reaver into the darkness of the alley.

When he was sure that they were alone and fully engulfed in shadow, Reaver turned and spoke. "Go ahead, Meyral."

"Guys, there's a bounty on our heads. We need to get out of here."

"What do you mean?" Alberto asked. "There's no way that guy with the giant turtle thing woke up yet!" He looked behind him, as if expecting the driver to be chasing them.

"Turtle-snatching isn't serious enough for a bounty, Bert," Maxine said as she smacked her brother's arm. "If anything the constabulary would come looking for us."

"Maxine is right, as usual," Reaver said, earning him a smile from Maxine. "It's Nordcross—they're looking for Old Kingdom Remnants." He walked toward the rear of the bar and tore a poster down. Reaver handed it to Maxine, who gasped.

"Well, what is it? What does it say!?" Alberto asked. He didn't like being left in the dark.

"Sorry, I keep forgetting you can't read," Maxine said. It was as much an insult as it was honesty. "It's a poster offering a thousand pieces of gold to anyone who can deliver Ardänian refugees to Nordcross."

Alberto kept staring, not quite catching on.

"Bert, *we* are Old Kingdom Remnants!" she said.

"There's no denying you're Ardänians—look at your clothes!"

Reaver gestured to Maxine's shirt and Meyral's vest. "Looks like I'll be staying away from any Ardänian garb for a while…"

"You said we'd be fine here," Alberto said as he ground his teeth.

"Guess not." Reaver shrugged. "But we need to go."

The four of them sneaked around the backstreets of Gate Five until they were running through the countryside under the cover of night. They only came to a halt when the city was out of sight. A moment later, the crickets erupted in their nighttime orchestra.

"That was a nice job, Meyral," Maxine finally said. "Very good intel. I managed to find out that Mantrych is about a night's walk northeast from here from some…some old man." She shuddered. "Apparently we go right at the next two forks and we're there. How'd you do, Bert?"

"I didn't get far. But I got her name," Alberto said, finally mastering his tongue since they left the alley.

"What?" Maxine asked quickly. "Whose name?"

"…huh? What? Never mind. Which way are we going? I'm starving!"

They reached a large oak tree that marked the first fork in the road.

"We take the path to the right," Reaver paused a second, "like Maxine said."

"So, whose name, Bert?" Meyral asked quietly with a sly grin. "Don't think I forgot about that."

But Alberto was done talking for the night. He took off down the road without answering their questions. Meyral chuckled at Maxine, and the two companions continued on behind him. None of them noticed the tall, broad-shouldered figure hidden up in the tree, watching and listening.

* * *

They walked in silence for several hours, all the while in fear of being pursued. Just after midnight, while the smallest moon set, their fears came true.

"Shit! I think I hear someone coming." Alberto dove off the road and into the high grass along the side.

"Are you sure, Bert? Might just be your heart or something," Meyral muttered.

This was the third time that Alberto or Maxine had heard something, and Meyral was getting fed up with diving into ditches.

"Either way, might as well get off the road." Reaver yawned and steered a reluctant Meyral into another ditch.

Meyral was just happy that their guide hadn't turned into another animal and left them. To their surprise, three riders approached on beasts that Meyral was unfamiliar with. They looked like hairy, overgrown pigs with huge paws, but it was hard for him to see them in the dark.

"I thought you said you saw something!" a gruff voice asked.

"I did," a high-pitched voice responded.

"I know those voices," Maxine said with a scowl.

"What?" Alberto whispered loudly.

"Quiet!" the high-pitch voice yelled. "I think I heard something."

Maxine and Meyral glared at Alberto, who shrugged apologetically.

"You ain't heard shit!" the gruff voice responded.

"I think you're both full of shit," a slightly muffled voice said.

Maxine's eyes went wide and she mouthed to Reaver, "They were in the bar!"

Meyral ventured a peek through the grass he was using as cover. He could make out a tall, toothless man, a short man who was picking his nose, and their scruffy friend who had just finished telling them they were "full of shit."

"Look, that old guy said she was heading to Mantrych. They've got to be on this road somewhere!" The gruff voice belonged to the short man, who was examining whatever he'd picked out of his nose.

"If you two didn't mess it up with that green-haired hooker, she'd already be in our warm room. Instead we're out here in the middle of the night, freezing our asses off because you guys have no game!" The high-pitched voice belonged to the toothless man.

Maxine and Alberto joined Meyral in risking peeks through the weeds while Reaver searched his pack for something.

The short man flicked whatever used to be in his nose off of his glove and spoke again. "You two are a disgrace to manliness."

Maxine covered her mouth, but her body still shook with silent laughter.

"Go back if you want. I'm getting that Nordcross reward for

Ardänian refugees. Then maybe I'll be able to afford a decent pair of dentures…"

"If you hadn't eaten those damned mushrooms like we told you, you'd still have your teeth," the scruffy man snapped back.

"And maybe if you didn't spend all your damned money on booze—"

"I saw the poster! I deserve more of the reward!" the short man butted in.

"Who cares? I recognized her Ardänian outfit, so if anything, I'm getting the whole reward!" The scruffy man was getting angrier.

"Because only people from Ardänia wear black? We should just turn back now." The short one seemed fed up with the whole thing.

"The whatchamacallit on the sleeves is what makes it…you know what," the toothless man started pointed wildly back down the road, "just go! Go on, that way there's more money for me!"

"You mean us!" the gruff man added.

"She can't be far now." The toothless man changed the subject. "Just wait 'til I get my hands on that sweet ass…"

Meyral could practically hear the short man panting. The scruffy man grunted and the three riders rode away on their animals, leaving their prey behind, still hidden in their ditch.

"Hooker?" Meyral asked when the riders were out of sight.

"I know!" Alberto whispered. "She sounds sexy, but I didn't see any green-haired girl. Plus, what are the odds that there'd be another Ardänian in that bar?"

A flash and a low, muffled string of curses drew their attention to Reaver. He had his forefinger in his mouth, and Meyral glared at him.

"You're still after the staff, aren't you?" he snapped at their guide.

"Always," Reaver said as he pulled his blistered finger from his mouth and slipped it into his glove. "Relax. I was just trying to light this." He held up a thin cigar with a bright blue flame at its tip. He looked at Alberto and added, "To answer your question, they were talking about Maxine, you load of buffalo dung."

Alberto's hand twitched and he angrily hopped up to his feet. He grabbed Maxine by the collar. "Why are they calling you a hooker, Sis?" he shouted in her face.

"Calm down! They were just pigs! They were too drunk to even carry a conversation." She pulled herself out of Alberto's grasp and dusted herself off. "They thought I was a hooker. And why would it matter? Do you really think it's true?"

She glared at her brother, and the tension was so thick Meyral was sure a fire would start beneath them.

"Forget it." Alberto turned to leave, but Maxine grabbed his elbow.

"If you ever grab me like that again, little brother, I will beat the living shit out of you."

"Maybe we should stay off the road from now on," Reaver intervened as Alberto was about to respond.

"Good idea," Alberto said. "Maybe you'll be useful yet." He turned, and this time he succeeded in storming off angrily.

Maxine took a deep breath and let it out slowly. Meyral reached out to touch her, but she batted his hand away gently.

"Just…don't. I'll be fine in a moment." Her eyes were closed, but Meyral knew there were tears behind those lids.

"Give her some time," Reaver told Meyral. He pulled the cigar from his lips and blew a few smoke rings. "Women are much stronger creatures than we often give them credit for."

CHAPTER EIGHT: NOSTALGIA

28th day of Anatra in the 507th Year of Dengen

My empire has been as it is for an eternity; a stone, a rock, a solid frame within the cosmos, forever constant, so it seems. What is its true history? Will I ever know how or why this place was created?

I'm sure there is some mythology surrounding its creation—perhaps a phoenix being slain on a mountaintop, or a moon giving up its immortality to grant us the power to thrive, or the gods singing life into the universe. Regardless, this empire is what it is—the most powerful nation in all of Cygnus. We are militaristically superior, our laws are perfect, our citizens are respectful and have pride in their empire, and civil wars have never touched our shores. We have settled into Utopia.

Why then, am I so discontent?

Is it because I am alone?

I know it. No matter what happens from here on out, I will forever be alone, trapped with myself and what I let happen...what I've done. But really, what is the difference? If you let something like that happen, if you did nothing to stop it, isn't that just as bad as doing it yourself?

We had met ten years ago...this month. Perhaps this is why I have taken up writing. Her death makes my own seem near, and lacking an heir, I want to leave some sort of a legacy.

29th day of Anatra in the 507th Year of Dengen

Azrael, my stone fortress, has served as my family's home for as long as any of us care to remember. My father actually attempted to use it as a military institution, but my mother would not even hear of it. Her dying wish, in fact, was to let me grow up inside of this fortress as my home, not some army base. Father never talked about her much...in fact, he rarely talked at all, unless it was about some political move he was going to make.

The irony in this is that his political strategies were futile. There was nothing that needed changing—it was perfect. He simply wanted to know that he had the power. He loved to pretend...he was a pathetic man. It was sick to be happy at his funeral, I know, but I couldn't help it. How is it fair to make such easy feelings a bad thing? You can't help your emotions. They are simply a byproduct of who you are.

Like my addiction...some would call me a drunk. Maybe I am.

The other night I relapsed. I started drinking again. This time, I wasn't alone. Sera was with me. We drank for most of the night, and she slept in the guest chamber down the hall. She seems to want to stay here more often during these cold, wintry nights. There seems to be another woman in my life...but even if things progressed and I remarried, I would still be alone. Sera would never understand me....

Not like she did. Oh, how I miss her.

I am the last of my kin. The Erranko bloodline ends with me. Who will rule Nordcross in my wake? My last wife, my only love, was perfect in every way but one...she was barren. I have no children.

Early morning, 34th day of Anatra in the 507th Year of Dengen

I still remember the first time I laid eyes on my beloved. She had been a citizen of my empire, not of a royal bloodline, but I was convinced that she was a gift to me from the heavens. Her stunningly white eyes, encircling her ruby irises, placed ever so delicately upon her perfect, angelic face. A few small freckles dotted the tops of each cheek, and her eyebrows were perfectly arched to match her haughty personality. Her bright blonde hair shone in the sun like the wings of a thousand angels visiting our lowly planet in some rare, celestial dance, flowing with the breeze.

She had a thin neck, graceful like a swan, but her shoulders gave her an air of power. Her figure was shaped perfectly, as if the gods had spent extra effort molding her. Her hands were slim, her fingers long and agile; had the circumstances been different, I have no doubt that she would have been an incredible harpist.

She had a certain way that she would stand—both hands on her hips, head tilted to the right, her eyes boring right into your mind...like what you were saying was so blatantly wrong that you had to have been beaten over the head to think such a thing.

This was the stance she took when we first met.

At the time, my father had seven years before he would be killed in battle. A fitting end for such a barbarous man. It's no wonder our country is so hated...

My father sent me to Iblis. The farmers had been unable to pay the taxes they owed, and my father thought they were simply holding out. He sent me as a kind of local authority to make sure they weren't trying to sneak anything past him.

What a selfish man.

That particular town was famous for its vineyards, and more importantly to my father, wine. This unfortunate fact meant that my father had taxed these farmers mercilessly as a way to keep his stores stocked and his subordinates drunk.

A sizeable manor had been erected upon the farthest hill to serve as my office during my stay. The manor's caretaker lived on the grounds with his family, and when I went to meet with him...that's when I saw her.

She was so beautiful. I walked inside, my speech carefully prepared, but upon laying eyes on her, I was struck dumb. I couldn't say a word! Never in my life has such a thing happened to me!

She stood there, her feet angled out, right hand resting on her hip, ponytail trailing in front of her left shoulder, her left hand clutching her right arm. Gods have mercy...she was an angel.

Iblis is set on a series of large hills, in the middle of a massive, grassy plain. Toward the north of the town, the largest hill rises and levels off at the beginning of a vineyard, which leads into the Arneus Forest. Off in the distance, past Arneus, is the beginning of the Osdorf Territory, beyond Nordcross' reign. From that hill, you can see sunsets and moonsets that seem like previews of heaven itself. The scenery truly is beautiful there, but only a fraction of the beauty I saw within her.

She was so stubborn at first. She ignored me, she avoided me, she treated me like I was the most annoying suitor in the world. It took months, but I eventually befriended her and gained her trust.

One day I went to her room and asked if she would accompany me on a walk. Instantly, I imagined all that I had worked for falling to pieces. The look in her eyes was so wary, so suspicious. I thought for sure that she would deny me and slam the door, never to speak to me again. To my surprise, she smiled that perfect smile and said yes.

She wore her traveling cloak, since it had been raining lately. We walked for about an hour before I led her to the town well, where we sat and watched the moons trail through the sky like giant comets. We talked about everything...I learned more about her that day than I'd learned about anything or anyone else in my entire life. She became my life.

Evening, 34th day of Anatra in the 507th Year of Dengen

Within a month, I had proposed to her. I took her on a walk just before sunset to the highest hill, behind the manor. I told her to look around and watch the moons, to survey all that she saw. She gave me that stare, that intimidating, wary glare. I told her that this entire empire, and if I had my way, the moons as well, would be hers if she would do me the honor of becoming my wife, my everything. She was beyond perfect....

She put her hand on her hip, flipped her hair over her shoulder, and said that she didn't care for empires. She asked what she would do with the moons. She was rejecting me!

I made to turn my head, to hide my face that would no doubt give away my breaking heart. She flung her arms around me and gently brought my chin up to hers. We shared our first kiss then; it was deep and passionate, and it seemed to last lifetimes. She wanted only me. She didn't care about the empire. I was ecstatic.

It was the first time in my life that I had truly felt happiness.

The wedding took only a month to plan, and I spent that month pacing my bedchamber. I was so nervous...I let her and her newly appointed staff plan out exactly what she wanted. Rather than inviting the entire empire like we were expected to do, she only invited a few of her close friends. She also invited what was left of my family, despite my grievances. As luck would have it, this only consisted of a half-crazed cousin and my extremely spiritual aunt that I had never had an honest conversation with.

I convinced her that I wanted my father to play no part in my personal life. It took a while, but she finally conceded. My father was much easier. I told him I didn't want him there, and the most noise he made during our little "talk" was a grunt.

My love wanted to invite my friends and was shocked to find that I had none—she told me that she would have to "fix" that.

We were to be married in the temple where I was born and blessed, a few miles from the fortress. She would go on about how perfect that place was, with its history and its deep foundation that reached back to the dawn of the empire. I saw an old building with a crumbling wall, but she saw the beauty in the rough stone. It was…poetic.

The day finally came, and, after a small breakfast that I almost lost due to nerves, I found myself waiting for my bride. She walked in to the sound of a single harp, which she thought was splurging. I didn't tell her that my grandparents had had a full orchestra complete with twenty young children performing at their ceremony. Whether we had a single harp or a sea of instruments didn't make any difference in the world; all my senses were focused only on one thing. Her.

Her dress was a simple ivory gown that was laced up in the back with crimson ribbon. It had long sleeves with a low neckline that revealed just enough of her porcelain skin and her strong shoulders. The skirt crept down to her ankles, but it did not puff out or try to hide her slender body in any way, nor did it cling. Instead it flowed with her like a feather on the north wind. Her face wore no powder or pigment, which would only take away from her perfection, and on her feet she wore nothing. If you just happened on the ceremony, you might have thought that perhaps a wood nymph had seduced a man into marriage.

It was the longest six hours of my life, but that night was pure bliss. I won't even dare to write about that night, for fear that they turn out to be a dream, or some old man's weak fantasy. I alone will be the keeper of those memories….

We tried for many years to conceive a child, with no success. Despite this, I was never happier. She was perfect, and as long as I had her, I had no need for a child.

And now, as I sit here writing this…without her…I want a child. Her only other imperfection…was her mortality. What had I done to anger the gods? Why did they see it fit to take her from me? I let it happen. I let her die. I killed her.

I'm not ready. Not tonight.

1st day of Verro in the 507th Year of Dengen

I was with Sera again. She reminds me of *her* in so many ways…I promised myself that I would never love another woman. I won't have a problem fulfilling that promise. However, Sera is proving to be good company. She comes over, we have a few drinks, we eat, we talk, and we go to sleep. Lately, it's been…different. No longer does she sleep in the guest chamber, but in the bed that I've only shared with one other woman. I almost feel guilty, but like I said before…why should one feel guilty about one's feelings? I can't help them.

She would want me to be happy, to move on. Unfortunately, those are things I can't wholly do. Does that make it like cheating? No…it can't.

Sera even looks like her, except for her eyes. Sera's are a bright emerald green, nothing compared to that soft ruby red. Some nights, I can't stand to look at her. It hurts too much, and I send her away without explanation. She never holds it against me. She has no idea why, but she knows it's a necessity.

What a sweet woman…so forgiving. Am I deceiving her? Leading her on? Letting her think she's getting somewhere, letting her think she can melt my icy heart? She doesn't know I am forever grieving for my love. Perhaps if I talk to Sera, she will understand. Maybe I should send her away. Whether or not she stays is of no consequence to me, but she deserves a whole man, which I can never be again.

I can't keep doing this to her.

2nd day of Verro in the 507th Year of Dengen

Last night I was plagued with an awful nightmare, and when I woke up all I could remember was dread. But why? Was it a sign? What in the hells was it?

For some reason, it reminded me of my father's funeral. That day, there was a full ceremony, and the entire empire was in mourning. Well, aside from me. It was…a relief.

Is that wrong to say? It's how I felt. Relieved.

My love didn't want to join the funeral procession, and neither did I, but I couldn't escape my duties. She never really liked the spotlight, but she loved me enough to become my bride. To love so much that your fears become inconsequential…gods be praised.

I refused to speak at his wake, but I had to give a speech at my own coronation the next day. That went well. To tell the truth, I would have been fine if somebody else had taken over. As long as I could just continue living in peace with her...maybe if I had stepped down, everything would have been different.

Maybe she wouldn't have had to die.

7th day of Verro in the 507th Year of Dengen

I don't even know what to think anymore. First off, I told Sera everything. Everything! And she was fine with it. She almost seemed to expect it! Hah! I should have known—I am the emperor, she would have known. Everybody had heard about the murder.

She slept with me again. This time, however, was the first time that it wasn't platonic. It wasn't as good as when I was with...her...but it did wonders to soothe my loneliness.

Before sunrise, the 8th day of Verro in the 507th Year of Dengen

I had the nightmare again. I was on what I could only guess was a moon. I have determined that it was most likely the smallest moon, Klyntar, supposedly the most powerful of the three. I was above myself, standing before a tall, blond man who was sitting in a chair.

He wore a striped shirt and had a small, strange medallion around his neck. In his arms he held a guitar, and he was concentrating on playing. The music he emitted was unlike that which I had ever heard before—it was full of sorrow and pain, yet comforting at the same time. It was smooth and rhythmic, absolutely beautiful.

He seemed to have not even noticed my appearance. I glanced at myself from above; I was wearing my royal garb—the black boots with gold buckles, black silk pants, gold- and silver-embroidered purple tunic, and my black-and-white fur cape draped down my back, drawn together in the front by a gold cord.

My broadsword was sheathed at my hip with its handle exposed. Around my forehead was my silver crown with the onyx stone in the center, which I use for hunts and other such endeavors. My thick, black hair was tied back, and my beard was neatly trimmed, like I haven't seen it in years. I returned to myself to watch the tall man play his guitar.

Without missing a beat, he looked up as soon as I entered my body. He looked straight at me, and then beyond me. He looked back down at his guitar. His music sped up slightly and my heart began beating faster. Clearly he wanted me to turn around.

My eyes lit on the world we were revolving around—my world, Cygnus, the house of my empire. Suddenly a small sphere appeared in front of me. It grew larger and larger, until it took up my entire view. It began to shimmer, and it formed a sort of vision.

I saw myself, and then I was myself. I was standing in the middle of a desert, with a horde of people around me. There was another person in the circle that the throng had formed. It was my love.

She was standing there, looking at me with those lovely red eyes. But something was wrong. Something was very wrong. Her hair was a silvery white, and her skin had taken on a greenish tinge. It seemed to be stretched directly over her skeleton, giving her a very hollow look. Her flesh, or what was left of it, had large gashes in many places, where bugs would crawl out and back into other wounds.

Her lips were not the supple, beautiful ones that I had kissed so many times. They had become rotting bits of flesh, pulled over blackened and yellowed teeth. Her clothes were moth-eaten and falling apart, and when she opened her mouth, dust and flies spilled out. The look in her eyes was sad, a sadness that I had never before seen in them.

I could witness no more. I turned away and found myself facing the man in the chair once again. His music had been picking up speed, although it was still soft and full of sorrow.

"What do you think you're doing?" I screamed at him. "Why would you show me this? What kind of sick joke are you playing at? No one in their right mind would do this to any man!"

He continued playing his instrument. He never relented. His right hand began strumming even faster as the fingers on his left flew over the frets. The song became louder. Pain replaced sorrow, hate replaced pain. His music was either controlling or reflecting my emotions, it was hard to tell. He looked up for a second. His face was unreadable. He made no sound other than that of his music.

"You aren't even going to talk to me? You won't even justify this…this vile vision you've shown me? By the moons—"

After I had said this, his strumming became frantic and angry. The music became caustic and disturbingly loud. I felt compelled to spin around, or maybe it was just morbid curiosity. Either way, the next image was coming into view.

I was walking forward in the desert, and the throng of people closed in on me. I reached out to touch my love, and she reached out to touch me. As soon as our hands met, she turned to ash, and I could do nothing but watch as she crumbled away. I had lost her again.

"You bastard! Stop it! Send me back! I don't want to see any more! ARE YOU LISTENING TO ME?"

At this point I had gotten so close to him that I could feel the heat emanating from him as his hands worked furiously. He looked up and our eyes locked. His music suddenly changed. It slowed and became more harmonious. It filled me with the deepest of melancholies. I became sick to my stomach. He nodded, signifying to me that it was time to awaken.

I woke up and my head was throbbing. I quickly leaned over the bed and vomited until I had nothing left to expel. I guess I drank too much the night before....

But I swear, I could still hear that freak's music playing, echoing throughout my bedchamber.

19th day of Verro in the 507th Year of Dengen

It was nearly three years ago, my darling died. It was so unexpected. I can't imagine a day when I will be used to the fact, when I can live again and be happy.

We had taken a vacation to the western outskirts of Nordcross the first summer that I'd spent as the emperor. On her request, we went to a lake that cuts through a small section of the Wolke Mountains and separates Nordcross from the Old Kingdom Ardänia. It was so remote that it didn't even have a name on any map that I knew of.

Everything that was there we brought through a small mountain pass—there wasn't even a road, and it all had to be hauled in. I assured her that we had much faster ways of transporting luggage, but she was insistent. She wanted land tortoises to bring us in.

Looking back, it added a certain unique element to the trip. The use of tortoises as transportation was so outdated...but simple. Simple and quaint, just like her.

It was our own secret escape.

We had built a magnificent house there, and we were having the time of our lives. Every morning for nearly an entire month, we would take our small sailboat to the island in the center of the lake.

It was the most beautiful place I had ever seen. It was surrounded by lush trees and huge green ferns. A spectacular network of waterfalls poured down from the northern end of the mountains, which created a certain ripple effect. The sky reflected in the water shimmered with the tiny waves.

Once we got to the island, we would make a snack out of the luscious fruits that grew on its trees. We would spend the whole morning there, and we'd head back when the sun was directly above us. In the afternoon, we would often jump in the water and swim around, scaring the ducks that landed on our shore.

Seven years together, and that woman was still just as wonderful as ever. We were far from any village or town, and nobody came to bother us. It was bliss.

Something still plagues me though. The last few days of her life...she acted so strangely. It was as if she knew, perhaps, that her end was near. She became adventurous and wild and...so different. Was it bad? I don't know. She could have become anything, and I still would have loved her just the same.

That last night...that horrible night, I remember waking up and feeling for her, but only finding a cold spot where she should have lain. Disturbed, I got out of bed to find where she had run off to. I searched the house for what seemed like hours, but to no avail. My curiosity became worry and I ran outside, but she was nowhere to be found. My worry became panic when I realized that our small detail of guards was also missing. Finally, I went to search the lake—but before I'd even gotten into the water, a horrific sight met me.

Her body, mutilated beyond recognition, was floating facedown in the water about ten feet from the shore. I pulled her out and flipped her over, but her body was already ice cold.

She had been slashed in a million places—the only way I was able to identify her was by what remained of her left eye. A dull, red iris looked blankly up at the sky, her soul having parted long ago.

I knelt there for hours, holding her wet, bloody body in my arms, howling with rage and despair. Her blood soaked my clothes, but there was no way I was going to let her go...someone had just killed the only person, the only thing in this life, that had ever made me happy. In essence, they had killed me too.

A search was conducted, but I never found her killer. We never even knew of a motive. Nobody had been found in the area; the only tracks around the house were ours from that day. The closest person we found was some deaf old hag in a cottage about thirteen miles away.

The search was called off after a month. Everyone had decided that whoever it was, they weren't going to be found.

Should I find that person…what they did to my wife will look like a papercut.

27th day of Verro in the 507th Year of Dengen

I've been alone for several weeks now. Sera never came back after she left to check on her family…why did she leave? Maybe she didn't take what I told her as well as she seemed to. Perhaps I scared her off. I shouldn't have told her I could never truly love again.

I shouldn't have been honest? How does that make sense? I feel like I'm going mad. I wish she would come back….

36th day of Verro in the 507th Year of Dengen

Yearend. A day of new beginnings. Ten months passes and we realize how far we've moved in only a year. And with every passing year, I am amazed at how time seems to be slipping past me more and more quickly.

A letter from Sera arrived today. It came from Abon, the only civil town in the Island Nations. I'm on my way to meet her. Apparently she has something for me, and it's quite urgent.

At least she hasn't just disappeared….

19th day of Mucca in the 508th Year of Kaosu

JASPAR.

Sera had been disappearing the last few months for days at a time. She had been searching for clues, and it led her to the Island Nations, to a broadsword coated in dried blood—my wife's blood. The bastard was bragging! He and his stupid clan of Old Kingdom Remnants were rejoicing in her death. Bragging in his collapsed kingdom wasn't enough. He had to take it south, to another realm. The nerve….

That night, he had gotten drunk and passed out. Sera searched his room and found the sword, but she didn't take it. The next morning, she sent for me. A week before I arrived, the son of a bitch had disappeared, undoubtedly back to his nation of demons.

Sera was able to find out that the murderer's country was still in celebration. Apparently they recreated some sort of order throughout and were continuing to call their decaying nation Ardänia, after the Old Kingdom.

Sera told me that the lake we were staying at was considered a holy site by the Ardänians, and the Remnants still believe it to be a part of their nation. The fact that my love and I were staying there was an immediate threat and a declaration of war, so they killed my wife.

Jaspar killed my wife!

20th day of Mucca in the 508th Year of Kaosu

I keep going over things in my head.

The land around the Wolke Mountains has always been neutral territory!

Why her? Why would they have killed her and not me?

Jaspar. The Ardänians. I will have their heads. And before I'm finished, Jaspar will beg me for death!

22nd day of Mucca in the 508th Year of Kaosu

I left for Azrael with Sera. It's time to assemble the troops. If the Ardänians think that we were at war before, then they are sorely mistaken.

I will have my revenge.

28th day of Mucca in the 508th Year of Kaosu

Sera offered to help. She wants to take command of the army. Let her become the commanding officer? Why not?

This will leave me more time to search on my own. She has agreed to take Jaspar alive and inform me when they have him, so that I may take my revenge personally.

10th day of Ruolo in the 508th Year of Kaosu

Sera is training the troops on her own. She is very secretive about it, but they have become these powerful, mindless…for lack of a better word, monsters. I don't understand it, but it hardly bothers me. She clearly knows what she is doing. Perhaps she is a former commander from the Islands….

She offered me my own squad of men. They are simply amazing! Six trained assassins, killers through and through. They wear leather and bone armor that has been dyed black, protecting them and allowing them to stay agile at the same time. Their heads are wrapped in black cloth, exposing only their eyes…but they are the eyes of the dead. They move silently, making them practically undetectable in the shadows.

Each has a specialty, I was told, and I was given a demonstration of their abilities. The soldier was huge and held a sword the size of his own body. I didn't expect much…but I watched as a group of five convicts we had gathered were ripped to shreds in a matter of seconds!

He was remarkably fast. There was no sound, save for the screams of the last two of the condemned and a sickening squishing of limbs hitting the ground.

Bravo.

They were assigned to protect me and do my bidding. I told her I didn't need them, but she insisted. We compromised and split the guard—three for her, three for me.

Jaspar will be mine soon enough. In the meantime, they can protect me all they want.

32nd day of Ruolo in the 508th Year of Kaosu

When I woke up, Sera was gone. When I went to look for her, the guards advised me to stay inside, saying that she had gone to escort a troupe of scouts to the border. When the morning came, the sky had turned a dark, sickly green, something I had never seen before.

This is too much for me to handle. I'm going to lose it all soon….

19th day of Maiale in the 508th Year of Kaosu

I almost feel bad for Sera...all she has ever wanted to do is make me happy. Yet here she is, in the middle of a war for the sake of my dead wife that she never knew.

Will revenge make me happy again? Will I be able to let go of her and become happy with Sera? Is that even feasible?

30th day of Aquila in the 508th Year of Kaosu

The end of another month, and there is still no news. My hate is boiling inside of me—I fear I may crack soon. What would happen to Azrael without me?

28th day of Erranko in the 508th Year of Kaosu

The news came a few days ago, during my birthday celebration. Sera sent two of her assassins straight into Ardänia, where they found an old doxyl breeder. He said he knew of a great warrior named Jaspar who lived in a village near the Errigan River. I know not of what happened to the man, but for his reverence of Jaspar, I hope he was killed.

23rd day of Drago in the 508th Year of Kaosu

The search for Jaspar seems futile. The village that the doxyl breeder described is absent from any map we have.

Sera is brilliant, but she can only do so much, even with the help of her guards.

5th day of Corvo in the 508th Year of Kaosu

They found him. I will personally escort the entire army and my own squad as we assault the village. This is it. Sera's reports included something about an artifact that makes the Ardänians more powerful, though I doubt it exists. It's probably just more of their Old Kingdom rubbish.

Sera took ill the day after the report came in. She will not be able to accompany me into Ardänia...it's probably better that way. She shouldn't see me avenge my love's murder.

29th day of Corvo in the 508th Year of Kaosu

I finally made it to the small village where Jaspar was said to live. He knew we were coming, and he had all the villagers flee ahead of time. He apparently had it in his head that he could take on this entire army by himself. The fool....

Well, he certainly was skilled, I'll give him that. However, our army was much too powerful for him, as he should have expected.

When we entered the town, I thought the coward had run like the rest of them. The screams from the westernmost part of this village told me otherwise. By the time we converged on the noise, we found that a squadron of foot soldiers had already been wiped out within minutes. We hadn't even a chance to negotiate. He clearly was not coming quietly.

As we swarmed around him, he rushed at the nearest platoon. He jumped in the middle of them, landing on one man's face and crushing his skull. As soon as he hit the ground, he executed a perfect sweep kick, tripping every soldier around him. By this time, the ones that were still standing had finally drawn their swords.

He launched himself off the ground and grabbed the head of the nearest man, spun around and snapped his neck, finishing it off by landing on the back of another man with an audible crunch. He stole the sword of his latest victim and lopped off three of the closest soldiers' heads with it.

The remaining ten or so men, out of the initial thirty, finally joined the fight. Jaspar kicked at one of the dead soldiers, and a second sword launched itself from the corpse. Without any hesitation, he snatched it out of the air with his free hand. He was wielding two swords like some fantastical beast!

He used his left sword to deflect attacks and his right sword to jab and slash. As soon as I thought I saw a pattern, he would change his style. In a few short minutes, that whole squad had been impaled or beheaded.

When the yelling stopped, he stood on the pile of bodies, his mangy hair dripping with blood and hanging in his face. I was horrified at this point. This man killed my wife, and now there was nothing in his way to stop him from finishing me off as well!

In one swift motion, he threw a sword right at me, leaving me no time to react. I thought I was dead—but one of Sera's assassins, who only uses his bare hands, jumped in front of me and caught the sword by the handle, with its point merely inches away from his face.

My lead assassin, the one from the demonstration, emerged from the woods at the same time the one with the throwing knives appeared from behind a tree. Jaspar clearly recognized that he was more than outmatched, and he dropped his other weapon.

The soldiers weren't too keen on letting him live—in fact, one of the smaller units defied my orders and charged him. Before they made it within striking distance, however, one of the guards sprang into action. In a flash, a slew of blades had found their way into every soldier's neck, killing them instantly. I can't honestly say that I saw him move when he threw the knives....

Sometimes, these guards of mine scare me. They terrify me.

But I wanted Jaspar to suffer. We bound him and threw him in the back of the carriage.

The generals believe that his fighting was a stalling tactic...I don't care. I have my prize, and as soon as we get to the fortress, that heartless bastard is going into the dungeon to rot. I will make it a point to go down there every morning and cut him, just like he cut my wife, until the day he dies.

He deserves nothing less.

30th day of Corvo in the 508th Year of Kaosu

The Ardänian dog escaped my grasp!

He was in a steel carriage with no windows and chains all around. I had the only key. My lead assassin was guarding the carriage, along with a squadron of our most experienced soldiers. We chained Jaspar's hands and feet to the vehicle, but he somehow freed himself.

He fought off the squad that was guarding him, and the people in front never heard a thing. Sera and I were baffled that he actually bested that assassin—he was one of the best. And then it hit me.

Jaspar was an Ardänian Remnant for a reason. The royal knights of Ardänia had escaped the kingdom's collapse. I have no doubt that these men are masters of survival and the fight for life. Their teachings were passed down to the current generation...perhaps there were even some knights still among them. This man was no fool, and treating him like one was my mistake.

We made it as far as the Wolke Mountains by the time we

realized he was gone. A group of horses from the rear convoy, the one that housed the murderer, reached us. They had no riders.

We couldn't pursue him at that point. It would have been too risky. I have no doubt he knows he can use the terrain to his advantage, and it would be stupid to search for him. It's damn near impossible to travel through the range, let alone track someone....

This one man is evading my army, a truly impressive feat. Sera is furious that her troops weren't able to contain him. Her letters were enough to scare even me. Even her handwriting looks like hers....

If we don't see any sign of him in a week, I'm going to have to retreat. He'll take us all out by night if we stay here too long. To the right people, those mountains are a stronghold in and of themselves.

This cannot go on any longer. I need my vengeance NOW!

13th day of Mulo in the 508th Year of Kaosu

Sera said that the troops had captured someone with information about the weapon. I'm not getting too involved—this is Sera's area, and she is rather adamant that I shouldn't bother myself with it. As long as it leads me to this "weapon" of theirs so that I can use it against Jaspar, I'm fine.

The information she got from the captive was minimal, so she let them go. I'm not sure why Sera was being so lenient, but that prisoner should be thanking the gods they're still alive. She assured me, however, that a mercenary would be checking up on that information.

18th day of Anatra in the 508th Year of Kaosu

Sera is a godsend...she knows so much. She found an ancient scroll that contained a piece of Ardänian mythology. Apparently, there is always some kind of staff in each of the histories. This staff has enormous power whose limits are unknown. She has suggested that obtaining this artifact is our top priority, as it seems to be the only chance we are going to have to destroy Jaspar. That man is the devil himself!

According to her, there is a book of records that was found in the town of Tem when her assassins raided it. The tome was half destroyed and barely legible, but we were able to glean at least one piece of important information. Jaspar was the last known Ardänian in possession of the staff—the Keeper, they called it.

Another scroll that they had found told of a tale in which a man named Kain had once wielded the staff. He seems to have fought off an entire army with that weapon alone. After seeing what these Ardänians are capable of, that doesn't seem like too much of an impossible feat.

I cross-referenced the dates of the scrolls with some tomes that my personal assistant Gideon brought me. I found that there are records even in our empire of such an event. The Tribes of the Monolith were all but destroyed during that battle, and the powers unleashed scarred the planet itself.

Jaspar, however, did not have the staff when we faced him. Good thing, too, for he might have destroyed us all.

He is ruthless.

Where has the staff gone? Even Sera isn't sure. We need to find it—it should have been in that village, if Jaspar truly did still have it. Since he knew we were coming, maybe he had someone take the staff somewhere safe?

Damn him!

25th day of Anatra in the 508th Year of Kaosu

The staff is apparently heading toward Mantrych. I don't want a global war on my hands…Sera needs to either keep it in this country or sneak in and take it. We can demolish Ardänia for what they've done, but we can't just waltz through all the other nations chasing bandits and rebels.

I'm going to bide my time, until I decide we can strike again. Sera is forever gathering information, which helps to ease my nerves. She feeds me updates about what we're after, how we're getting it, when we project that we'll get it…and every once in a while, she comes back home. Then it's like old times with her—we talk, we drink, we sleep.

Those nights, I feel like I have my wife back…almost.

CHAPTER NINE: TARYN

"Halt! Who goes there?"

"My name is Meyral, and I have a message for Taryn," he said after a second's pause to bring himself back to reality. They had been walking for so long that he had forgotten they had a destination.

"Taryn? You're friends of Taryn's?"

In the early light of dawn, Meyral could just make out a troubled look cross the watchman's face. The guardhouse he sat in was attached to the village wall, but the guard left the comfort of his fire when he heard "Taryn."

"Red and black...Ardänian knots...some silk to boot," he mused as shadows played on his wrinkly face. "You're from the Old Kingdom. There's a bounty on your heads, you know that? In fact, a few hours ago I had to run off three morons who claimed to be waiting for a green-haired whore from Ardänia." The old man looked at Maxine and grinned. "You know anything about that?"

Meyral drew the staff and set it on the ground as Alberto tensed up next to him. He didn't have to look to know that Reaver was fluttering overhead.

The three of us could take one guard before he could raise the alarm.

"Take it easy, boys." The guard held out both hands. "If you really are friends of Taryn's, you'll be fine. Not many even know she's here. I'll have someone escort you to her since I can't leave my post."

The old guard put two fingers in his mouth and whistled. A shadowy figure moved in the hut on the other side of the gate. Meyral turned warily as another guard stepped into the light of the morning sun, bow drawn and aimed right at him. Despite the fear he felt prickling its way into his stomach, he took a moment to admire the new warrior.

Unlike Cathari, there was no mistaking her budding, womanly figure underneath her leather armor. Meyral blinked a few times and pulled his staff closer to his body.

"You have *children* guarding your walls?" Maxine asked with a hint of outrage in her voice.

The new guard turned her aim to Maxine. "If you question my abilities, I would be more than happy to demonstrate them on you."

"Rubi, relax. It was an innocent question." The old man chuckled and turned back to Maxine. "Rubi is one of our best fighters. I feel safer with her around than I would with many of the adults here."

Rubi slung the bow onto her back. Meyral's eyes caught the two sword hilts poking out from behind her other shoulder. He marveled at the dedication it would have taken someone so young to master both dual blades and a bow.

She noticed Meyral staring at her and she frowned. "I'll take them to see Taryn. As long as we have one person here, we're fine," Rubi said. She eyed the trio suspiciously. Her eyes lingered on Maxine for a fraction of a second longer than the rest before she finally turned back to the old guard. "I'll be back as soon as Taryn gives me the okay."

Meyral caught a glimpse of short, auburn hair beneath her helmet as she turned and walked toward the town. As his eyes trailed down, he saw her short swords strapped side by side down her back diagonally, beneath her ebony bow.

Before he had a chance to finish giving her his onceover, she rounded on them. "Follow me and stay close. No wandering, or I'll kill you and collect that bounty myself. Until Taryn vouches for you, I don't trust you."

She stepped up to Maxine. Her orange, steely eyes locked with Maxine's violet ones in a staring contest of sorts. Maxine gave a haughty scoff and crossed her arms. She looked away pointedly until Rubi turned and walked down the main road.

"Girls," Alberto mouthed to Meyral and rolled his eyes.

As the four of them walked toward their destination, Meyral gazed in wonder at Mantrych.

It was a town whose structures seemed like a congregation of wooden leftovers from decades past. Maxine explained the night before about the cities beyond the Wall being modernized, using steel and stone to build structures several stories high, but here everything was still made of wood and mud, with straw roofs. Only a handful reached beyond one story.

Each house was painted some shade of blue or green and had a little garden in front. Most had an old oak or two growing around them. Maybe it was the calming nature of the town, or that it reminded Meyral of home, but he felt secure as he took it all in.

Father must have sent me here to drop the staff off with Taryn. It seems like the safest place we've been to...it certainly explains all the security. Maybe Reaver knows where he is!

When they made it to the town square, which was nothing more than a wide patch of dirt lined with stones and surrounded by large plum trees, their escort came to a stop and faced them once again.

Rubi bit the inside of her cheek as she re-evaluated the travelers in front of her. "There's something I don't understand," she wondered aloud. "Why aren't you armed? You were traveling at night with little more than a walking stick, a bow with only a few arrows, and a hunting knife—you must know there are people after you."

Alberto shifted uncomfortably as she looked him up and down.

"You look strong, but the others, not so much. Are you stupid, or am I missing something? You certainly don't look like rogue mages."

They looked at each other, suddenly very aware of how vulnerable they were.

"Mages? No, we just..." Maxine started before rethinking her response. "Well, we never really gave it any thought. We sort of...left in a hurry." She blushed, embarrassed to have missed such an important detail.

"Where did you leave from in such a rush that you didn't properly arm yourselves?" Rubi asked as her eyes narrowed.

"We were—" Alberto began, but quickly changed course when Meyral delivered a swift kick to his leg. "—going to see Taryn."

The relief on Meyral's face was unmistakable. Rubi stepped up to Alberto, and even though her head only reached his chest, she was quite menacing.

"You may be big, but you'd be no match for my blades. Remember that." Rubi jabbed a finger into the big man's chest.

Alberto nodded his head, but even Meyral wasn't sure what he had done to deserve being threatened.

"Taryn's house is down this street. Let's go."

They walked to the northeast corner of the village and passed through another break in the town wall. A young man watched them from the gate as they left town and headed for a house flanked by orchards. As they walked, Meyral noticed a magpie perched in a nearby tree, but it flew away when he looked at it.

The nearest dwelling was far enough away that Meyral could hardly see it. Rubi reached the humbly painted porch and waited for the others to catch up. Then she reached forward and knocked on the heavy front door. Each knock echoed in Meyral's head. His pulse started to race.

This is it. I've traveled so far, and we were almost killed for this moment. What if this Taryn person laughs at me? What if I'm not worthy of the staff, and it's given to Alberto or Maxine? Either of them has to be a better candidate than me...I never would have made it this far without them.

Meyral ran through scenarios in his mind, each one worse than the last, until he heard shuffling footsteps from inside. They were quickly followed by the sounds of locks being undone, and then a face wrinkled by age peeked out from the doorway. She had a braid of silver hair draped over one shoulder, and her light red eyes brightened considerably upon seeing Rubi.

"To what do I owe the pleasure of seeing my favorite pupil this early?" she asked. "Did Tyler fall asleep at the gate again?"

Rubi shook her head. Her demeanor had become even stricter than before. She was as stiff as a board, her arms pointed straight down her sides.

"Then please, come in. I'll put some tea on."

"No thank you," Rubi responded curtly. "I'm here on official business. You have visitors."

The door opened more, bathing Meyral in the light from within. The old lady stared at him until he couldn't stand it anymore. He looked away, hoping one of the others would say something.

The old woman turned back to their escort. "Thank you very much, Rubi dear. I can take it from here."

Rubi lost some of her rigidity, unnerved by her teacher's trust. She stood back, allowing the travelers to enter the house. Meyral could still sense tension coming from her, as if she expected them to suddenly attack.

The old lady closed the door without a backward glance. "You'll have to forgive her, friends. In fact, you'll have to pardon this whole nation. The Federation is very nervous about an invasion, and as you probably already know, they're not letting anybody through the Wall." She cast a knowing eye at the three of them and smirked. "You have a request for me, do you?"

"My father sent me to see—how did you know I had a request for you, ma'am?"

"Please, just call me Taryn. Don't make me feel any older than I already do." She winked at Meyral and headed deeper into her house.

The trio followed her to the kitchen.

"Would you like some tea?" she asked.

They all nodded in unison.

If she hadn't told us to call her Taryn, I would have assumed she was the maid, or that we came to the wrong house. There's no way this old lady is a warrior...maybe a long, long time ago...what in the world did Father want me to come here for?

The banging of pots and pans came from the stove, and Meyral decided to get to the point. "Taryn, my father sent me to see you. It...it may have been his dying request—"

"May have been? You don't know, so don't lose hope, boy, never lose hope." She wagged a finger at him over her shoulder. "Do go on, though."

"Well, he didn't say. He only told me to come to Mantrych to find you. He stayed behind..." Meyral trailed off. He looked to the ground, trying to find solace in the dust around his feet.

Taryn turned around with a tray holding four mugs of tea. The smell was sweeter than any drink Meyral had known, and his mood brightened a bit. They each grabbed a mug.

"Did you travel this whole the way on your own?"

"No ma—I mean, Taryn," Meyral answered. "We were helped by a man who called himself Reaver."

"Ah, yes. I'm sure he's hiding around here somewhere. Though it was wise of him not to show. I may be old, but my mind is as sharp as ever." The old woman looked up at the rafters. "And unlike some of my students, I don't forget, even if I forgive."

A long pause followed, during which Alberto looked around the house, as if expecting to see Reaver's feet poking out from behind something.

"It was a long journey, then. I'm going to guess all the way from southern Ardänia. And just to see me? My, my, you're very dedicated."

Alberto nearly spit out his mouthful of tea. His sister froze, her mug barely touching her lips. Meyral's eyes grew wide with fear and he let out a gasp, but it went unheard as Alberto coughed and pounded his chest.

"Oh, now, don't worry. I know you aren't here to cause trouble, and I won't tell anyone. You're safe with me," Taryn said with a smile.

Alberto finally caught his breath and Meyral relaxed, but Maxine wasn't pleased. The look on her face was one of absolute mistrust.

"You must be wondering how I knew?" Taryn's smirk lit up her wrinkled face. "It's very easy to recognize your own people. Here, the citizens are a combination of different nations, but you never forget the distinct looks of your own countrymen." She chuckled at the looks of surprise on their faces. "Yes, I too was born and raised in southern Ardänia, but that was ages ago."

"Our mother would have called you a traitor for leaving. Why didn't you stay with the Remnants?" Maxine demanded, still displeased with the old lady.

"Some things are beyond even my control, dear." Her eyes darkened and silence momentarily fell.

Meyral heard running water, although he didn't remember seeing any stream around the house. He turned his head to see where the sound was coming from, but nobody else seemed to have noticed. The edges of his vision started to fade and he felt himself falling. He heard birds chirping and animals rustling through the underbrush, but he felt like he was drowning, deep under all the rushing water. His lungs shrieked in agony.

He woke to find himself lying on his back in Taryn's living room. The old woman was peering into his eyes with the concentration of a blind man trying to read.

"Aw you aright, Meyral?" Alberto asked as he chewed on a biscuit. "Dish ishn't da firsh time dish hash happened, man. I'm shtartin' to worry a bit."

Maxine smacked the back of his head and the biscuit slipped down his throat, making him choke a little.

"Bert, you are such a dolt!" Maxine said.

"Why are you here, Meyral?" Taryn asked suddenly. "Your father must have had good reason to send you so far at such a young age. Does it have to do with the war?"

"War?" Meyral muttered. It hadn't dawned on him until then that Ardänia was actually in the midst of a war. "Nordcross…yea. They attacked Ardänia, and they destroyed our homes. We managed to escape and I…"

Meyral looked around frantically. The sheath was no longer on his back. A second later he saw it poking out from under the couch next to him. He grabbed it, untied the top, then pulled back the flap, revealing the blue gleam underneath.

"I took this," he continued. "My father told me to bring it here."

Taryn took a few steps back as fear spread across her face. "You brought that here?" she whispered. "Where did you find that staff?"

"I found it in a tree," Meyral answered. "Wait, do you know something about this?"

Taryn mumbled something under her breath, apparently debating with herself, before she looked back down at Meyral. "I have no doubt that this is what Nordcross is after. You three are in grave danger. Did you tell anyone? Does anyone know where you are and what you have?"

"No," Meyral said, "except for Reaver and my father."

"Reaver?" Taryn's lips pursed. "That thief cannot be trusted. He'll steal it and sell it to Nordcross the first chance he—"

"With all due respect," Maxine interrupted, "he led us here without stealing it. He's had plenty of opportunities. He may not be entirely honest at times, but he won't betray us."

"How can you be so sure?" Taryn asked. "He has stolen it before."

"It won't happen again," Meyral explained. "He can't touch the staff without it burning him."

"In that case," she stared fiercely at Meyral, "I will have to train you to protect and properly use that staff. As long as Nordcross cannot find it, we will be safe. I will become your teacher."

"You?" Alberto blurted out exactly what Meyral was thinking. "No offense lady, but you're old." The big redhead ducked just in time to dodge his sister's open hand.

"That's quite alright." Taryn smiled. "It's nice to see that one of you has the good sense to question the world around them."

Alberto was shocked. That was the kind of thing people said about Maxine, not him.

Taryn set down her tea and walked over to Alberto. The big man looked around, confused, and she simply jabbed her thumb into his stomach near his hip. After a second, Alberto gave a small yelp and hit the floor like a sack of potatoes. He was back on his feet a moment later as Taryn walked back to her tea.

"She's good," Alberto said with a grimace. "You listen to everything she has to say, you hear me Meyral? I'm, uh, going to sit now."

153

Alberto limped over to the couch and sat gingerly, apparently still feeling the effects of whatever Taryn had done to him. The old woman shook her head and tittered before bringing her tea up to her wrinkled lips.

"It's settled then. Your training will begin tomorrow. Meet me out back at dawn. Today you will all stay with me, and by tomorrow morning I will have arranged other boarding. You're going to be in Mantrych for a while. I'm already training two others, but a third pupil shouldn't be much of a problem. I believe you've already met one of them." She turned to Alberto. "I have only one rule: under no circumstances are you to tell anybody who you really are, where you're from, and especially why you're here. I will not risk the entire village. Got it?"

The trio nodded their heads simultaneously, surprised by her sudden severity.

"I'm assuming you didn't sleep last night. You'll find some bunks in the first bedroom on the right."

* * *

When they woke the next day, there were piles of fresh clothes waiting for them, along with a hastily scrawled note that Maxine had to read to the boys.

Your Ardänian attire will give you away in an instant. Try these clothes. Your new rooms are located at Number Twenty-Eight, down the lane. Gold won't be a problem, I will provide you with everything you need.

Alberto looked at the dull brown tunic on top of his pile and gagged. "What beautiful colors," he said. "What did you two get?"

Maxine held up a simple, cream-colored dress. Meyral inspected his brown leather vest with matching pants and white shirt.

"Well, at least we'll blend in. After all, that's what matters right now. We have to be…incognito." Maxine laughed under her breath, but the other two didn't share her joke.

An hour later, Alberto and Maxine stood outside of an L-shaped, two-story house.

"Number Twenty-Eight, right? I guess this is it." Maxine looked at her brother, but he was too busy staring at the house to listen to her.

The peaked roof was covered in grass and dandelions, and large windows looked out onto the main road. Ivy crawled up the longest side of the house, and a tree with indigo flowers stood in the courtyard. Large rosebushes covered the front, giving it a slightly secluded feel. A grey cat leapt out of a rosebush and rubbed against Maxine's shins.

"Well, I'd say this is a vertical movement, much bigger than our old shack!" Alberto ran around the house, opening gates and looking in windows as eagerly as a child on his birthday.

Maxine reached down and picked up the cat. She cradled it in her arms and rubbed its stomach. "We're going to be here a while, huh? Who would have guessed?" she asked, staring into the cat's bright, orange eyes. "How long do you think?" Maxine sighed heavily as she looked back to the ivy.

CHAPTER TEN: PASSION

I never knew it could be this cold. Why the hell is she making me wait so long?

A light fog was passing through town and Meyral shivered again, covering his body with goose bumps. He pulled at his new vest. The leather was tight, but his back felt naked without the staff and sheath on it.

By the moons, if that hag doesn't come out soon I'm just going to—

"Hey…Meyral, isn't it?" a female voice said from behind. "Sorry about yesterday. I hear Taryn's already taken you under her wing, yea?"

Meyral turned around and saw Rubi jogging toward him. Her short, reddish hair shone in the early sun, exposed without her helmet. She slowed to a walk and a young man appeared slightly behind her.

"This is Tyler," she said as she motioned to the other student, who gave Meyral a slight bow. "You might have seen him on the back gate last night."

Meyral waved awkwardly. "Well," he began, turning back to Rubi, "you look nice without your guard gear on." He regretted saying it before it had even left his mouth.

"What do you mean by that?" Tyler scrutinized him with the same look Rubi had used when she asked him why they were unarmed.

"I was just saying…that she doesn't look as…as…" Meyral mumbled as Tyler's glare became more intense.

"Well, I'm not the only one in new clothes, it seems." Rubi clapped him on the back and sent Meyral forward with unexpected force.

Tyler and Rubi exchanged skeptical glances as he tried to regain his balance.

"How old are you, kid?" Tyler asked with a sneer.

"I'm fifteen," Meyral responded.

Tyler held a hand to his mouth and grinned.

"How old are you?" Meyral replied defensively.

"Seventeen," Rubi answered, not catching on.

"I'm twenty," Tyler proclaimed as if he'd just won a contest. "Tell me, Meyral. How much training have you had…ever?"

"Well, my dad trained me a bit in some basic self-defense and pole-fighting, but that's about as far as I got before…before I had to leave."

"Really now?" Tyler asked with a note of doubt. "Because Taryn doesn't just take on anyone, you know. What'd you do, pay her?"

Rubi locked eyes with Meyral, but some of the steeliness was gone. This time it was curiosity he saw.

"Perhaps it's a family thing," Tyler added. "Are you related to Taryn? That would explain why you two kind of look alike."

Rubi tilted her head and considered the resemblance. "You're right. Now that you mention it, I can see it. They've got the same cheeks, and their noses—"

"We're not related," Meyral interrupted as he stared at Tyler. "Why did she accept you? Then again, I guess every class has to have at least one failing student, right?"

Rubi gasped as Tyler dropped down low and swept Meyral's legs out from under him. He hit the ground with a thud.

"H-hey! What gives? That was a cheap shot!" Meyral looked at Rubi for support, but all she gave him was a wry smile.

"I see you've begun without me," a voice spoke out from the fog.

Tyler and Rubi both snapped to attention. Meyral dragged himself off the ground, thoroughly embarrassed, as Taryn strolled into view with a plain staff in one hand.

"And I must say, Meyral, I'm a little disappointed. Maybe if you had been paying attention to *his* attack rather than *her* form, you would have seen that elementary move coming. My, my, we have a long way to go with you, young one."

Meyral instinctively looked over at Rubi when Taryn mentioned her, but he stopped when he caught the sour look on Tyler's face. Meyral snapped his head forward, instantly aware that he was representing his father badly. He could feel everyone's eyes on him, judging him.

"Lady Taryn, shall we begin?" Tyler asked with a slight bow.

"Yes. The moons Sintar and Yidtar have set, and the magic of the night has disappeared. You two will be getting off light for a while— Meyral has some catching up to do if he wants to be able to spar on your levels," Taryn said. "I think we'll start with a test to gauge how much your father has taught you."

Tyler and Rubi took a few steps back and sat down. The old lady tossed Meyral the staff she had been carrying. She gave it a spin as she threw it, and Meyral narrowly avoided a blow to his head as he caught it. He let the spin guide him into a twirl, ending with him in the defensive stance that his father had shown him so many times before. He had gotten so used to the smoothness of the other staff that the rough, wooden pole felt foreign in his hands. He was slightly nervous, but thoughts of his father helped keep him steady.

Taryn quickly spun around, sweeping her right foot in a long arc. A cloud of dust rose around her, and she snatched a clay sword out of the air. Meyral recoiled and almost dropped his weapon.

"What's the matter, kid? Never seen magic before?" Tyler scoffed. "Where the hell are you from, the river?"

"Tyler, why don't you go for a run?" Taryn asked politely. "Let's say...the banks of that river you seem to like so much. Thirty miles might do you some good, teach you to watch your tongue. You're welcome to watch the rest of the test before you leave, if you wish. Silently."

Tyler resigned himself to following his teacher's orders. He shifted slightly, and again Tyler's face turned sour.

Before Meyral could explore that strange look, Taryn brought the stone blade level with her face and motioned for Meyral to begin. He rushed forward with the pole at his side and attacked with a series of quick jabs. Taryn matched every shot with her blade almost effortlessly.

"Feel it, boy, absorb the staff. Make it your own, an extension of your body."

Meyral wasn't paying attention. His father had always taught him to focus on the fight at hand and to ignore that which is extraneous.

She's fast, but let's see how much strength is left in those old bones.

Meyral spun the staff above his head and brought it down with as much force as he could. There was a loud crack, and he briefly thought that he had somehow broken the old woman. The noise, however, had come from a notch carved into the staff as it collided with her weapon. She held him back with only one arm supporting her blade.

She may be ancient, but she's still faster and stronger. I wouldn't stand a chance if she were really comin' at me...

His father had said that speed and strength were elementary skills—improvisation and fortitude, those took lifetimes to gain. He hadn't lost yet.

He spun the staff above him, bringing it down for another strike to her head. At the last moment, he changed directions and swept at her legs. Like a strange dance, she matched him move for move and finished with a side flip. He pulled the staff back and brought it parallel with his arm.

She's evading all of my attacks. I have to find an opening.

Meyral took two deep breaths, focused his strength, and unleashed a series of lightning-quick attacks. The two combatants became a blur of stone and wood, sword and staff.

He quickly grew tired, but he knew Taryn would be feeling it too, even more due to her age. This thought gave him the motivation to keep up until he finally landed a sharp blow to Taryn's shoulder.

She let go of her sword, and it turned back into dust as it fell to the ground. Taryn raised her hands, admitting defeat.

"I think I underestimated your father's training," she said. She closed her eyes and took several deep breaths.

Meyral was breathing hard, but he knew he had just done something extraordinary when he saw that Tyler and Rubi were both staring at him openmouthed.

"I see," Taryn muttered, drawing Meyral's attention back.

"Pardon?" he asked.

"Jaspar trained you well, boy, no doubt about that."

"I never told you my father's name!"

"You didn't need to. Your fighting style told me more about you than I needed to know." She waved her hand and Meyral took a seat next to her other pupils. "Tyler, get a move on or there won't be any food left by the time you get back."

Tyler jumped to his feet and sprinted away.

"Rubi, Meyral, we're going to start on meditation today."

"Lady Taryn, I've trained with you for two years and I only just started meditation! I don't—"

"Rubi, do you have a problem with Meyral like Tyler does?" Taryn asked.

Rubi shook her head.

"Then it's my judgment you take offense to?"

Again she shook her head, her eyes never leaving Taryn's face.

"I should also point out that in those years that I have been training you, you've never landed a blow like he has," Taryn added with an air of finality. "Allow me to continue. After you clear your mind for a bit, you'll start on some chores. Take a seat under the almond tree and focus on becoming one with nature. Release your spirit. You never know when a tree can come in handy. I'll join you in a moment."

Meyral followed Rubi to an almond tree. He didn't know why, but tension clamped his muscles.

"What brought you to Taryn?" he asked in an attempt to calm his nerves.

"I never gave it much thought," Rubi said as she stopped walking. "I guess I just want to protect this town. It's everything to me." She looked intently back at him. "Why? What about you?"

"I-I didn't really have a choice. The responsibility was just thrust on me." He looked up at her, suddenly full of resolve. "I'm just trying to survive."

Meyral could see the questions behind Rubi's eyes, but she kept them to herself. For that, Meyral was grateful as they sat in the tree's shade. The day had somehow become even colder than it had been earlier that morning.

It's gonna be one hell of a long winter.

* * *

While Meyral dueled with Taryn, Maxine was resting her head against the copper rim of the bathtub. She had to drain and fill the blasted thing three times before the water stopped turning into mud, but it was well worth it to feel normal again. All she wanted to do was lie back and let the warmth of the water soak deep into her bones.

As she closed her eyes, the smell of her childhood wafted into the bathroom. She sat up and sniffed the air. The scent was crawling up from the kitchen. She recognized the tang of spices she hadn't experienced since her father had left. Her stomach made a loud groaning noise, reminding her that she hadn't had a truly decent meal since their brief stay in Misty Pass.

She decided to investigate and reluctantly left the comfort of the bath. She toweled off, slipped into the cream-colored dress Taryn had left for her, and then headed downstairs. She found Alberto tending to two different pans on the stovetop while a pot boiled away over an open flame. Her brother looked over at her and grinned.

For a moment, Maxine's mind slipped back to when she was a child, when Alberto had been inseparable from their father. He had taught them both how to cook, but it was her brother who had fallen in love with the art of it. She still remembered waking up every morning to the smell of them cooking up something new, using wood they had chopped before the sun had risen.

"How was that bath?" Alberto asked, bringing her back to the present. "I thought you might just spend the entire day stewing in your own filth."

Maxine let out a slow, sarcastic laugh. "Where did you get all this food?" she asked.

"It was just sitting in the cupboards. I figured since nobody was using it, I might as well."

"You've always been like a raccoon, you scavenger." Maxine meant it as a friendly jest, but Alberto shrugged in response and turned back to his pots and pans. "I can't believe you remember how to make that stuff. You haven't cooked since Dad…"

When their father abandoned them, only one thing about Alberto had really changed. They continued to practice hand-to-hand combat as if their dad was still around, with Jaspar occasionally standing in as their teacher. Alberto, however, had lost his love for the kitchen and hadn't cooked any of those special recipes. He, like Maxine, generally avoided discussing anything to do with their father, but there was something different about that morning.

"I know, but it's a special occasion. Today starts a new chapter in our lives. I figure we'd better start it off with some good food," Alberto said with his back still turned to her.

Maxine approached him and hesitated. She wrapped her arms around her brother. "It wasn't your fault, you know. Dad did what he wanted, and there was—"

"None of that matters now," Alberto muttered. He shrugged his sister off of his back and scraped some meat he'd been cutting up into a large bowl of spices. He mixed it around before throwing it into one of the pans, where the meat sizzled on the hot surface.

Maxine stood where she was, wondering how to comfort her brother, or if he even needed it.

I knew feelings were overrated. Maybe my hug wasn't tight enough. Maybe I shouldn't have used the word "fault." That probably put him on the defensive. This was a mistake.

Alberto jerked the pan around, and the noise brought Maxine's mind back to the kitchen.

"All that matters is today," he continued as he tossed the meat around in the pan. "The past is the past, right? So let's move on."

He forked the meat onto two plates and slid one across the counter to Maxine, who instinctively caught it. She was suddenly hungrier than she could ever remember being, and she ravaged her plate like a wild animal.

"I thought you didn't eat meat, Sis."

Maxine turned bright red and choked on a slice of bacon. "I don't," she said. "Well, I stopped after Dad left. But I'm just really hungry. And like you said, it's a new chapter and..." Maxine trailed off.

The big man began picking at his food. Maxine knew something was wrong. She racked her brain, but she couldn't think of anything comforting to say. She quickly ruled out hugs and a conversation about their father.

I could tell him the history of barbeque. That would be quite a distraction for him...no, no, no, what are you thinking, Maxine? This is Bert, he doesn't want a history lesson!

Her face lit up as she thought of something. "I think we should find something to occupy our time here. You know, it's going to be a while before Meyral finishes his training. We might as well do something useful."

Alberto ignored her first attempt to distract him, but she wasn't daunted.

I just need to find the right combination of words to fix this.

"I've always wanted to learn how to shoot a bow, maybe you—"

Alberto pushed away from the table, and without looking back, he exited the house. Maxine craned her neck to see through the open window, but her brother was already out of sight. The only living thing she could see was a cat perched on the windowsill. She frowned before deciding that she had been at least moderately successful. The cat slipped into the house and sauntered toward Maxine, then hopped into her lap.

"Well, I got him out of the house, probably just what he needs," she cooed to the cat as she scratched its head. "But I'll never figure that kid out.

She returned to her plate and was disappointed to find it already empty. She looked out the window once more to make sure Alberto wasn't coming back before she grabbed his unfinished food.

"You saw nothing, you hear me?" she said, pointing to the cat. Then she paused. "Great. Now I'm threatening small animals."

* * *

By the moons, Maxine needs to learn to just shut her trap. She's gonna drive me crazy one of these days.

Alberto had been walking for hours, letting his feet take him wherever they wanted to, with his head down and his hands stuffed in his pockets. When his thoughts began to wind down, he stopped to see where he had gone.

He found himself at the western edge of the town square. A small gift shop stood to the left of him, where a woman was admiring a blue dress behind the glass display window. Alberto wandered over.

The woman had jet-black hair with streaks of red entwined in it. Her slender legs were encased in tight pants that stopped at her calves. The shirt she wore hung off of one shoulder, revealing part of a red tattoo on her back.

Alberto briefly marveled at how she could wear so little and not be cold, but he continued to stare. She wore black stiletto heels, and he wondered if they were what made her backside look so good or if that was just all her.

As if she felt his eyes on her, she turned and greeted his stare with a brilliant smile. Her light hazel eyes, surrounded by incredibly dark lashes, brightened as her plump, red lips curved upward into a gorgeous grin. She raised a tentative hand and wiggled a couple fingers at him.

Alberto clumsily lifted his hand in return, feeling very out of place. Before he could say anything, a man walked out of the shop and whispered something in the woman's ear. She gave him a peck on the cheek and the two walked away, hand in hand, as the girl stole one last glance back at Alberto.

Of course, a woman that beautiful would never *be available for me.*

He watched as a beast the shape of a huge dog bounded from between two houses. If he hadn't been so absorbed by the seething flood of dark thoughts constricting his mind, he would have called out to warn the lovers. To his surprise, the woman reached out and petted the thing as if it were an old friend.

Alberto turned from the odd scene.

That must be what those guys that called Maxine a whore were riding. By the moons, is there any place I can go to get away from my sister?

Alberto continued meandering until his thoughts stopped racing. He closed his eyes, still facing the ground. He wondered if his feet had taken him somewhere safe, to a place where he might find solace in silence.

He looked up and found another shop. He gazed into the window, fascinated by the multitude of shelves stuffed with roll after roll of parchment.

Alberto opened the door, and the light tinkle of a bell met his ears. A pair of overly magnified, watery eyes behind thick glasses was the first thing he noticed about the small old man. Alberto looked up at the shop's owner behind the high counter. When the old man finally realized he wasn't alone, he gave the big redhead a toothless grin.

The geezer had about eight hairs left on his head, but somehow they'd managed to all become entangled with one another. His clothing would have made him look like a nobleman, aside from the layer of dust on his shoulders and the mismatched buttons on his coat, whose sleeves didn't reach past his elbows. To complete the bizarre image, he had seven watches stacked on one wrist.

"Welcome, m'boy! I got all kinds o' maps here. Ya interested in geography? Traveling p'haps? Come, take a seat." He lightly patted the stool next to him behind the counter.

Alberto sat down, but he only looked at what was on the counter for a second. His eyes were already searching the large room, taking in everything they could.

"What is this place?" Alberto asked.

"Carter's Archives," the old man answered. "You're in the only cartographer's office fo' miles around. People call me Carter, tha's right." He handed him a piece of parchment. "Take a look at this. It's a basic world map—anyplace in particular that piques your interest?"

Alberto scanned the map. He couldn't read any of the names, but he still recognized Ardänia sitting on the west coast. Above Ardänia, he saw a cluster of dots. Each had a name scrawled above it, and there was a thick line that closed them in. Apparently he'd just found the Northern

Federation.

To the east of the Northern Federation was a valley, and south of that was a vast blank spot with a single word written. He figured it must be Nordcross. Beyond that, even farther east, was a massive island, a place he'd never heard of.

Below the continent, though, was what really drew his attention. There were no names written there, only a large title written in light pencil.

"Ah, you have exotic tastes, I see. Yap, the Island Nations. Just a heap o' island states really, each with its own little government, and some with none. Not even Nordcross has any jurisdiction out there. It's said to be a wild and adventurous place, a very dangerous region for the unskilled and the unaware. Far as I know, I'm the on'y one to have mapped it." He patted his breast pocket. "I keep that map in my safe, and I've got the on'y key."

The Island Nations. That's where I want to go. Far, far away from everything.

Alberto sat in silence, studying the map. He wanted to know what was above the Northern Federation, because the page seemed to run out before the land did. He wanted to know what that eastern island was, and what all the names meant.

His eyes were constantly drawn back to the islands in the south. Something inside of him ignited, and he realized that to find the freedom he sought, he would need to learn to read.

And he figured that this was the perfect time to start.

We might as well do something useful...I hate it when Maxine is right!

* * *

Meyral sat underneath the almond tree with his eyes closed, feeling like a child playing make-believe. He didn't understand the point of meditating, but he didn't say anything. Pissing off Taryn was not on his to-do list.

"Excellent. Now open your eyes."

Taryn's voice surprised him—he hadn't even heard her approaching. As soon as Meyral opened his eyes, he saw Tyler running through the garden at the back of the house.

"Now that we are all here again, we can start on our chores for the day," their teacher announced.

"I believe we left off in the library last time," Tyler said as he lined up with Meyral and Rubi, making sure to separate the two.

"Ah, Tyler, good to see you made it back," Taryn said. "I was wondering what I would do without you always answering questions I never intended to ask."

Tyler was still breathing heavily as he lowered his eyes.

"You are correct though," she continued, and Tyler's chest puffed out a bit. "Let's get to the library."

Meyral followed the others back into the house. Taryn opened a door that led into a room without windows. Rubi and Tyler entered, and in an instant they had a few lamps lit. Meyral was amazed at what he saw—every inch of wall was obscured by books and scrolls.

"When I come back, I expect this all to be dusted and in order." Their teacher exited the room without giving any further instructions.

Tyler shot Meyral an impatient look before picking up a few pieces of cloth and grabbing several books off the shelves. Rubi did the same, and together they started moving everything. They would grab a book and dust it off, then look at the clean cover and replace it on the shelf...except they were putting them back in a different spot from where they had originally taken it.

Meyral grabbed his own rag and headed for a shelf on the other side of the room. He grabbed a book and dusted it off, then cast a furtive glance over his shoulder to see if the others were watching him. He looked back down at the cover, which was bound in green leather and had gold writing on it, and he put it back on the shelf at random. He continued on like this until he almost had an entire row done, and then Rubi quietly leaned over his shoulder.

"What are you doing?" she asked softly.

"I'm dusting off the books and putting them back. Isn't that what we're supposed to be doing?"

"You're supposed to put them in alphabetical order, by author."

Meyral gave her a blank stare and she sighed.

"This one is by Stanley Adler, so it goes over here," Rubi explained. She grabbed the green book that he'd grabbed first and put it at the far left of the shelf.

"Right," Meyral said.

"Yea, you'll have to redo the whole thing." She made a tutting noise and backed away, but Meyral still didn't move.

"Seriously? Don't you know how to read?" Tyler asked with an overdramatic sigh.

"No," Meyral said. His face seemed to catch fire, but he tried not to let his shame show.

He had seen books before—Maxine had a couple in her room. His dad had always meant to teach him, but he never got around to doing it.

Tyler laughed and quickly covered his mouth. Taryn wasn't in the room to hear him, but Meyral got the feeling that the old woman had a knack for knowing things without needing to be told.

"Tyler, don't be an ass." Rubi shot him a nasty look and his face dropped. "Just dust them off and hand them to me. I'll put them away for you."

Meyral nodded, grinding his teeth.

* * *

Taryn appeared in the doorway two hours later. She looked around the room, nodding and muttering to herself. Then she looked at Rubi and Meyral with a twinkle in her eye.

She stared at them for a whole minute before she finally spoke. "That's all for today. You're dismissed."

It was already dark outside when Meyral walked into the house that Taryn had acquired for them. He stopped when he saw the cat stretched out on the stairs.

"Don't let Taryn see you," he muttered to it. "I'm pretty sure she can see through your tricks."

The cat meowed and bolted up the stairs. Meyral laughed and followed the familiar sounds of his friends bickering into the dining room, where he found them in the middle of a shouting match. He took a seat next to a plate of lukewarm stew and was halfway done before the siblings noticed he'd come home.

"All I'm saying is that the beds aren't gonna make themselves, and you *are* a woman—"

"And what does that mean, you oaf? I'm busy too, why can't you make your own damn bed?"

"Yea, that's what I really want to do, spend ten minutes fixing the sheets so I can mess them up again at the end of the day."

Maxine looked like she was about to throw her fork at Alberto when Meyral sneezed and drew her attention away from her brother.

"How was your day, kiddo?" she asked as her voice returned to a more normal volume.

Meyral was taken aback at hearing that nickname, seeing as it was usually Alberto who called him that.

"We're not done talking!" Alberto shouted.

"Yes we are," Maxine said as Alberto seemed to deflate a bit. "Go on, Meyral."

"It…I…" Meyral stared into his lap. "Not so good. I need to ask you a favor."

"Anything." Maxine's brow creased with concern.

"Could you teach me how to read?"

Alberto went quiet and shoveled some mashed potatoes into his mouth. Maxine closed her eyes and pinched the bridge of her nose.

"Is that a no?" Meyral asked, defeated.

"Yes. I mean, no…it's a yes. Gladly. It's just that this buffoon," she jabbed a thumb at Alberto, "asked me the same thing not ten minutes ago. That's how our dinner conversation started."

"And what did she tell me? Not 'yes', like you. No, she tells me," Alberto started wagging his finger as he put on his mock-old-woman voice, "I can't teach you with some silly tide chart. Is it me, or do you seemed a little bi-assed?"

"It's biased," Maxine managed through clenched teeth. "And you didn't let me finish, *Bert*."

Alberto shoveled another forkful into his mouth.

"I was about to tell Meyral that I would need books to teach from. Just like I told you."

Alberto was about to shout something when Meyral interjected, "I know where we can get some."

"You do?" Alberto nearly choked on a small carrot. He looked at his older sister with bright, hopeful eyes.

"Alright, you guys get the books and I'll teach you."

Maxine sat back in her chair and watched the two boys ecstatically wolf down the rest of their meals. A quiet smile formed on her lips. She reached into her pocket and touched the note she had found that morning, which read:

Dearest Maxine,

I've heard that you want to learn how to use that bow you've been lugging around for so long. Meet me outside of the city, south gate, tomorrow morning. I can teach you how to shoot.

If you haven't heard, Taryn isn't very fond of me, so I hope it goes without saying that this needs to be discreet.

—R

* * *

A week later, the bell above the office door jingled and Alberto looked up. Standing in the doorway of Carter's shop was an angel. Her hazel eyes reflected the light pouring in through the windows. Her red-streaked hair flowed over her shoulders, and her long, thin legs seemed to stretch on forever.

"Is my uncle around?" she asked.

"Who…who is your uncle?"

It was the fifth time he'd seen her, but it was the first time that they'd actually spoken to one another.

"He's the owner of Carter's Archives…you know, the shop you're taking up space in." Her tone was light, and a wry smile played on the corner of her mouth.

"He left for lunch, like he does every day around this time."

"Well, if he's not here…then why are you?" she asked as she made her way over to the counter.

He couldn't help but notice the way her hips swayed as she walked.

"Well he, ah…that is to say…I…I like maps." Once it was out, he was relieved to have at least said something.

"You must be the apprentice he mentioned. Well, when Uncle Carter gets back, let him know that Chloe was looking for him, will you?"

"I will…Chloe." He said her name like it was a secret that he would never let go of, relishing the way that it resonated in the air and how it made his lips tingle.

The raven-and-scarlet-haired beauty turned, sending a scent of lavender and roses into Alberto's face, and she left.

* * *

Maxine stood in waist-high ryegrass as the sun just broke through the dark clouds. Her left arm was locked straight and holding the bow. She had the string drawn back, her thumb against her jaw and her index finger almost touching the corner of her mouth. It had been two weeks since Reaver had given her the task of holding that stance for as long as the sand in his hourglass fell.

As she glanced down at the hourglass, sweat dripped into her eye and she tried to blink away the stinging without losing her focus. Her arms were trembling and her back muscles were screaming, but she was almost there.

The stinging stopped and she looked down at the glass again. The sand seemed to fall impossibly slow. When the last grain fell, Maxine dropped the bow and collapsed into a ball. She smiled and giggled between gasps for air.

A bird warbled in the distance and roused her from her thoughts. She composed herself, reset the hourglass, and resumed her stance.

* * *

Maxine reached the south entrance several hours after the sun had set. Rubi was on duty, and she stopped Maxine at the gate.

"This is the fifth time in two weeks. Where do you keep sneaking off to?" Rubi demanded.

"I don't really see how that's any of your business," Maxine replied.

"Mantrych's safety *is* my business, and you sneaking around is its biggest threat right now."

Maxine laughed shrilly. "Do you listen to yourself when you talk?" she asked. "What could I be doing? The nearest town is two days away on foot. I'm only outside the walls for half of that. You can see all around for miles! There's no army out hiding in the grass!"

Rubi said nothing. Maxine waited for a retort, expecting Rubi to argue with her like Alberto would, but all this redhead did was stare. Finally, Rubi sighed and let her shoulders drop. Maxine watched her for a moment and took a step forward.

What have you done, Maxi?

"Rubi?"

"I'm sorry," Rubi said. She raised her head. "Sometimes I forget I don't have to be so harsh. I feel underestimated sometimes...you can

171

understand that, right?"

No, not really. Why did it have to be more feelings? Maybe less is more. Just don't say too much, keep it simple.

"Sure..."

Rubi smiled. "Thanks," she said. She reached out and pulled Maxine into a hug.

By the moons, what HAVE you done, Maxi?

Maxine put her arms around Rubi and smiled.

* * *

Meyral was quickly getting accustomed to the schedule that Taryn had laid out for her three students—it wasn't so different from the things his father used to have him do.

His mornings consisted of a small breakfast, followed by a quick lecture from Taryn about the mental state of a battle. Elements of surprise, knowing your enemy's weakness, strategy and tactics...it seemed like she had even more experience in battle than Jaspar himself.

After the lecture, they would begin their training with sparring matches, which included unarmed fighting and wrestling, along with lessons on the use of every weapon Meyral could imagine. Afterwards they went into skills: swimming, forging armor and weapons, botany, anatomy, and archery, which was Rubi's forte.

Their runs were usually fifteen miles or so, halfway to the river and back. The path went slightly downhill for most of the way there, which made the trip back a bit more strenuous. It took Meyral a month to finally get used to the treks—he vomited at least once a week on that trail.

After running, they had a brief break for lunch. Then they focused on meditation, another round of sparring, and Meyral's least favorite part, the mundane chores Taryn always had them doing. He never complained about any of it, though, because he got the feeling that Taryn would be about as forgiving as Jaspar was when it came to whining.

Night after night, no matter how tired he was, Maxine would drag him into the living room to teach him and her brother how to read. Meyral would borrow a book from Taryn's library and bring it home for Maxine to use with them. Every week, he would take it back and grab a new one, each time hoping that Taryn wouldn't notice.

Alberto kept bringing in more maps and charts. He knew the alphabet and most small words, but he was still having trouble remembering the sounds of a couple letter combinations. Meyral was picking it up much more quickly, which only aggravated Alberto. He tried giving up at least twice a week, but Meyral and Maxine always talked him into staying.

* * *

Maxine marched through the ryegrass, shaking her head every few steps.

"Where the hell are you, Reaver? Are you ever going to teach me anything?"

Step...step...step...step.

"I can hold the bow, you know. I can outlast the hourglass. I've been doing it for weeks!"

Step...step...step...step.

"I don't need his permission. It's not like he's here to stop me." Her voice picked up as she got farther and farther from town. "I'll just take a few practice shots and teach myself."

Step...step...step...step.

"Well, well, my favorite student," a deep voice called out.

Maxine looked up from her angry musings. Reaver was leaning against a wooden target that she could have sworn hadn't been there a few moments before.

"Where have you been?" she asked.

"Do you want to talk or do you want to shoot?"

Maxine sighed dramatically. "Is that even a choice? Shoot."

"Good. Now, show me what you've been working on."

Maxine hesitated and faced the target. She pulled back on her bowstring and aimed.

"Well, you have the strength, but your form is sloppy at best. I've seen slugs with better stance!"

She lowered her aim and glared at Reaver.

"I didn't tell you to relax."

"Right," Maxine said as she resumed her position.

Reaver grabbed her shoulders and tilted her right side back half a step.

"This is your shooting stance," he explained. "Now, draw an

173

arrow and notch it."

Maxine reached for her quiver and Reaver stepped behind her. He hugged her from behind and laid his arms over hers. "Your movements are too sudden, too jerky," he said. "You have to flow."

He guided her hand up and back in a smooth arc. They grabbed an arrow and pulled it against the string. "No wasted movements," he said. "Always know your next move. Grab the arrow, but not like Alberto with a chicken bone. Use only your first two fingers and thumb."

Maxine put the arrow back, then pulled it out like he had explained.

"Good. Notch the arrow and pull back the string with three fingers—make sure your pinky is out of the way." Reaver took his hands off of Maxine's and reached up from under her arms. He held her shoulders back so she was flat against him. "Now breathe."

Maxine's breathing slowed until she was in sync with Reaver.

"Try to visualize a line from yourself to the target. Once you can see it, raise your arrow along that line."

Maxine tilted her head so her eyes were level with the arrow.

"Take a deep breath and hold it. Once you're completely steady, relax your hand on the string. Let it fly." Reaver stepped back.

Maxine became overly aware of the wind at her back when the warmth from his body disappeared. She held her breath three times, then finally relaxed.

Thud.

"Not bad," Reaver said with a nod. "You managed to hit the board, at least." He slid behind Maxine again and corrected her aim.

* * *

"Alberto…" He heard his name floating across the room, spoken by his ancient teacher, whose throat was as dry as the papers he worked with. "The west wall needs to be organized. Fix it, would ya, m'boy?"

He had worked at Carter's Archives for two months and the old man finally trusted him with bigger tasks, like organizing whole parts of the shop on his own. He knew it would be a day's worth of work at best, but Alberto didn't argue. Sometimes, during those arduous tasks, he would come across a long-forgotten chart or map, and he would sneak them home to pore over with Maxine and Meyral to learn the odd names of faraway places.

Around noon, Chloe wandered in on the arm of a new man. The two split up, Chloe walking toward her uncle and the new guy toward Alberto. Before the man even opened his mouth, Alberto answered his question.

"The maps of the Black Iron Mountains are behind the counter," Alberto said. "I presume you're looking for the hot springs there."

"How did you know?" the man asked.

The shocked look on his face gave Alberto a certain amount pleasure. He gestured for the man to come closer.

"You're not the first guy to ask for 'em. This chick's been to the springs at least a dozen times in the past month, and each time it's with a different man. Not very original, if you ask me. But, feel free to try your luck."

It may have been an exaggeration, but the effect was exactly what he wanted. The man paused for a moment, inched away from Alberto, and sneaked out of the shop. As the bell rang, Chloe noticed that her escort had disappeared. She stomped over to Alberto, and the look in her eyes made him a little scared.

"What did you say to him, Alberto?" Chloe demanded. She put her hands on her hips and glared.

Alberto smiled stupidly. This was the first time she'd used his name, and something about it sent tingles down his spine. "I, uh…just…you know…I told him you had gallphyre."

"Really? That's it?" She laughed her dark laugh, turning his tingles into goose bumps. "I expected a better story. I'm kind of disappointed."

Although her tone was casual, her eyes had a fire burning in them. Alberto's hands started to sweat.

"So you think that lowly of me?" she continued. "That I would catch some whore's disease?"

"No! I think…I think…you're perfect!" he blurted out before he could stop himself.

"Because I'll have you know, I…what did you just say?"

Her eyes widened and Alberto could see shock flit across her face. It gave him just enough of a chance to notice how deep and stunning her eyes really were.

"Everything about you is amazing! I mean, sure, you're beyond beautiful, but I've also heard you when you talk with Carter and

I…you're brilliant. I've never met anyone like you."

"Really?" For a moment, Chloe was speechless. "Well, I'm not surprised. Because I am!" She flipped her hair, and the scent of lavender and roses returned. "Tell me, Bert, have you been to the Black Iron Mountains?"

"Can't say that I have," he said with a wink. "But I know of this nice spot, complete with a hot spring."

She let out a low, coy laugh. "And tell me, did you know that it's customary to bathe in those springs nude?"

"I didn't…you…" Alberto's eyes widened and his left hand gave one twitch before he fainted against the wall of shelves he'd been organizing.

Chloe grabbed a blank piece of parchment, scribbled a time and place, and slipped it into his breast pocket. "This is gonna be fun, big boy," she whispered into his ear.

"What'd ya do to Bert?" Carter asked as he looked over her shoulder. "That boy has work to do, y'hear?"

"I think it's just exhaustion. You should take it easy on him, Uncle."

* * *

Maxine stood in the tall grass and watched the sky as Reaver threw plates into the air. He had started with serving platters, then dinner plates, bread plates, and finally tea saucers. When she could hit all of them in one go, he began to throw multiple plates into the air at once.

Maxine had no idea where he got all of it, but she knew better than to ask.

* * *

A week later, Alberto met Chloe at the place she described on the piece of paper. He'd asked Taryn for some nicer clothes, and she managed to find a black silk shirt for him. It looked surprisingly like the one he was wearing when they had arrived on her doorstep, only this one still had its sleeves and a full set of buttons. He attempted to comb his hair for the first time in years, but he eventually gave up. He shoved his head in a bucket of water and let it dry in its usual style.

Alberto stood on top of a hill on the outskirts of town that overlooked Taryn's orchard. He kept biting his cheek to try to calm his nerves, but it wasn't working. Thinking he'd found the wrong hill, he dropped down, sat in the grass, and began talking to himself.

"Way to go, Bert. You sure you can read? Maybe she meant the other side of town." He lay onto his back and sighed. "East. West. Shit, I ruined this one. By the moons—"

"I haven't heard anyone say 'By the moons' in a long time. Aside from that old lady you're all so fond of," Chloe's voice called out to him from the shadows. "Every time, it reminds me of a lullaby my mom used to sing to me." She began to sing quietly before he could say anything.

> *"Celeste, Celeste,*
> *Three moons, they reign.*
> *Klyntar, smallest,*
> *Sent down four kings.*
>
> *Lawrence, Lawrence,*
> *Cygnus, they reigned.*
> *With fire and ice,*
> *Our land they claimed.*
>
> *Ragmor, he came*
> *From o'er the seas.*
> *The humans, they reigned,*
> *Klyntar displeased.*
>
> *Waters rose and winds fell,*
> *Old ways were lost.*
> *This story I tell,*
> *For humans forgot."*

"My mom used to sing that to me and my sister when we were kids," Alberto said. He stared at Chloe with his mouth open as the moonlight cast her silhouette in a strange yet beautiful glow. "I didn't think Northerners believed in the power of the moons."

"It's an old myth," she said. "The stuff of children's stories. Nobody really thinks it's true." Chloe giggled as she knelt down beside him, and her black, form-fitting dress moved up her thighs. When she saw the hurt look on Alberto's face, she stopped laughing and leaned back onto her forearms. "Sorry. But really, it's a ridiculous story. There's no reason to believe it any more than the other legends, like how the mountains were forged by giant mole-people."

"That's not funny." Alberto's eyebrows were so scrunched that they almost touched.

"I think it is." Chloe pointed west, where a bright light shone in the distance. "Look over there. That's Vent, where the Northern Senate meets. One day, I want to be the first female senator." Her hazel eyes sparkled and reflected the stars. "I've studied all my life to learn the laws and regulations of the Federation, and soon I'll have a part in running it."

"What's a senate?" Alberto asked.

Chloe held a hand up to her mouth to stifle another quiet bout of laughter. "The senate is a group of people, politicians by nature, who make decisions on how the Northern Federation functions. There are forty senators, and they've always been old men. Maybe they just need a woman's touch to turn it all around."

"What does that have to do with the moons?"

"Oh. Right, I sort of got sidetracked." Chloe took a deep breath and let it out slowly. "Well, the point I was trying to make is that you need to think for yourself. You can't just believe everything you hear. People tell me all the time that a woman would make a terrible leader, but I don't let that kill my dreams, you know?"

She continued to smile at him, and all Alberto could do was agree.

"In all my years of studying, the main thing I've learned is that the ability to objectively analyze and make your own decisions is something to be valued above all others."

Alberto only really understood about half of what she was saying. It was like she was talking in riddles, and he'd never been able to pay attention when Maxine started to talk like that. It was even worse with Chloe, because he was so distracted by her beauty.

"So you don't believe that the moons are the reason we exist?" he finally asked.

"Definitely not," Chloe said with a serious look. "There are hundreds of legends about how we came to be, but really, there's no factual evidence to back any of it up. That's the tricky part."

"Then you believe in nothing?"

She shook her head vigorously, whipping her womanly scent toward him. "I believe in my five senses. If I can't touch it, taste it, smell it, see it or hear it, then what use is it to me? It's impossible to prove, either way. I don't mean to get you down, Bert, or tell you what to believe. If you were raised that way, there's no reason you should change just because of me."

She leaned forward and kissed him—a full, passionate kiss.

"In fact, if you did, I don't think I'd like you quite so much."

"You're amazing," he muttered as he stared into her hazel eyes. "I've never met anyone as smart as you…except maybe my sister."

"You're kissing me and thinking of your sister?" She raised one eyebrow and smirked.

Alberto grabbed her head and pulled her back into another kiss. "Oh yea, you know how I like it."

The two of them giggled and rolled around in the grass until the moons began to set.

CHAPTER ELEVEN: ALMONDS

The trio had been living in Mantrych for four months before Meyral actually pinned Tyler in a wrestling match—something he had been trying to do since they'd started training.

"Congratulations," a voice said from a few feet away.

When Meyral looked up, he was surprised to find it was Rubi holding out a helping hand and praising him.

"Oh…thanks," he replied awkwardly.

Meyral still wasn't used to her rare softer side, and neither was Tyler. When Meyral glanced over at Tyler, he saw the same sour look that he always wore when Meyral was close to Rubi.

Rubi seemed completely oblivious to the constant competition that existed between the two boys. There was no denying that Tyler now found himself outmatched by Meyral on an almost daily basis.

"Wipe that look off your face," Rubi said. "You can't expect to win every time, after all."

Father always said too much pride was an ugly thing. He's still a better swimmer, and I'm not as good with a knife…

"Again…let's go again!" Tyler shouted.

Meyral's thoughts were interrupted by a red-faced Tyler. He was huffing like a bull and gesturing for a rematch. It wasn't that he didn't like Tyler, it was just that something about his rival made Meyral want to prove himself.

"Really, boys?" Rubi asked. "Why don't I just go get a ruler and get it over with?"

Rubi's remark took some steam out of Tyler, but Meyral was certain he'd misunderstood what she said. He was about to ask when Taryn arrived.

"It's the last day of the month," their teacher announced, "so tomorrow morning we will do things a little differently and start with a swim. The cold waters should invigorate your weary muscles and refresh you for the new moon cycle ahead. For now, let us return to cleaning up the music room."

Meyral's shoulders slumped. He hated swimming more than any other type of training.

* * *

The next morning, they all stood on the banks of a large reservoir, shivering in the chill of dawn's darkness. Meyral saw a scalekat bobbing in the water.

Great, an audience.

When Taryn looked out, the critter dipped below the surface.

"Which method are we using this morning, Lady Taryn?" Tyler asked with a grin.

"The backstroke sounds about right," she answered. Her eyes landed on Meyral, who could have sworn she had read his mind about hating swimming.

"And how many laps are we doing this morning, Lady Taryn?" Tyler asked.

"Tyler, stop kissing my ass," their trainer snapped. "In any case, twenty-five laps. Begin!"

Tyler, Rubi, and Meyral all hit the glassy surface of the lake at the same time, each silently gasping as the freezing water stabbed at their skin. A lap later, to everyone's surprise, Meyral was neck and neck with Tyler. Eight laps later, Meyral was actually out in front by half of his body length.

After four more laps, Tyler had closed the gap. They were even once more as they turned around for the second half of the swim. Every other lap or so, the two boys would trade places at the lead, up until the final round.

Halfway across the reservoir, Meyral's left leg cramped and the rest of his body locked up in response. He splashed in the water feebly and Tyler shot forward, taking advantage of Meyral's misfortune. Tyler popped out of the water near the shore and waited eagerly for Taryn's praise.

"Congratulations, boy," Taryn said, her tone impassive and cold. "You came in first—but at what cost?"

She questioned him as her eyes trailed toward Meyral, whom Rubi was dragging through the water. Taryn's wrinkled hands clasped together over her stomach as Tyler turned to follow her gaze. Rubi emerged from the reservoir and a look of shame dominated Meyral's face. Both of them were pale and out of breath.

"Winning isn't everything," their teacher said. "Comrades are and always will be your most effective tool. Leave them behind and you may as well leave yourself behind."

Taryn's lips pursed and Tyler hung his head.

"Yes, Lady Taryn. I understand," he replied.

Meyral could hear the struggle in his voice as Tyler held his anger back. He could only imagine how Tyler felt after winning and still being reprimanded.

"As for you, Meyral," Taryn continued, and Meyral snapped to attention. A hint of devious pleasure found its way into his teacher's eyes. "What happened out there?"

"My leg cramped and…I panicked. I'm sorry." Meyral coughed quietly and rubbed a shaky hand across his face. Across the way, a scalekat climbed out of the reservoir and sauntered off into the morning mist.

"Do you expect someone to always catch you if you should fall?" she asked as she glared in the direction that Reaver had gone. She brought her stormy eyes back to Meyral's bright blue ones. "I don't care about your apologies, boy. What I need you to do is master your emotions—fear, anger, hate. Even love. All these things will only distract you in battle." She leaned in close and whispered in his ear so the others couldn't hear, "And if you want to master that staff, it is imperative that you understand this."

Taryn turned her back to the boys and looked to Rubi. The old lady winked and nodded, and Rubi did a sort of half bow. She pointed to the blossoming almond tree in front of the house, indicating that meditation was next. The three students ventured to the shade of the tree and sat, waiting for their master to join them.

* * *

Maxine was surprised to see Reaver waiting outside in the courtyard as the sun rose. His salt-and-pepper hair was slicked back, giving him an air of regality that seemed strange on a thief.

"Are we not practicing today?" she asked as she stepped outside. She didn't bother concealing her disappointment.

"Oh, we are. But we're moving on. Trying something new today, just for my favorite pupil."

"You mean your only pupil," she muttered.

"Same difference. It's time for you to shoot something more than just dinnerware. I know of a lovely meadow where the pheasants are as fat as can be. It's almost impossible not to hit them."

"You mean…kill them?"

Reaver laughed. "If you took up the bow in hopes of tickling a lover, you've chosen the wrong instrument. But this is merely hunting."

* * *

Spring came back around and Alberto was practically running Carter's Archives. The bell above the door jingled and he looked up from his desk, which was littered with parchment. Standing in the doorway was his angel. Her luscious lips were a glossy black, her red-streaked hair was pulled up into pigtails, and her long, thin legs protruded from a light blue dress.

"Is my uncle around?" she asked.

"No, but he has me rearranging his scrolls anthropologically, whatever in the moons that means," Alberto answered.

Chloe walked over to him and leaned over the counter, letting Alberto's eyes trail down the top of her dress. "Good," she said. "I wanted to have a little time alone with you today. You don't think anyone will mind if we close the shop for a bit, do you?" she asked as she placed her hand lightly on his thigh, her face only inches from his.

"It hasn't been too busy today, so I guess…" Alberto grinned and ran across the room, pulling the shades down and locking the door.

An hour later, the two of them were lying naked on the floor and holding each other, red faced and out of breath. Chloe lay with half of her body on top of Alberto, their pale skin seeming to melt together. Her head rested on his chest, just below his chin, but her feet still barely reached his shins.

"I should go now. Uncle Carter will probably be back soon. Wouldn't want you to lose your apprenticeship or anything."

She lifted herself off of his body and Alberto rolled onto his side. He grabbed her wrist and pulled her in for one last playful kiss before letting her go. He lay where he was, admiring her lean body. The red compass rose tattooed on her back was fully visible as she wiggled back into her dress. When she was done, she tossed his clothes on top of him.

"Get dressed, you lump," Chloe said. "It'd be even weirder if he walked in on you rolling all over his maps naked and alone." She turned on the spot and walked out of the office, leaving the door wide open.

Alberto scrambled off of the floor and lunged after her, slamming the door. He took a deep breath, and once again the scent of flowers filled his nostrils.

* * *

Meyral was finally able to read on his own, save for some bizarre names on a few of the maps that Alberto had brought home. He had even moved on to reading the thick, old books that Taryn had on obscure subjects, like psychology and the abandoned practice of water worship. It had been a month since he'd studied with Alberto, though. His friend had come home one night, raving about hot springs and sacred traditions. Since then, he spent all his time with that Chloe woman.

She liked to read, and at first she sat in on some of their lessons. She would find a spot where Alberto could stare at her, and she would read history books while Maxine tried to get the big lug to understand the difference between assonance and alliteration. Meyral had mistakenly taken this as a good indicator that Alberto would continue his studies, but Chloe never seemed to take much interest. Before long, neither did Alberto.

The lovesick redhead was cooking almost every night now. Nobody minded not having to rely on Maxine's soups, but the big guy hardly ate with his companions. Instead, he would put enough food for two in fancy tins and head off to see Chloe, leaving Meyral and Maxine to serve themselves.

As Alberto left one spring evening to see Chloe, Meyral picked at the mutton on the plate in front of him.

They can all jump in the reservoir for all I care. No, that's not right. I do care...I'm actually proud of the big guy. He deserves a little happiness after everything that happened.

Meyral continued to play with his food, trying to avoid the root of his foul mood.

Where in the moons is my father? He said he would send word, but it's been almost half a year and I haven't heard a thing. Was he captured? If I don't hear from him soon, I'm going to take the staff and go looking for him...

185

"…he'd do the same for me."

"Say again?" Maxine asked from across the table.

He realized he must have said the last part out loud, because she was looking right at him. "Nothing…I was just wondering what prepositions were."

Maxine started to buzz about something while Meyral's mind continued to wander.

I'll find you, Father. Even if it's the last thing I do.

* * *

Maxine was surprised by how quickly she and Rubi had bonded. It mostly stemmed from Rubi needing someone neutral to listen to her and Maxine having a surplus of free time. Maxine actually enjoyed their visits more than she would admit. Rubi took her out to new places and forced her to talk to people she would normally ignore. Maxine spent this time practicing conversations without mentioning anything Ardänian.

"Have you noticed how much Meyral and Tyler compete?" Rubi asked Maxine as the sun set. Maxine had taken to visiting Rubi during the first few hours of her night shifts. "Why is that?"

"They're men. It's the same with dogs—there always has to be an alpha male."

"Well if we're talking about the best body, it would have to be Tyler. Have you seen that boy shirtless?" Rubi asked with a laugh, and Maxine blushed.

"I have," said a third voice from behind them.

The two women turned to find Chloe with a smug look on her face.

"Of course you have," Rubi said. "Who *haven't* you seen shirtless?"

Maxine cringed, but Rubi grinned. Chloe laughed and turned her glare to Maxine.

"Sorry, that's not what she means," Maxine said, stumbling over her words. "I mean, it's what she said, but I'm sure didn't mean…she was joking, and…"

"Maxi, calm down." Rubi turned back to Chloe with a smirk. "The truth hurts, am I right?"

"I wouldn't know," Chloe said. "But after all those nights you've spent with Tyler, it's no wonder you'd be so defensive about your...*housemate*."

Rubi's jaw dropped comically.

"But I bet he's nothing compared to my Bert," Chloe continued. "That boy is proportional, if you know what I mean."

"Why must you do that?" Maxine asked as her face switched to a frown. "It's like you intentionally say things just to get a reaction."

"I think...you think too much," Chloe shot back.

"I know there's more going on under your perfect hair and behind your goddess-worthy makeup," Maxine snapped. "Why are you hiding it? What are you afraid of?"

Rubi waited with her eyebrows raised. After a moment, Chloe pulled Maxine into a hug and laughed.

"I love this bitch!" she yelled. "Now I know why you've been keeping her all to yourself, Red." Chloe pushed Maxine back and held her at arm's length. Then she threw an arm around her neck. "Come on, I heard the Bowan twins just got a new boarhound. I want to ride it."

Chloe steered Maxine away. Rubi was holding her stomach, doubled over and trying not to make a sound. As her laughter started to pick up volume, Maxine looked back and mouthed, "Help me!"

* * *

"I've anticipated this day for a very long time, students." Taryn eyed each of her pupils one by one, beaming with happiness. "Today is not practice. Instead, it's a test, and I wish to see how you all do." She pointed at Rubi and Tyler. "You two, stand."

They stood as they were commanded. They faced each other, but Taryn shook her head.

"No, today you do not fight each other," she said. "The two of you will be fighting Meyral. Begin!"

Meyral scrambled to his feet without a second thought and pulled his training staff from the ground. Tyler slashed before Meyral could even take a breath.

Meyral quickly rolled backward, narrowly dodging his opponent's sword, and then finished by raising his staff. He deflected the four quick strikes from Rubi's two wooden blades before spinning on his knees and sweeping Tyler to the ground. Rubi, however, saw it coming, and she jumped in time to avoid him.

While Tyler tried to regain his ground, Meyral jabbed Rubi in the stomach with the pole and launched himself into the air. He landed a safe enough distance away to survey the situation and catch his breath.

To his right, Rubi ran toward him with her swords at either side. Closer on his left, Tyler staggered toward him and picked up his pace. Meyral's rival was taller and stronger, but he was a lot slower. Tyler wielded a greatsword the length of his body as if it was a club; it was his weapon of choice.

Meyral ran forward as Rubi swiped at his head and Tyler swung at his feet. He dove in the air between their weapons and landed behind the two of them, then switched his stance from defense to offense, readying his weapon for an attack of his own.

Tyler's head was the perfect target—a weak spot, lightly guarded, and big as life. Meyral struck out at it, but Rubi knocked his staff to the side before it connected with her partner. Three wooden swords barraged him like a flock of angry birds.

Meyral took his chance. He used the staff to vault over his opponents as they both pulled back to attack at the same time. He landed and did the splits, effectively avoiding Tyler's two-handed chop, and started to spin around on the floor with his feet out like a frenzied, horizontal windmill. It didn't take long for him to trip Tyler yet again.

He rolled as Rubi poked at him with her swords. Each time she missed, she formed a divot in the hard dirt. Meyral struck back unexpectedly and missed Rubi's face by several inches. The redhead took a defensive stance as Meyral continued to press his advantage with several jabs of his own.

Rubi danced around his weapon, and Meyral realized that she was luring him into a trap. He had to dive to avoid another slash from her partner, who was still on his back. As he hit the ground, he found himself within striking distance of Tyler. As soon as his nemesis lowered his weapon to lift himself from the ground, Meyral sprang to his feet and easily brought his staff down on Tyler's face. When the staff was a hair from his nose, Meyral slowed it to a stop and waited until Tyler dropped back to the ground, accepting defeat.

One down!

Taking out Tyler was a risk, as it left his rear vulnerable. Rubi took the opening and became a whirling blur of swords and feet. Meyral was only able to keep up with her intense speed through instinct and dumb luck.

She can't maintain a pace like this for long.

When he saw his chance, he delivered a quick jab to her left hand. Rubi let her sword drop to the ground, and Meyral closed in while she tried to pull the blade in her right hand back around. She ducked and knocked Meyral's staff aside with a high kick. Meyral rolled to his left and raised the staff high above his head, then brought it back down on top of Rubi.

She raised her weapon to defend herself. Her knuckles were turning white, letting Meyral know that she was focusing all her might on keeping him at bay.

This is it!

He pulled back a bit to make her think she was making progress, and then he switched tactics. Meyral swept at her legs and took her by surprise. Rubi went down with a small yelp. Meyral brought his staff around and gently laid it on her neck. She let go of her remaining sword as she lay panting on the ground.

"Impressive," Taryn said. "You performed admirably, Meyral, as I expected."

Meyral bowed as the other two lined up for their teacher's inspection. A magpie warbled overhead and Taryn's face turned stern. She turned to them, and Meyral saw a look of shame on Tyler's face and sadness on Rubi's. He almost felt bad for beating them so quickly.

Not Tyler, but I could have let Rubi go a little longer.

"You two..." Taryn's voice was harsh, and all three students snapped to attention. "Cheer up." Their old teacher's demeanor switched from angry to proud. "Teamwork, improvisation, fortitude...you did very well against such a skilled adversary. It might also help if you cleared your minds a bit," she nodded to Tyler. "Now," she pointed to the almond tree again, "let's take our spots..."

* * *

As Taryn escorted Tyler and Rubi off of the property that evening, Meyral sneaked into her library to return his latest book and grab a new one. He slipped the old, brown book with the odd bird on the front into the middle of a shelf, then grabbed another one at random. The new book's cover was bound in black leather worn by years of use, and it felt heavier than Meyral expected. It smelled strongly of mildew and decay. One glance at its stained pages stabbed fear into his heart, and chills ran down his spine.

"Now I know where my books have been disappearing to," a voice said from behind him. "I really wanted to brush up on my ornithology last night. I hope that this is no indication that you are taking advice from a thief."

Meyral dropped the book and turned around with fear in his eyes. Taryn was standing in the doorway with a crooked smile on her face.

"I do hope you treat them better than that," she added as she pointed to the book on the floor. "However, this one seems to get dropped more often than one might expect."

"My apologies, Lady Taryn," Meyral said. He bent down to gingerly pick up the book, but Taryn intercepted him and pulled it away. "I don't usually...what I mean to say is...my father always taught me that stealing—"

Taryn waved her free hand and chuckled. "Why do you think I set you all to work organizing these rooms? I ask you to clean my house because I know it is packed with extraordinary things. Furs of exotic animals, ancient statues and busts, spices, perfumes, musical instruments that nobody's played in centuries...I have a shrunken head, for Klyntar's sake! And then, of course, there are the books."

She smiled and clasped her hands behind her back. Meyral's confusion must have shown on his face, because she sighed and rolled her eyes.

"I was trying to inspire you all to try something new, to be more than just mindless warriors. And you, young man, you have been here for only a fraction as long as the other two, and you've been the only one to overstep the boundaries of your orders."

Meyral opened his mouth a few times to speak, but he didn't know what to say. Finally, Taryn grabbed a small book bound with brown leather and placed it in his hand.

"Next time, try asking first," she said with a wink.

Meyral raced home, and when he got inside, he narrowly missed kicking Reaver as he practically sprinted to his room. He examined the little book like it was his most precious possession. The leather was old and dried, but the pages still had gilded edges. There was no title on the cover, which he expected, since most of Taryn's books lacked any kind of introduction. He opened to a random page and read aloud.

"Our lips met,
Our souls departed;
Like a breeze,
A breath of life
Had slipped in and out
Unnoticed.
For only the first bright star
Of the dark, dark night
Catches the eye.
Love departed from this world,
Speeding like the cry of a crow
But still our hearts beat on.
Never again this face
Did a smile touch,
Never again his laughter
Did meet these ears,
Never again."

He shook his head with a look on his face like he smelled something rotten. Reaver jumped into his lap and practically demanded to be petted. He set the book down and sat back on his bed, absentmindedly running a hand along the cat's back.

"What in Klyntar's name did all that mean?" he asked out loud.

Reaver only purred.

* * *

The next day, Taryn paired Tyler and Meyral against Rubi. The results were disastrous. As soon as they began, Meyral ignored Tyler and focused completely on Rubi. Tyler must have done the same thing, because they only seemed to get in each other's way. Rubi defeated them quickly without even struggling.

"Amateurs!" Taryn shouted as Meyral's forehead throbbed. "You're too old for this nonsense," she snapped at Tyler, who averted his eyes.

She rounded on Meyral, but he didn't look down. Instead, he looked past his teacher and saw a smirk growing across Tyler's face.

"And you don't have the luxury to act like a child!" she yelled at Meyral.

I bet he did this on purpose. That son of a goat got in my way just so he could laugh at me.

Anger boiled up inside of Meyral, and an image formed in his mind of him kicking Tyler into the reservoir in full armor.

"Are you listening to me?" Taryn stood so close to Meyral that he could smell her breath. She whispered, "Do I need to remind you that your father is out there somewhere? Do you want to save him? Because if you think I'm going to let a child who can't control his emotions take the Staff of Ardänia, you're wrong."

Meyral completely forgot about Tyler as the idea of Taryn keeping his staff ransom eclipsed all other thought.

"Did I hit a nerve?" she asked. "Are you going to kick me into the lake?"

How did she know that?

"If I teach you anything," Taryn said to the other two, "it should be this: your worst enemy is yourself. Remember that. You're all dismissed for today."

* * *

Maxine walked slowly along the banks of a wide, slow-moving river. Reaver followed a few steps behind.

"Today is the day," he said. "You will hit all of your targets today."

"What's wrong with me? I was so good with the plates," she muttered.

"Plates don't have souls," Reaver said as he pulled her back. "You are missing because you *want* to miss, because you *need* to miss. But that might all change under different conditions."

"What does that mean?" she asked.

"A pheasant runs from danger. The intuitive and caring heart that beats inside your chest screams at just the thought of harming such a creature. It seems nothing short of an atrocity. So you miss. And that, dear, is what makes you human."

Could it be? Do I actually care about these birds?

"But the Venstrum geese will not run. They are proud creatures that have lived in the shallow waters of the North since the beginning of human history. They will stand, and they will fight. I have heard tales of a chorus, their name in mass, of these birds killing fearless warriors.

They peck at you from every direction, and once you succumb to the multitude of shallow wounds, the feeding frenzy begins. They take your lips, your eyes, your nose, and the soft flesh of your belly, all while you're still alive. By then you'll be praying for death."

"So," Maxine said, finally breathing, "where would we find these Venstrum geese?"

"Right here, of course," he said. He spread his arms, faced the river and let out an inhuman roar. Every bush within sight came alive.

Maxine's world was engulfed by grey, flapping wings and beaks made shiny with blood. She pulled an arrow and steadied it as a massive goose flew her way. The bird was large enough that a small child could ride it comfortably. She took a deep breath, held it steady, and then she released. The arrow found its mark and the goose splashed into the shallows a few feet from where she stood. Maxine drew another arrow, but something caught her attention. Reaver still stood at her side.

That rogue never sticks around when there's danger. He even caused this bird riot…

As she pulled the string back for her second arrow, the two geese speeding toward her veered to the side. Their wings blasted her with air as they took to the sky and flew away.

"You lied to me!" she shouted.

"There was some truth," Reaver said with a smirk. "These were Venstrum geese, and they are quite dangerous…to anything smaller than a wolf."

"So why the story? The chorus of Venstrum geese?"

"I needed to give your logical mind a reason to take a life. Self-defense. And now that you have," he gestured to the large bird floating nearby, "how do you feel? Fine? It's not like you died. Your aim was true. Your soul is still intact, so far as we can tell, and the bird is not suffering nor is he haunting you from the grave. Correct?"

Maxine thought for a moment and shook her head. "It's just inherently wrong—what gives me the right to choose what lives or dies? The rest of his life can't be lived because of me."

"Do you worry about the life of a berry when you pick it? The seed will never sprout; a whole generation of vines will never grow. Every time you bite into a strawberry, you take the lives of countless plants, but do you care? No, because you must eat.

"Meyral tells me that you have started to eat meat again. How do you think it got to your table? Killing is not evil when there is justifiable

193

reason. It's called self-preservation."

She hesitated, then nodded.

"Besides, that was an amazing shot. Right in the chest, and it was flapping all over the place. You're getting a lot better."

"You think so?" she asked. Her voice was timid, but her smile was genuine.

Reaver pulled her into a celebratory hug. "Yes, your progress has been nothing short of miraculous. The way you're picking this up, you—"

Maxine cut him off with a full kiss. He pushed her away with incredible force, though his fingers handled her as if she were made of porcelain.

"I am flattered, Maxine," he said slowly, so unlike his usual gregariousness, "but this will never be."

Maxine stood where she was. Her mind was racing, trying to figure out why she had even done it and what Reaver was saying. But mostly she was trying to figure out what that empty feeling in the pit of her stomach was.

The thief continued, "I take full responsibility. I am too open with my words. I never thought that…"

"Forget it," Maxine muttered as she strode away without a glance backward.

* * *

Meyral walked home slowly and plopped down on his bed, where Taryn's book still sat. He opened it, but he quickly changed his mind and he set it aside. Every few seconds, his eyes would find their way back, and eventually he opened it again. He read aloud, hoping that this time something in it would make sense.

> *"The monster under my bed,*
> *The creature inside my head,*
> *The It that wants me dead,*
> *It fills me with dread.*
> *As long as I run, it can't catch me,*
> *When I'm done, I'll become the enemy.*
> *Stay fast, this feeling can't last.*
> *When the die is cast,*

Forget the past,"

Meyral read it again three more times, sure that he was missing something. On the third time through, it still didn't make sense, but he felt slightly comforted. He turned the page to finish it.

"Don't let It get you,
Don't let It win.
Their numbers are few,
And stained in sin.
I lowered my defense
And let the pain commence,
It got so intense,
It stopped making sense.
If you should go,
Abandon this hate.
What I do know…
This is my fate."

He read the second half again, then read the entire thing once more. He finally gave up and set the book aside. Meyral rolled over and closed his eyes, the passage continuing to play in his head.

* * *

"He's only been here a little over a year, and he's already won everyone over," Tyler said. "But do we know anything about him? Where did he come from? And his friends? Why are they here? Has it ever struck you, Rubi, that they may be spies, or…or assassins?"

"You're being ridiculous," Rubi said. "We've trained with him every day nonstop for all eleven months that he's been here. I highly doubt he even has the energy to sneak off at night to conspire, let alone the motive. Would you?"

"There's no reason to trust him. There's a war going on just to the south of us, in case you haven't noticed, and for all we know they're planning to drag us in. Are you willing to risk it?"

Tyler stomped the ground angrily as Rubi used a branch from the almond tree to help herself up.

"Is this because of what happened earlier?" she yelled into his

195

face. "Or are you just mad because you have to share some of the glory now?"

"I've always shared with—"

"No you haven't! Other than archery, which you have no interest in, I have *always* been number two. And that was fine with me, because it meant that Mantrych was that much more protected. But apparently you can't handle being number two!"

"Look, I'm...I'm just being skeptical," Tyler said.

"Why would they bring us into the war? They have no reason!"

"Then where are they from? Has he ever told you that?"

"He's done nothing to wrong you!" Rubi shouted.

"Nothing to wrong me? He's stealing my...my..." he trailed off.

"What is he stealing, Tyler? Your glory?" Rubi scoffed.

Tyler stood where he was, battling some raging beast inside of him.

"You're so paranoid!" she shouted after a moment of silence.

"YOU, alright? He's stealing you...from me. Rubi, I'm in love with you!" He said it without thinking and cringed.

"Tyler, I...you're like my brother." Rubi's eyes widened and tears began welling up inside them. "We've been best friends and training partners our whole lives! It's...it's not like that..."

"It's him, isn't it?" he asked quietly. "You love him. Don't think I haven't noticed you sneaking off in the afternoon to do who knows what!"

"I'm not with him...it's not like that."

"Then what is it like?"

"Listen! I don't *love* anyone, not like that...especially not him!" she said as she backed up defiantly.

"Then why do you stick up for him all the time?"

"Just because he's clumsy with a blade and awkward with his speech doesn't mean we should exile him! What the hell is wrong with you?"

"Meyral. Meyral is what's wrong!" he shouted as he stepped forward.

Rubi took another step back. "Then stop training. I'll keep going. I'll keep this town safe and you can have your paranoia!" Rubi's voice quivered and tears streamed down her face. She turned away so he couldn't see.

She could feel Tyler trying to say something, trying to comfort her. He must've opened his mouth a dozen times, but nothing came out. Finally, he gave up, and without even a goodbye, he left.

When he was out of sight, Rubi sat down and cried harder than she had in years. He had been her best friend since they were children, and she did love him, but not the way he wanted her to. Now he was going to leave, just like that, and for no reason that she could understand.

She couldn't help how she felt, and damn him for thinking otherwise.

* * *

Maxine finally made it back to Mantrych, but she didn't want to go back to Number Twenty-Eight, just in case *he* was there. She nodded to Markus, the oldest guard, before heading toward the temple. She knew nobody would show up there so late, but more than that, Reaver would never show his face there.

"Praise be to the Great Mother," a man in a green, hooded cloak near the entrance recited his usual greeting as he lit a line of candles against the wall.

Maxine smiled, but it only lasted a fraction of a second before faltering. She entered the nearly bare chamber and sat in the first seat she reached.

What the HELL was that, Maxi? Of course he doesn't want you, you're...you're...broken.

The empty feeling in the pit of her stomach grew and the pain she felt deepened. She looked down at herself through eyes blurred by tears. She was wearing the same plain dress that Taryn had given her when they arrived.

He would want Chloe. He wouldn't push her *away. Bert certainly doesn't. But no one looks at me like they look at her. No one notices poor, responsible, ugly, broken—*

"Hey, Maxi," a female voice called out, "I don't want to alarm you, but you're crying...in a temple. It's kinda depressing."

Maxine turned around and wiped a hand over her face. "Sorry, Chloe." She shook her head and made her best attempt at a grin. "What are you doing here?"

"Reading," she answered with a shrug. "People in this suffocating town have spent so much time and energy 'thanking the

197

planet' and studying nature that this is the only place you can find actual books. I mean, other than Taryn's, but I'm not exactly welcome there. Not since a certain student took me skinny dipping."

Maxine couldn't help but laugh. Although Tyler probably thought he was the one doing the convincing, he was wrong. She could make men eat out of the palm of her hand if she wanted them to.

Maybe I should be more like Chloe.

Maxine looked up and found her brother's girlfriend studying her face.

"Just as I thought," she finally said. "Boy trouble, am I right?"

"Why would you think…I mean, it's not…what?"

"I've seen that face a million times, and I've even made it myself once or twice. I don't need any names. Who doesn't matter here—only what he did. Let me guess: he promised you the world, and when you finally gave in, he left. Maybe for another woman?"

"No," Maxine said with a short laugh, "I've never…well, just no."

"What's wrong with you?" Chloe put a soft hand to her mouth. "Sorry. I mean, you have the looks and you have the brains. You could have anyone you wanted…provided I didn't want him as well, of course."

"Of course," Maxine agreed.

"From what Bert has told me," Chloe said as she took the seat next to Maxine, "maybe it's about time you did something for you. Stop worrying about the rest of the world."

* * *

When Meyral woke, it was dark outside. The voices coming through the floor meant that it was one of those rare nights when everybody was in the same place at the same time. Meyral grabbed Taryn's book and scampered downstairs. He entered the dining room with a huge smile on his face.

Chloe was in a bright red top and shorts that were so short it gave Meyral chills just looking at them. She stood behind Maxine, putting her green hair up in a complicated braid. As Meyral walked in, Maxine turned bright scarlet. She nearly toppled over Chloe to get out of her chair. She stood awkwardly while Chloe held up her hands and scoffed.

"Maxi, I was almost done," she said. "Sit back down."

Maxine did as she was told and tugged at her lavender dress.

"Where did you get the dress, Maxine?" Meyral asked.

"Isn't it gorgeous?" Chloe said with a smile. "It makes her eyes practically light up."

Meyral shrugged. "Yea, sure."

"That's all? Wow, way to lay it on thick," Chloe snapped.

"Hey Alberto, need any help in there?" Meyral scrambled across to the kitchen to escape.

Alberto was just putting the finishing touches on a goose he had cooked, and apparently he hadn't heard a thing.

When Chloe was done with Maxine's hair, they joined the boys in the kitchen. Alberto gave his sister a strange look and turned back to the food.

"Hey," Meyral started as he held the book up, "I found something I've been meaning to show you guys. I got a new book from Taryn and, well…it doesn't make a whole lot of sense."

He handed the book to Maxine. She opened it and flipped through a few pages before she cleared her throat.

"I tried not to hear
But I heard
The ever-loud pounding
Of a heart's distress.
The most feared of all sounds
Is that of the broken heart,
The cries and wails
Drenched in sorrow
Of a pain so deep
Of a loss so strong
Of a grief, unbearable.
So long, I say
To the wielder.
So long, I say
To the tormenter.
So long, I say
To the one I once loved."

"You sure you read that right, Sis?" Alberto scratched the back of his head and raised an eyebrow at her.

"Yes, I'm sure. By the way, the beans are starting to burn," Maxine said with a hint of impatience. She pointed behind Alberto and he returned to his food.

"It all sounded like gibberish to me," Alberto muttered as he stirred the pot.

"That's because you're more of a literal man, and I love you even more for it," Chloe cooed. She walked across the kitchen and hugged Alberto.

Maxine pursed her lips and shook her head behind their backs.

"I couldn't make any sense of it either...what does it mean?" Meyral asked. He was mildly surprised when it was Chloe who answered.

"It means that love is fleeting," she said. She turned so she was back to back with Alberto, leaning dramatically against her love. "It's easier to deal with heartbreak and separation than the trials that life throws at you. It kind of mourns the fact that the author lost someone they once loved."

"I'd say it's pretty open to interpretation," Maxine said as she bit her lip. "But I think it's saying that it's a painful, yet sometimes necessary thing to become enemies with someone you love."

"How is it even possible to become enemies with a loved one?" Meyral asked, trying to imagine hating his friends or his dad.

"Sometimes people do things...things that others can't, or won't, forgive." Maxine's eyes darkened. "Some people will do some unforgivable thing, and they lose their loved ones forever. They become enemies to distance themselves, so that they won't hurt as much in the long run."

Alberto set the food on the table and rejoined the conversation. "So why didn't they just write that?" he asked.

"It's a poem, Bert." Chloe gave the big guy a light kiss on the cheek before continuing. "It's supposed to be...pretty. Deep. Meaningful."

"Still sounds like gibberish to me," Alberto repeated.

"So...they're like codes then, with hidden meanings?" Meyral asked with a spark of understanding.

"That's exactly what they are, Meyral," Maxine said.

They waited for Chloe to add something, but she was too busy spooning beans onto Alberto's plate to respond.

"Maxine, have you seen the new dresses they just imported from

Ardänia?" Chloe asked as she set the bowl of beans back down. "I hear they came from some place called Bonthon."

Alberto choked on a mouthful of goose. Chloe slapped him on the back until he coughed and slobbered down his chin. Maxine engaged Chloe in small talk about fashion to distract her while she kicked her brother in the shins.

As soon as the discussion changed course, Meyral's thoughts enveloped him and he focused on the plate in front of him.

"Hey, has anyone seen that cat?" Alberto asked.

"He hasn't been here all day," Maxine answered.

"He'll be fine." Meyral smiled to himself. "Don't worry about him."

After dinner, Meyral spent the night studying the strange book, but he still had trouble making heads or tails of the thing. He fell asleep frustrated once again.

* * *

Rubi was crying by the dim glow of torches when a shadow fell over her. She looked up into a pair of violet eyes. Her sobbing stopped, but the tears continued to fall.

"Rubi? Why are you crying?" Maxine asked as she sat beside her. "Are you hurt?" she added while inspecting her body for some sign of injury.

"Tyler's done. I…I lost my best friend." Her lip trembled, but she managed to hold back the hurt she felt welling up inside her.

"I'm sorry." A moment of silence ensued until Maxine broke it. "You should come over for dinner tomorrow night. Alberto's cooking again, and his meals have gotten phenomenal. But if you tell him I said that, I'll deny it," she said with a smile.

"I guess that would be nice. I don't think my housemate will be coming home anytime soon." She crossed her arms and pouted.

Maxine tilted her head and put an arm around Rubi.

"I live…well, I used to live with Tyler." Fresh tears started to fall again. "His parents took me in after my father died, and then after they passed away, it was just us. And now…now…" Rubi broke down into complete hysterics and buried her head in Maxine's neck.

"I think we might have an empty room if you need a place to stay," Maxine muttered as she clumsily rubbed her friend's back.

"I appreciate it, but that would just make it worse."

"How would that make it worse?"

Rubi pulled back from their embrace, and she couldn't help but stare into Maxine's eyes. They smiled at each other as Rubi pushed a lock of green hair behind her ear.

* * *

The next day, Tyler didn't show up for training again. Rubi's eyes were red and puffy from crying, and before Meyral could ask, their teacher interrupted.

"Where's Tyler?" Their teacher had appeared behind them, as silent as usual. Her eyes scanned the orchard, looking for her third pupil. "Did he finally quit? He lasted longer than I expected. I'm actually kind of impressed," the old woman said with a smirk. "He'll come crawling back once he realizes he's being ugly. I guess this means testing is over, which is a shame. I was really looking forward to how you two would work out as partners…"

Taryn paired them up for their sparring lessons, and as Rubi and Meyral faced each other, she grabbed Meyral's staff and handed him an angular blade with a slight curve.

"It's called a katana," she explained. "You need to learn to diversify. What would happen if you lost your staff in battle?"

Taryn's words made him feel uneasy, but not quite as uneasy as the unfamiliar equipment. Before he could focus on his discomfort, Rubi attacked.

Their sparring matches only lasted about an hour that day. Rubi didn't hold back against Meyral, and she kept knocking him onto his back like a helpless turtle.

"Enough. To the almond tree," Taryn finally announced.

Rubi helped Meyral up from the ground for what seemed like the hundredth time that day. The three of them then took their positions underneath the shade of the tree.

When Meyral closed his eyes, he felt a pulling sensation and immediately reopened them. He realized he was no longer in Mantrych. He was still sitting under a tree, but instead of the almond tree he'd become so accustomed to, he found himself looking up at an ancient ash, whose branches were as bare as any he had seen in the depths of winter.

The staff was on his back for the first time since it had been locked in Taryn's basement. He took it out of its sheath and spun it a few times, happy to have it back in his hands...but something was amiss. Taryn stood next to him, wearing a red, Ardänian-style dress that reached her calves.

"I was wondering when you would get here, dear boy," the old woman said with a smile as she turned his way.

"Where are we?" he asked, hoping to finally get some answers. He recognized the place, but he still didn't know where it was.

"I have no idea. This is your mind, after all." She closed her eyes and frowned.

"But...why are you here? Last time I was alone."

"I'm not here. Not really. I'm actually just somewhere in your consciousness, a figment of your imagination, if you will. This just happens to be where *you* are."

"I have so many questions, Lady Taryn."

"All I can do is try to answer them." She smiled again, creating a network of wrinkles stemming from the sides of her eyes and crawling back toward her ears.

"Can you tell me about this?" he asked as he held the staff out. "Like what the inscription says, maybe?"

Taryn took the staff and looked at the inscription for a long time. She pinched the bridge of her nose and sighed. "It's not my place to tell you, young man."

"Can you tell me why I dream about this tree then? It's not the first time I've been here."

"I told you, this place is only between you and this stick." She heaved the staff back at him with an air of neglect.

Meyral felt a certain twinge of pain at the way she so poorly treated it.

"No offense, Lady Taryn, but why are you here if don't have any answers for me?" Meyral asked.

"My job isn't to hand you things, dear boy. I couldn't just hand you the fighting skills you have been acquainted with any more than I could just answer all of your questions. What I can do, however, is give you the tools for you to better understand the things that you experience."

Meyral nodded.

"The tree is of significance, I believe. The rest," she waved her hands at nothing in particular, "well, that's up to you. The sky, the moons, the simple fact that we're breathing air and not swimming under an ocean is because of you and your mind. So if you wanted to be up in that branch…"

As she spoke, the new world shifted and Meyral found himself on a branch of the tree. "We could be!" he shouted.

He watched Taryn walk around the tree, nothing more than a black dot far below him. A red squirrel ran up the trunk and scampered along the branch where he was sitting. As his blue eyes met the squirrel's beady black ones, the world started to spin. He felt dizzier than he'd ever felt before.

"What is this?" he cried as he felt himself almost fall to the ground.

"The vision is fighting back," her voice floated up to him from below. "It doesn't like the position you've taken. Come back down!"

He closed his eyes and focused on the ground below. He didn't open them until he felt the tall, soft grass under him like a cushion against the hard dirt.

"So…I can't control these visions?" he asked, crestfallen.

"Not necessarily. I said you can control your part of the vision. But just like during a battle, there is a balance. With enough practice, you will be able to tell what parts of the vision are yours to control and which aren't."

Meyral's face scrunched up for a moment as he thought about what she'd just said. "I think I understand what you mean…can I ask you another question?"

The old woman nodded.

"Can you tell me how to get back to the real world without the painful headaches or the sensation of…not existing?"

"It will take training—the pain you feel is the vision's way of letting you know it's over."

Meyral nodded.

"You can wake up whenever you want, but it would be in your best interest to trust the visions and to witness what they have to show you."

"So is this why we meditate?" he asked.

"Precisely. I'm glad you're finally getting it. Anything else?" The old woman glanced over her shoulder anxiously, turning a small stone over in her hands.

"Is there any way to control *when* I get these visions? Because they could come at some really bad times, you know?"

"If you ever figure that one out, be sure to tell me," she said with a chuckle. "I still have the same problem. About a year ago I passed out in a plate of green beans just so *they* could tell me you were coming."

Meyral tossed his head back and laughed, and when he opened his eyes, he was back under the almond tree. Rubi was glaring at him through her red, swollen eyes.

"Sorry," Meyral muttered. He could have sworn he caught a smile on Taryn's face.

* * *

It had been fifteen months since Meyral, Alberto, and Maxine had wandered into Mantrych. Chloe gave Alberto the idea to throw a party to celebrate the year-and-a-half anniversary, and after some pleading, Taryn agreed to help.

When the sun set, the guests began to arrive at Number Twenty-Eight. Taryn turned up with the first wave, carrying a basket of fruit to supplement what she rightly assumed to be a meal consisting wholly of meat, potatoes, and beans. After a few polite greetings, she headed for the kitchen, where Alberto was putting the last few spices into a boiling stew.

"I'm not sure you are aware of this boy, but the North is just as capable of growing fruits and vegetables as anywhere else in this world," Taryn said.

The large man hovering over the smoky pot didn't even look up. "I haven't seen a single lemon tree," he grumbled.

"You know what I mean."

"Alright, alright," he said. "Put it on the table. Salad won't be too terrible."

Alberto had six different pots and pans spread throughout the kitchen, some over the stove, one over an open flame, and some on the counter either marinating or finishing. Even Taryn had to admit that it was an amazing thing to watch the big redhead successfully manage each item without burning a single dish.

"You'd be surprised at how many flavors there are out there. Maybe you should explore something outside beef, pork, and mutton," Taryn said as Alberto nodded and waved a hand at her, still not looking up.

She left the kitchen and quickly returned with Maxine and Meyral in tow.

"Alberto, turn around!" the old woman commanded and, to everyone's surprise, he listened. "These two will watch over your meat for a few minutes while I teach you a thing or two about cooking."

Alberto opened his mouth to protest, but Taryn held up a hand and stopped the words before they came. Maxine and Meyral reached for a few of the pans, and Alberto mumbled directions to them before he followed Taryn.

Twenty minutes later, he was incorporating handfuls of previously foreign fruit into three of his dishes. Taryn nodded in approval before leaving him alone. As she exited the kitchen, she grabbed Meyral's ear and pulled him close.

"I was hoping to meet a certain cat I've heard so much about," she whispered. "Do you know where he might be?"

"I think we both know we won't find him within shouting distance of you," Meyral said with a laugh. "What is it between you two?"

"That, young man, is not my story to tell. I'm sure if you asked him, you'd get an answer. Maybe not the truth, but it hardly matters. Some things are better left a mystery." The old lady winked before walking away.

As the living room came alive with activity from the many guests scrambling to get a piece of comfortable furniture, Maxine left them to set the table. When she walked into the dining room, she found Taryn already there.

"Taryn, please, you really don't have to. I can take care of it! You've done more than enough for us," Maxine said as she tried to pull the plates away from the old woman.

"No, no, dear, it's my pleasure to help. I'm just as spry as ever, you know."

Maxine tried to think of a way to get Taryn to leave the plates alone without insulting her, and just as she was giving up, the front door opened.

Chloe strutted in like she owned the place. She wore a short, black dress that hugged her body tightly, showing off her womanly curves. It had a low back, and when she headed for the kitchen, both women at the table could see her entire tattoo. Taryn's lips pursed and

Maxine rolled her eyes.

"Very rude, very rude, just walking in like that unannounced," Taryn said. "She's always been a tad strange, you know? Very into herself, and lives with her crazy uncle. That man is out of his mind, drawing new maps all day." She shook her head and made a tutting noise. "Come to think of it, I don't know if I've ever seen her without a man courting her. Distasteful, if you ask me."

Maxine smirked as she remembered Chloe's story about Tyler and their moonlit swim. Her eyes strayed across the party and the people amusing themselves with liquor, food, and small talk. The mismatched armchairs and sofas that Taryn had brought in were scattered throughout the living room, which gave the place an odd look, but they served their purpose. Almost everyone had a comfortable seat.

She uncrossed her arms and tried to smile a bit, then leaned against the wall to seem more casual. When she spied Rubi walking toward her, Maxine's smile turned true. She smoothed the front of her dress and pulled her hair back. She opened her mouth to greet her newly arrived guest and the first real friend she'd made in years, but Meyral intercepted Rubi from the kitchen.

"Where've you been?" he asked. "I wanted to show you these crazy bugs I found! I swear their butts glow in the dark!"

Meyral dragged her away by the elbow as Maxine's smile disappeared.

* * *

"I think it's so sexy when you cook." Chloe grabbed Alberto's shoulders from behind and kissed his neck. "Nobody else is here in the kitchen…"

"I would, but the food…I already had Taryn in here distracting me, and unless you want everyone to be eating lumps of burnt meat, I'm gonna need full concentration."

A high whistle sounded. Alberto picked Chloe up and sat her on the counter before bounding across the kitchen. He pulled a pan off of the fire and mixed in some herbs. Chloe sat pouting, her legs slightly parted.

"Alberto?"

"Yea?"

"So, I was wondering…why is Taryn taking care of you all? Are you family of hers or something?"

Alberto paused for a moment, then tossed a few more spices into the pan. "She's related to Meyral, on his mother's side," he explained. "It's like a third-cousin thing. We brought him here because he happens to enjoy stick fighting, and Taryn is the best around."

Maxine had invented that back story during their first few days, when Meyral mentioned that Tyler thought they were related. It was the first time Alberto had actually had to use it, though, and he turned away so she wouldn't see him cringe.

"Where are you from originally?" Uncertainty clouded Chloe's eyes and she bit her lower lip.

Alberto lit the contents of the closest pan on fire and played with it a bit, trying to buy time. "Can you pass me that bottle of wine?" he asked without looking up.

Chloe grabbed the bottle and walked it over to Alberto. He reached for it, but she didn't let it go.

"You avoided my question, dork. Is there some reason you don't want to tell me?"

Alberto looked up from his meat and locked eyes with her.

"You ever been to Padscott?" he asked, continuing their alibi.

Maxine had picked one of the biggest cities in the North, so even if they met a Padscott native, nobody would question them.

"Can't say that I have…" Chloe muttered.

"Maybe we'll make a vacation out of it. Go there sometime and just relax," Alberto said.

At least that much is true.

She nodded her head. "I'll ask you again later. See if your answer is the same." She kissed him and let go of the bottle. "I just want to know you better. You understand that, right?"

"Of course I do, babe." Alberto watched her as she headed into the living room, then turned his attention back to the meal.

* * *

A few more people trickled in, mostly friends of Taryn and Rubi, and the house quickly filled with merriment. They feasted on fruit and meat, and Alberto even brought out a couple extra bottles of wine. Rubi seemed determined to stay out of the same room as Maxine, and when the party started to thin out around midnight, she was one of the first to leave.

As the first light of day started to peek over the horizon, those who hadn't had that much to drink sobered up and stumbled home, while others fell asleep on whatever marginally soft furniture was available in the living room. Alberto had passed out facedown at the large wooden counter in the kitchen, a chicken leg still clutched in his right hand.

Chloe was the last person awake. Taryn had engaged her in a long conversation about the myths of the moons—specifically the history of "The Four Kings of Men," and how that story is related to the druids of the North. But at some point the old woman had fallen asleep, much to Chloe's relief.

She stood and stretched, then walked around the various sleeping people, letting out a quiet giggle at the absurdity of the scene in front of her. Most of the people who'd drunken themselves to that black sleep were the "important" people of Mantrych. The ones who looked down on her social life, judged her, called her names behind her back and whispered about her when she walked by...and yet there they were, passed out, some in rather suggestive positions.

Chloe accidently kicked the town's Healer, who had fallen asleep with his face buried in the breasts of a woman who'd once told Chloe that her son was too good for trash like her.

She finally reached Alberto and rubbed his cheek, but he refused to wake from his drunken slumber. The most she got out of him was a noise that was either a grunt or a snore. She straightened up and turned away, discontented with going to bed alone. As she walked toward the front door, the back door opened and shut quietly. She slipped into a corner and hid in the shadows.

Maxine slinked past Chloe, her feet bare and her dewy boots in her hands. The green-haired woman stopped and glanced around the house as if she was waiting for something to happen. After a few moments, she quietly headed upstairs.

Chloe took off her high heels, walked to the bottom of the stairs, and sneaked through the back door. The footprints were obvious in the grass, but there was only one set. They stopped just inside the casing of the weeping willow's branches, then headed back toward the house. A grey cat meowed from a shadow next to the door. Chloe jumped a bit before stooping down and picking him up.

"You didn't make those prints, did you?" she asked as she

stepped out onto the dewy grass. "I guess you're keeping quiet about what Maxine was up to, aren't you?" She dropped the cat unceremoniously and re-entered the house.

Alberto was still snoring like a bear the size of a mountain. With a little pushing and prodding, Chloe finally managed to climb into his lap. She shivered a bit before she lifted Alberto's arm and snuggled up to his warm body.

CHAPTER TWELVE: PROPHECY

Taryn found herself in a familiar place, a place she hadn't visited in years. She looked around and saw the endless stretch of a rocky, grey and brown surface. All that broke the monotony was the man in the chair, sitting and playing a guitar that sounded akin to a harp.

"Hello, old friend. How have you been?" she asked the man as she brushed a lock of silver hair out of her face. "I can't imagine that you're here on pleasant business. You never are."

The man with the guitar said nothing. He continued strumming his instrument, the light from the stars twinkling off of a medallion around his neck. The song was low and soft, and it seemed to soothe her very soul. He looked at her and then past her, like he had done so many times before.

"What if I refuse to look this time, Iggy? What if I just...ignore you? Continue about my business?"

He said nothing and continued to look at the sky behind her. The longer she avoided his message, the louder he would play. The faster the chords, the more powerful the melody. Eventually the song would drill into her head, and she would hear it even while she was awake.

She knew. She'd tried before.

Taryn turned around and sighed. "I'm too old for this. Why don't you find some young kid to play with?" She watched as the well-known orb appeared in front of her and began to form a series of images.

She saw a vision of Nordcross from the air, and as the ground came rushing up to her, a million little black dots met her eyes. The dots grew and grew until she could see them clearly. An army of men marched, clad in purple and silver armor. The orb shifted slightly and she watched the army's destination come into view.

"They march north...to the Federation?"

The image zoomed beyond the army, along a mountain ridge, and stopped just short of the long, stone border. It turned and headed through a vast expanse of marshes and swamps before it stopped near a lone peak in the center of the wetlands. She watched as the army trampled through a small town at its base.

A man with shaggy, black hair stood on a pile of bodies amidst a cluster of burning buildings. Time seemed to reverse until she saw the man standing in the middle of the town, untouched by war. A medley of shabby-looking men and women surrounded the man, completely oblivious to their oncoming doom.

"It's time, then. You've always been a harbinger of sorrows." She sighed and turned around, but he only played faster. "You aren't done? Oh, dear."

When she returned to the orb, it showed her Meyral. The staff floated on his left, and its tip shone a brilliant blue. On his other side, flames erupted, and a red glow lit up his right.

She watched, fascinated as the light of the staff and the flames consumed Meyral. When the whirling snowstorm of color faded, a scarlet cobra and a green viper appeared where the staff had been. The snakes made to strike each other, but they entwined themselves in a figure-eight and bit the others' tail. They spun around in the twisted circle until the cobra released its jaws. It burst into flames, and the viper withered into smoke.

"Yes, yes, I know. Anything else?" she asked. She had always ended her meetings with Iggy the same way.

This, however, was the first time he had given her an answer. He shook his head and she heard a deep voice resonating in her mind.

"I have shown you what you need to see, but our work is not finished. Don't expect to come back here until it's all over…"

"And why do I need to see it? Is it some grand master plan you've concocted? Why do you interfere?"

"I have no answer for you. It is not in my power to see that future…what shall I call you this time?"

"You needn't call me anything. I'm leaving, and I hope to never see you again, Iggy."

Taryn awoke to find herself standing in a road. She looked up and twisted her face into a hateful glare, her eyes locked onto the smallest moon.

"You don't leave much up to free will if you start sending me places I don't mean to go!" Taryn whispered. She looked back toward Number Twenty-Eight and sighed.

* * *

Alberto woke to the sound of someone tapping on the front door. At first, he tried to ignore it and he rolled onto his side. He pulled Chloe close to his body. He found it so much easier to fall asleep with her in his arms...at least, that's what he told Meyral and Maxine when Chloe had taken to sleeping at his place instead of at her uncle's.

Alberto inhaled that sweet scent of lavender and roses that hung around his love's hair. He was about to drift back to sleep when another bout of knocking came.

Moons be damned, who the hell's buggin' us this early?

He left his warm bed and stomped down the stairs. Their cat hissed and bolted past him, almost causing Alberto to trip down the last few steps. By the time he reached the bottom, the knocking had turned to pounding. He threw open the door, ready to wring the neck of this burglar of peace. Alberto looked down and his anger dissipated instantly.

"Taryn!" he said. "What are you doing here so late?" Alberto started to yawn, but he stopped quickly and scanned the yard behind the old woman. He couldn't see anything out of the ordinary.

"Alberto, who is it?" Chloe's angelic voice called from the second floor. "Come back to bed."

Alberto blushed when he caught the disapproving look on Taryn's wrinkled face.

"I need to speak with Meyral," she commanded.

No lecture? Shit, this must be serious. The old hag never passes up a chance to yell at me.

"You might as well hear it too," she added as the cat snaked between Alberto's feet. "He'll probably ask for your help anyway."

Alberto was about to yell to wake the others, but he heard footsteps on the floor above him. Seconds later, Meyral bounded down the stairs with Maxine right at his heels, each looking frazzled. When all five of them—including Chloe, much to Taryn's displeasure—finally gathered in the living room, the old woman stood and spoke.

"Meyral, your father is safe in Trosloth," she said. Meyral's face lit up, but Taryn continued before he could speak. "He thinks he's safe, but Nordcross has found out where he and the Remnants he has gathered are. I suggest the three of you—"

"Oh no, you crazy old bat! How do you know that all this is true?" Chloe planted her hands on her hips.

Oh boy, this isn't gonna be pretty.

213

"Yea, how do you know that? And isn't the mighty Wall supposed to protect the North?" Maxine inquired.

Alberto did a double take at his sister.

I think this is the first time since they've known each other that Maxine and Chloe actually agree on something!

"It was in a dream I had," Taryn answered simply.

Alberto expected the disbelief on Chloe's face, but he still nodded along with his sister and Meyral. His mother had always taught him that dreams were more than just random and meaningless.

"The Wall can protect the North, but Trosloth is outside of it," Taryn explained as Maxine's face went scarlet. "Which is exactly why Jaspar chose it—it's protected by Northern treaties, but not governed by them."

Nobody moved or said a word.

"If you don't trust me, then don't go. It's simple," the old lady added.

Alberto looked at Meyral, and he could tell by the gleam in the kid's eyes that his friend was as tired of hiding out in Mantrych as he was. Unfortunately, Chloe didn't share their enthusiasm.

"Alberto isn't going anywhere!" she yelled with enough ferocity to stop even Taryn, and then she rounded on the big man. "We're getting married in three months, and I'm not letting you get in the middle of some stupid war that you're not even involved—"

"Chloe, we're already a part of this war!" Alberto yelled back.

Years of arguing with Maxine had trained him to act first and think later. His eyes met Chloe's, and he was surprised by the look of hurt she wore. He closed his eyes so he wouldn't have to see her tears.

"I'm from Ardänia," he blurted out. "Nordcross burned down my village and killed my mother. Then I found you...and I couldn't risk you. That's why I didn't say anything."

Alberto glanced at Taryn. She nodded as if she'd expected it a long time ago.

"But now it's time for me to go and fight." He took a knee so his face was level with Chloe's. "It's my responsibility to keep Nordcross out of the North, and it's my duty to protect you. I can't have them invading your home...our home."

Alberto felt something in his chest release. There was a long pause and he swallowed anxiously. He reached out and took one of her tiny, delicate hands with his own rough ones, and he waited for her to respond.

"I don't care about that. Just please…please come back in one piece." Chloe choked and put her other hand in his. "You are coming back, right? I don't want to be a widow before I'm even married." She wrapped her arms around him and kissed him.

"Don't worry. I can take care of myself." He pushed her back lightly and flexed. "See? I'm big. I'm bad. I'm awesome. Nobody can beat me." Alberto winked.

"Alright. Alright, go," she said. "But come back safe…and a hero…with treasure, lots of treasure. Then we can leave this place." Chloe smiled her perfect smile, and Alberto hugged her close. "I…I love you, Alberto." She looked up and kissed him again, this time with all her might.

* * *

The room went silent, aside from the sloppy sounds of the lovers kissing. Maxine turned and walked away. Meyral scratched the back of his head and turned to Taryn, who wore a peculiar look as she watched their teary embrace.

"I want the staff," Meyral said, eager to put his training to use. "I want to help my father as best—"

"No," Taryn said as Reaver meowed from his spot at the top of the stairs. "I'm sorry Meyral, but to give you the staff and send you into battle so unprepared would be a disaster. You'd either kill yourself or everyone around you…probably both."

"I can't go to my father empty handed. He entrusted it to me," he argued.

"I'm sorry, Meyral. I can't do that. I've seen enough death in my life and—"

Rubi burst into the entryway and drew everyone's attention to the front door.

"If there's a fight, I refuse to be left behind!" she shouted. Rubi was already decked out in her leather armor, with her dual blades and bow strapped to her back. A decently sized quiver was slung over her shoulder.

"Isn't tonight your night at the northern gate?" Taryn asked with a smile and Rubi blushed. "Abandoning the gate, that's something I'd expect more from Tyler or Markus, you know."

Before Rubi could open her mouth, Meyral stepped forward. "I know you want to go," he said. "I'd want the same thing if I were in your position. You're more than capable, but you can't...not on this one."

"Meyral, I'm going with you. I'm one of Taryn's students too. Even if I have to kick your ass and carry you, I'm going!" She crossed her arms.

"You can't abandon your guard duty," he said. "If Nordcross is willing to attack Trosloth, they clearly have no problem attacking the Northern Federation. It's war. Would you leave Mantrych's safety in the hands of that old guard? You're this town's best defense, and you know it."

Rubi chewed on her lip for a moment. She cracked her knuckles and sighed. Meyral was about to say something else, but she reached out and hugged him—something she had never done before.

"Don't die!" she whispered into his ear.

Maxine returned from her room. She strolled past the group and out of the house. Nobody had even noticed that she had left, but she now had a bow in her hand and quiver of arrows slung over her shoulder. She had pulled the Ardänian shirt her mother had given her over her dress, and it was all held together with a thick leather belt. Her green hair streamed behind her in the slight breeze, and the light of the moons shimmered off of it like some exotic string of emeralds.

Rubi pulled away from Meyral with a look of apprehension on her face.

"Whoa, wait, what? You shoot?" Alberto asked as he stood back up.

"Yea. I told you when we got here that I wanted to learn." Maxine realized that Alberto was still confused, so she added, "Where do you think I've been sneaking off to all year? I found a master that's been teaching me to shoot. I killed that goose we ate a while ago. I even bragged about it to you when you were cooking it!"

The big guy stared around the room, hoping he wasn't the only one surprised. Taryn shrugged and his sister scoffed.

"You're such a dolt, dearest brother of mine."

"I thought you were kidding."

Maxine spun around, notched an arrow, brought the bow up, and released before anyone could react. Alberto felt a gust of wind by his right ear, and Meyral turned in time to watch as the shaft buried itself in a map that Alberto had brought home. The arrow had pierced the dot labeled "Trosloth Peak."

For a moment, Alberto stood completely still. Fear filled his eyes. Then his chest puffed out with pride and he stared at his sister.

"Oh, big muscles," Chloe muttered. "I feel so much better sending my man off to fight with you alongside him."

Maxine glared and stuck her tongue out.

"Before we leave, Taryn, do you know when the army should be getting there? Can we even make it in time?" Meyral asked, suddenly unsure about heading out on foot.

"Trosloth is about a seven-day walk from here, assuming we can get through Gate Nine," Alberto answered, much to his sister's surprise. "There are no mountains or rivers in the way for either us or Nordcross, until we get to the actual wetlands themselves. We can assume a steady pace for both parties up until then.

"It would take our same group two days to get from the Nordcross border to the Clarion Swamp, so I'm assuming it will take a well-trained army the same if they pushed. I doubt they sent a squad from the border though, so let's say they left from the capital, which seems more likely considering Azrael doubles as a fortress. That would take an extra day or two."

"So you're saying we don't have a chance to get there before the battle starts?" Meyral asked. He didn't care if the fear he felt was obvious in his voice.

"No, no! I've seen various maps of Clarion, and I'm positive I can get us to Trosloth in time. The army doesn't have a chance in that bog. It'll probably be the better part of a week before they make it through. I think we should have at least a day to get things organized before the battle even starts."

Maxine stared at her brother and smirked.

"I've been working a lot with Carter," Alberto added with a grin. "I spend a lot of time looking at these countries."

Chloe grabbed his hand and squeezed it. Alberto looked at her, and she smiled back with tears in her eyes.

"Well, I might as well give you a bit of a head start on the enemy," Taryn interrupted with a slight air of annoyance. "I have a few boarhounds in the local stables. Take them and you should get there in a couple days' time."

Meyral had no idea what a boarhound was, but they all followed his teacher to the stables. Inside, they found the beasts she was talking about.

"Are we supposed to ride these?" Meyral asked as he stared at a creature with a particularly bad drooling problem.

The boarhounds stomped around their stalls on all fours. They were each the size of a small bull, but longer. Their shaggy coats varied in color and style, but they all had the same ugly head, like that of a bald boar. A single long tusk poked out of either side of their mouths, and each protrusion had a rein attached at its middle. Meyral guessed that their huge paws were slightly bigger than Alberto's hands, which was an impressive feat in itself. He found himself a bit apprehensive about getting too near.

"Don't worry," Taryn said. "They're very gentle creatures. They only look intimidating because their bodies had to adapt to the harsh winters." She emphasized her point by kneeling and petting its snout. It let out a low rumble and its tongue lolled out of its mouth. "The long hair keeps them warm, and the paws," she grabbed the beast's paw in a kind of handshake, "are for the snow. That way they don't sink in the drifts."

"Those horns don't look so harmless to me," Meyral said as he pointed to the nearest hound.

"They're called tusks, actually, and they're used to forage for their favorite food."

"What would that be?" Alberto asked, his interest in food always shining through.

"Mammoth grubs!" the old woman exclaimed as she pulled something out of a barrel.

It looked like a foot-long bag of pus. She tossed it to the white-and-brown hound that Meyral had just been warming up to. It caught the grub out of midair and Meyral turned away in disgust. The boarhound swallowed and licked Meyral's whole right side playfully, and Alberto laughed at the look on his face.

"They're the preferred method of transportation here in the North, especially because of their paws," Maxine explained, already saddling up a very shaggy boarhound with a golden coat. "Is this how you do it?" she asked Taryn as she tightened one of the straps of her saddle.

"Yes, dear. Well done." Taryn nodded at Maxine before she turned her head to Alberto and yelled, "You'll want to watch yourself around their hindquarters!"

Alberto didn't waste any time getting to know his boarhound. He walked right up to it and patted it on the head, then ran his hands through its coarse, black hair. He put his head right next to the animal's face and stuck his tongue out. It grunted and licked his whole face with a flat, purple tongue, and Alberto toppled backward.

Meyral noticed their cat near the entrance, staring intently at Taryn. It waited a second and then slinked outside. Meyral sneaked away from the group and followed Reaver into the shadows. He found the thief back in human form, slicking his hair back and stretching his neck.

"I'll follow you to Trosloth, just in case the big guy doesn't really know where he's going," Reaver said as he nodded toward the doorway. "But if there really is going to be a battle, I won't stick around for it. I'm a thief, not a warrior. Besides," he added with a grin, "I only promised to get you to your father. No more babysitting for me."

"Thank you, Reaver. For everything." Meyral extended his hand and stood up straight.

The thief stared for a moment, then grabbed and shook Meyral's hand.

A few moments later, the trio was sitting atop their beasts, ready to head out. Taryn slipped Meyral a note in a sealed envelope.

"This should help you at Gate Nine," she whispered. "Good luck, mysterious travelers." Taryn winked at Meyral, who was still trying to get his boarhound to turn about-face. As he struggled, he saw Rubi hand Maxine something.

"My father gave this to me before he died," she was saying. "It's made from real dwarven silver—from the Black Iron Mines—and he told me the hilt is made of giants' bone from Quercus."

Maxine unsheathed the small blade and inspected it. There was a red insignia on the hilt, but it was too faded for her to make out what it was. "Thanks, Rubi," she said as her eyes watered.

"Good luck, everyone," Rubi said as she took her place at Taryn's side.

Meyral finally got his beast under control, but before he could steer his boarhound away, Chloe grabbed his reins. She shot a worried look at the siblings, who were already lost in another argument about who should lead.

"Don't...don't let him do anything stupid. I know how he is, especially about his sister." She bit her lip. "Just be safe. Please."

Meyral nodded and led his boarhound to the other two.

Father...I'm on my way.

A few minutes outside of town, Alberto broke the tense silence that had fallen over them.

"I can't tell whether I'm more nervous or excited," he said. "I mean, I can't help it. I haven't been away from Chloe for almost a whole year."

"You're so whipped, Bert," Maxine said. "You've got to learn to do things on your own. She'll be fine without you protecting her from everything that might scrape her knee."

"Aw, thanks Maxi. You really know how to cheer a guy up." Under his breath he added, "Bitch."

* * *

The trio set up camp in a sea of rye grass just outside the south end of Gate Nine. The guards were reluctant to let them through, until Meyral shoved Taryn's letter into their hands. As soon as they read it, they apologized profusely. One of them even bowed.

With nothing better to do that night and thoughts of the upcoming battle chewing at the backs of their minds, they talked and joked, pretending to be carefree friends again, a luxury they hadn't had since they'd left Ardänia.

Alberto had just finished telling a cartographer's joke, which only he found funny, when he turned suddenly to Meyral. "So let me get this straight. You're like, some badass fighter, and that ginger is in love with you?"

"That's a huge simplification for a year and half of my life, but yes, I am pretty skilled. By the way, if you call her a ginger to her face, she'll make you limp for the rest of your life." Meyral adjusted his pants with a pained look on his face. "Trust me."

"But you two are in *love*," Maxine teased.

"No," Meyral said as he scrunched up his face. "To be honest, that hug she gave me was the first time she's acted like a friend instead of a rival. It's nothing!" He stared into the fire, unable to wrap his mind around the feelings that swarmed his gut.

"And Sis, you're like a ranger or a huntress or something? How did this happen?"

"Well," she blushed, "it turns out Reaver stuck around. He kept it secret because of Taryn, but he's been teaching me to use the bow. I'm pretty sure I could give him a run for his gold nowadays."

"Such modesty, Maxine," Meyral said. "Old men are tough to beat, you know."

"You've been hanging out with that thief?" Alberto asked as he scrunched up his eyebrows. "I still don't trust that guy…"

Maxine threw a pebble at her brother as a magpie warbled in the distance. "Don't be a jerk. You're the one who spends all his time with Carter and Chloe, never enough free time to talk to *your* family!"

"Yea," Meyral said with a mischievous grin. "Is it Alberto the Wise, or Alberto the Heartbreaker?"

"I've always been pretty bright," Alberto said with a wink. "I just never had access to the proper resources. Now the girl, I ain't breakin' no hearts there—we're set to marry next fall. I was gonna tell everyone, but all this," he gestured around him and looked up at the sky, "kinda got in the way."

Neither of the two men noticed that Maxine's face had turned into a light scowl. The darkness hid her weakness, and she silently thanked the night.

* * *

"Yuck!" Meyral shouted as bog water splashed him. "Gross!" He slowed his hound to a crawl to wipe his face with his shirt.

"Don't worry, Meyral, this water's good for you. Full of nutrients and whatnot." Alberto patted the side of his steed. "Know where it all comes from?"

Meyral shook his head.

"The Frozen Wastes in the North. It's made up of these things called 'glaciers.' Giant blocks of ice the size of whole cities rise up through the snow like mountains."

Maxine sighed as she passed her brother.

"What, you don't like it when other people explain stuff?" Alberto asked as he shook his head. "Anyway, back to the ice…when it gets far enough south, it melts, creating a body of water that borders the eastern side of the North—the Great Lake. The water that runs out of there goes here, which creates this swampland. Now," he wagged a finger at Meyral as they bounced along on top of their hounds, "the ice extends over a huge part of the land, and it even covers a whole range of mountains. When the ice melts, it releases this water that's insanely packed with nutrients. Then rivers bring it all the way down into the eastern part of the continent, now known as Nordcross."

Alberto spat at the mention of the enemy.

"That's why those ass-hats have no problem growing anything they want. That water comes here first, though, which is why this place is so fantastically overgrown and lush. In fact, most of these plants can only live right here. It's really kind of amazing when you think about it."

"I could have told you that," Maxine said. She had slowed down and was riding alongside Meyral.

"This new jealousy thing is ugly on you, Sis, you know that?"

"Ugly? Ugly? Have you looked in a mirror lately?"

"Chloe likes the way I look!" the big man shouted back.

Meyral looked around him, trying to ignore the siblings' bickering. The luminescent green moss that grew on the water and hung in the trees was only slightly less impressive than the giant ferns that grew in between the tall cypress trees. He'd seen a few dark things swimming around in the deeper waters that, to his credit, Alberto had managed to keep them out of. Meyral tried not to think about it. He didn't even want to know what lived down there.

"This place creeps me out, Bert," Meyral said under his breath.

Alberto laughed and clapped him on the back, almost falling off of his hound in the process. The beast let out a low grunt and shifted to counterbalance him.

"See that?" Alberto pointed ahead of them. "That's Trosloth Peak. The town is at its base."

"It used to be a volcano, a long time ago. It's the only one this far southwest," Maxine finished.

Meyral had his eyes set on the tip of the peak in the distance, hoping that its namesake was on higher ground…or at least a little drier.

* * *

They arrived at the town shortly after lunch on the third day of their journey. They rode their boarhounds into the center of the shabby, deserted place. They scanned the area, but Trosloth looked completely vacant.

"Hello?" Meyral shouted as he dismounted his hound. The low warble of a magpie was the only response he got.

"Hey, we're here to help! Don't hide from us!" Alberto yelled as he dropped to the ground and led his beast, his deep voice much more impressive than Meyral's.

Only silence followed as Alberto absentmindedly scratched his animal's head. The boarhound grunted its approval and rubbed its massive head against Alberto's thigh, covering it in thick and goopy slobber.

"Meyral, I'm gettin' kinda creeped out," Alberto said. "Are you sure Taryn wasn't makin' it all up?"

"I don't like it here either. It feels wrong," Maxine added as she dismounted.

Meyral shot them both a sharp glance and they shut up.

Trosloth consisted of less than twenty or so buildings, set up like a big cross. In the center was a temple, and at the north end was a whole slew of what looked like sheds full of mining equipment resting against the side of the mountain. A small bird took flight from the top of the highest shed.

Meyral turned to face the temple and began shouting again. "We have reason to believe Nordcross is on their way! We wish to speak with Jas—"

"Stop it! Don't say that out loud!" An old man rushed out of the building behind them and wildly waved a cane in the air. "You never know who's listening...there could be goat-suckers all over these swamps!" The old man winced and grabbed his lower back. He held this stance for a few long seconds before continuing to hobble toward them.

Alberto looked to Maxine and mouthed, "Goat-suckers?" but she only shrugged.

When he reached the trio, he stared at each of them one by one. He looked to his left, and then to his right. Finally, after apparently deciding they weren't spies, he began to speak more freely.

"You don't look like Nordcross bastards, but sayin' that man's name here...it might get you killed. He is a wanted criminal. He slaughtered one of the royal guards and escaped the emperor," he spat at the floor, "after being falsely imprisoned, mind you."

He looked to his left and right again, then motioned for them to come closer. "Around these parts, though, he's a damned hero. He's also been rallying other Remnants from the surrounding territories, and our little town is more than happy to help. Damn Nordcross!" His curse echoed back to him and he quickly looked around, suddenly frightened. "We know what they've been up to, with their senseless murders."

The old man beckoned them back toward the store he had just left. They tied up their hounds and followed him into the building.

"My name is Lazlo, by the way," he called back as he led them into his office. He pulled back an ornate rug on the floor, then struggled to pull up some of the exposed floorboards. After a tense moment, he pried them loose, revealing a stone staircase that descended into darkness.

The basement was dimly lit, and it took their eyes a few moments to adjust. When Meyral finally focused, he saw a man with black hair, a muscular build, and familiarly brilliant blue eyes. He had a broadsword resting by his side and looked like he had a few wounds still healing on his face.

"Father!" Meyral shouted as he rushed toward the man.

Both of his arms were immediately grabbed, and he was held in place by several large men.

"Let him go!" Jaspar commanded. "He's not here to kill me. He is my son." He strolled forward and grabbed Meyral's shoulders. He looked him over with a joy so powerful that his eyes watered, and then he pulled his son into a strong embrace.

"Dad..."

"I'm sorry I sent you away on your own. I shouldn't have abandoned you." Jaspar squeezed Meyral. "And I'm sorry I didn't send word. Lazlo was willing enough to help, but he couldn't risk word spreading too far that he was harboring fugitives. It would have put the entire Federation at risk. I'm so glad you're alright."

"I wasn't exactly alone," Meyral said with a warm smile. "I had Alberto and Maxine. And Reaver helped us, just like you asked him to."

"Ah, Reaver," his father said as he pulled away. "I wasn't sure if he would get my letter in time. It was a tough decision to even send him..." Jaspar eyed the siblings suspiciously. "Which reminds me, how did you know I was here?"

"Taryn told us—" Alberto started.

"Ah, you found Taryn then?" Jaspar asked. "Good. I take it she has some bad news, though, from the looks of it."

"Nordcross knows you're here," Meyral announced grimly.

"They're on their way, and they're supposed to arrive in a few days."

A loud murmuring rose up from the small crowd.

"Lies!"

"Why should we believe him?"

"Says who? Nobody knows we're here!"

"HEY!" Alberto shouted, his voice reverberating throughout the stone basement. "Look, this chick hasn't been wrong yet. Clearly she was right about you all being here."

The murmuring ceased, and Jaspar sighed. "It was foolish of me to not expect them so soon. We need to prepare. How long do we have?" he asked.

"I guess about four days…maybe more, depending on how they're doing in the swamp," Alberto said quietly as laughter filled the basement.

Jaspar's eyes strayed from Alberto's muscular build to Maxine's bow and arrows to the sheath on Meyral's back. "And I take it you've come to help? I appreciate that, but Meyral, I can't allow you to fight. Not only would it be wrong to ask a young man like yourself to go into battle with such low odds, but…you don't have the proper training to handle your weapon."

His eyes locked onto the sheath, and Meyral could see fear creeping into his father's face.

"Don't worry," Meyral explained. "Taryn wouldn't even let me bring it. This is just a staff that I've been training with, per your orders."

"A damned smart woman. I hope Reaver knows better than to try to take it from her. Wouldn't be the first time he…" Jaspar frowned. He crossed his arms and stared down at his son. "I don't know what you're thinking, but I still can't let you fight."

"You don't have to let me, Dad. But I'm going to. I'm not running this time. I want to protect my friends and my family. And I'll do everything in my power to do it. Nordcross can't walk on us forever!"

A few appreciative cheers and scattered claps echoed off the walls. Meyral felt his face turning red, and then a hand grabbed his shoulder. He turned and looked into a familiar, wrinkly face.

"You're more like your father than you know," Guillaume said. "It's good to see you again." The old man pulled out his handkerchief and spat a glob of phlegm into it. He pulled the cloth apart, stared at his snot, and shoved it back into his pocket.

"*You're* here?" Meyral asked. "There's gonna be a battle. What are you going to do?"

Guillaume paled noticeably, but when he looked around furtively at the warriors standing beside him, he straightened up and squared his shoulders. "I will fight! I won't run this time. I owe it to your father—to Ardänia!"

He raised an old, gnarled fist in the air and soaked up the cheers that erupted around him.

CHAPTER THIRTEEN: TROSLOTH

For three days, the small rebel army prepared for battle. Most of the warriors had armor and weapons, but they were in need of repair. There was a forge, but the blacksmith had run off a week before Jaspar had arrived, smelling war in the air. Meyral and his father had some skill in forging, so they set to work.

Alberto, with the help of some of the younger men, worked on defenses. They dug a large ditch and flooded it with the most foul-smelling water they could find. A mound of dirt surrounded the whole town, and Alberto gathered sharpened poles to set into the newly formed wall.

Maxine wrangled the archers together, set traps, and kept watch over the road.

Between strategic discussions with Lazlo and forging sessions, Jaspar continued to train the rebels, the siblings, and his son.

* * *

"Like this, Bert!" Jaspar shouted as he sparred with the big redhead.

"Watch it!" Alberto yelled as he dodged Jaspar's right hook.

A sizeable crowd had gathered around the two men, and Meyral watched with glee. It had been a long time since he'd watched anyone spar with his dad.

Alberto dodged another couple of punches and charged forward. He caught Jaspar in a tight headlock, and from the look on Alberto's face, he was as surprised as everyone else that he had gotten the upper hand.

Jaspar punched Alberto in the kidney and the big man winced. It was all Jaspar needed to slip out and get behind him, but before Jaspar could take his advantage, a meaty elbow flew at his head. He ducked and dove sideways as Alberto kicked out wildly.

Alberto turned around, but Jaspar wasn't where he expected him to be.

"Lookin' for me?" Jaspar asked as he kicked low.

Alberto jumped and dodged the attack, but it left him airborne and vulnerable. Jaspar capitalized and buried his fist in the redhead's jaw. Alberto spun as he fell, but he managed to land on his feet. When he recovered, he grabbed Meyral's father around his waist and slammed him into the ground. The redhead jumped on top of Jaspar like a kid doing a belly flop.

"I think you're gettin' slow, old man!"

"Not a chance," Jaspar growled.

Meyral's father strained and lifted his arms, taking Alberto by surprise as the big man found himself once again in the air. The crowd gasped as Jaspar slipped out from under Alberto. He fell back to the ground with a heavy thud, and Jaspar quickly grabbed the redhead's arm and twisted his wrist. Whatever he was doing sent an immense amount of pain through Alberto's whole left side.

"I give! Let go, I give! Damn!" Alberto shouted.

Meyral's dad let go and he brushed himself off with a chuckle. "I think you're getting better!" he exclaimed as he helped Alberto to his feet. "But you don't defend your head enough. From your chest up can be a vulnerable place. Spears are excellent for quick jabs into your weak spots—and that's the default weapon for most Nordcross soldiers."

"Yea, and that makes you an even easier target, Bert," Meyral cut in, "with such a big head and all!"

"I don't see you fighting unarmed!" Alberto shot back playfully. "Maybe if you ate that raw fish like I told you to…"

The three of them laughed and made their way to the local bar, which had been turned into a mess hall. Inside, Lazlo and Guillaume oversaw the cooking.

When they entered, Jaspar spotted Maxine in a corner booth by herself. She was smeared with mud and her hair was caked with dirt.

"I'll catch up with you two later," Jaspar said to the others as he dropped back.

He approached Maxine and tapped her gently on the shoulder. She jerked like she had been roused from a deep sleep.

"Sorry, I must have—"

"Don't worry," Jaspar shrugged, "you're working hard. I know that."

"It's just that sometimes I'm afraid it won't be enough," Maxine said.

228

"That makes two of us," he said, "but a little luck can go a long way."

"Luck favors the prepared," Maxine mumbled with the hint of a smile.

"That it does!" Jaspar laughed.

He paused and waited for her to say something. It took a few moments for her mouth to start up again.

"I saw my first mammoth grub the other day," she said.

"You're going to sit there and try to tell me the life cycle of the ice beetle is what's really on your mind?"

Maxine rearranged the potatoes on her plate as Jaspar waited patiently. It wasn't the first time he'd had to push for Maxine to express herself.

"Mother is dead," she finally said, staring right into Jaspar's blue eyes.

Maxine had always found a certain amount of safety and comfort in his eyes. She felt as if he was the one person she could tell anything to and not be judged for it.

"It wasn't even the sickness," she continued. "It was a man dressed in all black."

Jaspar's eyes widened. "I'm so sorry. That must have been devastating, after your father—"

"It's no big deal. Death is part of the cycle of life. Everybody has to die, you know."

"I know you don't feel so indifferent inside, Maxine."

There was another long pause. Then she looked back up at Jaspar, her eyes clouding with doubt as she chewed the inside of her cheek. "She loved him until the day she died," Maxine said. She waited, but Jaspar didn't respond. "To the last day, she still believed that I should forgive him. I asked her...I asked her what she would do if he came back. She said that she would continue loving him as if nothing had happened, and that she would expect us to do the same. She blamed herself. I always wondered what I would actually do if Dad ever did return..."

"Your mother had a good heart, Maxine," Jaspar said.

"Jaspar..." She bit her lower lip and looked back down at her potatoes. "Is it possible to...to love wrong?"

Jaspar shook his head slowly. "Love can't be wrong. It's really the only reason this life is worth living." He frowned. "Although sometimes love doesn't work both ways, but hey, there are plenty of good things other than love. Like mashed potatoes." He winked as he forked a chunk of her food and shoved it into his mouth with a grin.

Maxine smirked, glad to see the tension lifting. "Sometimes I wonder if I'm like her and I just—"

"You listen here, Maxine. You are beautiful, kind, and the moons know you're smart. Someday you'll find the right person who will see all of that and love you the same way you love them."

A smile formed on Maxine's face, but it quickly fell as she saw the boys walking over. Alberto and Meyral took the seats directly across from them and their conversation quickly dissolved. The two were dragged into the boys' debate on whether buffalo or doxyl dung smelled worse. Jaspar gave Maxine a knowing look before he left to get his own lunch.

* * *

"So what brought you to this little town?" Alberto asked Guillaume as he lay back against his boarhound that night.

The old man had invited the trio to live with him while they were staying in town. They spent their downtime resting by the fireplace, too tired for much else.

"Diamonds mostly. Gems of all kinds…" A greedy twinkle found its way into Guillaume's eyes. "Hell, we were pulling all sorts of goodies out of this here volcano before my associates had a series of very unfortunate accidents." He pulled out his handkerchief and spat into it. "Soon I'll have enough to retire to someplace nice. I just need more workers. This little war is pushing back my schedule."

"I'm sorry my father's life is such an inconvenience to you," Meyral snapped. He was growing less and less fond of the old man as time went on.

"You're twisting my words around, young man! I'm just trying to say that war is a burden for all of us."

"That might be the first intelligent thing you have ever said, Guillaume," Maxine said. She looked like she was gearing up for a long lecture on ethics, but Alberto hastily intervened.

"Time for sleep, guys," the big man said. "Nordcross could be at our doors as early as dawn, and we'll want to be rested to greet them properly."

* * *

The next day, the entire rebel army gathered outside to watch Jaspar test Maxine.

"I heard Reaver trained you," Jaspar said. "He isn't much in the way of a decent human being, but he's certainly good with a bow. Let's see what you learned."

He had gathered ten targets and scattered them throughout Trosloth. Two were nearby and at eye level, and a few were on rooftops. One was on the very top of Guillaume's mining equipment.

Maxine smirked and shot three arrows before anyone had seen her aim. The closer targets were hit just as she turned to aim for the one on top of the tools.

The crowd waited with baited breath, and finally she fired. The missile sailed through the air as she reached for her quiver and drew two more arrows. She set them both and shot toward the last of the rooftop targets. All three arrows hit their marks at the same time with a resounding thud.

She shot another target that was hanging out of a window, then turned toward Meyral. Some of the other archers leapt to the side and an arrow whizzed by Meyral's head. He turned to watch as it barreled down the alleyway and hit another target on top of a cart.

Jaspar stepped out from between two targets set next to each other. Maxine pulled two arrows out of her quiver, then shot. She hit both marks perfectly, leaving Jaspar unscathed. Cheers and Alberto's deep whooping broke the tense silence.

"That son of a goat taught you well," Jaspar shouted as he fixed her with his piercing stare. "But killing a man is not the same as shooting a hunk of wood."

He walked quickly down the road, his eyes never leaving Maxine's. A few people near the edge of the crowd walked away, but most stuck around.

"You must search your heart," he said when he reached her. "When the battle comes, I will have to ask you to kill. There will be enemies as young as your brother, maybe even Meyral. They may even remind you of them. Despite that, you will have to end their lives. Can you do that?"

Maxine's arms shook. She could feel everyone's eyes on her and her face flushed. She looked into Jaspar's dark eyes and tried to protest, but her mouth made no noise.

"Maxine," he continued, "we all have to make decisions for ourselves. There is a fine line between cowardice and nonviolence, just as there is one between murder and self-defense. But I will tell you this: a fight is coming either way. If you or the others want to survive this, you're going to need to take someone's life. It's the way of the battlefield."

Maxine dropped to her knees, set the bow on the ground, and shook her head. Rivulets of tears ran down her face, and when she heard people in the crowd whispering, she sobbed.

"No," Jaspar said quietly as he dropped down beside her. "You don't need to answer to me, or to anyone here. If you can't do it, then that's fine. I would never tell you what to do, and I would never want you to do something you didn't feel comfortable with."

Jaspar reached down, grabbed the abandoned bow, and pulled Maxine to her feet. He held her in front of him by her shoulders as her tears slowed, then finally stopped. For a few seconds, he said nothing. When her eyes dried a little, he handed her bow back.

"I would hate to see your talents wasted. Think about it, ask yourself who you are, and find your answer."

He strode past her as the rest of the crowd dispersed and made its way to the mess hall.

* * *

That evening, the entire town was filled with tension as they all waited for the oncoming invasion. The defenses were set, the traps were laid, and the armor was mended. Some men had plucked ferns from nearby and nervously chewed them while others told jokes that landed without response.

Meyral set off to find his father to invite him to join the group around Guillaume's fire. He searched the barracks, then the mead hall, but it wasn't until he came around a dark corner that he finally heard Jaspar's voice. He seemed to be alone, until a second man appeared out of the shadows. Meyral recognized the tan, half-bearded man as he took a puff on his skinny cigar and blew a smoke ring. The look on Reaver's face told him that the conversation probably wasn't going very well.

"Hello, Meyral," Jaspar said with a strained smile. "We were just saying our goodbyes."

Reaver glanced coldly at Jaspar, then looked back to Meyral. "Yes, well, I don't want any blood on my hands. It seems like I ought to pack up and leave before this unpleasant battle starts."

"I understand," Meyral said. "You're a thief, not a warrior. Nonviolent, not a coward, right?"

Jaspar's smile turned true and he laughed, although Reaver continued to frown.

"Where will you go?" Meyral asked the old thief.

"Who knows?" Reaver's mood finally broke and he shrugged with a slight grin. "Maybe head back to Nordcross and rob them blind while the troops are stationed elsewhere. Maybe I'll go back to Mantrych and await my owners' return."

This time Meyral laughed. "I have no doubt we will meet again," he said.

"Why not someplace warmer?" Jaspar butted in. "I hear the Island Nations are nice this time of year."

"Oh, ha-ha," the thief said slowly, turning back to Jaspar. "I heard you the first time. And with that, I bid you goodnight." Reaver slipped back into the shadow and seemed to melt away.

"Maxine says she has her answer," Meyral said after a few seconds. "The others are at Guillaume's. Care to join us?"

"Does she?" Jaspar asked with a slight smile.

A few moments later, Jaspar and Meyral had joined the others around Guillaume's fire. Guillaume fetched an ornate pipe, and before long, a lavender cloud surrounded them all as the two older men passed it back and forth.

"Why is Nordcross after you, anyway?" Maxine asked, breaking the silence and pulling Alberto from the brink of sleep.

Meyral and Alberto both perked up.

"I never figured that out," Jaspar said. "But if I had to guess, I'd say they're after the staff. They must have found out that I was the last Keeper, but that doesn't explain the whole war. Also," he smiled, "I think I pissed them off."

Alberto and Meyral laughed.

"Right, how did you escape?" the redhead asked.

"Yea, that must have been some battle," Meyral said as he smiled up at his father.

"So there I was, surrounded by four squads of Nordcross soldiers and the emperor himself. I made a beeline for Erranko—taking him down would be an instant victory. Unfortunately, he'd brought along three of his royal guard. Assassins, to be more precise. I was outmatched.

"I could take two of those monsters," Jaspar shrugged, "but three? Not a chance. I had to change my strategy, but I had only a few seconds to do it. I surrendered, knowing full well that they would take me east, away from the rest of Ardänia and my son.

"They searched the entire town, looking for something that was long gone. I was forced to watch as they pillaged every building and broke everything they could get their hands on. Eventually they gave up and torched the whole damn place," he looked pointedly at Guillaume, "including the mill."

Guillaume took a long pull on the pipe and slowly let out the smoke. The purplish haze clung to the humid air around them, and mixed with the glow of the fire, the ambiance had become rather dreamlike.

"Two assassins dragged me toward the fleet of wagons and threw me into a caravan reinforced with steel. Then they threw a sack over my head and forced me onto my knees. My hands were shackled and my feet were bound together. They wrapped more chains around me, and when they pulled them tight, I was stuck lying on the floor. A few minutes later, the whole thing started to move."

The small group listened intently. Not a sound was audible, aside from Jaspar's story and Guillaume's slightly labored breathing.

"During the skirmish, I noticed that one of the assassins wielded a familiar blade. It had been mine at one point, and I decided then that I had to take it back before I could escape.

"I picked the locks to the chains that kept me attached to the caravan…but I dropped my pick before I could free myself completely. My hands were still connected to each other, and so were my feet."

Guillaume handed Jaspar the pipe and he inhaled deeply. He blew a few smoke rings and handed it back.

"Don't get me wrong," Jaspar said. "I have no love for Nordcross, but their craftsmanship is something to be admired. Those chains were practically indestructible. I tore that damn sack off of my face, and then I looked through the little crack between the door and the wall," he squinted and held his hands up in front of him, "and I saw three men on horseback riding behind my carriage. I spent a few minutes planning out my escape, and I grabbed a couple coils of chains that I had loosed. Then I got on the floor and started kicking the door, timing it with the dips and bumps of the road."

Jaspar stomped the floor rhythmically as he spoke.

"On the seventh kick, it broke free from its hinges. The door bounced twice on the road before it crashed into the horseman directly behind it. I had little time to spare at this point, so I threw a long bit of chain at the rider who was farther behind. It caught him by the arm, so I yanked forward and pulled him from his horse. With only one enemy left, I jumped.

"Time seemed to slow down. In my mind, the next few seconds seemed to last for several minutes. I could see the tiny particles of dust kicked up by the wagon wheels, the froth at the bit in the horse's mouth, the miniscule movements of the horseman's armor as he took his final breaths...I could see everything in such vivid detail.

"I sailed through the air and angled my body just right. I landed on my feet behind the last rider, right on top of his horse. It was impossible to keep my balance at that speed, and I nearly slipped right off. I caught myself with the chain around the rider's throat and my body off the side. It had finally registered with him that his comrades were gone."

Jaspar pantomimed choking an invisible man. Alberto gulped audibly.

"As soon as he stopped struggling, I tossed him aside and grabbed the reins, but I didn't have any time to adjust my position." Jaspar pointed at Maxine. "You ever ridden a horse sidesaddle?"

Maxine shook her head. He looked meaningfully at Guillaume, but the old man was fast asleep with the pipe clutched tightly in his hands.

"Well," Jaspar sighed, "imagine doing it at a gallop. Anyway, I pulled my horse into the shadow of the caravan and inched my way forward until I could see what was up ahead. There was a team of four horses guiding us, and five Nordcross knights out in front. Along with the three men that I had just dispatched, we had a standard unit. Fortunately, the guard I was after was sitting at the front of the caravan."

Jaspar carefully plucked the pipe from Guillaume, but it had already gone out. He pulled a twig from a log in the fireplace and lit the piece.

"Where was I?" he muttered. "If I could just kill the leader and take my sword back, the five up front would never even have to be alerted that I'd escaped. I jumped from my newly acquired horse, and the stupid beast immediately stopped. I was stuck dangling from a speeding wagon with my hands and feet shackled, in the middle of the night, and my only way out of the whole mess was falling farther and farther behind. My only option was forward."

Jaspar closed his eyes and sighed.

"Before I saw him, I saw his blade." He laughed loudly. "*His* blade...he cradled it in his arms like it was a baby. I approached him cautiously, trying not to make any sudden movements despite the shaking caravan. The plan was simple: choke him out, throw him overboard, and ride away with my sword.

"I didn't think he'd heard me, but he slashed behind him without even looking. I narrowly dodged the attack, and when I looked down, I saw that he'd cut through the chains binding my feet.

"I dove to the side and he followed me, hacking and slashing the whole time. He nearly beheaded me at least twice...fortunately, we were on the straightest stretch of road I could have hoped for, so the horses kept guiding us as if nothing was happening.

"I kicked at his head and he dodged me, but he didn't account for my chains. I whipped him in the face, and as he recovered, I snatched my sword away from him. I leapt down to the horses, cut one of them free, and rode away."

Jaspar took another drag from his pipe and exhaled slowly.

"I rode across the grasslands as fast as the horse would carry me. I thought I'd made it. But soon I heard the sound of hooves behind me. The assassin was riding fast and catching up, and I knew that this time, he wouldn't take me as a prisoner.

"Before I go on," he looked to his son, who had slowly been inching toward him, "I want you to know that I had no choice. It was either kill or be killed."

Meyral nodded. "Trust me," he said, "I get it."

"He caught up to me and I slashed at him, but he ditched his horse. Somehow he dodged my blade and tackled my steed. My sword landed some distance behind us, and that bastard was at least twice my size.

"I ran back toward the sword, but he was right on my heels. I knew if I grabbed it, it would leave me vulnerable and I'd be a goner. So

I ran past it, and as he grabbed for the hilt, I spun and roundhouse kicked him in the face. He stumbled back and I grabbed—"

Meyral coughed loudly and drew Jaspar's attention. He reached down, pulled the pipe from his son's hands and laughed.

"I grabbed the sword and ran the monster through," Jaspar continued. "Only one of the horses had stayed behind, so I saddled up and disappeared."

"And then what, hmm?" Guillaume asked sleepily, rubbing his eyes.

"I knew it was only a matter of time before Nordcross found out I'd escaped, but I didn't want to draw them north. So I lost them in the Wolke Mountains, an area I know fairly well."

"That's amazing…" Alberto said.

"So how did you get those nearly indestructible shackles off?" Maxine asked with a raised eyebrow.

"Maxi!" Alberto shouted. "And people say I'm the rude one!"

"Hold on, Bert. That's a fair question," Jaspar said. "It's actually the exact reason I'm here. Lazlo used to be a Nordcross engineer before he got fed up with the place and moved for some peace and quiet. I've brought him many, shall we say, *interesting* projects in the past, so I knew a few cuffs wouldn't be a problem. Turns out I wasn't the only Remnant who'd fled to the swamps."

"Is that the sword you took?" Meyral asked, pointing to the massive blade leaning against Jaspar's abandoned chair.

His father grabbed the broadsword and raised it in the air. "This is the blade Abaddon, which once rested in the halls of Sepulchro Regum. It was given to me for my coming of age and stolen years later. This is the assassin's blade that freed me from Nordcross' tyranny. This sword took countless Ardänian lives on its way back to find me…and now I will use it against our enemies."

"Where do we draw the line?" Maxine asked quietly.

Every head snapped toward her.

"What determines whose life is more important than someone else's?" she continued. "You said it yourself, that sword killed Ardänians, and now you're going to use it to kill the people of Nordcross. All this war and killing…how are we supposed to decide who lives and who dies?"

"Every life is sacred." Jaspar's voice softened as he leaned on his sword as if it was a crutch. "But at the same time, we have to acknowledge that there are those who don't abide by this unalienable fact. We have to be able to protect ourselves. What would you have us do when they threaten our lives, or the lives of our loved ones?"

Maxine sat silently and mulled over Jaspar's question.

"We fight!" Alberto blurted out.

"But it's never that black and white," his sister said.

"Sure it is!" Alberto slapped the ground. "They're bad, we're good. What's wrong with you? They killed Mother!"

"Take it easy, you two," Jaspar intervened.

"I think that's enough excitement for one night," Guillaume said loudly.

Everyone had forgotten the old man was there. He coughed weakly and spat into his handkerchief before stuffing it back into his pocket.

"Jaspar," the old man nodded, "always a pleasure."

With a nod, Jaspar exited the house with Alberto following close behind him.

"Sorry about Maxi," Alberto said when they reached the road out front. "She just…sometimes, you know…I mean…"

Jaspar turned around and nodded sternly. He pulled his sword level with their faces. "Do you see this?" he asked as he pointed to the hilt.

Alberto's eyes trailed along the silver inscription engraved in the handle. Despite his recent brush with literacy, he couldn't make out what it said.

"What does it say?" Alberto asked.

"'Blood means nothing,' in the old language. It was your father who gave me Abaddon."

Alberto didn't say anything. He stared at the inscription and tried to imagine his father carving it.

"Alberto," Jaspar said, "family isn't about whose blood runs in your veins. It's about a bond between people, one that drives them to protect each other. Family is who loves you, understands you, and would do anything for you. A family isn't necessarily who you're related to."

Alberto's mind drifted back to Chloe. He quietly nodded at the ground, suddenly unable to face Jaspar.

"Maxine loves you, she understands you, and she is willing to do anything for you. Meyral and I, we feel the same about the both of you. We understand as much as you do. We aren't just your companions—

we're your family. After all," Jaspar sighed and lowered the blade, "it's what Derek and Eden would have wanted."

The big man wiped tears from his cheeks. He watched Meyral and Maxine inside Guillaume's house, lying on their bedrolls. Meyral glanced outside, then reached down and fluffed Alberto's pillow.

Alberto imagined the lot of them growing old at their house in Mantrych, watching all of their kids live out their easy lives. The thought made him smile and tear up at the same time, and he wished with all his willpower that that future could become a reality.

"Thank you, Jaspar." He looked up at Meyral's father with watery eyes. "That…means a lot."

* * *

Later that night, the scouts spotted smoke rising slightly to the south as dark storm clouds rolled in from the north.

"A lover, a fighter, and now a decent geographer. You're a triple threat, brother of mine," Maxine said as she stood next to Alberto.

"Meyral, did you just hear something?" Alberto asked. "It sounded like a fart in the breeze to me."

Maxine kicked her brother in the shin and headed toward the center of town. A crowd had gathered once again around Jaspar, who stood on top of a stool.

"Tomorrow, we fight!" he announced.

The small army roared with inspiration.

"No more hiding, no more running! They outnumber us, but we outmuscle them! We *will* be victorious!"

Another roar of approval rose up from the crowd.

"The women and children have left to the various Gate Cities to spread word of Nordcross' invasion. We will send the emperor a message—we will *not* be oppressed!"

The crowd cheered its loudest yet.

"This is my son," he motioned to Meyral, "and he is what I have sworn to protect, more than Ardänia itself. I know you all have something you love, something you wish to protect above all else. Find your reason for fighting, because survival is no longer enough."

They shouted in admiration and lifted their weapons.

"Get your rest, because tomorrow we fight with all our hearts!"

The group broke apart and everybody headed to their quarters, each knowing that there would be no sleep that night. Meyral stood in the moonlit road as the storm clouds and smoke threatened to extinguish the light. Jaspar, Guillaume, and Lazlo approached him and his companions.

"Alright kids, this is going to be an uphill battle," Lazlo explained. "They'll probably outnumber us at least ten to one, but we have the terrain on our side. They also don't expect us to know that they're comin', but thanks to you, we have the upper hand there as well." The old man's eyes glimmered in the moonlight. "We definitely have a chance. A small one, but it's there."

"I expect great things from you three," Guillaume said with a smile that revealed numerous gaps where teeth used to be.

Off in the distance, lightning struck. A few seconds later, thunder rumbled, filling them with an ominous sense of dread.

"You kids understand that nothing is being asked of you?" Jaspar asked as he looked down at his son with mixed emotions in his eyes. "You don't have to stay."

The trio nodded their heads in unison.

"Son, I want you to come with me," Jaspar said quietly. He headed toward an abandoned shop, then motioned for Meyral to stay behind as he went inside.

A few moments later, Jaspar returned with two poles in his hands and a stern look on his face. Without a word, he tossed one of the staves to his son and they immediately took up their battle stances.

Jaspar swiped at Meyral's head, but he ducked and rolled to the side. Meyral leapt to his feet as his father pulled his weapon back. They lunged forward at the same time and their staves met with a loud crack. Meyral spun and swept low, but Jaspar blocked the hit. Within seconds, Meyral had become a whirling mess of wood and Jaspar was forced onto the defensive.

They broke apart and stood still, eyeing one another.

"I'm impressed," Jaspar said. "A year and a half with Taryn and your fighting style has almost completely changed."

"Maybe you're just getting rusty," Meyral replied with a slight grin.

Jaspar charged and they sparred again, this time with more enthusiasm. Both father and son were using their best moves, their fastest attacks, neither one willing to give an inch. Jaspar scored first— he barely clipped his son's shoulder, but he had landed the first blow.

Meyral didn't stop. He pushed Jaspar onto the defensive again, and suddenly Meyral's world collapsed in on itself. When he regained control, he found himself surrounded by absolute blackness.

Taryn's lessons rang in the back of his mind and he took hold of the vision. Slowly a blue light illuminated the darkness around him—it looked like an arena with a sandy floor. Three figures stood in the center, brawling with fists and feet. As Meyral closed in on them and the light became brighter, he noticed that two of the combatants were covered in scales, as if they were giant lizards. The third fighter was human, and he wore only black pants. His entire right side was riddled with scars.

The scarred man dipped down to avoid a punch from the larger of the two lizard-men then he tackled the beast to the ground. Manic laughter rose up from the fight, and after a second, he realized it was coming from him. He looked down at his own scarred torso as he stomped on the lizard's legs. A loud crack resounded throughout the cavern. The second lizard closed in, and Meyral reached his fist back. Something grabbed his arm, and when he spun around, he came face to face with his father.

"Your eyes…" Jaspar slowly let go of his son's arm as Meyral returned to his own place and time. "You called me Yiddi."

Meyral fell to his knees with a grunt, his mind spinning. "Ever since I found the staff…I've been having these visions."

"I know," Jaspar said.

Meyral looked up, but his vision was still blurry. He blinked several times, trying to focus, and Jaspar helped him to his feet. When he finally regained control, Jaspar had both hands on Meyral's shoulders and was staring intently into his eyes.

"Meyral, you've grown so much since Berrywillow," Jaspar said softly as he led his son to the shop's porch.

"I was so worried about you, Dad!" For the first time since they'd been reunited, Meyral was alone with his father, and he wasn't ashamed to show his emotions. Thick tears ran down his cheeks as he tossed his weapon aside and hugged Jaspar.

"I'm glad you're alright," Jaspar said. "I knew you would be, but sometimes, duty—"

"That's no excuse!" Meyral stopped and looked at his dad with watery eyes. "You always talk about your duties, but what about your duty toward your family? You're supposed to be there for me!"

241

Jaspar chuckled quietly and turned to face his son. "You sound…just like her."

For a moment Meyral didn't understand, and then it hit him. "Like…Mom?"

"She said the same thing to me before she died," Jaspar said. His eyes became unfocused as he tried to remember something.

"How did she die?" Meyral asked quietly.

Jaspar shook his head and looked toward his son. He opened his mouth a few times before he actually spoke. "We come from a long line of warriors. Men and women both. In fact, your grandmother Andrasté helped defend the Great Moon Temple when it was torn down in the revolt. She was studying to become a priestess. A man spoke to her in her dreams and woke her up. Most of her peers…were not so lucky. After that, all magic was seen as evil, so they started to hunt your grandma and the few other survivors."

"Grandma knew how to do magic?" Meyral asked. "Did she teach you any?"

"No," Jaspar shook his head, "she gave all that up long before I had even been thought of. That's why she moved to the Northern Federation, to start a new life. But I left her to join the Remnants…"

"Does that mean," Meyral's voice filled with awe, "that I could do magic too?"

"It is in your blood, yes. Along with the natural ability to wield almost any weapon and a powerful sense of dutiful obligation. You, my son, come from a long line of Ardänian knights." His speech had taken on that strong tone that Meyral had grown up hearing. "It's not like Guillaume, whose father was a miller and his father before that. No, our fate is bound to war, the Remnants, and that staff in a way that nobody understands."

"Like destiny?"

Jaspar nodded with a small smile.

"But what does all this have to do with Mom?"

"When I was a bit younger than you, I abandoned your grandmother and I became Taryn's student. She was a powerful woman, and my devotion to her was absolute. So much so that I…I wasn't there when you were born. I was out on an errand for her that was so trivial I can't even recall what it was. I came back a week later, and Derek found me."

Jaspar's voice softened and he sighed.

"You were born a few weeks earlier than predicted. The town's Healer did all she could, and she managed to save both of you, but your mother's body had grown weak. She could hardly move when I came to her, but her spirit was as strong as ever.

"She yelled at me. Told me that I had failed her as a husband. Then she pointed to a bundle of blankets next to the bed, and with a voice so full of love and hope that my heart nearly broke just to hear it, she told me to hold my son."

Meyral had never seen his father cry, but there were tears in his eyes as he spoke.

"I thought I was doing the right thing—serving my home and the Remnants—but sometimes…you have to ask yourself. What is truly important?" Jaspar fell silent for a moment as he composed himself. "Even then, being berated by your mother, I thought serving Ardänia was the most important thing. By morning, she was gone, and you were all I had left. I'm pretty sure she held on to those last few days just to set me straight."

Meyral's hands shook and tears streamed down his face. He'd never heard his father speak so frankly.

"After she died, I vowed to abandon my place as Taryn's student and stay with you. But it's like an addiction for me. Still is. And now, more than ever, I wish I had taken your mother's wishes to heart. I probably should have spent more time teaching you things like how to read instead of how to kill a man—"

"You've always been a good father, Dad."

Jaspar pulled his son into another embrace. Meyral cried into his father's chest.

"You don't know how much that means to me, my son."

CHAPTER FOURTEEN: SKIRMISH

"Everybody up! The enemy is on the move! Suit up and take your places!"

Dawn had broken, but the land was still blanketed in shadow. Jaspar finished rousing any troops that weren't already awake before he rushed to the center of the village. A select few of the bravest warriors were waiting for him there. Their armor was dull and pitted, but their blades gleamed from a night of incessant polishing and sharpening.

From Maxine's position at the top of Guillaume's sheds full of mining equipment, she had a view of the entire, swampy battlefield. The first banner appeared on the horizon, and within the hour, Nordcross had surrounded the entire town. Lazlo was certainly right—Nordcross had more than five hundred troops, as opposed to the forty or so rebels that they had gathered together.

"This is it," Alberto said as he stretched his arms out and clapped his fists together. "Have you ever seen such a ragtag bunch of soldiers? They call themselves an army? I hope for their sakes they fight better than they look."

He glanced down at Meyral and thought the little guy looked extra pale that morning.

"Hey, you alright?" the big man asked. He pushed Meyral gently and chuckled.

"I'll be fine," he responded.

"If you need to puke or something, you do it," Alberto said with a grin. "These bastards are going to get all of my wrath today, and I'm gonna need you to watch my back. I haven't forgotten what they did to my mother. I need you to be ready."

Some of the color returned to Meyral's face.

* * *

Maxine watched as a large man stepped forward from the Nordcross forces. He wore bright silver armor and a white cape trailed from his shoulders. He held his helm in his right hand, letting his shaggy, dirty-blond hair blow in the light breeze. In his left hand he carried a long sword that was polished to a mirror finish, reflecting the lightning that crashed overhead.

A wave of murmurs started among the men. At its height, Maxine could make out pieces of what was being said.

"…must be the commander…"

"…and check out that cape!"

"…one hell of a sword…"

As the rain started to fall in heavy sheets, the commander walked half the distance to the village with two knights under a white flag. Lazlo strolled forward rather jerkily to meet him and Guillaume followed.

"You can't be Jaspar," the commander shouted in a booming voice when the old man got close enough. He looked from Lazlo to Guillaume, and Maxine could see the boredom on his face.

"No, I'm not, you filthy son of a whore!" Lazlo yelled back. He wasn't as loud, but he could still be heard over the sporadic thunder. "What do you want with this village?" he spat.

"I thought you would send someone more…intimidating," the commander said. "No matter. My name is Rios, Commander of the Special Recon Forces. I hope you don't mind, but we've come to take Jaspar back to Nordcross for the crime of—"

"Who says he's here?" Guillaume asked.

Maxine shifted in her tower. She was surprised to hear the old coward speak.

"Come now, do we have to go through all of that?" Rios asked. "Why don't you just hand him over so justice can be served?"

"Whose justice? Yours?" Guillaume shouted fiercely. "I do believe your jurisdiction stopped at the border. As far as the township of Trosloth is concerned, Jaspar is an innocent man. You're quite mistaken if you think you can just take him without a fight! If you haven't noticed, there are a few champions here who are ready to die to stop you."

"Well, that certainly is unfortunate. Because in case *you* haven't noticed," Rios grinned and spread his arms, "I, too, have a few…champions, you said? To be absolutely honest, I was hoping you'd fight. Even the Northern Federation wouldn't mourn the loss of such a pathetic little town…and my blade is too sharp anyway." The commander threw his head back and laughed.

"Looks like only half of what we expected to show made it to the party. Did y'all have trouble in the swamps?" Lazlo asked with a grin.

"This cursed place is hardly suitable for even rats to live in!" Rios sneered.

Lazlo opened his mouth to retort, but Rios gave a small nod. One of his knights sliced through the old man's neck with a swift flick of his blade. Just as Lazlo's body hit the ground, Maxine released an arrow that pierced through the knight's head.

The knight's blood drenched Rios' pristine armor. Rios staggered backward, slipping a little on the mud and gore. The white flag had been stained crimson with the blood of both sides.

Maxine cursed as Guillaume shrieked. The old coward crawled backward in the mud and sobbed. He looked from the elder's body to Rios' furious face to the enemy soldiers lying in wait, and he began hyperventilating.

"No, no, no. This is not okay. I'm an old man, what am I doing here?"

The look of rage on Rios' face dissipated a tiny degree as he watched the old man trip over himself in an attempt to run away. Before he got very far, he stumbled into a deep pool and disappeared.

"Anybody else? Run now, or face a—" Rios shouted as another arrow found the second knight's head in response.

Jaspar stepped forward and grabbed the hilt that jutted out from behind his shoulder. He pulled, and his huge blade tore through the straps that held it in place. He swung Abaddon around and held it in front of him.

"*CHARGE!*" Rios roared, and drums were beat and horns were blasted to get his men to move.

"Hold your positions!" Jaspar yelled.

Maxine was impressed that Jaspar's words were all he needed to keep the Remnants at bay. She felt the tower begin to vibrate as the Nordcross army started its frontward assault. Their boots slapped the mud in perfect rhythm. Soon the cries of dozens of enemy soldiers filled the air as they stumbled upon the bear traps that the archers had placed outside of town.

"Leave them, they're useless now!" Rios shouted as he pointed to his soldiers sporting bloody stumps for legs.

As soon as the words had left the commander's mouth, the ground opened up in several places. Almost three entire squads fell into pits of quicksand that reeked of death and decay.

"Your tricks show just how desperate and weak you truly are, maggots!" Rios sneered as the rain pounded against his face. "Archers, ready your aim!"

* * *

Alberto was practically vibrating with anticipation. He and Meyral, along with a unit of some of the older warriors, hid in swamp water up to their chests beneath giant ferns. There were three other groups like them that had been stationed there all morning.

The big man walked himself through his orders one more time, trying to calm his nerves.

Wait until the main force has passed our position…

Roars, heavy footfalls, and metal clanging reached his ears and died down, signaling the main force's advance.

Hold our positions until the archers get the signal to shoot…

They had told him that the mission was to not only disarm Nordcross' archers, but to cause general chaos and pandemonium. As soon as he had heard this, Alberto jumped out of his seat and was the first to volunteer. Meyral tagged along with him, of course, and Alberto wouldn't have had it any other way.

Maybe Jaspar was right. Maybe we really are a family.

It was only when Meyral sprang into action that Alberto jerked himself back into reality. His thoughts had managed to pull him away from battle, and he missed Rios' signal for his shooters. Alberto closed the gap between him and Meyral quickly and was impressed by the kid's skill.

Meyral's fighting had improved immensely from when they had left Westmore. Alberto could still remember when the assassin had broken in, and Meyral hadn't been able to do much more than stand by and watch. Now the little guy could hardly stop himself.

Meyral bounced from person to person, his staff whirling in a blur of pure pain. He swept through a unit of archers like a knife through hot butter. What remained of them tried to retaliate, but he was too fast. Before they even lifted their bows or drew their blades, he jabbed every one of them in the stomach, which temporarily incapacitated them.

Alberto saw his chance. He charged into the mob of soldiers and slammed his fists into the backs of their heads. Rain poured down his face, partially blinding him. It didn't slow him down in the slightest—he started punching at random, all the while hoping that Meyral and the rest would manage to stay out of his way.

He relished the feeling of steel being pounded under his fists, and the muffled sounds of helmets breaking and skulls cracking open. Alberto clamped his hands on one soldier's arms and put his foot against his chest. He pulled back with all his might until he heard a splintering noise and his enemy's arms shattered. He pulled the sword from the dying man's broken hands and spun clumsily, slashing through two soldiers charging at him.

Alberto glanced at the mess of guts spilling out onto the wet ground and let the rage overtake him.

You'll pay for Mother. You can't beat me. You'll pay for Mother. You can't beat me...

* * *

Maxine stood in her tower, nearly frozen with disgust at the scene that played out beneath her.

Lazlo was a brilliant tactician, there's no denying that.

When she had first heard of his plan to station her brother outside the walls, she thought the old man was an idiot. But, like she expected, Alberto refused to listen to her and started shouting about being a "grown-ass man."

He always thinks he can just do whatever he wants. And he does. He's just lucky that Lazlo knew what he was doing...

In the chaos of the sneak attack, Maxine saw the Nordcross army panicking. Their movements became random and order started to break down. Rather than trying to fall back and regroup, Rios ordered a full frontward assault. The panic must have reached him as well.

The Nordcross army finally began climbing the barrier around the village. The rain was so powerful that the dirt mound was quickly turning into mud. Soldiers slipped and fell, knocking their companions down with them.

Maxine was amazed and filled with a small amount of pride when Alberto's sharpened sticks that he'd hidden in the muck actually worked. Soldiers slid and the stakes impaled them, which forced a second wave of troops to climb over their fallen allies.

A high whistle sounded. Arrows launched from the treetops

surrounding the village—the rebel archers had begun their assault. Maxine pulled back on her bowstring and tried to ignore the faces of her enemies, twisted in pain and desperation. Her arm shook and she lowered her bow with a frustrated sigh.

Shooting the two knights had been easy. It was more instinct than anything, and they were fully armored. They were faceless enemies that had just killed one of her comrades.

It was justice.

Then she heard her brother roar. She scanned the battlefield until she found her worst fear. Alberto clutched his left forearm as a soldier charged him. Maxine notched an arrow in a split second and let it fly. Immediately her reluctance melted away, and any feelings of regret she had disappeared.

Her task was simple: keep her friends safe.

* * *

A quarter of an hour passed before Nordcross reached the center of the village. They were cold and wet and panting, but they didn't slow their advance. The last of the Remnants waited patiently, fresh and eager, and Jaspar finally gave the order to attack. The two sides collided in a mesh of steel, blood, and grime. The Remnants hacked and slashed with expert precision, and they dodged blades with killer instinct.

Jaspar evaded an axe aimed straight for his chest, and then he kicked it out of its owner's hands. He launched himself onto the soldier's shoulders and dove into the mass of enemies. He spun with Abaddon as he spiraled downward, decapitating a few and amputating others' legs.

He sprang back up and smashed a nearby spearman's face with the hilt of his sword. As Jaspar fought to regain his footing in the slippery mud, a soldier raised his maul. Before he could strike, an arrow pierced through the soldier's chest, spraying blood onto his would-be victim.

Jaspar lunged with his sword out, disemboweling another handful of soldiers. Their blood ran through the wet dirt as the rain continued to pound and lightning flashed nearby.

* * *

Alberto was on a rampage. He tore through the masses of Nordcross soldiers with ease. The bright red blur that the others could see through the rain acted like a beacon of inspiration.

The big man leapt over an ally and landed on an archer, whose arrow was poised to fire. He drove his elbow into the throat of another archer and lunged toward the last one, who seemed determined to get his final shot off. As Alberto closed his hands around the puny soldier's throat, he let it fly. The arrow flew almost straight up and came back down in the center of the town.

An eerie roar met their ears as Alberto stopped beside Meyral. Bodies flew into the air from where the arrow had landed. They didn't have to wonder for long who had gotten hit. Alberto had never heard Jaspar roar like that, but there was no doubt that the voice belonged to him.

* * *

Jaspar flew into the air from the battle, covered in mud and blood, with an arrow sticking grotesquely out of his right shoulder. His broadsword was clutched in his left hand, which he used with as much expertise as he had with his right.

He brought the sword back down in a diagonal slash, cutting the soldier in front of him into two pieces.

* * *

Jaspar's roar had broken Alberto's bloodlust and returned him to reality.

"By the moons, that could have gone badly!" Alberto yelled to Meyral. "They could have really pissed him off or something!" The big man smiled and let out a hearty laugh that seemed completely out of place on the battlefield.

An enemy with a sword and shield screamed as he struck out at Alberto. Surprise dawned on the big man's face as he turned to meet his attacker. Just before the blade slashed Alberto's torso, an arrow poked out from right between the soldier's eyes. His limp body fell to the ground as Alberto silently thanked his sister.

* * *

Maxine stood in her tower, communicating with whistles and hand gestures to her comrades in the trees. Her sharp eyes focused on the battle below, and she shifted from ally to ally to make sure each one was in no immediate danger. When a weapon rose up, her arrows would fly.

Nobody gets hurt on my watch. Especially not my brother, and especially not Meyral.

She heard a light whistle behind her. Maxine whirled around and looked at the level below to find three soldiers slowly climbing the equipment toward her. She notched an arrow, raised her bow, and her arms became a blur as she released three missiles, one right after the other.

The first hit one climber in the neck, which exploded in a gory rain of red. His limp body fell to the ground and made a small crater in the soft mud. The next two arrows hit their marks in the center of their chests. Each soldier flipped backward and landed facedown, splintering the arrows.

Maxine turned back to the battle and let a few more arrows fly. She reached down, still keeping count in her head. She didn't have to look to know that the arrow in her hand was her last. She heard two sharp whistles followed by a low whistle—she wasn't the only one out of ammo. The other archers dropped from their trees and rooftops. As each one landed, they pulled out small blades and joined the fight on the ground.

All of Maxine's training had only been for hunting. She had no knife-fighting skills. Dress a deer, sure, but she didn't know if she could bring herself to stab a man. She looked at her escape route and found two more soldiers already on the level below. She readied her final arrow and let it fly, taking down a soldier preparing to strike Meyral from behind.

"You're on your own, little one," she muttered to herself. "Okay, you twice-baked thunder turds!" She pulled Rubi's blade from the sheath at her thigh. "Let's dance!"

The first of the two men reached her landing and she spun blindly around with the dagger held out at arm's length. It cut straight into the enemy's neck, forging a deep, crimson line in his soft flesh. Blood spurted onto the ground at her feet, and he let out one last grunt before dropping to the muddy ground below.

She felt her stomach rumble and she dry heaved. The second

soldier made his way up and shouted something, but Maxine didn't hear. She was wholly focused on not vomiting. Suddenly a hand wrapped its way into her ponytail and pulled her head back. The smell of steel and old blood reached her nostrils and she finally lost it. Vomit spewed from her mouth and the hand let her go.

"You sick bitch, what's your deal?" the soldier cried.

A sword slashed at her, but it missed as she dropped to the ground. Her head cleared and she saw a dirty man standing close, his sword perched uncertainly above her. She kicked straight up, nailed him in the crotch, and shoved him over the edge. He yelled the whole way down, until she heard a splat at the bottom.

"That's my deal, asshole," Maxine muttered as she climbed down the side of the building and dropped to the battle below. She held her dagger at the ready as adrenaline pumped through her veins.

* * *

Jaspar's right arm had been rendered useless by the rogue arrow, but he refused to stop fighting. The enemy had learned to stay out of his way, as each assailant was immediately cut down. He found Rios and began taunting him.

"Rios! Is this the best that Nordcross has to offer?" Jaspar shouted. "You're pathetic! Leave now and minimize your casualties!"

Rios looked at him with contempt and hatred. He motioned to signal a retreat, and the rebel army cheered with their victory.

* * *

Maxine, spattered with blood, pulled an arrow from the nearest corpse and took aim as Nordcross retreated.

"This is for my mother!" she shrieked as she let go.

The arrow sailed all the way from one end of the village to the other, where it landed in Rios' left shoulder.

"Damn, a little to the left," Maxine said with a sigh. "There must have been a breeze."

The rebels cheered again as Rios screamed into the pouring rain, but their joy was short lived. They turned to find their town in flames.

"Let us collect our fallen brethren and put out these fires," Jaspar said, his voice rising above the din, "then we can celebrate our victory and mourn our losses."

No cheer rose up this time. The warriors who remained collapsed to the ground, amazed to still be alive.

Maxine walked slowly through the heart of the battlefield. Only twelve hours earlier, it had been the town square, but now the burning, broken scenery reminded Maxine of what she always imagined hell would be.

Men lay about, some screaming, some moaning. A few writhed quietly, waiting for death's merciful hand to take them. In the mud and blood, it was almost impossible to tell who belonged to which side.

I guess it's poetic, in a way. Death chooses no side.

The living weren't doing much better. Formerly fierce men now wept openly. Others stared at the sky in hopes that the rain would cleanse them of their pain.

Then she heard it. Faint, but unmistakable, it was her brother's laugh. She spun until she spied the giant redhead standing on the mud wall. He was laughing and tossing balls of muck at Meyral.

Maxine instantly forgot the horrors of war and ran to join her brother. She flung herself into Alberto's arms. "You're alive! Thank the moons!" She kissed Alberto on the cheek and reached down to inspect the wound on his forearm.

He swept her into a powerful hug, which took her by surprise, then pushed her away gently. "I'm fine, Sis! Relax!" Alberto laughed. "Thanks, by the way. I know it was you that killed the little bastard that did this to me."

Maxine nodded as she turned and grabbed Meyral. "You two fought so bravely!"

She was trying to mop the mud off of Meyral's face with her hands when Jaspar limped over. He cleared his throat and Maxine pulled away from his son. Jaspar grinned at the trio while he used his good hand to support his bleeding shoulder.

"You guys fought like heroes. I'm so proud of you," he said as his grin transitioned into a loving smile. His eyes lit up as his joy rippled across his face.

"Sorry about your shoulder," Alberto said as he eyed the broken arrow still inside Jaspar's flesh.

"Ah, this?" Jaspar squeezed the wound and winced. "Yea, if you don't mind, could you find the Healer and get him out here? My arm is killing me."

"Yes sir!" Alberto saluted him and the two boys ran into town.

"And tell him to keep his blasted leeches away from me this time!" he shouted after them.

The rain finally stopped. Maxine and Jaspar looked at one another in silence.

"We are all in your debt, Maxine," Jaspar finally said.

"You owe me nothing," she replied. "The town owes me nothing. I was fighting like everyone else."

"Yes, you were…are you okay?" Jaspar asked as concern lined his face.

"I'm fine." Maxine smiled, surprised that what she said was actually true. "You were right. When it comes to the lives of our loved ones…we don't really have a choice. It was easy."

As if Jaspar knew what was going on inside her mind, he shook his head. "Not easy. Maybe tolerable, but never easy. How you feel right now is a good thing. Battle isn't supposed to be something enjoyable. It's a necessary evil sometimes…" Jaspar trailed off and smiled at Maxine sheepishly.

The two of them laughed genuinely for a moment, then turned back to the smoldering remains of Trosloth.

Jaspar was still laughing when the boys returned with the Healer in tow.

"Wow, you really did a number on yourself this time," the Healer scolded. "No problem though, I've seen worse. I'll have it fixed in a few months, as long as you take care of it."

"Now that this place is demolished, what are you and the Remnants going to do?" Maxine asked stiffly.

"Not sure," Jaspar said. "But since Nordcross has taken the war outside of Ardänia, it won't be too terrible to spread the news about our rebellion…"

"Father, come back to Mantrych with us!" Meyral shouted. "With Taryn on our side, the Remnants would be unbeatable!"

"No. We're going to a place where it would be more ideal to regroup. I think we're going back to Arntim. Back to Ardänia, to try to contain the war…and where the rebellion would be the strongest." He paused to hug his son with his uninjured arm. "You three get back to Mantrych and continue training. You won't be useful to the rebellion if you're dead. It's your duty to learn to use the staff." Jaspar winked and then let out a mighty yelp. "For Klyntar's sake!" he shouted.

The Healer held an arrow up, its shaft stained with blood, and he pressed a towel against Jaspar's open wound. "The good news is I think I got it all, so there aren't any worries about problems later down the road. But there appears to be more damage here than I thought..." The Healer saw the worry in Meyral's face and added, "Get on your way, boy, your father is in good hands."

Maxine took over and led the boys to their boarhounds. The three of them mounted their steeds and rode west. A light drizzle was all that was left of the storm.

With one last backward glance, she saw a town engulfed in smoke as its flames diminished. The smell of victory was faint, yet undeniable.

* * *

"Dammit! Meyral, Alberto! Get back here! I don't understand why we have to ride so fast!"

"It's because you don't have a gorgeous woman waiting for you back home!" Alberto yelled as he rode hunched over his hound. He threw his head back and bellowed laughter.

The moons shone brightly over the grassy plains, and the three of them raced home at breakneck speed. As the middle moon, Sintar, reached its highest point, Maxine convinced them to stop and rest for a while.

"Jeez, you're such a pushy woman, Maxi. How's 'bout you..."

Alberto never finished his thought. Dark clouds started to block out the light of the moons.

"Another storm?" Meyral asked.

"Those aren't storm clouds," Maxine said slowly, shaking her head.

Smoke rose in the west, and Alberto was already back on his beast, riding as fast as his boarhound would let him.

"Let's go!" Meyral shouted at Maxine, but she was rooted to the spot.

When her paralysis finally broke, she jumped onto her hound, already far behind the other two.

CHAPTER FIFTEEN: TREASON

Fear pumped through Alberto's heart as he continued to kick his boarhound, willing it to go faster. He reached the last hill and his eyes widened. The entire town of Mantrych was in flames, and at the gate, the old guard's bloodied corpse hung from the walls. Alberto rode right past the suspended carcass—his focus was elsewhere.

When he reached his destination, he leapt off of his hound and ran for what remained of Carter's Archives. The flames reflected off of his pale, sweat-covered face.

* * *

Maxine brought up the rear. She lost sight of Meyral as he disappeared behind the city walls. By the time she entered the burning town, she had no idea where either of the boys had gone. Acting on instinct, she headed toward the one place they all had in common in hopes that the others had done the same.

When she reached Number Twenty-Eight, she found it deathly quiet. Maxine entered stealthily and headed upstairs. She didn't find anything as she scoured the top floor. The house had at one point been on fire, but the rain had extinguished the flames. The roof had burned away in several of the rooms, exposing the interior to the brisk night air.

She headed back downstairs and heard the sound of someone rifling through the kitchen drawers. As she rounded the corner, she saw a man with yellow teeth and a long, wiry beard. He snickered and talked to himself as he filled a sack full of silverware and a few of the trio's personal possessions.

Maxine shot him through the heart before he even noticed she was there. She looked at his dead body on the tiled floor and gasped. He was wearing the same plum armor with a snapping turtle engraved on the breastplate as the troops invading Trosloth.

* * *

Meyral arrived at Taryn's house and found a spear that had been stabbed into the ground a few feet from the porch. He stepped forward reluctantly to see what had been mounted upon it.

Tyler's head had slid halfway down the pole, the wood protruding through his mouth. Blood had dripped down and dried from the heat of the flames, making it look like a grotesque shish kabob.

"The Nordcross army is here!" Maxine shouted breathlessly as she ran up behind Meyral. "Is there anybody left?"

Meyral positioned himself between her and the bloody sight. "Not alive," he muttered.

"We need to find Alberto!" Maxine cried. She turned and sprinted down the road, leaving Meyral dazed in front of Taryn's house.

* * *

As Alberto took a few steps toward the burnt shell that used to be Carter's Archives, he heard voices from around the corner. He slowly made his way over to the alley.

"I've already had my fun. You do what you want with her."

"Damn, it's too bad we can't take prisoners. She'd be quite a gift for Rios."

Time itself seemed to slow to a torturously sickening crawl as Alberto stepped into the shadows. Terror's icy cold hands gripped his impossibly loud, beating heart as he saw two half-armored soldiers holding something between them. He walked a little closer and realized that they were holding a woman's body that was drenched in blood.

"Put her down, man. She's already half dead."

"We don't get chances like this every day, y'know? Maybe I'm not content with just one go."

Alberto stepped even closer. He saw firelight reflecting off of the blood running down the body's thighs. Her eyes were glassy with shock and her clothes had been torn. The flames made her skin glow a sickly orange, but he still recognized her.

"Ch-Chloe?" Alberto asked, unaware that he was barely speaking out loud. His hands shook violently as he slowly walked forward.

The soldier holding Chloe by the legs dropped his arms, letting her stand and lean against the other man. "We should go," he said. "Rios expected us back hours ago."

Rios? The bastard we were fighting? How...how did he...Chloe...

"Chloe?"

"You're such a"

"Chloe?"

"buzzkill,"

"Chloe?"

"y'know that?"

"CHLOE?"

He found his voice and it shook the ground beneath him. The soldiers looked up, wide eyed with surprise. They each took a step back. Chloe remained standing like some mutilated mannequin.

"You know her, eh?" the first soldier asked.

"WHAT HAVE YOU DONE TO CHLOE?"

"Is that her name?" the soldier continued. "Y'know, she didn't talk much. I don't think she enjoyed herself—" He punctuated his last word by jabbing his sword through her chest and tearing her open all the way down to her navel.

Blinded with rage, Alberto lunged. He tackled the man, ignoring the blade that pierced his shoulder. Alberto bashed the soldier's head into the ground and stabbed his thumbs into the man's eyes. Then, with one great heave, he tore the soldier's head off.

The redhead stood up with the man's detached skull still clutched in his hands and he howled into the night. He turned to the other soldier, whose sword lay forgotten in the wet grass.

The man turned to run away, but Alberto threw the bloody head at him. It hit him square in the back and sent him crashing to the ground. The man flipped onto his back, but Alberto was already standing over him.

Baring his teeth like a wild animal, Alberto grabbed him and lifted the man into the air by the legs. Using the soldier like an axe, Alberto bashed him against a tree, over and over, until his armor crumpled in on itself.

Within seconds, the soldier had become a bloody, broken ragdoll. Alberto finally dropped him to the ground and turned back to Chloe. She had fallen limply into the bushes, and Alberto crawled over to her lifeless body, weeping the whole way.

Her hazel eyes had lost most of their color, and her streaked hair was matted with blood and dirt. Alberto held her body to his and stroked her face as he sobbed. She took her last breaths in his arms, without saying a word, and he wailed helplessly into the night.

* * *

Maxine was frozen behind her brother, having just stumbled across the bloodbath.

Alberto dropped Chloe and dug his hands into the ground, as if he was grabbing for his past, desperate to turn back time. He let out a final, massive roar before collapsing onto the ground in a body-wrenching sob.

* * *

Meyral heard voices carrying from inside Taryn's house, which had been untouched by the raid. For a moment, he thought that he'd gone insane.

"What happened to that old bitch? She was supposed to be here with that staff Rios wanted."

Meyral's head started to throb at the mention of the staff. Just the thought of it missing made him sick to his stomach.

"It's not our fault," the other voice said. "That guy in black was the first one in, and he didn't find her. Far as I can tell, she was already gone when we got here. It's like she knew we were coming."

"Well, yea, but why wouldn't she have warned anyone else? That's what I don't get."

"Maybe she didn't want to risk anyone telling us where she...what's this?"

The two soldiers who had been searching the house emerged to find Meyral looking up at them with glowing, solid blue eyes.

"You bastards."

A strange, deep voice emanated from Meyral's throat, and he was no longer aware of what he was doing. A monster was writhing inside him, itching to get out and to destroy. Meyral let it take over.

"How...dare...you..." He picked up a broom handle that had been broken in half.

"Doing some spring cleaning, boy?" one asked as the other laughed.

"I think you should start with the upstairs bedroom. It's a bit messy."

Both soldiers laughed again, but one of the men fell silent only a second later. Meyral had hurled the broken broom handle and impaled him in the throat. He advanced toward the other soldier without missing a beat.

Meyral pulled the handle out of the first man's neck as he passed and blood poured onto the porch. The other soldier pressed himself against the wall and begged for his life. The blue-eyed monster wasn't listening.

He bashed him across the face with the stick, hard enough to splinter the wood. The soldier fell to the ground and scrambled backward.

"Gods, help me!" he shouted.

"They'll do no such thing," Meyral bellowed as he reached his hand into the man's mouth and tore his jaw from his face.

The soldier gurgled as blood poured out of the gaping hole that used to be his mouth. Meyral dropped the jawbone to the ground and stepped down from the porch, leaving the man to drown in his own blood.

When his boots hit the gravel of the road, the blue faded from his eyes. He watched in horror as the last few minutes played in his head.

Did I...? By the moons, what's happening to me?

He looked down at his hands, desperately hoping he was dreaming, or that his body was invisible again. Instead he found solid flesh. He cringed as he heard the sound of the man behind him gasping for air.

What have I done?

Before he could consider helping the dying man, he heard a voice to his left. It sounded vaguely familiar, but he couldn't place it. Meyral turned slowly and his eyes lit on the edge of the orchard. He saw someone dressed in a long, deep red cloak. A tuft of light hair poked out of the hood and he realized it was Taryn. She held the staff in her right hand and beckoned him to follow with the other.

His feet dragged on the ground as he walked toward her. He felt like he was stuck in some hellish dream, some terror that he would never wake from. Reality itself had become a daze of horror.

* * *

Where am I?

Meyral looked around, but he was shrouded in darkness. Suddenly a brilliant flash of light appeared, and the inside of a cave came into focus. A familiar-looking man in a dark cloak stood before him, holding a walking staff that Meyral knew he'd seen before. A bundle of blindingly bright, golden fire floated above the man's head. Meyral already knew that the man with the perfect smile and curly hair wouldn't be able to hear him if he spoke, so he resigned himself to watch.

"Happy birthday, girls," Shraka announced ominously, his eyes flickering back and forth.

Meyral turned to see who he was looking at, and he found the two young girls from his last vision—King Thessius' daughter Marie and her cousin, Marguerite. This time, however, they were a little older than Meyral.

"I'd like to show you some magic. I think you're old enough to grasp some of its power…"

Meyral noticed that Marie looked nervous, but Marguerite almost looked hungry.

"What are you going to show us?" Marguerite asked eagerly.

"Well, let me ask you this. How do you feel about death, young ones?"

Marie responded quickly, "It's a natural part of life, and to grieve excessively is—"

"It shows our humanity, our frailty. It's disgusting," Marguerite interrupted.

"I like that answer!" He snickered before moving on. "Well, I'm going to teach you how to beat death. Really, it's just a simple bit of magic, but I think…"

The vision started to fade again, this time to white.

* * *

When he woke, Meyral was lying on his back in wet grass, not far from Mantrych. He rolled over to find his staff lying next to him. Using it to prop himself up, he got to his feet and looked around.

Memories of the previous evening flooded into his mind, but everything went fuzzy, and he couldn't remember anything past riding in through the town's wall. He doubled over and vomited, spewing bile onto the grass.

When he returned to the village, all of the houses were nothing more than hollowed out and torched shells of what they used to be. In an alleyway by Carter's Archives, Maxine sat with her knees pulled up to her chin, rocking back and forth. Alberto lay facedown in the grass, next to what Meyral could only guess was Chloe's body.

He sat next to Maxine and waited for the sun to rise. He waited for the most hellish night of his life to end.

* * *

Drazin stood in a room lit by torches. He had been there many times before with the previous emperor, Falco, who had called it his war room. Really, it was just another throne room used specifically for producing horrendous ideas.

This was his first time there since Erranko had taken over, but everything was still the same. The room was perfectly round, with alcoves where windows should have been. No outside light reached that room, and Drazin was certain that this second throne was deep underground.

For a moment he watched the room in silence, and then it dawned on him what had changed. Instead of the usual orange glow, the torches cast a green light that gave everything an ethereal look.

He glanced down at his watch and reminded himself how he wound up in this mess in the first place. It all started when he was a kid—more specifically, with his brother.

Drazin loved his older brother, and, even though they were nine years apart in age, Jon had always found time to teach and inspire him. They worked on puzzles, went on adventures to the library, and he even helped his brother design machines when he started working for the empire.

When Drazin had begun his life as a full-time student, his brother left home to work on the Nordcross Rail. Drazin applied himself to his studies more rigorously than any other student. Their parents were so proud of him—of both of them.

Before long, he was at the top of his class, but all he hoped was that his brother was proud. He wasn't able to write to Jon because he never knew where he would be, but Jon wrote to him. Every month, he would get a letter from some far-off place. It seemed as if his brother had been everywhere from the Island Nations in the south to Osdorf in the north.

During his last year at the University of Icarus, the letters stopped coming. Fear gripped Drazin like the tentacles of an evil sea beast. More than that, he knew it in his soul...he knew that his brother was dead.

Spring came, bringing with it an official package in the mail. Inside was his brother's charred watch and a letter from Emperor Falco himself. The letter explained that there had been an attack by land pirates on the Nordcross Rail during its operation. There were no survivors.

The day after the package had come, the attack became public knowledge. The newspapers had printed the tragedy and made him relive the pain for weeks. There was even a list of those killed in the attack—one hundred and thirty-eight, including Jon's wife and child. A whole part of Drazin's family had been taken from him before he ever had the chance to meet them.

Drazin decided then that he would enlist in the army to defend Nordcross against the very things that killed his brother. Summer came, and he was a cadet. His family, his friends, everyone he knew thought he'd gone insane.

Looking back...maybe he had.

Once they made it through the initial boot camp, the up-and-coming soldiers were to take an aptitude test to decide how their talents would best be used. Drazin failed every physical task he was given, and he was going to be placed in the front lines to absorb the initial wave of enemies.

When he was finally given a written exam on tactics and strategy, he passed with a perfect score. Drazin had to take seven different tests before the commanders would accept that someone could even get a perfect score. The emperor took notice, and Drazin was immediately promoted to Strategist of the Seventh Unit of Nordcross.

A few months later, Drazin made his first trip into the war room. He was invited to Azrael, but instead of entering the throne room, he was led behind a tapestry and down a winding staircase. He walked for what felt like days, until they reached an ancient door with bizarre carvings on it. Upon entering the bare chamber beyond, only three things caught his eye: the onyx throne and the two small archways behind it.

Carved into the Black Throne were horses and chariots, scenes of fires and wars from the past, and depictions of beheadings. He knew enough to know that the markings explained the history of Nordcross' rise to power. He guessed that the story carved into that throne was the one they didn't teach in school.

Emperor Falco had been a decent man—Drazin came to know him on a personal level. But when he sat on that throne...the Black Throne...something took hold of him. He would rage against towns and lords and order their executions for the most insignificant reasons.

Drazin realized too late that protecting his country against land pirates and wrongdoers was not on the agenda, but he had seen too much and he knew too many secrets to leave. He was trapped in a cage without bars.

"Drazin!"

He jumped at the use of his own name. He'd been so lost in thought that he forgot where he was.

A woman in a revealing dress sat on the Black Throne, her left leg crossed over her right. Her head, topped with blonde, flowing hair, rested on her right hand, giving her an air of boredom. Her emerald eyes, sparkling with the light from the torches, shot back and forth between the two men in front of her.

"Why are you so quiet?" Sera asked. "This was your idea, and it seemed to have worked rather well, don't you think? Shouldn't you be the one telling me what a success it was?"

"Your Highness," the tall, broad-shouldered man continued from his spot next to Drazin, "I can assure you..." Rhett wore a suit of black armor, a heavier style than most of the other officers' uniforms. He maintained eye contact as he delivered his message.

Drazin stood to Sera's left. He was portly, with a great deal of facial hair, and he kept nervously spinning the watch on his wrist. When Rhett finished the report, Sera waved at him listlessly.

She turned her eyes on the portly man. "Drazin?"

"Eh...ma'am...I...it wasn't...we didn't obtain the staff," he responded.

"I know you didn't get the staff, but you certainly pissed those kids off, didn't you?" Sera chuckled and raised her head off of her hand. "To think, the split attack was your idea...of course, they could only successfully defend one place with their numbers, and the staff was bound to be in one of them, but..." Sera waited for Drazin to explain.

"We won the battle at Mantrych, yes," Rhett interrupted, "but we suffered quite a few losses at Trosloth."

"Losing at Trosloth was not the fault of any of our present company." Sera surveyed the room with narrowed eyes. "I know who was responsible for that. What I'm saying is that the *idea* behind it was quite a gem, you brilliant, little man."

Drazin coughed into his hand and his watch clattered to the ground.

"We expected the kid to be using the staff, like you warned us," Rhett said, "but he didn't have it. When we searched Mantrych, we didn't find the old woman you ordered us to capture. Perhaps she took the Staff of Ardänia and ran, expecting us?"

"No, that old hag would have alerted the town if she had had sufficient warning. Anyway, Drazin, what shall we do next?" Sera asked.

As she pointed to the short strategist, Rhett stepped back and took his place against the wall.

Drazin bent down to pick up his watch. He thought to himself about the irony of how people in charge often said "we" when they didn't actually do anything. From what Drazin could tell, Sera rarely left the Black Throne, let alone Azrael. She had no blood on her hands. She didn't know what it was like to burn a house down and listen to the people inside screaming, or to torture information out of a man...

"Drazin?" Sera called to him. "Are you still with us?"

He realized he was still bent over to retrieve his watch and he blushed. "I haven't figured that out yet, Your Highness, but we know their movements are going to become erratic after being separated from Jaspar and...I believe you called her Taryn?" He straightened up and met Sera's face, which had lost some of its humor.

"I could have told you that. I have a team of Trackers at my disposal, after all. Your job is to find out where they're going ahead of time so we can beat them to it," Sera snapped. She brought her hands together and tapped her nails against each other in front of her face.

"They are children, ma'am," Drazin continued. "As such, they will most likely seek out the places that feel the most safe and familiar. They are probably headed back to Ardänia, but since their homes no longer exist, it's hard to say where they will go from there."

"That's more like it, my hairy brain of a man. Maybe you should take over a unit…become a commander?" Her tone implied that it was more of a command than a question.

"I'm a strategist, Your Highness, I wouldn't know—"

Sera waved her hand. "Of course not, you're a philosopher."

Drazin knew what kind of person it took to become a commander. Every one he'd ever met was the same. They were all obsessed more with their image than anything. Just the fact that they were fighting for Nordcross gave them the idea that they would always come out victorious.

Drazin knew better.

"You couldn't command a single soldier, let alone an army. I forget these things sometimes." She smiled, but there was nothing happy about it. "But I still need a replacement for our latest…failure." Sera's grin broadened, and her eyes once again caught the light of the torches surrounding her. A lock of her hair fell down, obscuring part of her cheek as she turned her head to one of the spear-bearing soldiers that flanked the throne.

Drazin took his cue and backed up into his spot against the wall, finally breathing easy.

"Bring me…Rios." She seemed to take extra joy in pronouncing his name.

The temperature in the room dropped significantly, and the flames withered into small embers. The blood ran out of every soldier's face and nobody made a sound. The soldier she commanded stepped forward, but he immediately stopped as two figures entered through the small arch on Sera's right. A tall, gorgeous woman waltzed into the room with a man behind her, who looked quite out of place in the sterile environment of the Black Throne.

He was bound with strong rope and covered with so much mud that it was hard to tell if he was even human. What little of his armor that showed reflected the green light so perfectly that Drazin was reminded of the lizards that used to sunbathe outside of his window as a child. He cringed a bit when he saw the arrow that stuck out painfully from one of the muddy man's shoulders. His face was pale, as if he'd been stricken ill.

His escort's purple hair was pulled back in a high ponytail, and her revealing armor grabbed the attention of everyone in the room. Her dark skin remained unaffected by the green firelight.

"I believe that you're looking for this man?" the huntress

announced with a deep and exotic voice. "I caught him attempting to flee the battlefield at Trosloth. I figured you might want him."

If not for the massive axe slung over the woman's shoulder, Drazin might have been attracted to her. The weapon was an unnerving sight.

"Yes…excellent job," Sera said while she eyed the bounty hunter like a prized buffalo. "I should have expected as much from a woman of your talents. My offer still stands. You don't need to keep up with these contracts—"

"No," the woman answered. "I gave you the refugees' locations for the bounty on their heads. I only want my reward."

"You really could have a place in this army," Sera said as she stared into the bounty hunter's eyes. She clapped her hands once, and from behind the Black Throne a mousey man appeared with a large bag of gold.

"Here, take it," Sera commanded. "I do hope you reconsider though. You could even have your own regiment…or something else, perhaps?" She raised an eyebrow as she ran a talon down the front of her dress.

Drazin wondered if he was the only one who realized what she was implying.

"I have no allegiances, and that's the way it stays," she responded indifferently.

"Alright, Aldomein. You may be needed in the near future," Sera said as she stroked her nails along the armrest.

"I'll be around. Bounty hunters tend to know when they're needed." Aldomein spun on one foot and gracefully left the room, leaving the soldiers agape.

Sera beckoned the guard next to her to bring the traitor in front of the throne. "Rios…what a pleasant surprise. Tell me, why were you trying to flee? What could possibly make you want to desert your ranks?"

"Your Highness, I wasn't fleeing, I-I was trying to gain a better vantage point so I could strike again," he mumbled quickly.

Sera glared until the silence was unbearable. Rios struggled against the ropes, but it was no use. He dropped to his knees.

"They knew we were coming—"

"Stop. I don't want to hear it," Sera said as she held up her hand. "I know what happened. You lost miserably. You knew it, and that's why you fled. Luckily, Aldomein was there to escort you back to me. Well, maybe not luckily for you…"

Sera stood and walked toward Rios, who shook uncontrollably. His dirty hair swung in his face and hid his fear in shadow. She extended her right hand with all the love of a worried mother, but Rios instinctively cowered away.

"There, there, it's going to be okay," she cooed.

Despite her soothing tone, a shiver ran through Drazin. Rios began to sob as her hand caressed the side of his face. Sera knelt down in front of the dirty man.

"Yes, I know, I know." She reached around and pulled the arrow out of his back quickly, and blood spilled onto the polished floor.

Rios yelled in pain and convulsed within the ropes.

"See, isn't that better?" she asked.

Rios' eyes widened as her other hand caught fire. Her fist burst into green flames and she jammed it into his chest. When she pulled her arm back, Rios saw his own beating heart clenched in her fingers. His body went limp as Sera pierced the heart with the arrow. She dropped the bleeding organ onto Rios' face and grimaced.

"Although I do thank you for the pleasure of seeing Aldomein again," Sera added.

Drazin noticed that she had avoided getting any blood on her.

"Do not fail me, any one of you. I am determined to see this war out to the very end, and I am determined to win. Do I make myself clear?" She looked around the room slowly, making eye contact with every soldier present, until she stopped on the tall man in black armor. "Rhett."

Rhett stepped forward with a look of pride as Sera finally addressed him.

"The remainder of Rios' unit will be added to the Seventh Unit. You will act as commander with Drazin as your strategist. Make me proud."

Rhett stood tall and saluted her. "Thank you, your Highness. I will not let you down."

Drazin saw Rhett's eyes wander back toward the green embers still glowing inside Rios' wounds.

"That's enough for today," Sera said quietly. "You're all dismissed."

The soldiers exited single file, and she extinguished all the flames with a flick of her wrist. After the last soldier left, she grabbed the partially charred carcass and dragged it through the small archway that Aldomein hadn't used.

* * *

Later, when she reached the highest spire of Azrael, Sera hurled Rios' corpse out of a window and into the moat. She wiped his blood off of her hands and onto a tapestry just outside of a stone door. She quickly checked her clothes and entered Erranko's bedroom, where she began undressing. A flicker of annoyance crossed her face when she saw that the emperor was still writing in his journal.

"Darling, it's late. Come to bed..." She circled her hand on the purple satin sheets.

"Just a minute, I'm busy," he said without looking up.

"I am without adornment, Your Highness."

"I said I'm busy!" he snapped.

Pouting, she rolled over and threw the blanket over herself.

A few minutes later, she felt a tap on her shoulder and saw her lover undressed, his journal closed and locked inside his desk. She sighed and pulled the blanket back, accepting his unspoken apology.

* * *

Drazin stood on a stool and watched through a peephole as Sera climbed onto Erranko. He had found a labyrinth of hidden tunnels in Azrael many years before, but for some reason the peepholes were much higher than normal eye level.

He used the tunnels to spy on his superiors, often to see if they were lying to him, or if they knew anything they weren't telling him. He also liked to get a handle on his commanders' personalities. Just because he worked for the empire didn't mean he agreed with everything they did.

Suddenly Sera looked up, her eyes seemingly locked right onto the peephole. It was as if she knew Drazin was there, watching and listening.

Bitch.

He had been watching her for months, but he still had no idea what she was up to.

* * *

The sun had just risen above the Wall when Alberto started to stir. Meyral, still sitting cross legged and meditating, had been waiting for his friend to recover.

His black and bloody hair hung loosely in his face as he looked at Maxine. She was still transfixed on the same small patch of dirt she'd been staring at all night. She stared on with her jaw slack and an almost comical look of fascination on her face.

Alberto lifted himself into a pushup position and rolled over onto his back. Sighing, he turned onto his side and came face to face with Chloe's body. He jumped to his feet a moment later as reality set in.

His face paled and he glanced around. Meyral started to rise, but Alberto held a hand out as he uncrossed his legs and he stopped. Alberto turned and gagged a few times, then looked back to Chloe. He bent down and picked her up, his left hand supporting her head and his right supporting her legs.

"She's my angel again." He paused and sniffed. "This dress…did you put this dress on her?" Alberto asked with a nod to the white dress that Chloe now wore. Its middle and the hem had both dried dark maroon.

"It was all I could do," Meyral muttered.

"M-Meyral. This time, she gets a proper sendoff. We aren't in a rush like…like with my mother. I'm going to do it myself. Take care of Maxine for a bit, would you?" His words fell out of his mouth with minimal emotion.

"Bert," Meyral said as Alberto flinched, "I'll go with you. Let me help."

An unbearable silence followed, until Alberto nodded his head, tears falling off of his nose. Meyral pulled himself up with his staff and pushed it into its sheath. He tugged at Maxine's arm in an attempt to rouse her, but she continued to stare at the ground in a catatonic state.

"Leave her for now," Alberto said. "We'll come back when we're done."

Meyral followed his friend through Mantrych. He silently wondered where Alberto was taking them as the big man stopped in the town square and looked toward the sky. After a minute, he started again, this time walking with determination.

They came to a hill high enough to see over the charred remains of the town and across the plains to the west. Alberto carefully set Chloe's body down in the center of the knoll and wiped his nose with the back of his hand.

"This was where we began," he told Meyral as he patted a patch of dirt just beyond her body. "Right here is where we fell in love."

Alberto's hands shook as he dug them into the soft ground. Meyral stepped forward to help, but Alberto shook his head. Meyral sat and watched his friend toil away, digging his love's tomb.

Alberto finally stopped and lowered Chloe's body into the shallow grave. An onslaught of tears worked its way down his face, but he made no sound.

"We'll avenge her," Meyral said, breaking the deafening silence. "Nordcross won't get away with this."

Alberto nodded and waited for him to continue.

"I...I fought in Trosloth to save my father, but at what cost? You and Maxine and my father are the only things that I have left, but I'm not going to give up. I will protect you three for as long as I can fight."

"Damn right, kid, damn right," Alberto muttered, his lips barely moving.

The big man bent back down and pushed the damp soil over the open grave, sealing Chloe under the surface. Meyral watched as his friend pulled out his hunting knife. He began carving something into one of the boulders overlooking Chloe's grave.

"Even if it kills me...even if it's the last thing I do, I will kill the men responsible for this. Not just the soldiers, no. I want the emperor himself."

Meyral nodded solemnly.

Alberto continued to cut into the stone and his voice picked up. "This stupid war is meaningless. The only thing that's going to come of this is more death and destruction. I know why they're fighting—it's that staff." He pointed at Meyral with a scowl. "But I'll be damned if I'm going to give them what they want. That's why I have to fight back. Vengeance...justice...call it whatever you want, but that bastard can't just do whatever the hell he wants."

Alberto put the knife back into his boot and rested his head against the cool granite. Meyral stood completely still as his friend looked for the words to express himself.

"I promise you this..." Alberto's voice wavered, and Meyral noticed blood dripping from his clenched fist. "I won't stop until I have my revenge."

As the big man walked away, Meyral took a moment to read the inscription that the redhead had carved into the rock.

Chloe. Taken before she had the chance to see all the beauty in the world that she deserved.

They returned to find Maxine sprawled out onto her back, mumbling nonsense under her breath and giggling. Alberto bent down next to her and whispered in her ear, but Maxine continued to giggle.

He reached out one of his large, meaty hands and patted the side of her face gently, and she began shaking with laughter. He pulled his hand back and smacked her hard, knocking his sister onto her side as she gasped for air. She hopped up and glared at Alberto as the manic humor disappeared and her damp, dark green hair swung in her face.

"What the *hell* was that for?" she yelled.

Alberto towered over her and she fell back. "It's time to go."

"It's not like the army's coming back, Bert," Meyral said. "We can rest at Taryn's. We'll be safe."

"We need to leave, dammit," Alberto growled under his breath.

Maxine watched the two apprehensively. Her face relaxed and she stood up straight, her violet eyes regaining their former sheen. "You...you're right. Let's go." She looked around nervously and added, "Meyral, where did you get the staff? Didn't Nordcross take it from Taryn?"

Meyral pulled the sheath around and tied the flap down. His eyes clouded over and his face contorted in concentration. "I don't remember anything after reaching Taryn's house," he mumbled.

Maxine went silent and Meyral could almost hear the cogs in her head spinning furiously.

"How did Nordcross get through the Wall in the first place?" Alberto grumbled. "I thought it was supposed to be impenetrable..."

"Bert, we got through the Wall," Maxine said. "Lies, disguises...who knows what they did. But it wouldn't have been hard to send them in small groups. It wouldn't have taken much to win here— Rubi, Taryn, Tyler, and that old guy would have been the town's only defense."

"Taryn wouldn't have been an easy target," Meyral exclaimed, jumping to his old teacher's defense. "And Rubi's no pushover, either."

"I didn't say they were. But if Taryn was busy protecting that

273

staff..." Maxine stopped when she realized what she was implying.

Meyral shook his head violently, tears appearing in his eyes. Nobody moved for a moment.

Maxine took a calming breath and spoke again. "Meyral. Where *is* Taryn?"

"I-I don't know." He sighed shakily. "Rubi's gone too. There weren't any bodies at the house. Rubi wouldn't let Taryn get captured..."

"So they ran—" Maxine started.

"Rubi wouldn't abandon her home!" Meyral shouted. "She loved this place! She—"

"She wouldn't abandon her duties, either. If Taryn ran—"

"In any case, we need to figure out where we should go next," Meyral said abruptly. "I think we need to get out of the Northern Federation to keep the casualties down. We're like a plague." His shoulders sagged.

"We go back to Ardänia then," Alberto said. He looked to the other two and squared his shoulders. "You know how well we fight. We could start some guerilla warfare while Jaspar does whatever he's doing in Arntim. It'll throw Nordcross off his trail. It's the best way for us to help!"

"For once, you meathead, you have a good plan. Now I can be proud to call you my brother." Maxine flipped her hair out of her face and chuckled.

"Shut up, Maxi," Alberto muttered with the hint of a smile.

Once again the siblings pushed their problems aside with a few jokes. Although they didn't let their anxiety get to them, Meyral couldn't help but wonder what actually happened to Rubi and Taryn.

CHAPTER SIXTEEN: REDEMPTION

Meyral looked up as the leaves above him rustled quietly. His heart raced as he waited for the imminent, muffled sound of an arrow being shot from above him.

It hadn't quite been a month since the fires of Mantrych had gone out, and now the trio was about to exact a small measure of revenge against Nordcross. They'd planned out their attack over the course of the last three days while squatting in the surrounding forests. Every step was supposed to happen at just the right moments—these soldiers never missed a beat, so there was no room for error.

Maxine would be taking aim through the trees with her sights set a few feet from the door of the closest building. A guard exited right on time. He waited a moment, then turned right along the wall to take his post observing the boundary between Qellnorm and the LaBarbe Forest.

The second the soldier stopped moving, an arrow flew from Maxine's bow and lodged itself in his throat. He fell back against the building and tried to cry out, but with his neck punctured, he made no sound. Another arrow pierced his chest immediately afterward, pinning him upright and ending his life. If not for the bloody arrows sticking out of him, one might have thought he was just an unobservant sentry.

Meyral sped out from his hiding spot, broke the arrows off, and quickly mopped up some blood from the dead man's face as the guard's partner stepped outside. The new guard noticed him immediately, but Meyral continued to fix the dead guard's knees into a standing position as instructed.

Suddenly the second soldier was facedown in the grass with an arrow sticking out from the side of his chest. His mouth was moving, but no sound came out.

Alberto took his cue and sneaked out from behind a boulder. He dragged the second body back, leaving the first sentry dead at his post without any witnesses. The three of them had just silently murdered two guards and commandeered a Nordcross building.

"Step one of Operation Qellnorm is a success," Maxine whispered as she dropped down from the branches. It had been her plan, and she knew it would work perfectly. "You guys ready? We've got to be quick."

"You got it, Sis," Alberto said. "But I still say all this sneaking is pointless. I'm ready for a good fight." He stretched and cracked his neck as he entered the building.

"Relax, we've got at least ten minutes," Meyral said. "Then you can cause some real commotion." He grabbed a piece of jerky from the rations inside the building and tossed it to Alberto. "Here, chew on this. It oughtta calm your nerves."

"Alright, be quiet." Maxine peered out of the window that faced the rest of the town. "As soon as the next guard comes around the corner to check on the sentry, we're on..."

* * *

Two weeks before they reached Qellnorm, while Mantrych was still spewing little banners of smoke into the sky, they passed through Gate Five. Around the fire that night, they tried to decide where to start their counterattack. Meyral had suggested Bonthon, but Maxine pointed out that there were only three of them, and Bonthon was a big city. A few more ideas were tossed around, but they didn't come up with anything concrete. As it was, they had no idea what was going on inside of Ardänia.

That night, Maxine had a dream—a nightmare, really. She found herself on what she guessed was a moon. The sky was awash with stars, even though it was as bright as day out. The other two moons dominated the horizon, and off in the distance was a blue-and-green orb that could only be Cygnus.

Behind her, a blond man sat on a small wooden chair and held a guitar. This man showed her images, and she quickly understood that they were telling her stories of the past, the present, and the future.

She tried to ignore them at first. Her logic overpowered every emotional fiber inside of her. The more she resisted, though, the more powerful the music became, until Maxine understood that her only option was to watch.

There was a village in the center of the vision, where she and the boys stood victoriously over a force of Nordcross soldiers. The music slowly changed as she became determined to make the vision a reality. She wasn't sure if it was her mood that influenced the music or the music that influenced her mood—either way, when she woke, her mind was set.

The next day, they came across a large trade caravan that had an inordinate amount of women and children with it. The carriages had the Raven and Moons draped down their sides, much to the trio's relief.

Maxine sold their boarhounds and gave the boys some of the gold. She instructed them to purchase supplies, and whatever they had leftover was theirs to keep. She stuck with the caravan, gathering information on the political state of their home country. As she eyed some of the women and children, she noticed that the cloth bracelets they wore were black and had Ardänian knots woven into them—they were Ardänian refugees. Polygamy wasn't unheard of in the North, and she instantly distrusted what the man she was talking to had to say.

They must be marrying for citizenship in the Northern Federation...could things really be this bad back home?

The boys returned in the same bushes where they had stolen the wagon and tortoise so long ago. They came back with large bags on their backs and even larger smiles on their faces. Maxine was already waiting for them.

She passed the information from her dream along to her brother and Meyral, under the guise that it was a new rumor she had heard from some of the women.

"So tell us already," Alberto demanded.

"There are eleven buildings in a circle," Maxine explained. "In the center of that, there are four larger buildings. The outer ring is residential, but the inner ring is made up of storehouses. The...the young lady couldn't remember the town's name." She bit her lip.

"Do you remember her saying anything about the surrounding stuff, like lakes or hills?" Alberto asked.

"Mountains!" she said with a gasp. "There are mountains on one side, to the east I think she said, and trees surround it. The woman said they were tall and skinny, and had strange, needle-like leaves—"

"Those sound like redwoods, which means you'd be describing Qellnorm. It's at the north end of the LaBarbe Forest." Alberto chuckled. "Redwoods grow everywhere there, and it's set right next to the Wolke Mountains."

"Any shortcuts, Bert?" Meyral asked.

"Nope. We'll just have to go back through Misty Pass and..."

Alberto trailed off as his eyes clouded over.

"Misty Pass?" Meyral tilted his head. "Criminals from Nordcross...can we trust them to keep their mouths shut? We can't risk Nordcross getting information from them."

"We don't have a choice," Alberto said, "unless you think we can sneak through. But they have guards stationed at those gates all night." He rubbed a hand over his face.

"It won't be a problem," Maxine muttered. "They were sentenced to death. 'The enemy of my enemy is my friend.' Chances are they'll welcome us with open arms."

"Maybe we should bring some fish, just in case," Meyral said and nudged a scowling Alberto.

The music continued to play in Maxine's head, drawing her out of the conversation.

* * *

"Quick!" Maxine shouted. "He's out!"

She threw herself onto the floor as Meyral launched out of the side window, his staff at the ready.

He ran along the border of the forest, using the trees as cover. He watched the houses glide by until he found his mark. As soon as the guards at the bottom of the signal tower looked his way, Meyral pounced and smashed their heads with his staff. At the same time, Maxine fired an arrow through her window. The missile flew straight into the top of the signal tower and embedded itself in the sentry's head.

The guard that would have seen the assault on the signal tower was walking toward the sentry they left pinned against the wall, shouting something about napping on the job. When he realized his comrade was dead, he doubled back and waved to the tower to raise the alarm, but nobody was there to receive his warning.

While the soldier waved frantically, Meyral watched Alberto sneak up behind him and snap his neck. They were still undetected.

Maxine burst out of the back door and headed straight for Meyral, who used both of his hands to boost her partway up the tower. She moved up the ladder as the remaining guards began to realize that something was wrong.

Maxine reached the top of the lookout, where she had a perfect view of the whole town.

"Let's hope this is a quick battle," Meyral muttered to himself as he looked up at the other six towers. He started to feel exposed.

* * *

Eight days prior, they made it to the base of the Wolke Mountains as another column of smoke climbed into the sky.

"That makes four now," Alberto said through ground teeth. "One a day since we left the North…what do you think it is?"

"I guess I was wrong," Maxine muttered, "Nordcross *is* stupid enough to attack the Northern Federation. I'm sure everyone is nice and safe behind that Wall, though."

Albert let out a laugh. "Meyral, you're here as my witness! My sister just admitted that she was wrong!"

He laughed again and Meyral joined him, but Maxine didn't. She seemed driven by something other than the thought of sleeping somewhere comfortable again.

That night, they reached Misty Pass as a light snowfall started, adding a fresh layer of powder to the already annoying sheet of slush and mud beneath them. Luckily, Maxine had anticipated rough weather and they were all wearing thick, woolen coats to fight the biting cold.

Meyral was still having trouble since he was the shortest. The snow almost reached his knees, and three times Alberto had to lift him out of a hidden divot in the road. They quietly crept along the edge of the highway to try to avoid alerting the Guild, but as soon as they got within twenty feet of the north gate, a voice called out to them.

"Who's there?" A thin face with brown, shaggy hair and thick glasses peered over the gate. "Who—Alberto?"

The gate swung open and Arthur ran forward with open arms. He wore what looked like a buckskin parka and matching gloves. Arthur opened his mouth, but Alberto held up a hand and pressed a finger against his lips.

"Arthur, by the moons, don't say a word," Alberto warned.

Arthur froze where he was as concern formed on his face. Within moments, Cathari appeared behind him.

"Arthur, who—Meyral!" Cathari laughed. She was wearing a similar parka, but Meyral could still see her trademark blue armor underneath it. "You came back!"

Meyral copied Alberto and made a shushing gesture.

Cathari narrowed her eyes. "What's going on?" she asked in hushed tones.

"Look, the less people that know we're here, the better," Meyral whispered. "It's for everyone's safety."

Cathari's eyes shot between each of them, but it was Arthur who gasped. "You guys!" Arthur said. "You're the fugitives that Nordcross is after in the North! So...you're fighting back?" His eyes gleamed with excitement.

Alberto and Maxine exchanged nervous glances, but Meyral answered right away. "Absolutely," he said as he puffed his chest out. "We aren't going down without a fight."

"Well, take that fight somewhere else," Cathari snapped.

"Cathari, you know this is the only way through the mountains," Arthur told Cathari with a stern look. "Be reasonable."

She pursed her lips and fell silent.

"We need to pass, but we don't want to risk being discovered," Meyral explained. "Can we trust you?"

Cathari and Arthur both nodded.

"How did you hear about the attacks?" Maxine asked as she rubbed her bow.

"The merchants have been talking about it nonstop," Arthur answered. When the trio stared at him with confusion lining their faces, he continued. "We've been doing really well since you all came through. Nordcross set up camp in Ardänia and started calling it the Western Frontier. Trade has been booming—we've made quite a small fortune just from the people passing through."

"Come to think of it," Cathari said with a backward glance, "those wanted posters they've made could definitely be you three. They've posted them all over the fort, which really has these gold-grubbing merchants excited. I see them practically wet themselves every time they glance at the bounty on your heads."

"Shit, they have posters?" Alberto banged a fist on his knee. "We'll get caught in no time..."

"Unless we move by night," Meyral assured him.

"You've got that right," Cathari said. "Everyone's looking for you three and one other guy." She looked around again. "Why are you leaving the Northern Federation?"

"We can't risk any more casualties," Maxine answered. "We

can't keep dragging innocent people into this war."

"Admirable," Cathari muttered. "This is assuming that they are after you...how exactly did you manage to piss off Nordcross?"

Suddenly the staff felt heavy on Meyral's back. He looked to Maxine, hoping that she could find the words to properly deflect Cathari's question.

"You said it yourself. We're on their wanted posters..." she answered.

That seemed to satisfy the blue-haired woman's curiosity. Meyral silently thanked Maxine.

"By the way, who's that other guy on the posters?" Arthur asked.

"It must be my father," Meyral answered without thinking.

"Alright," Cathari said after a pause. "We'll escort you to the south gate and you can be on your way—just don't talk to anybody. You got it?" She placed one hand on her hip, where a weapon was undoubtedly hidden underneath her parka.

The five of them quietly trudged through the fort, listening to the drunken shouting of old men in the mead hall. Fortunately, most likely due to the cold, everybody was already inside, stuck in the places where they would be staying for the night.

"I'm diggin' the new bandana look, Cathari. Me-ow!" Alberto said with a smile, despite the scathing look that Cathari gave him.

"Those of us who don't have long hair like Xander or Howler have to wear these, so long as Nordcross soldiers are here," Arthur said. "It's part of our uniform now." He pulled his hood back to show his own bandana.

"Soldiers? What the hell are soldiers doing here?" Maxine asked.

"They're trying to protect Misty Pass from rebel factions," Cathari explained. "Apparently it's a prime target, seeing as it would block all trade coming from the North." She eyed Maxine warily.

"Forget the fact that before we fixed that bridge across Devil's Gorge, all trade went by ship." Arthur rubbed his temples. "We keep the soldiers here sufficiently drunk, and so far they haven't been much of a bother. Xander keeps telling us that this might be a good opportunity to make 'contacts.'"

"Regardless," Cathari seemed agitated, "that's why we're escorting you. Merchants are easy to persuade, but soldiers...especially Nordcross soldiers. They're in a whole class of their own."

For some reason, Meyral couldn't shake the feeling that he was being watched. To his right was the side of a mountain, where a few buildings and the abandoned temple were carved out of the rocks. To his left was the mead hall and the rest of the houses. In front of him was only darkness.

This would be a great place for an ambush…

Finally they reached the south gate, which was flanked by torches. Cathari ran ahead toward a rock covered in snow.

Arthur leaned in close and whispered with exasperation in his voice, "Second time this week Howler's fallen asleep at his post. Lucky for you, I guess, but Cathari's gonna kick his ass later."

When the three of them reached the other side of the gate, they turned and waved to Cathari and Arthur.

"Really, thank you," Meyral said. "And if you could just not tell the others…the Guild is better off not knowing anything." He gave them a slight bow.

"Go," Cathari said as she waved back. "The quicker you leave, the better."

* * *

Maxine shot six arrows around the camp, silently eradicating the six scouts. The last arrow knocked its mark back into a bell—Alberto's cue. He ran into the back of one of the shops as soldiers poured out of its front.

Meyral had taken down the first two guards from the tower without breaking a sweat, but the second wave had him vastly outnumbered.

* * *

"Do you really think they'll keep quiet?" Meyral asked in the silent darkness of the pass. "I like them and all, but…"

"There's just something suspicious about criminals," Maxine interrupted, finishing his thought. Meeting Alberto's glare, she added, "Reformed or not."

She noticed the music was fading with every step they took toward Qellnorm. Even so, her mood was still as sour as if the haunting melody was at full volume. The snow slowed to a slight drizzle as the trio moved past an old lookout. Then a voice from in front of them broke

Maxine's concentration, expelling all thoughts of the music and the man who played it.

"It's not four people like the posters are talkin' about, but it's a man, woman, and child, with a staff to boot. Well, well, boys, I think we've hit the jackpot."

A scrawny man emerged from the shadows with two older men behind him. Each of them sported long, grey and brown beards. Behind them sat a forgotten cart full of odd pieces of wood and silver.

"You bet, boss. That bounty sure is somethin' amazing," the old man on the boss' left mumbled.

"Bounty? No, you've got the wrong people, we—" Maxine started.

"Don't lie to me, you whore!" the main merchant shouted as he pointed a curved knife at her. "Don't even try to talk your way out of this!"

Maxine unsheathed Rubi's dagger and Alberto stepped in front of them with his fists raised. Just then, more voices came from the direction of the fort.

"What's all this shouting about? The pass is a trade route, not a battleground."

Two men in purple armor approached them. Each breastplate was engraved with a snapping turtle.

Maxine gasped. They were surrounded.

"We found the terrorists!" the two older merchants shouted.

"Terrorists?" the commanding soldier repeated.

"Yea, now give us the bounty!" the boss exclaimed.

"We'll do no such thing," the second soldier shouted back. "You old men and your stories are getting more and more ridiculous, always sending us on wild goose chases…"

The first soldier stopped his partner. They whispered to each other as the traders fidgeted in the cold. The soldiers turned back to the merchants and the commanding officer addressed the man in charge. "Come to think of it, they do fit the description," he announced. "It looks like we'll be taking them into custody."

"And the bounty?" one of the older men asked greedily.

"Nordcross has strict policies about paying criminals. You three are under arrest for the crime of theft," the commander said, pointing to their cart.

"If you come along quietly you might be able to keep your hands when this is all over," the second soldier added with a sneer. "As for you three rebels, you won't be so lucky."

Weapons were drawn all around them and the old traders roared. The soldiers made it one step before they stopped and fell to the ground, their bodies suddenly motionless.

Arthur popped up behind them, looking oddly out of place with his glasses askew and a morning star clutched in his hands. Meyral turned around and found Cathari standing over the bloody merchants' corpses with a sai in each of her hands.

"Get out of here. We'll take care of the bodies." Cathari made a shooing gesture with her hands. "Go!"

Without a second glance back, the trio headed down the pass as fast as they could.

* * *

From Maxine's vantage point, she shot down eight of the soldiers closing in on Meyral. The kid held his ground as the rest of the men surrounded him.

Alberto flew out of the building he was hiding in and plowed into four soldiers, knocking them to the ground. He joined Meyral and they stood back to back, Meyral's staff drawn and Alberto's fists at the ready.

"Aw yea! This is what I was waiting for!" Alberto launched away from his comrade, sprinting from one enemy to the next in a red blur of pain. He smashed their heads together and carved a path of destruction through the small battlefield.

Meyral put all of his staff training to use. He bludgeoned his half of the soldiers while Maxine climbed down from the tower. She left the boys to their work and went to check the buildings for prisoners and ambushes.

Within minutes, only five soldiers remained. They threw down their weapons.

"We surrender!" one of them shouted.

Alberto grabbed him by the breastplate and dragged him up so they were eye to eye. "How many surrendered to you and begged for mercy?" he asked. "How many did you cut down as they cowered before you?"

Alberto's voice was so clogged with emotion that Meyral barely recognized it. An arrow flew past his face and cut the straps holding the breastplate to the soldier. He fell to the ground, leaving Alberto holding an empty piece of armor. The man crawled away and grabbed his sword, but Maxine kicked him in the face while Meyral held Alberto back. The big man continued to struggle until Maxine smacked him across the face.

"What!" her brother yelled.

"Bert, we don't kill in cold blood. They surrendered," Maxine said calmly.

"They killed Mother! They killed Chloe! They destroyed Tem, Mantrych, Westmore, and Klyntar knows how many more! Am I wrong?" Alberto looked to Meyral, daring him to argue. He turned back to his sister. "You wanna just let them go? It's not like we can take prisoners!"

"Maxine, he has a point," Meyral said. "We can't just let them go. We'd have to fight them again eventually. At the very least, they'd give away our position as soon as they got back to Nordcross."

Maxine bit her cheek and watched the five soldiers squirm on their knees. A few of them were shaking their heads.

She drew Rubi's dagger and shouted, "Strip!"

All eyes turned to her in amazement.

"I said strip!" she shrieked as she brandished the dagger.

The five men took off their armor and then stripped out of their clothes. Maxine stepped forward and cut the nearest man just under his right eye. Blood poured down his face and the others backed away.

"Stay where you are!" Maxine shouted. She went from soldier to soldier and cut each one under their right eye. "You've been marked. If we ever find you in Ardänia again, we will make you wish you had been killed today."

The last soldier cowered as Maxine approached him.

"Look at my face! As far as you are concerned, this is now the face of death. Don't forget it."

Her companions stared at her with open mouths.

"Now leave, before I change my mind!" she shouted.

The five naked soldiers ran away, bleeding from their faces.

Maxine let out a long sigh and beckoned the other two. "The prisoners are being held in the storehouses. Come on."

"Have you come to save us?"

"Oh, thank the moons!"

"Those bastards were torturing us."

"Where have you all come from?"

A prisoner with long, blond hair rattled his chains, a smile forming on his pale, scruffy face for the first time in months.

"We're Ardänians, just like you," Maxine answered. "We're leading the liberation front with Jaspar—"

"Jaspar?" the blond man interrupted. "Is he here with you? We heard rumors that he escaped Nordcross and defeated them in the North!"

"He certainly did, but he's not here with us," Meyral answered. "He's gathering any Northern and Ardänian resistance he can find and bringing them back to Arntim to form an army."

Maxine bent over the talkative man and released him from his chains, using a key that Alberto had found in the barracks.

"Now, when do the scouts come?" she asked the newly freed man quietly. "There's no way they're letting this camp function independently."

Meyral and Alberto looked up from releasing the prisoners and exchanged intrigued glances. It was the first they had heard about any scouts.

"They come once a week," he answered. "They're due back in two days."

"Perfect. Alright, gather everything you can loot and get as far away from here as you can," Maxine ordered as she pointed west.

"Yes, to Arntim! Join the resistance!" Meyral shouted as he looked out on the haggard men and women. "Don't let Jaspar's struggles be in vain. Fight, not for us, but for your kingdom. For Ardänia!"

He held the staff above his head and Maxine was reminded of Jaspar's rousing speech in Trosloth. Excited chatter broke out among the freed prisoners.

"Wait!" The blond man approached them nervously. "There's a stronghold east of here. Every time the scouts came, they would take another prisoner there. I don't know why, because nobody ever came back, but please, save them if you can!"

"Yes, they took all the children first!" a dirty woman yelled.

Others nodded in agreement. The blond man ran forward and grabbed Maxine by the shoulders.

"They took my wife," he said. "By the moons, they took my

Eleanor…" He broke down and cried on Maxine's shoulder.

She patted his back carefully with a hard look on her face before turning to her brother for help.

"Don't worry, we'll save your wife. And the kids!" Alberto shouted gleefully. "You guys get outta here and leave it to us. We're gonna save everyone!"

At that, Maxine rolled her eyes.

"Thank the moons!"

"Thank Jaspar!"

"Thank me!" Alberto added as the prisoners helped themselves to what was left in the store.

"Alberto?" Maxine leaned over Meyral and whispered into her brother's ear, "We're going to 'save everyone,' you said?"

"So I got a little carried away," the redhead answered with a shrug. "It can't be that hard, right?"

"We're just supposed to storm this stronghold then?" Meyral asked as he joined the conversation.

The boys both looked to Maxine and she winked at them. "We'll have to be quiet at first when we follow the scouts," she explained. "Don't worry. It won't be heavily guarded…I think." She spun and left toward the barracks to refill her quiver.

"Is she alright, Alberto?" Meyral asked timidly. "I mean, she just agreed with you."

Alberto shook his head. "No idea, kiddo. She'll always be a mystery to me."

* * *

At the first mention of the stronghold, the music inside Maxine's head stopped. It was like hiccups—once it was gone, she was relieved, but she kept expecting it to restart every other second. Regardless, her mood began to lift very quickly.

Over the next two nights, the trio slept in the officers' quarters, enjoying their food and whiskey. Every time Maxine closed her eyes, she expected to see the guy with the guitar, but he never showed. She convinced herself that it was a good thing, that they were going in the right direction.

On the third day, the scouts arrived. When they found Qellnorm empty, they frantically sprinted out of town with three new shadows in tow.

Everything about it felt strange to Maxine. She was no great general like Jaspar, but she knew enough to know that storming an enemy base with no plan was a bad idea. She didn't want to question the music, though. As long as it was gone, she felt safe.

* * *

After almost a day of traversing ground riddled with roots and trails overgrown with foliage, Meyral approached a familiar-looking temple set against the dull rock of the mountains. It was covered in vines with large, red blossoms, and as he marveled at them, his vision began to swim. He stopped for a moment to catch his breath as fragments of a broken memory tried to invade his mind.

Two arrows whizzed past him, nailing each of the scouts. Maxine strutted past them and climbed the stairs, not even stopping to look at the vine-strewn walls surrounding her or the corpses of the two men she'd just shot.

"C'mon, Meyral, we don't wanna get left behind. At this rate, it's almost like she's trying to lose us." Alberto put a hand on Meyral's shoulder and nudged him toward the temple.

They reached the top of the stairs, which Meyral thought was strangely unguarded, to find Maxine waiting for them. She seemed to be unfazed by the lack of soldiers.

"Hurry up," she called back over her shoulder. "I want to be out of here by nightfall."

A massive stone door stood in front of her, with an odd fixture in its center shaped like the handle of a teapot. Maxine grabbed the handle and pushed, and when the door opened, the trio found themselves staring into a dark hallway. None of them moved.

After a moment, Alberto broke the silence. "Let's get out of here, guys. This just feels wrong…it's too empty. Sis?"

Before Maxine could reply, Meyral dropped to his knees. A memory of the temple flooded his mind with perfect clarity.

Meyral found himself behind a hooded figure outside of the same temple they'd just entered, its walls still covered in ivy and colorful flowers. The woman turned and handed him the staff, her face still obscured by the hood.

288

He grabbed his weapon and she beckoned him inside the pyramid-like building. She reached for the door handle with one smooth hand, and without turning it, the door swung open. She led him into a dark hallway, dimly lit by torches with green flames.

Meyral reached out to touch her, to make her turn around, to make her explain what was happening. She whirled around as if she could feel him reaching for her and she tore back her hood.

She wasn't Taryn.

Meyral's first thought was that she was the most beautiful woman he'd ever seen—she was how he'd always imagined his mother would have looked. She had bright blonde hair, striking green eyes, and dark, thick lips.

She shook her right hand and blades sprang out of her cloak along her fingers, clacking together with a sickening metal-on-metal screech. He looked into her eyes and he felt his vision fade from the edges inward.

He dropped to the ground.

When he looked back up, his mind had cleared, and whatever was bothering Maxine wasn't anymore. The siblings were both staring down at him with concerned looks dominating their faces.

"This is where I got the staff the night Mantrych was attacked! A woman in red led me here, she—"

"Well, well, visitors. We certainly don't get many of those here, do we?"

A high, crisp voice met their ears, and they looked back at the door they just entered. In the dim light of the setting sun, the woman from Meyral's vision stood before them. She was flanked by two men clad in black, just like the assassin they had killed in Westmore. One had a spiked chain-whip on his hip, but the other one seemed to be unarmed.

The unarmed assassin gripped a man with long, blond hair by the elbow.

"I did what you said! I told you everything I know and I sent them here! Where's Eleanor? You promised me my wife!" the blond man shouted.

"I did promise that you would be reunited with her, my apologies for forgetting," the woman responded lazily. "Boys, reunite the lovers, would you?"

The assassin with the chain-whip snapped his weapon and tore the man's neck open in one swift motion. His limp body fell to the floor and his head bounced onto his back.

"I've been expecting you," the woman said as if nothing had just happened. She raised her arm, her jade dress that matched her eyes billowing around her, and she snapped her fingers. Her long, talon-like fingernails flashed a brilliant emerald as rings of fire enveloped the trio's wrists. When the flames dissipated, they left behind shackles.

"YOU!" Meyral shouted and lunged forward, but he collapsed to the floor at her feet. "Who are you? What the hell do you want with us?"

"I don't believe we've met. My name is Sera. You must be Meyral, and you're Alberto, which means..." Sera inhaled slowly and deeply. "You, my green-haired beauty, are Maxine. You're all awful traitors and war criminals with massive bounties on your heads. How did I do?"

"You...bitch..." Meyral gasped as the flaming cuffs bound themselves closer to his wrists.

"You should probably relax. You'll be in much less pain that way. Men, take them into the dungeon. I'll take care of the lady over here."

"Don't you touch my sister!" Alberto shouted. "I'll kill you, you evil wench!"

Alberto tossed his entire weight at the approaching guard and slammed the man's head into the wall. Ignoring the pain of the flaming cuffs, he turned on the spot and lunged for Sera. The unarmed guard stepped in front of him and kicked with enough force to send him back three steps. Alberto's howls echoed off the stone walls surrounding them as he tried to attack again.

He felt something tug at his ankle and he fell to the ground. The whip had wound its way up his calf, leaving streaks of blood and broken flesh. The unarmed assassin jumped on top of Alberto and put him in a chokehold.

"I told you to relax. You're only going to the dungeons to wait for me. In the meantime, I won't hurt your precious sister." Sera gripped Maxine's upper arm, her nails digging into her skin. "I wouldn't dare bruise such a delicious piece of fruit...I just have a few questions for her."

The woman's laughter echoed as she led Maxine away.

CHAPTER SEVENTEEN: CONSEQUENCE

Meyral once again felt the familiar weightlessness that accompanied his out-of-body visions. He was standing beside a throne occupied by a man with a long mane of crimson hair—King Thessius.

"Enter," the king said to nobody in particular. His booming voice echoed magnificently around the golden chamber.

A knight entered and knelt in front of Thessius. "Your Majesty, your younger brother, Lord Theron, is dying," he announced. "The curse seems to be taking effect in a most gruesome way."

The king's face suddenly changed as if he were the one who had been stricken ill.

"His hair has turned a sickly green, and he is too weak to eat or get out of bed," the knight continued.

"By the moons…what of his daughter?" Thessius asked as he stroked his magnificent beard.

"We have been keeping her from him, as per your orders, Your Majesty. She wants desperately to see him, however."

"Let her. I don't believe that he is going to make it. Have you spoken with Shraka?"

"The court magician has said, and I quote, 'For the last time, there is absolutely nothing I can do about this dark magic.' My apologies."

"It is as I feared. Malachi, if there is nothing more…"

"My king, there is one more thing," the knight said hesitantly. "In his feverish state, Theron has been plagued by…visions. He claims the kingdom is doomed, and I'm inclined to believe him." The knight could no longer maintain eye contact. He continued as his eyes studied the floor. "Rumors are spreading. There are many stories being told about your brother and how he came to be cursed, none of which I would repeat to you, Your Majesty. The worst of these are causing unrest and dissent throughout Ardänia. There are even whispers of a revolt."

The king paused for a moment, considering what Malachi was telling him, his hands still working through his dark beard. "Thank you," he finally said. "You are dismissed."

The room vanished and Meyral was left alone with the king.

"First my wife, and now my brother. A plague sits upon this house..." Thessius hung his head. "Damn you, Theron! If it's not keeping company with prostitutes, it's dealing in the illegal slave trade." Thessius sighed heavily. "It seems we can never escape our past. It's as if you are singlehandedly bringing destruction to everything that I have strived to create. And poor Marguerite, the truth would devastate her. She's so young..."

Meyral felt the vision ripple and he let go. The room reappeared, draped in banners and set for a massive celebration of some sort. A young man with a long, brown cloak entered the room, a swagger apparent in his step.

"Shraka, please tell me you bring some good news on this night, the eve of my daughter's birthday," Thessius begged as he took a long drink from his goblet.

"Your Highness, I bring only the best of news. Your brother is dead!" Shraka did a little jig around his staff.

"The best...dead? Was it...are you to blame for this?" Thessius knocked his goblet over as he rose from his throne and drew his sword.

"I wouldn't do that, *Your Highness.* Remember? I told you that your brother couldn't be trusted. He was a bad apple, and we all knew it. He needed to be...silenced."

"How dare you!"

The king rushed Shraka, but he was immediately lifted into the air by an unknown force. The look on Thessius' face was one of pure hatred.

"Yes, yes, boohoo," Shraka said. "You should know that you're no match for me. I have stolen your wondrous power, old fool!"

"My...my power? You mean—"

"Yes. It's mine." Shraka tapped the stick on the ground, and Meyral noticed a familiar blue glow at the tip. "And so is Ardänia."

"Are you mad? You will doom us all!" Thessius shouted as his face reddened with rage. "There is no way that the citizens will trust you after everything you've done!"

"I have done nothing!" Shraka spat back. "It is *you* who have set these things in motion. I will be nothing more than a trusted steward of Ardänia, and when the time is right, I will marry Marie and become king!" He cackled wildly. "As for Marguerite...I think the pain of having her heart broken a second time will be enough to send her over the edge. Suicides are such tragic events, you know, and the people will have to turn to someone for peace of mind."

Thessius' eyes went wide as Shraka continued to laugh.

"All I need now is to set the stage," the magician continued. "When Marie finds out her father has been murdered by a ruthless rebel knight, she will be mortified. Her defenses will be down." Shraka wrung his hands together and grinning. "Remember that slave that your brother knighted, the one he employs as his personal bodyguard? Malachi, wasn't that his name? You've grown so fond of him lately...he'll do nicely.

"Marguerite was much easier—all I had to do was tell her the truth. What's that old saying? 'The truth will set you free?' Well, I guess in her case, the truth has only enslaved her. Oh, how I love irony! Both girls will be under my control, and all of Ardänia will be mine!"

Shraka walked under the suspended king and prodded him with the staff. Thessius grunted, but he was unable to move. Then Thessius' own voice issued from Shraka's mouth. "Malachi, come quick!"

Thessius dropped to the ground and immediately lunged at the wizard, but all he grabbed was air as Shraka laughed and teleported in a flash of blinding light. With a light snap, he reappeared behind Thessius just as a knight burst through the doors.

"Your Majesty!" Malachi shouted.

"Give me that!" Shraka yelled as he summoned Malachi's broadsword right out of its sheath.

The knight ran at the two men, unarmed, but he was too late. Shraka ran Thessius through with Malachi's own blade. The magician pushed the king off the sword as Malachi reached them, his steps faltering. Shraka tossed the sword back to the knight, who caught it on instinct.

"Oh, no..." Malachi whispered.

"Oh yes," Shraka muttered, still grinning. "Murderer! Treason of the highest degree! Guards, come quickly, the king is dead!"

Knights emerged from every doorway, and they looked back and forth between Thessius' desecrated body and Malachi's bloody sword. There was no hesitation as the knights drove their weapons through the alleged traitor's body. Nobody noticed the court magician as he sneaked out of the room.

There was a tiny snap as a knight strode forward from the chaos and addressed his brothers. "From the moment Theron knighted this bastard, we knew he was different. A murderer, though? Damn him!"

Many helms nodded in agreement. Another knight entered in a hurry, unfazed by the scene in the throne room.

"I bring morbid news," he announced. "Lord Theron has been found dead in his bedchamber."

Another voice yelled, "The king and prince are dead. According to Ardänian law, Marie is our new queen. We must inform the remaining royal family."

"Long live the queen!" the knights shouted in unison.

All but three knights vacated the room. The ones that stayed were those who had spoken. The first raised his visor, and Meyral was shocked to find Shraka's face inside.

"My, what impeccable timing…"

The second knight raised his visor as well, and again Shraka's face peeked out from inside the helm.

"…both brothers dead on the same day!"

The final knight lifted his helmet completely off. Shraka's thick hair fell down to his shoulders.

"Long live the queen, indeed!" he shouted.

The last knight looked toward Meyral, and he got the feeling once more that Shraka was looking at him. The three knights started to laugh, a laughter that permeated the air like a sick gas filling the chamber. It turned into a familiar screech, and Meyral felt something pulling him back. He reached out with his mind and found his physical body.

* * *

"Meyral? Meyral?"

Meyral opened his eyes and tried to remember what was going on. "Alberto?" He coughed weakly.

"Yea, it's me. We're in the dungeon." Alberto's voice was glum.

Meyral could barely make out his large friend's outline in the darkness. "How long was I out?"

"An hour, a day. It's hard to tell," Alberto answered. He rubbed a large, callused hand across the stone floor.

As Meyral's eyes adjusted, he noticed that he could see bones scattered around the cell by the dim firelight. "Where's Maxine?" he asked. He sat up and winced as the flaming cuffs flared up in warning.

"Still gone with that Sera bitch. I have no idea what's going on..."

"Where's the staff?" Panic stole over Meyral and he leapt up, ignoring the flames licking his forearms. "Alberto?"

"They took it. I couldn't stop them," the big man answered quietly.

"By the moons, no!" Panic turned to despair, and for the first time since he had left home, Meyral was truly lost.

"Call it."

"What?" Meyral looked around, expecting to see the owner of the voice.

"I didn't say anything," Alberto answered. "Sit down before those cuffs kill you, man."

"No, I heard—"

"Call it to you."

Meyral froze. "I think I have a way out of here," he whispered to Alberto.

"What are you talking about? Meyral, are you okay?"

Meyral closed his eyes and concentrated. He visualized the staff and could feel its weight in his hand.

Come!

Blue flames engulfed Meyral. Alberto jumped up, bumping his head on a hanging shackle in the process. When the flames died down, Meyral's chains had disappeared and the staff had taken their place.

"How did you do that?" the big man asked as he gawked at his newly freed friend.

"No idea. Let's just get out of here!"

Letting instinct guide him, Meyral closed his eyes again and concentrated on freedom. A soothing blue light emanated from the staff and Alberto's restraints disappeared. An audible click told them that the cell door had just unlocked.

"Whatever you're doing, keep it up." Alberto rubbed his wrists and tried the door, which swung open almost automatically.

The two captives exited their cell and came face to face with the two royal guards. Without even thinking, Meyral tapped the staff on the ground and cracks immediately formed in the floor. The fissures traveled up the walls and across the ceiling, bringing huge stones down on the guards' heads. One was knocked unconscious immediately and the other raised his arms to defend himself. Meyral and Alberto slipped past them in the chaos.

Alberto reached the doors at the end of the hall and shouted back to Meyral, "They're locked!"

Meyral felt the staff vibrating in his hands. A fireball shot out of its tip toward the doorway to the staircases. Alberto dove to the side with a frightened shout as the door blew open. He pulled himself up from the floor and brushed off the debris that had settled on him.

"Alright Meyral, that's enough destruction," Alberto said. "We're gonna bring the whole place down!"

"I didn't do it!" Meyral screamed as Alberto glanced back at him with wide eyes. "It did that on its own!"

The staff clattered to the floor as Meyral finally let go. The burning sensation that had been winding its way up his arm dissipated. The weapon lay on the ground, once again nothing more than a harmless piece of wood.

"Leave it!" Alberto shouted.

"Are you insane?" Meyral scrambled across the dusty floor and retrieved the staff.

Alberto grabbed his arm and brought Meyral to his feet. "Look at your hand," the big man commanded as he shook him.

Grudgingly, Meyral looked down. The heel of his right palm was discolored and oozing.

"It's hurting you, and it damn near killed me!"

"Did you forget where we just were?" Meyral snapped back. "The staff freed us."

"Well," Alberto glanced over his shoulder at the rubble nervously, "maybe you should think about getting some gloves." He clapped Meyral on the back and walked toward the busted door. "They took Maxine upstairs, let's go!"

They sprinted as far up the stairs as they could go and eventually found ornate double doors blocking their way. Alberto lifted his leg and kicked with all his might. He knocked one stone door off its hinges.

"You rotten—"

Before Sera could finish what promised to be an interesting insult, the two men rushed in and grabbed Maxine. Sera screamed with rage and jade flames shot out of her hands. Alberto shielded his sister with his body. He waited for the pain, but it never came. He opened his eyes and saw a transparent blue shield had formed a kind of bubble around them.

Meyral stood up, his face contorted with concentration, as Sera launched two more fireballs from her hands. Meyral focused on blocking her shots, and they all watched in awe as the barrier absorbed the fire and turned momentarily green.

"Run!" Maxine screamed as she bolted past them and down the stairs.

"You don't need to tell me twice, Sis!" Alberto ran after her, but Meyral lingered for a moment.

"You…you returned the staff to me. Why?" he asked from behind the shield as another boil began to form in his right palm.

The woman only looked back at him with a gaze of pure malice that made his skin crawl. She hissed as she sent more fire his way.

"Meyral! COME ON!" Alberto grabbed the back of his neck and nearly threw him to the bottom of the stairs.

"We need to go southwest, toward Arntim!" Maxine shouted as Meyral passed her in the entrance hall. "Sera had maps pinned up on the walls, and I found another town where they keep prisoners!" Maxine stopped to catch her breath as Alberto caught up. "It's Beldin!"

"Good to know. Do you have a plan?" Alberto asked as he threw her over his shoulder effortlessly.

"Bust in. It's way smaller than Qellnorm was, we can take them head on."

"Just my style. Let's go!"

* * *

Maxine woke up the next night covered in sweat, unable to see anything except the faint outlines of the men sleeping a few feet away. The dreams kept coming, no matter how hard she fought. That man, the one playing the music…she refused to listen, refused to watch the horrible things he kept trying to show her. He wasn't pleased.

Once again, she found herself horrified at the thought of going back to sleep. How was it that his damned music could follow her outside of the dreams? It was like he was trying to punish her.

"Damn him," Maxine muttered to herself in the night, "damn him to hell."

She raised her eyes to the moons floating above her. A tear dropped down her cheek and into the soft dirt at her side.

CHAPTER EIGHTEEN: REVERENCE

Greg sat up too quickly and he hit his head on the bunk bed above him. He rubbed a cool hand on his sweaty brow as he tried to recount the dream he just had.

I was on that moon again...I was watching that green-haired Remnant argue with some guy in a chair. No, argue isn't the right word. He wasn't fighting back. She was yelling at him, and he just kept playing his guitar.

Just as the thought reached his mind, he heard the phantom music playing above him, around him, inside him. He remembered the things that the blond man had shown him.

The three of them are camped outside of Beldin! Damn! They're going to attack!

Visions of the wanted rebels floated through his mind. He and his friends had jokingly referred to them as "phantom enemies of the state." They never really admitted to themselves that it was all real.

The wanted posters that had gone up portrayed the three as savage beasts—especially the red-haired guy—but there was something...demonic, and altogether unworldly, about their leader. The look that the artist gave that kid was creepy.

He got chills again just thinking about it. Up until then, they were rebels without a name. Since the dreams had started, he knew the woman was called Maxine.

Does that make her more or less dangerous? It certainly makes her real, and that in itself is scary enough.

Greg knew about the things they'd done up north, bringing civilians into their war and hiding. Now rumor had it that they were tearing up the strongholds that Nordcross had started in the Western Frontier.

Greg focused on his dream once more, but all he could remember was the path into the forest where the three Remnants were waiting and watching. The images grew fuzzy after that and the whole dream broke apart...but he could still hear it. That music had haunted every waking hour of the past week, ever since the dreams had started. The last dream, however, was the first time that the guy acknowledged Greg's presence.

Slipping out into the night silently, Greg made his way along the path that the blond man had shown him. He hadn't woken anyone else, because there was a strict policy against mental illnesses amongst the trainees. If anyone found out he was seeing things, the captains would haul him away.

Right at the stump, right at the stump...listen for voices...

And then he heard them. The voices were faint at first, but as he moved forward quietly, the words became coherent.

"...at night seems kinda weak, doesn't it? I mean, we could—"

"Dammit, Bert, we have to do this tonight. I have my reasons, why can't you just listen to me?"

Greg recognized her voice, even though she was only whispering. The rebels were definitely attacking, and Maxine was leading the charge.

Boy, Nordcross has it wrong...she's in charge. She's the little demon we should be watching out for. The redhead too—he's got murder in his eyes. But the kid...no, that kid is innocent. I haven't seen eyes like his since I left home.

A few minutes later, "Bert" gave up his argument and set off with the kid toward Beldin. Maxine stayed behind, gathering the scraps of paper and whatever other traces they'd left.

"Maxine!" Greg whispered as he emerged from between two massive redwoods.

Her head snapped up and she drew her bow before she even saw him.

"Wait!" he said. "I'm here to tell you something."

He couldn't remember any more of the dream, but for some reason he knew that they thought Beldin was holding Ardänian prisoners. As if to agree, the music picked up again in his head and almost stopped his entire thought process.

"You have it wrong, we aren't holding any Ardänians here!"

"Likely story," she snapped. "I'm not buying it. But now that you know we're here, I have to kill you. You know that, right?" She pulled the arrow back against the string of her bow and aimed directly between his eyes.

"You should know something first." Greg tried to sound brave, but he wasn't sure if it was working. "He showed me that you're headed for Arntim after this, right? All you're going to find there is ash and rubble. The army attacked yesterday, it was all over the Nordcross papers. They've captured Jaspar and the war is pretty much over."

"Jaspar? Already?" Maxine's eyes grew wide and Greg saw a flicker of panic and fear cross her face.

"Maxine, if you would just watch what that dreamguy is trying to show you, you would know all of this already. Why won't you—"

"You don't know me!" she snapped at him as her arms began to tremble. A strand of hair fell in her face, obscuring her expression. "He showed me victory...and we were captured. I won't listen to his lies! Every time I fight, I get closer to losing what I love..." Her arms straightened out. She aimed back at his face.

"They're taking Jaspar to Nordcross for imprisonment and execution, alright? Now please, leave us and go!" he pleaded.

"Don't you think he's shown me that already?"

Then the rest of the dream flashed into Greg's mind.

I was looking straight at an arrowhead, held by a stranger. Then there was only darkness. Gods, she's going to kill me!

* * *

The dim firelight cast eerie shadows all around them, reflecting the darkness they each felt in their hearts.

"Arntim. That's our next stop, right?" Alberto tossed another log on the dying fire, startling the horses and sending sparks into the night sky. "Maybe then we'll actually fight someone who's a real threat...instead of civilians."

"Bert...I didn't know. I—"

"Save it, Maxi! We murdered a lot of innocent people last night," he said, cutting his sister off. He slammed one of his massive fists into the damp ground.

"They weren't innocent, they were the enemy! They want us dead all the same, we just got to these ones first. Don't you get it?" A crazed look sparked in Maxine's eyes.

"What happened to the sister I knew that wanted nothing to do with killing? What happened to the woman who told me that we, Maxine, *we* don't kill in cold blood?"

"But we were just...we were there to free Ardänian prisoners..."

"No! We attacked them at night and didn't give them a chance to fight back. Where were the prisoners? All we found were a bunch of scared cadets who wouldn't even know how to wipe their own asses on a battlefield!"

Maxine hung her head, resigning herself from the argument.

"And moons be damned, Meyral," Alberto rounded on his young friend, "if you lose control of that stick one more time, I don't care what people call it, I'm gonna snap it like a twig! You still don't believe in magic, Sis? How 'bout you tell me where all that blue fire came from!"

Maxine didn't move, and neither did Meyral. He hadn't said a word since leaving the enemy camp. During the attack, he had used the staff. He'd only meant to start a small fire for light, like Maxine had instructed him to, but things got out of hand. Before long, flames covered the whole encampment, and it felt like the skin on his hands had been peeled away. It wasn't until Alberto tackled him to the ground that he had been able to regain control.

Then Alberto tried to save the very people they had set out to kill. The blue flames refused to die, though, until the last structure had collapsed on itself. A look of horror dominated Alberto's face as he led the only other living beings from the encampment back to where Meyral lay. All that they were able to save were three horses, scared half to death.

Maxine hadn't even been there. She showed up late to her own surprise attack, but Meyral secretly thanked the moons. If she had been where she had planned to be, she would have been caught in the inferno, just like the others.

By the first light of day, the trio could see what had become of Beldin. Its destruction was complete, and nothing remained of the small town. Alberto started to berate his sister then, but she didn't say a word in response. The big man continued to yell, but she only ignored him and bandaged Meyral's hands. When she finished with the bandages, she turned, and Alberto braced himself for her response. All she did, however, was mount one of the surviving horses.

"I'm going to Arntim," she said before she rode away.

Meyral looked down at her bandaging job. His hands were throbbing and blood had already seeped through the rags. He'd never seen her do such a shabby job, but her mind was clearly occupied.

Why does the staff hurt me? Am I using it wrong? Why didn't Taryn show me anything about how to use magic?

Meyral pictured his old teacher pulling a stone sword out of a cloud of dust, and he regretted never having asked how she did it.

* * *

"Arntim..." Alberto whispered the word into the night like the name of a long-anticipated lover.

They'd set up camp in a clearing, and Alberto was already lying on his bedroll. The big man's stomach growled, but he ignored it. A flash of blue distracted him as Meyral's eyes lit up and the kid fell onto his back.

"Do you think he'll ever tell us what he's been seeing?" Maxine asked as she stared across the campsite to where Meyral lay, unmoving and unconscious.

"What do you mean, what he's been seeing?" Alberto asked with an alarmed look on his face.

"I mean he's probably having some sort of vision. I've been having them too. Nightmares really, over and over..." She lowered her eyes to the ground and emotion clogged her voice. "There's a man on the moon. He plays music and shows me...things."

Maxine's eyes wandered around the campsite and landed on Meyral again. She stared at him for a moment, and then looked back to Alberto.

"It can't simply be coincidence that his eyes light up the exact same color as the sapphire on that damned staff, or that my nightmares didn't start until that thing came into my life," she said shakily.

Alberto scoffed. "Really? What does this music man show you?" he asked.

"Death," Maxine answered in a low voice. "But who needs to dream to see that anymore..."

* * *

As the siblings sat in the dark, letting silence envelop them, Meyral floated through trees, once again a specter in a world long dead. He heard the familiar sound of rushing water and footsteps, and he floated down to follow them.

"C'mon, just a little farther!" an excited voice yelled from ahead of him.

The blonde woman leading the way was breathless from excitement. The one next to her was breathless from exhaustion. Each of them had aged quite a bit since the last vision that he'd seen them in, but he still didn't have to look hard to recognize the two women.

"Marge, can't we take a break? I'm tired…" Marie panted as she sat next to a tree and rested her head against the mossy bark.

Marguerite doubled back and grabbed her cousin with her free hand, the other clutching a walking stick. "It's right over here," she said. "I'm sure that our dear queen can walk a tiny bit more." At this Marguerite's face darkened, much like it had when Thessius had announced that her father was ill.

"Papa said we shouldn't go back to that cave. Shraka broke practically every law by taking us there, remember?" Marie stopped and put her hands on her hips.

"Well, both of our 'papas' are dead, so it doesn't matter what they said."

"Watch your mouth, Marguerite," Marie said slowly. "Never speak to me like that again."

"I'm sorry, milady," Marguerite said with a small bow.

Marie rolled her eyes.

"Come on," Marguerite urged.

She dragged Marie a little farther and the two women emerged from the foliage. They came out upon a vast, majestic lake with a steep waterfall at the far end.

"Besides, we aren't going into the cave. We're just going to have a little swim."

Marguerite stepped back and pushed Marie into the water. Marie laughed and dunked herself under. When she came up, the water reached her neck and her clothes were soaked through.

"I'll expect you to do my laundry when we get back!" she shouted to Marguerite.

"I'll have one of the maids do it," she muttered darkly. "I'll race you!" Marguerite dove into the water and came up next to her. "First one to the waterfall wins!"

The two women raced, and it was Marie who made it to the waterfall first. She looked up at the sky and bit her lip as she waited.

"We should really head back soon," Marie said when her cousin finally caught up.

"Wait, don't you wanna see what I found?"

"What?" A hint of curiosity crept into Marie's face.

"It's a surprise. Follow me!"

Moments later, they found themselves on a rock shelf set against the mountain. They were behind a solid sheet of water that overlooked the entire Old Kingdom of Ardänia. Meyral stared in awe as he took in the beautiful landscape.

To the west were blankets of forests and massive lakes, and in the distance he could see spires climbing into the sky. Ardänia was whole and beautiful, and Meyral realized more than ever why the Remnants were so adamant about restoring it to its former glory.

"Marge, we shouldn't be here. It's wrong!" Marie glanced into the cave behind the waterfall and took a step back the way they'd come.

She turned back to Marguerite, expecting her usual look of exasperation when Marie would mention rules, but only a glare of malice met the young woman's gaze. Marguerite lunged and pushed her cousin toward the edge. Marie lost her balance and tripped into the waterfall. Its force drove her down upon the rocks and into the lake below.

Marguerite pulled Shraka's old walking stick out of thin air and stabbed it into the solid rock as she spread her arms. Her voice was low and deep as she chanted in a language that Meyral had never heard before. The water behind him fell slower and slower, until it froze into a solid block of ice. The sheet of frost continued into the lake and froze the entire surface.

"That should do the trick." As she turned away from her cousin's ice coffin, Meyral heard a faint, "Bitch."

The scene at the lake faded, and Meyral found himself floating slightly above a marble balcony that overlooked a crowd of people. Footsteps behind him announced the arrival of Marguerite with two knights flanking her.

"People of Ardänia, I have grave news," she announced when the crowd fell silent. "I am henceforth calling off the search for the lost queen, on the grounds that after weeks of searching without a hint of what transpired, she is most probably dead. This announcement is made all the more disheartening due to the fact that today would have been Marie's twenty-first birthday."

A few loud cries rose up from the crowd.

"Instead of celebrating her coming of age, we will spend this day mourning for our great loss."

There was a great swell of emotion from the crowd below. Marguerite held up her hands and waited for the throng to settle down.

"Fear not, citizens of Ardänia, for your queen still stands!"

The crowd didn't move. A voice from the back yelled something incoherent, and a few people nearby responded with shouts that sounded treasonous.

"I expect absolute loyalty!" she shouted. She slammed her hands on the banister and the knights made a movement like they were going to hold her back.

A figure at the front of the crowd, dressed in a black, hooded robe, stepped forward. "Marguerite, I challenge your right to the throne."

"Who said that?" the queen shrieked as she scanned the courtyard beneath her. "On what authority do you make such a boast?" Marguerite motioned with her left hand for one of the knights to draw his sword.

The figure in the crowd tore the robe off and Marie stepped forward. "Thessius' daughter, Ardänia's true queen."

The crowd started to cheer, but Marguerite let out an unnaturally loud howl that drowned them out. The masses went silent with fear as she flung herself down from the balcony. She landed in front of Marie with enough force to crack the stone beneath her, the Staff of Ardänia held firmly in her hand. The two knights hesitated on the balcony, watching the girls circle each other like animals.

"You think the throne belongs to you, *cousin?* What about the *rules,* hmm? We're both of age now, and I'm in line—"

"You're insane, dear cousin," Marie interrupted. "Why would you do this?"

"I know what you had planned with Shraka, you harlot!" Marguerite shouted. "He promised himself to me! Why couldn't you just leave us alone?"

"Leave you alone? What are you—"

"You've never wanted it anyway! You would make a horrible queen! I *want* the power!" Marguerite cut in viciously.

"And that's precisely why you can't have it!" Marie said. "You give me no choice." She raised her hands and began chanting in a language similar to the one Marguerite had used to trap her in the lake. Marie's eyes began to glow a bright crimson, and the staff was ripped from Marguerite's hands by an invisible force.

"NO! You can't—" Marguerite froze in her tracks, paralyzed. In a flash of red fire, she disappeared before she could even finish her statement.

Marie dropped to her knees. Silence followed for a moment, until the crowd remembered that Marie had returned and was now kneeling on the ground.

"Your Majesty—"

"Are you alright?"

"Say something!"

"Queen Marie!"

She raised her hand and the talking ceased. "Do not fear. I have banished my cousin from Ardänia forever. She can never return to this land, so long as I live."

The vision began to fade as Marie walked back toward the castle, and all that remained for only a second was the staff embedded in the cracked stone beneath the balcony.

* * *

Meyral woke with a start and was momentarily disoriented. Every time he slipped into visions of the past, he found himself coming out more and more dazed and confused. Reality finally set in, and he remembered where he was and what had happened. He sat up and brushed his shaggy hair back with a trembling hand. He took a long look at his companions.

Alberto's face was stony as he savagely used his hunting knife to trim a stick into a fine point, as if it had done him a personal wrong. His once short, red hair had become a motley mat of dreadlocks, and his face was overcome with a gargantuan beard.

Maxine hadn't changed much outwardly, save for the dark circles under her eyes and the pale tinge to her face. What worried Meyral was that he was pretty sure she was only sleeping a couple of hours a night.

"Guys," Meyral's voice escaped his throat in no more than a pleading, raspy whisper, "I have something to tell you."

Maxine turned her head and her eyes widened, but Alberto made no sign of having heard him.

"I've been having visions. I've seen what happened when Ardänia fell. The legends are wrong—the court magician was behind it all."

Alberto froze mid cut.

Meyral shook his head and cleared his throat. "I don't know why I see these things. I just do. It has something to do with the staff...everybody was so eager to have its power that Ardänia collapsed." He put his head between his knees. His voice was muffled, but the other two heard him clearly enough. "It was greed."

"So?" Alberto grumbled.

Meyral's head snapped up. "I just told you that I'm having visions of the past, and that's all you have to say?"

Alberto stabbed his stake into the wet ground. "See, I'm no genius, but I know this much. The Staff of Ardänia is some kinda magic." He looked at Maxine, but his sister had apparently given up explaining away magic. "Sure, it freed us from that blonde bitch, but it also burned down an entire town of innocents. Now you tell us that it's giving you visions, but the visions are of the past. I don't need a history lesson. I need to know how to avenge the things that I've lost and how to save the few things I still have. Can the staff show you that?"

Meyral shook his head. He was sure that the staff could do what Alberto wanted, but he still didn't know how to properly use it.

"Then it doesn't really matter, does it? That staff may be the only damned thing left from the Old Kingdom, but it's causing us a hell of a lot of trouble. I say get rid of it!"

"Are you suggesting we just hand it over to Nordcross?" Meyral asked defensively.

"I'm saying we destroy it!"

Meyral stood, but before he could say anything, Maxine intervened. "Boys," she said, her voice timid and trembling. "It's been a long day. I think we just need some sleep..." Maxine trailed off as she noticed her brother's intense glare.

Alberto hurled his knife into a nearby tree and flopped onto his makeshift mattress without a word. Meyral and Maxine exchanged worried looks before rolling over. They both stared at the heavens quietly until sleep overtook them.

* * *

"That's right..." Alberto rustled in his sleep.

He was having the first pleasant dream that he'd had in months. He was walking up a lane to a little house covered in roses and jasmine. Playing on a swing in the garden was a young boy with jet-black hair, and a girl with long, red braids dug in the yard near him.

He'd never actually seen the children before, but he knew immediately that they belonged to him. As he gazed at them, the front door of the cottage opened up, and there stood Chloe. She was as beautiful as ever, pregnant with child number three, smiling and holding her belly. The children ran to Alberto as he cut through the tall, white flowers surrounding the house.

He lifted them up, one in each arm, and they clung to his neck. A smile lit up his face, and he carried them through the garden and toward his wife. As he approached the porch, a shadow passed behind him. He turned around to see who it was as his heart already began to fill with dread. There stood a man in black, and on his forearms were blades dripping with blood.

Alberto hugged the children tighter as the dread turned to terror. He backed up to the porch, trying to stay between the assassin and Chloe. His lover shrieked behind him and he whirled around, but it was too late. Somehow the assassin was already there.

The assassin swiped his arm down Chloe's back and she collapsed to the ground with a soft cry. She and the children disappeared simultaneously, leaving the two men staring each other down. Alberto tried to raise his hands, but they had become too heavy to lift.

"Why would you leave your family?" the man in black demanded as blood seeped from a bandana wrapped around his mouth.

"What are you talking about? I'm doing everything I can to protect them!"

"Then why isn't your sister here? Don't you care about Maxine?"

"She's my sister! Of course I care!" Alberto roared, but he still couldn't move.

"It doesn't look like it." The assassin spread his arms and looked around. "Shouldn't she be here, here in your paradise?" He pointed at Alberto with an accusatory finger. "You hate her. You always have. You've always resented her. You blame her!"

The house erupted in blue flames and the assassin disappeared inside. Alberto could hear the kids screaming for help, for his help, but he couldn't move. He was glued to the spot, doomed to watch his family perish in the fire.

Mustering all of his strength, he pulled himself away and rushed into the smoke-filled cottage, ready to die for those he loved. When he burst through the doorway, he found himself in the kitchen of his old house in Westmore.

His father was in the kitchen, teaching a young redhead with freckles how to prepare a steak. As Alberto turned around to look through the door he had just entered, his mind melded with that of his kid-self at his father's elbow.

He looked up into his father's face as he sautéed the steak and the two of them laughed together. The meat caught fire and a blanket of smoke filled his vision. His dad disappeared and he was left in a corner, crying.

Alberto rose up and looked out of a window. He saw a slim, green-haired man waving back at him. Derek bent over and picked up a young Maxine and hugged her close. She waved at their father as he began to walk away, but Alberto sprinted outside to catch him. No matter how fast he ran, though, the man was always out of reach.

Derek faded away into the shadowy boundary of their yard. All that was left was his dad's voice, resounding in Alberto's head like a gong.

"It's just what I have to do."

Alberto realized that Maxine, only about eight years old, still stood next to him, waving at a man who was no longer there.

"Where's Dad?" he asked, and a fresh, young voice filled with emotion escaped his mouth.

"He left us," she responded with a small smile.

Alberto balled his hands into fists. He ground his teeth as tears ran down his cheeks. "Why, Maxi? Why did he have to go?"

"Relax, Bert." She continued to smile as she looked down into her younger brother's face. "You know how he was. We're better off now. Mother will take care of us."

"But...but...he's Dad!" Alberto tried to think of something else to say, something more profound, but his undeveloped mind couldn't process the emotion.

"You'll get used to it. Trust me, kiddo." Maxine hugged her brother, but he didn't even lift his arms to reciprocate. "We don't need him."

If he'd been paying attention, he would have felt his sister's tears dropping from her chin onto his head.

Alberto watched as his dream-self entered his mother's room again and again, and each time he became slightly older. He would feed his mother soup that Maxine had made...out of obligation. She couldn't—no, wouldn't—look at her mother, even then.

Finally his dream-self became the Alberto that found his mother's body drenched in blood. Eden's throat had been slashed from ear to ear, and her eyes had become glassy. His anger for Maxine faded quickly as pain struck his heart like an arrow. At the window stood a man in black with blades running down his arms.

His?

The dream shattered like glass, and all that was left was darkness. The assassin appeared, illuminated by some unknown light in an otherwise dark world. He slowly unraveled the black wrap around his face and head.

Alberto watched Maxine take her black mask off. There was a sinister grin on her face, and she winked at her brother as if they were sharing some secret.

Her mouth looked the same as his mother's throat. A giant, bloody gash ran across Maxine's face, stretching from ear to ear, only there were razor-sharp teeth inside of it and blood pouring over her chin.

"See, Brother? It's all for the best. It needed to be done, and now we're free! You should thank me..."

The blood bubbled out of her mouth as she spoke, and Alberto cringed as his sister's demonic voice reached his ears. He screamed, eyes shut, fists clenched, and every muscle straining against him. His body convulsed until his nightmare collapsed and he awoke.

When he opened his eyes, it took him a moment to adjust to the darkness of the night. Slowly Maxine's worried face came into focus above him.

"Are you okay, Bert? Did you have a bad dream?"

He'd already forgotten the specifics of the nightmare, but he was left with a sour feeling in the pit of his stomach. He simply shook his head and rolled back onto his side.

* * *

The next day they reached the town of Sweetwater on the shore of the Bordo River.

"I don't think there's anyone here," Meyral said. He tried tying up his horse, but he was having some difficulty due to the bandages on his hands.

Alberto shoved him aside, finished the knot, and walked away without a word.

"Did everyone leave or…?" Meyral continued.

"What?" Maxine had been transfixed on a pot of dead flowers hanging from the roof of one of the surrounding houses. "You should see about some new bandages for your hands."

Maxine started after her brother, but she stopped after a step. She decided against it and headed down a side street instead. Meyral sighed and paused a moment, then headed off on his own.

He found an apothecary, where he was able to piece together some supplies to clean and rewrap his hands. He dropped a few pieces of gold into an open bin. Keeping an eye out for the siblings, he made his way to the river.

The Bordo looked just like the Errigan, only smaller. Meyral found a small dock and sat for a moment, enjoying the stillness. A wide bridge made of stone stood a short way down the stream, and as he stared, he remembered something his dad had once told him about Sweetwater.

"It's a decently sized town with a reputation for stubbornly defending itself from any laws imposed from outside of its own small government. Don't bother going there if you need anything. As a rule, they won't help outsiders. The only reason anybody keeps it in mind is for the bridge. It's the only place for miles where someone can cross the Bordo. That river looks shallow and mellow, but its waters are actually deep and swift."

Meyral sighed deeply as his tears fell on the wooden dock.

Don't lose hope. Never lose hope!

He wiped away his tears and unwrapped his hands. He stared at his raw palms for a moment before washing them in the clear water. He patted them on his coat until they were dry, and then he wrapped them in fresh bandages.

As he sat with his back to the abandoned town, he heard a wolf howl in the distance. As much as he wanted to avoid the negativity surrounding his friends, he figured he'd be safer with them.

When he made it back to the horses, he couldn't find either of the siblings. A tinge of fear stained his heart, until he noticed lights coming from the tallest house in town. Meyral walked through the broken front door to find Alberto stoking a fire. Maxine stood in a daze, completely silent.

"I hope you don't mind. We let ourselves in," Alberto said without looking up.

Meyral said nothing.

"There's food in the kitchen. It's not stealing if it's abandoned, right?" the big guy added.

Meyral grabbed a fallen bench, placed it right-side up, and took a seat.

"I'll bet Nordcross controls everything along the Errigan by now," Alberto grumbled. "How do you suppose we're going to make it west? Can horses even cross rivers? Or are we going to just leave them? I mean, not like we can do much worse at this point, right?" He tossed a couple heavy logs onto the small pile of smoldering wood.

Meyral hoped Maxine would say something to relieve the tension, but she only sat down next to Meyral, her eyes unfocused.

"Whatever," Alberto muttered as he got up and entered what Meyral assumed was the kitchen.

After their meal of possibly spoiled food, Meyral watched the siblings avoid each others' gazes as they set up their bedrolls. Soon they all slipped into an uncomfortable sleep.

* * *

"Where am I?" Meyral's voice echoed through the distorted landscape.

Most of the ground was dark brown and covered in rocks and stones, but smears of red and green were splashed all over the sky. He noticed a man in the distance who seemed incredibly familiar, but he couldn't make out what or who it was through the bluish fog.

He ran toward the figure, but the distance between the two of them remained constant. Meyral called out to him, but he didn't get a response. He saw sudden movement and sensed eyes watching him. A voice resounded in his head with music that was so twisted it sounded as if he was underwater.

"I don't have much time, Meyral. The rules are clear about directly contacting those in possession of its power, but I have to show you something. Turn around, kid."

Despite his hesitation, Meyral did as the strange man requested. He turned to look, but the world that he was standing on seemed to turn in order to counterbalance him. He fell to his knees and cried out.

"Look! You have to see before you wake up!"

Ignoring the rocks cutting into his knees and the blood floating up around him, he looked to the sky. As he squinted through the fog, he saw a line of caravans traveling on a road that was no more than a ledge barely wide enough for one wagon. The road jutted out from the middle of one of the most daunting cliffs Meyral had ever seen.

A vast, sandy expanse sat above them, and fifty yards below were sharp rocks and thundering waves. The waters stretched out past the horizon, and Meyral gawked at the lake whose size was unfathomable. The image zoomed into the center caravan, and he saw a mane of black hair encircling the face of a prisoner with bruises and gaping wounds.

"Father!" he screamed to nobody in particular, and again found that his voice was sickly distorted.

Jaspar stirred, but he took no notice of his son watching him. Tears welled up in Meyral's eyes and a single thought formed in his mind, the only clear thing he could process in the dream.

Where are you?

He knew not to expect an answer from the man in the mist. The rules were clear, apparently. But, to his surprise, the image morphed as he watched. Two soldiers talked, and a man in black with a number of small blades strapped to his body steered the lead wagon.

"I hate this damn pass," one of the soldiers muttered to his ally.

"It's the safest way home," the other soldier responded. "Would you rather take the short way and get swallowed up by the desert, or ambushed by bandits and renegades?"

"Leviathan Pass gives me the willies…"

"It's just a road, man. Relax."

Meyral gasped as he was wrenched into the sky. Everything faded to black.

CHAPTER NINETEEN: VENERATION

Alberto gathered the last of the pans and put them in his rucksack. He looked over at his companions with mixed feelings of disgust and remorse. Meyral, his little buddy, had both of his hands wrapped in cloth because of that staff on his back. The same staff that burned down an entire enemy camp filled with cadets…a camp that his brilliant sister had dragged them to.

Why won't anyone ever listen to me? I say leave the stick, and Meyral ignores me. Then he burns down a village and practically destroys his hands. I thought I was going to watch him burn alive…

Alberto stuffed his hunting knife into his boot with a small grunt as Maxine finally lifted her head. She stared out of the window for the thousandth time.

I tell Maxine we should wait until morning, gather some more information. But no, it had to be that night. She couldn't let it go. What was the hurry?

The morning had been filled with an unbearable silence, broken only when Alberto finally asked, "Arntim, right?" He glanced at Meyral, who was tending to the horses, and then at Maxine, who only shifted her weight nervously. Alberto threw his hands into the air with exasperation. "Isn't that the plan?"

What in Klyntar's name is wrong with them?

His mood became worse with every passing minute, but it wasn't just because he was being ignored. It was something else, something he couldn't figure out. All he knew was that he'd been having bad dreams. He couldn't remember what they were about, but he remembered feeling powerless and sick to his stomach.

"No," Meyral announced.

Maxine's head jerked toward Meyral as he entered and her eyes went wide.

"Arntim was attacked," the kid continued. "Nordcross has my father. They're taking him to their capital for trial…and then execution. We need to go to Leviathan Pass."

A full minute of silence followed, during which the only sound was the chirping of a lone bird high in the treetops. Maxine wrung her hands nervously, practically rubbing her skin right off.

"Did that stick tell you that?" Alberto asked with more spite than he intended.

"Yes."

"It'll take days to go that far south. You think we're gonna magically ambush them at just the right time?"

"We don't really have any other option," Meyral answered as he looked Alberto dead in the eyes.

"Oh yes we do...we can stick to the plan. We could ignore this goatshit plan and go straight to Arntim, where we know the resistance is gathering. Instead, you want me to put my faith in all this magic garbage. I don't know if you guys have been keeping count, but that stick has caused us—"

"It's called the Staff of Ardänia, Alberto," Meyral interrupted sternly. "If we give up on our faith in it, then what the hell have we been fighting for this whole time?"

The two men stared at each other until Maxine stepped forward.

"Bert...let's listen to him. I saw the same thing."

Alberto's jaw clenched as he looked down, trying to make heads or tails of the situation. He returned his stare to Meyral, who hadn't taken his eyes off of him in the first place.

"And when we realize that I was right?" Alberto asked.

"If you're right, then we'll only have lost some travel time. But if we're right..." There was a hint of concern in Meyral's eyes as he looked toward Maxine. "If we're right, and there's nothing left of Arntim, it'll be too late to save my dad. We can't exactly invade Nordcross to break out their most wanted war criminal." Meyral grabbed his staff and pointed. "So I'm going south."

Without another word, Meyral walked out the door, heading toward the horses. Maxine waited a moment, as if she had something to say, but then she grabbed her bag and set off after him.

Moons be damned, they're seriously trying to get me killed!

Alberto let out a loud curse and followed the others.

* * *

"Maxine?" Meyral turned his head to watch her push her green hair back behind her ears.

"Huh?" Her purple eyes locked onto his blue ones and the sunlight made little gold stars in her irises.

"You have visions too?"

Maxine nodded once.

"Are your visions the reason we attacked Qellnorm and Beldin?"

Maxine took a deep breath before she responded. "It's what I thought we were supposed to do."

"It really wasn't your fault. You don't always have to take responsibility for everything and everyone."

For a moment, Maxine looked utterly bewildered.

"I set those fires," Meyral said shakily. "I just...I couldn't...you didn't kill anyone. You weren't even there. It was the staff...I killed them all...me."

Maxine's demeanor finally softened a bit. "It doesn't matter. They were the enemy, and they were invading Ardänia."

"I know you believe that about as much as I do. Which is not at all," Meyral said. "If it were true, it wouldn't be sitting on our consciences so heavily. You know that. Maxine, we're in this together." He risked a glance over his shoulder at the big man, who was hacking at the underbrush with his knife as he rode by.

"I'm just scared," she explained. "That's all. It's just fear...I'm sure it's the same for him..." Maxine looked to the ground as if she'd lost something.

"I'm scared too. For my dad..." Meyral muttered. "I kept running my mouth. I led Nordcross right to him."

"Oh, Meyral," Maxine said. She shook her head and tears welled up in her eyes. "You know your father was destined to go up against Nordcross at some point. We don't even really know what happened."

"I'm supposed to have this great power, but it doesn't help," Meyral said after a moment of silence. "I can't even protect the things I love the most."

"It's not always possible to protect those we love. But we all want to." She sighed and closed her eyes. She took several deep breaths before continuing. "The moons have given us each our own parts to play. We can't argue or make requests...so we just trudge through the mud as best we can, hoping we're doing the right thing."

The two rode alongside each other quietly for a few moments before she finally spoke again.

"This war...my family, Mantrych, Arntim...why can't we just

end it?"

Meyral turned toward her and frowned, wondering what she was getting at.

"Why do we have to fight?" She waited for an answer, but Meyral didn't have one. "No, I guess that's a stupid question. It's because humans are just evil. I wish we didn't have to, though..." She snapped her reins and her horse moved slightly past Meyral's.

The rest of the day's trip was marked by silence, broken only by the sounds of hooves clopping on hidden stones in the dewy grass.

* * *

It had been Maxine's idea to travel through the harsh desert to reach Leviathan Pass—she had said it'd be easier to ambush them from above the ridge than to fight them from behind or head on.

Meyral was stunned as he stood at the edge of the desert, where the grass was swallowed up by sand. The dry, lonely expanse extended as far south as he could see. He looked off to the east, knowing that the desert pushed into Nordcross.

"We leave the horses here," Maxine commanded. By now the only time she spoke was to give orders.

"Right, because the desert is no place for *them*," Alberto said irritably as he got off his mount and looked directly at Meyral. "Sandstorms rage through it by the week, and new skeletons are added to the dunes every day." He looked off into the distance. "I'm so glad we're here."

"Why does the desert even exist?" Meyral asked, but the mood didn't lighten like he'd expected. "I mean, it doesn't seem to belong in Ardänia like the mountains and rivers."

Maxine pretended not to hear and she walked out onto the sand. Alberto gave him a strange look and followed after his sister.

* * *

After three days of walking through the desert, Meyral felt completely alone, despite the siblings' company. The night before they were supposed to reach Leviathan Pass, Meyral looked up to the sky for the hundredth time. The desert had one good quality—the skies were the clearest he'd ever seen.

Alberto, who had said nothing since they first stepped onto the shifting sands, tossed a sharp, wooden nub onto the ground. He reached into the bag on his back and pulled out a thick twig. Without even looking, he started shucking it with his knife. Maxine continued to cast quick looks at her brother, like she was waiting for him to do something, but she said nothing.

Meyral was about to speak when he collapsed to the desert floor, his eyes once again a bright blue. Alberto scoffed and turned away, still shredding his stick.

Meyral's eyes opened slowly. He was no longer in the desert, but somehow he knew that he hadn't moved far from where he fell. He stood up and took a look around.

He was in a large clearing, surrounded by a dense forest of oaks and willows. Strange flowers in shades of every color he could imagine poked though the grass, and above him birds were singing. A stone road cut through the far corner of the clearing, complete with pillars supporting several fires lighting the way.

It's the Grand Highway! Where does it lead...?

Meyral stepped onto the road as he once again found himself admiring its construction. Time lost its meaning as he followed the cobblestones, and soon red banners covered the pillars just below the torches. The spires that he had seen in his last vision were north of him this time, outlined against the vermillion sky. The glassless windows looked down on him and he felt oddly at ease.

He closed his eyes and took a deep breath. The vision shifted around him, and when he reopened his eyes, he was in the center of a forlorn and deserted city. All around him were empty shops and homes, crumbling stone walls, and stables occupied by pigeons. He walked the dusty streets until he came upon the castle gates.

Meyral let instinct guide him as he moved through courtyards, along battlements, and in the halls of the old castle, until he heard soft voices echoing from somewhere above him. He felt something right in the voices, something familiar. He again closed his eyes and embraced the pulling sensation.

An old, grand entrance met his curiosity this time. The doors were made of solid oak and were intricately carved, but they had been knocked off of their hinges, losing any illusion of majesty. Meyral entered, and at once he recognized Thessius' throne room.

The walls shimmered and he was shocked by what the room had become. It was no longer draped with illustrious banners and covered in gold; instead, the walls stood drab and bare, and it looked as if looters had stolen anything and everything they could. Had it not been for the roaring fire in the marble hearth, he would have thought he'd just walked into a crypt.

The thrones where the royal family once sat were gone. A large table occupied the center of the room, covered in a thick layer of dust. Around it sat a group of men and women, all wearing somber expressions.

The motley crew looked similar to the refugees that his father had gathered in Trosloth. Each person wore armor adorned with capes, desperately clutching some kind of weapon. They might have looked rather regal, had their armor not been worn and their garments tattered by age and use.

Meyral took another step into the room and looked around the table. Dread dominated the faces he saw. Nobody spoke—they all looked back and forth between one another, as if they were waiting for someone or something.

A large man with green hair leaned toward two others who wore black hoods and necklaces with X-shaped pendants. "You do know the Guild no longer exists, right?" he asked.

"As long as trade persists, we will be relevant," the stern-looking Guildsman replied.

The big man snickered until he noticed an old woman glaring at him.

"I am not surprised that a pirate would bring that up," she said with her eyebrows raised. "Such distasteful behavior."

"Pirate?" A handsome redhead jerked in his seat as he set his fearful eyes on the green-haired man.

Meyral lost track of the conversation after that. He was transfixed on a familiar face sitting at the table. Next to the redhead sat an older version of Rubi. He stared, knowing that nobody could see him. Her hair was brown and her eyes were grey, rather than the orange he'd grown so used to, but the face was unmistakable.

A loud cough resounded and the bickering stopped. "We have all come here from different paths, but our goal remains the same," the man who coughed said from the head of the table. "The Remnants have been backed into a corner." He rose to his feet and everybody turned to watch, including Meyral. The man surveyed his eagerly awaiting crowd before continuing.

"The Tribes of the Monolith have trampled their way as far south as the Island Nations. With their conquest has come a breed of dangerous religious fervor, resulting in the deaths of all those who refuse to bow to their god.

"They have destroyed what little progress we have made in trying to restore our beloved kingdom," he continued. "Nordcross has allied itself with the Monolith in a vain attempt to be spared. They even offered Svirdark as a show of good faith. In the Island Nations, Lilium and Jardim continue to burn in the night."

A few people shifted nervously.

"But no more," the man said darkly.

Taking a closer look at the speaker, Meyral noticed that he had striking blue eyes and long, shiny, black hair. His prominent chin reminded him of his father, and he had the same small ears as Meyral.

"I dreamt last night," he continued. "I dreamt of a final battle, right here in Ardan. A beast is on its way, a monster is woken. Its name is war, and it is stalking the night, ready to feed."

At that, mutters broke out around the table.

"I must end this," the man said as he sat down slowly. He took a deep breath and added, "Alone."

"I dreamt too!" one man shouted.

"I saw the same thing!" the old woman from before yelled as she stood from her seat.

A few heads nodded in agreement, but others shouted refusals.

"Madness!" one of the Guildsmen roared.

"I did not come all this way to tuck my tail between my legs and flee," the pirate added.

"No doubt you all saw the same thing I did," their leader said. "I am to fight this battle alone. Pack your belongings and return to your families. This is not the end. No, it is only the beginning."

The chatter came to a stop as a beautiful woman entered the room and walked right through Meyral.

"Kain," she said forcefully. Her blonde hair ran down her back in a solid plait, and her red eyes seemed to pierce straight through the man named Kain.

"You're alive!" Kain swiftly rushed forward to meet her and he put his hands on her shoulders. "We thought...I thought—"

"What little faith you have in me, then. I have always been more than capable of handling myself." Though her voice was cold, her eyes were filled with life. "I'm here to address the dream that I can only hope the rest of you saw."

"We have already addressed it. There is not much else to say," Kain said, locking eyes with her. "You should go, too. Return to the neighboring villages and help restore—"

"I'm here to fight with you," she interrupted with a raised hand. "And to bring you this."

She pulled a staff out of thin air and held it in front of her. Meyral could tell before he even saw the thing that it was the Staff of Ardänia.

Kain didn't move for a moment. He stared at the staff as gasps filled the bare chamber. One person twitched so violently that he knocked his goblet over. The two members of the Guild started talking to each other in harsh whispers. The green-haired pirate was the only one who seemed unaffected.

Meyral noticed that Kain's entire demeanor changed when he took the staff from the mysterious woman. The woman rested a hand on Kain's free one.

"Destiny is yours to control. Fate…is not predetermined," the blonde whispered to him.

Kain nodded and turned to face the table once more. "I suggest you all head out now," he said. "Get as far away from the battle as you can."

His voice was meek and much less sure than it had been only minutes before. The room started to empty, except for Kain, the woman by his side, and the man who had been accused of being a pirate.

The woman by Kain called out as the Remnants vacated the room. "Aurora, may I have a word with you?"

The lady who could have been Rubi's twin stopped, and the two women walked over to the fireplace.

As Meyral was about to follow them, the pirate approached Kain with the air of someone who knew his way around a fight. "I will not run," he said.

"It's not a matter of running, Gabriel," Kain replied. "You have a wife, and you need to see to it that she is provided for. Go to her, my friend. Be fruitful and live a long, boring life. Live, for the children of the Remnants are more important than we could ever hope to be."

"I am no Remnant. You knights—"

Kain only had to hold up his hand to silence the giant of a man. Gabriel had the build of a buffalo on two legs with violet eyes that seemed darker than coal. Kain was tiny beside Gabriel, but the colossal pirate seemed to be watching his tongue.

"It is my duty, Gabriel. You know that."

"What of your wife, Kain? And your daughter? Are the Remnants, or perhaps one person in particular, more important to you now?" The large man raised an eyebrow and looked toward the blonde by the fireplace.

Kain punched Gabriel in the jaw. Although the mountain of a man hardly budged, it was enough to silence him. The two women paused their conversation and looked toward them.

"My wife is dead, and our daughter with her," Kain said.

"My apologies," Gabriel responded softly. "I did not know. But my wife Xóchitl will share their fate should you fail here. I'm fighting, whether you like it or not."

Meyral wondered if Gabriel had ever had to convince someone to let him fight for them before. The pirate shifted his weight and stared. Meyral almost expected them to duel until Kain spoke again.

"You know that if you stay you will die?" he asked.

"Destiny is yours to control. Fate is not predetermined," Gabriel said with a slight sneer.

The blonde woman returned to Kain's side. Aurora strolled out of the room with a final glance back at Kain, who nodded.

"Fine," Kain said as he turned back to Gabriel, "they'll be here at sunset."

"Understood." Gabriel gave the blonde one last look and left the room.

For a minute, the two of them stood in front of the large fireplace, simply looking at each other.

"I know who you are," Kain finally said.

"I wasn't aware it was a secret." A girlish demeanor replaced the fearless warrior she had been only moments before.

"No, I—"

"You men and your titles." She stepped forward until her face rested against his chest. "All you need to know is that I'm yours."

"Bethany…" He sighed and pressed his hands against her face. "Don't fight. The children of—"

She laughed, although he didn't seem to understand what was funny about what he'd said. "Not without you," Bethany said. "I know I saw more than most, and there's a high chance you won't make it back."

"And I know you won't if you stay." He kissed her forehead and she stepped back. "I can't have you die. You're—"

"There are worse things than death. I won't let you go alone, Kain."

Kain held the staff out to her, and the sapphire in its tip gleamed a bright blue. "You take it. That way I know you'll make it back," he said.

"Absolutely not!" The look on her face changed to complete bewilderment. "It's not…meant for my hands." Bethany shied away and stepped out onto the balcony. "It's almost time. We should go."

Kain sighed and stepped toward her, but she walked back toward the fireplace. Meyral saw her wipe her eyes with the heels of her hands as she exited the old throne room.

The world spun once, and suddenly the sun was at the tops of the mountains. Meyral found himself in a deserted room. The fire had turned to ash, and the spilt wine had since dried. He was amazed by the strange flow of time in this other realm. He walked to the balcony that had just been occupied by Kain and Bethany, and he saw three people standing below him on the castle steps, waiting.

The man on the left, with his forest-green hair pulled back in a low ponytail, cracked his knuckles as he paced. Gabriel's legs were like tree trunks with arms to match. Next to him stood Kain. His black hair reached his shoulders, and the staff was slung on his back in a sheath. In his hands was a halberd that was longer than he was tall. Bethany stood on Kain's right, her bright blonde hair gleaming.

A horn sounded in the distance. Gabriel twitched in anticipation. He stopped pacing and stretched his arms, then took a few practice punches at the air.

Bethany swept her leg in an arc in front of her, and from the cloud of dust she pulled a blade of stone. She swung her other hand in a vertical motion and a column of water appeared in front of her. With another complicated motion, the column froze in the shape of a scimitar, which she grabbed and held at her side. Her battle stance, along with the two swords at the ready, completely changed her seemingly harmless manner into one of menace and bloodlust.

Kain stood still. He had his eyes shut, halfway up the steps, and he didn't move.

Meyral closed his eyes and focused on the courtyard below. In an instant he found himself on the ground, looking up at Kain. All around him, dark men in spiked armor ascended to the rooftops and hurtled around corners of the surrounding buildings.

A giant man walked slowly down the main street. He wore a skullcap with spikes the length of Meyral's arms. "Ardänia...mine...you...die..." he said. The man's words came out in growls, but his meaning was clear enough.

"I'll take the ugly one!" Gabriel shouted as he ran toward the man Meyral presumed to be the leader of the Monolith.

The two giants bellowed into the air and the fighting commenced. The leader was brawling with Gabriel in hand-to-hand combat, and Bethany had become a flurry of slashing blades, attacking anything within striking distance.

And still Kain only stood.

Bethany moved with fluid and deadly grace. After killing ten men that attacked her one on one, another dozen tried to swarm her all at once. The Monolith soldiers hopped down from the buildings above, only to have their limbs hacked off before they hit the ground.

Gabriel wrestled the chief to the ground and snapped his neck. He donned the spiked skullcap with a vicious grin. As he reached down to release the leader's morning star that was still strapped to his dead body, a man with a dagger sneaked up and attacked from behind.

Gabriel was too slow. The man stabbed the dagger into his lower back and the pirate let out a roar. Dark blood poured from his wound and spilled onto the ground. The fighter climbed onto Gabriel's back and continued to jab his blade into the pirate. Gabriel slumped forward against the wall of a building.

The little man stood triumphantly on his mighty foe. As he raised his hands in victory, five meaty fingers wrapped themselves around his head. The little man struggled, but it was too late—with Gabriel's last seconds of life, he crushed his enemy's skull, a grim smile etched onto his face.

And still Kain only stood.

Meyral floated over to Kain as a few more mutilated bodies were thrown through him by Bethany.

Why is he only standing there while his friends are fighting for their lives? Why does he refuse to act while his comrades are cut down?

Why are his eyes shut?

Meyral reached out to shake him in some vain attempt to get him to fight, but when he extended his arms, he received a shock.

My great-grandfather...the one who wielded the staff's power.

Meyral heard a shriek and he turned to see Bethany hurled across the street into a pile of decomposing wood. Her blades vanished as her concentration broke, and what seemed like an entire tribe ran at her with their weapons drawn.

Kain burst through Meyral, his eyes blazing bright cobalt. If Meyral had ever been able to see what he looked like when he passed out, he would know that Kain was just recovering from a vision.

As his eyes returned to normal, Kain put his halberd to work and sliced through the Monolith army with ease. His arms were little more than blurs as he whirled his weapon around with incredible skill.

Bethany watched Kain with fear in her eyes. That distraction was all that a man on top of the building next to her needed. He leapt off of the roof with his sword pointed directly at her chest.

Kain turned, and with lightning speed he caught the man out of midair on his halberd. His enemies capitalized on his turned back and a sword pushed through Kain's stomach. A dirty face appeared over his shoulder and yelled something in a foreign language. Although Meyral didn't understand it, Kain seemed to. He responded in the same language and the foreign warrior became enraged.

Bethany snapped back to the fight, Kain's blood dripping from her face. Kain spun and threw the man from his back, the blade still stuck through his core. He launched the halberd at another attacking warrior, pinning him to a wall.

Bethany jumped on the unarmed man who'd been thrown from Kain's back and her hand developed a bright, scarlet aura. The light solidified like a knife and she slashed the man's neck, beheading him.

Kain and Bethany were the only two people left alive in the courtyard, but Meyral knew it wouldn't last for long. Blood seeped from Kain's wound and dripped down his body as he panted for air. Bethany reached forward to help him, but he pushed her away and drew the staff.

"Don't," he panted. "If you pull that out, I'll lose too much blood."

"But I can heal—" Bethany started.

"There's no time. More are on their way. That was only the first wave, to test our strength." Kain took a deep breath and shuddered. "I know why you stayed. But you can't stop this..." He grimaced. "We both know that this is how it must end. You have to go! Now!"

Kain shoved her with what little strength he had left, but she didn't budge. Instead, she reached up and kissed him. Tears welled up in her eyes, but she refused to let them fall.

"You truly are a hero," she whispered as she caressed his face. Her tears finally spilled out as she ran past Meyral.

Kain approached the man pinned to the wall and removed the halberd. The body fell to the ground unceremoniously.

"Bring it on, you bastards," Kain muttered as he used his halberd to help himself stand. "You won't have Ardänia."

As if they had heard him, a myriad of Monolith tribesmen appeared.

Meyral was impressed by Kain's reflexes and power, considering he still had a blade stuck through his torso. With the staff in one hand and the bloody halberd in the other, he battled on until his injuries took their toll.

He stabbed the halberd into an oncoming soldier, but he was too weak to pull it back out. He was forced to abandon the weapon in the corpse. With only the staff left, he tripped a few warriors clumsily and knocked out the next few with a couple of uncoordinated swipes. Kain seemed to realize that he was losing, and as his attacks faltered, a blue aura overtook him.

A bolt of lightning came from the staff and struck the nearest man. He burst into blue flames and his armor disintegrated in a matter of seconds. Kain hesitated, and then he pointed the staff at his other enemies. He began firing more bolts of lightning and hurling cerulean fireballs all around him.

As he whirled the staff above him, dirt began to encircle his feet. The Monolith army started to fall back as the ground began to quake. Wave after wave of cobalt fire erupted from the staff and rolled over the fighters, incinerating them.

Kain was pulled up into the air, and Meyral could see the panicked expression on his face. Intense blue light radiated from the sapphire in pulses, each pulse sending an odd tingling sensation through the battlefield that even Meyral could feel.

The flames swallowed Kain's body and he screamed, but the blaze only grew more intense. The pulses sped up and became more powerful. The buildings began to give way and the castle caught fire.

The whirlwind of azure flames that swirled around Kain started to expand into a blazing inferno, and then...

Everything went white.

For several minutes, Meyral had no sense of direction, no sense of being. Then the light dimmed and the world came back into focus. Every direction that Meyral looked, all he could see was desert. Sand covered the flat land for as far as his eyes could see, and he finally understood.

The desert was a scar left by the power of the staff. His great-grandfather had destroyed the heart of Ardänia in a fool's attempt to save it. This was the power that his father had warned him about.

Why do I have the staff? Am I supposed to repeat the same mistake that my ancestor made? Its power seems impossible to control...it's nothing but a raging tempest of destruction.

And then another voice rang out in his ears.

"Destiny is yours to control. Fate...is not predetermined."

CHAPTER TWENTY: TEMPEST

Erranko sipped his whiskey as the gypsy woman danced in front of him, her smooth, erotic movements lulling him into a state of pure bliss.

They had found the dancer traveling Leviathan Pass alone. They arrested her under suspicion of espionage—as an added bonus, she happened to be gorgeous and hungry for gold. There were murmurs about what kind of woman traveled alone at night on such a treacherous road, but the emperor had dismissed them. He certainly wasn't any kind of gypsy expert, and he had learned long ago not to question a good thing.

The woman moved like a serpent, her body bending in ways he didn't even know was possible. Her thin, purple brassiere barely held back a set of voluptuous breasts that Erranko couldn't wait to get a hold of. Her veil covered the lower portion of her face and extended down to her navel. She would occasionally use her elegant fans to flip the veil aside to give him a peek at her luscious lips. High boots reached her knees, and a broad sash trailed down the front and back of her hips, hardly concealing her curves.

Erranko's eyes were glued to the fluid movements of the purple-haired dancer's body, but his guards remained unfazed and completely still, weapons sheathed. The guard on his left wore an ornate suit of plum armor, but on his other side stood an assassin with an arsenal of daggers and throwing knives. The assassins took orders from no one but Sera, and even though he trusted her, he didn't quite trust them.

"It's truly amazing what people will do for a little gold, am I right?" Erranko asked his men as he sipped his drink.

The dancer giggled and winked, then flipped around and whipped her hair into his face. The guard beside him tensed noticeably, but Erranko raised his hand. The soldier unwound.

The gypsy took a step back and sped up, letting her hair and sash whip around with her, lowering the emperor's gaze. A cloud passed across the two brightest moons, momentarily blinding the three men as their eyes attempted to adjust to the dark.

In one quick movement the gypsy spun and dipped. She flung two razor-sharp blades from the stash hidden in her fans, and the knives headed toward each of the guards.

One blade found its way into the gap between the purple breastplate and its matching helm. The missile pierced the guard's neck and he dropped to the ground almost instantly. The assassin caught the gypsy's other blade with his hand, then retaliated with a barrage of his own knives.

Erranko found himself half drunk and in the crossfire of what seemed like an endless stream of flying blades. The gypsy woman knocked away most of the missiles with her fans and dodged the rest.

She launched another two blades at the assassin, but he deflected both of them without difficulty. One stray blade grazed Erranko's cheek and the guard froze for a moment.

The gypsy capitalized on her opponent's hesitation. She leapt over the emperor and stabbed the assassin in the chest with one of her fans, bringing him to the ground. With a final smooth movement, she slashed his neck so deeply that she nearly beheaded him.

As his body fell, she flipped and landed behind Erranko. She wrapped her legs around his arms and chest as she held the other bladed fan to his neck.

"What...? Who...?" Erranko gasped fruitlessly as her grip tightened around him.

"I'm here to free the rebel leader. Say another word and I'll cut your throat."

Erranko lay back, admitting defeat. She pulled the first bloody fan from the assassin's body and sent it spinning into the cliffs overlooking Leviathan Pass. A poleaxe fell to her from the darkness of the rocks above.

She leapt off of Erranko, who tried to regain his footing, and she caught the axe in midair. The emperor struggled to his knees, but she landed in front of him and leveled her weapon at his neck. He froze.

"Goodnight, old man," she said as his vision went black.

* * *

Aldomein slammed the blunt end of her axe into the back of Erranko's head. She cocked her head, then looked up. Smirking, she raised one arm and beckoned to three people to drop down from their hiding places.

Right on time.

A large redhead slid down the cliff, a crimson bullet barreling its way to the bottom. A slight female with green hair hopped from rock to rock in a blur. Behind those two, a kid climbed down. When the trio finally reached her, she pulled off her veil.

"Aldomein!" the redhead exclaimed.

The woman smiled and winked at him. "I'm glad you recognized me, Red. Who might these two be?" she asked as she motioned to the others.

"Never mind that," the green-haired girl cut her blubbering brother off, "how the hell did you know we were there? We were completely hidden!"

The two women stared at each other, tense hatred radiating off of them.

"You're really not that good at hiding your tracks," Aldomein said with a shrug.

"Where's my father?" the kid asked.

Aldomein turned her head toward him and glared, but he didn't back down. She knew exactly who they all were the moment she noticed them on the cliff, but she always feigned ignorance if she could get away with it. Being underestimated usually worked in her favor.

"Well, Jaspar is in the middle carriage," she said. "You three can free him, but the emperor is not to be harmed."

"Really?" Maxine snapped. "You just bludgeoned him and he's bleeding. I'm pretty sure that falls under the category of harm."

Aldomein rounded on Maxine and the air grew thick with tension once again.

* * *

Meyral busted the lock on the carriage and threw the door open. A man who looked like he'd been through a meat grinder a few times was covered in chains and held down in about a dozen different places.

Meyral pointed the staff at him, hoping that it would respond like it had in the pyramid. Energy emanated from the sapphire and the chains slithered away from Jaspar. Meyral's father stumbled out, his face bruised and bloody. His exposed right shoulder had turned a sickening black color.

"Dad! I've got you. You're gonna be okay…"

"Meyral…I couldn't do it. I couldn't protect Ardänia," Jaspar whispered.

"Don't say that, it's not over yet. We can still—"

"No, we can't do anything. Rather, I can't do anything. My right arm," Jaspar shrugged and lifted his right arm with his left, "never got a chance to heal. I'm practically useless."

"Is that how they were able to capture you? But how did they know where you guys were hiding out?" Meyral asked.

"I suspected that we had a leak amongst our allies, so I tried to set up a trap."

Meyral rubbed his right hand, which had already developed another blister. Jaspar glanced at his son's bandages, but it didn't seem to register with him. He continued to explain, though his speech was slightly slurred.

"What I didn't expect was that almost a quarter of our force was either leaking information or Nordcross spies." Heavy coughs racked his body and a small amount of blood flew from his lips. "They overpowered us. The few Remnants that fought with me…it was terrible. Friends turning on each other, brothers forced to fight one another. We cut them down, but so many were lost…and then a whole damned Nordcross squadron attacked. Hell, even the emperor—"

Aldomein smacked Jaspar in the back of the head with her axe and his eyes closed. She caught his body with one arm as he exhaled and slumped to the ground.

"Sorry kids, story time is over," she said. "I really need to hurry this up. I've got to finish my contract." Aldomein swung her axe around, now guarding both Erranko and Jaspar's lifeless bodies.

"I thought you came to save my father! What the hell are you doing?" Meyral shouted as he pointed the staff at her threateningly.

She didn't even bat an eye. "No, I'm not *saving* anyone. I'm just doing what I was paid for—getting him into the boat at the bottom of this cliff."

Before anyone had a chance to react, Aldomein jumped over the side of the road with Jaspar slung over her shoulder. The trio was left stunned and speechless. A moment later, Meyral ran to the edge of the pass, but he couldn't see anything apart from the ocean. When he turned back, Maxine was moving toward the unconscious emperor, but Aldomein reappeared with her axe pointed right at her.

"Naughty, naughty," she taunted as she resumed her place guarding Erranko.

Meyral turned back to the sea and watched a small boat being rowed by a crew of men, one of whom was dressed in all black.

"Contract, huh?" The sad silence was finally broken as Maxine resumed her catty stance and berated Aldomein. "What are you, some kind of mercenary?"

"I prefer the term 'bounty hunter,' but they do mean the same thing, don't they?"

"Who are you working for this time?" Maxine asked.

The purple-haired woman strutted past Maxine and scoffed. "Like I would tell you," she whispered before putting her face within kissing distance of Alberto's. "One more thing before I go…"

She caressed the big man's cheek with a supple hand, her dark skin standing out against Alberto's pallor. It looked like Alberto was trying to talk, but no sound came out of his mouth.

"I need your word that you won't let anyone harm the emperor when I leave," Aldomein whispered in his ear. "Can you manage that?"

"A-anything you say," Alberto stuttered as Aldomein slipped a letter in his pocket and sauntered away.

A door to one of the wagons opened and a soldier stepped out. He paused a moment to take in the scene before panic took him.

"What the…? Everyone up! We've been ambushed!"

Aldomein spun on the spot, covering Erranko with her weapon again. Maxine drew her bow as Alberto and Meyral took up defensive stances.

"Run! You three are no match for them!" Aldomein's shouted, though her warning was ignored, even by Alberto.

Out of each carriage came a squad of six soldiers, forty-eight in all, with their weapons drawn. In only moments, the trio and Aldomein were surrounded.

Just as Maxine was about to release her first arrow, a high-pitched cackle sent the temperature around them plummeting. Emerald flames erupted at the edge of the road and Maxine groaned. Sera stepped gingerly out of the fire with the whip-wielding assassin behind her. She surveyed the scene before her with amused eyes.

"Aldomein, what a lovely surprise," Sera said. "Although, where there are criminals, there are always bounty hunters. Have you completed our contract yet?"

"Don't doubt me so easily, Sera. I'm not a drone like him." Aldomein pointed to the assassin behind Sera, but he made no sign that he even heard her.

"Of course, my apologies. It looks like the emperor is…" The cut on Erranko's face and the bump forming on his head caught Sera's eye and her lips pursed. "Who is responsible for this?"

Every soldier on the pass looked around nervously, but Aldomein was the one who answered. "That cut on his face is courtesy of one of your boys in black pajamas," she said.

Sera waved her hand as if Aldomein was a bug buzzing in her ear. "Ah, Maxine," she tittered, "I've been meaning to talk to you again, seeing as our last conversation was cut so short."

The blood drained from Maxine's face as her brother lunged in front of her.

"Thanks to you, we tracked down the resistance in Trosloth, removed that bitch that lived in Mantrych, and found Jaspar in Arntim," Sera said with a grin. "Really, you're the best player on our team right now."

Stillness followed. It was as if time had stopped altogether. Alberto's head turned and he looked at his sister, whose face was expressionless. The expression on Alberto's face was pure heartbreak. He dropped his massive fists at his sides.

"What is she talking about, Sis?" he asked.

Maxine bit her lip and shook her head slowly as tears filled her eyes.

"Aldomein, did you deliver that letter to our green-haired friend like I asked?" Sera asked with a hint of sarcasm.

"No, I gave it to Alberto like you—"

"An understandable mistake," she interrupted quietly.

Meyral thought he saw confusion in the bounty hunter's face, but it quickly disappeared.

The blonde looked at Alberto and continued. "Bert, dear boy, why don't you read that letter the pretty bounty hunter gave you? When you're done," she pointed to Maxine, "you can give it to its proper recipient."

Sera crossed her arms and ran her talons down her biceps, relishing in the moment. Alberto pulled the note out of his pocket and raised the piece of paper with shaking hands.

We have Jaspar, thanks to your information on Arntim. You've done very well so far, but we need one last thing from you if this war is going to end—turn your brother and the traitor Meyral in to the proper authorities. They are the last of the rebel faction, and if you deliver them to us, your crimes will be pardoned and you can live as a free woman.

Don't forget our other little deal. I never go back on my word.

Sera & Erranko

Alberto looked up from the paper, his eyes blazing with rage. "After what they did to Mother…our village…our home…Ardänia? You led them to us? You let us abandon Mantrych?" Alberto's entire body shook. "YOU KILLED CHLOE! *YOU KILLED MOTHER!*"

"Bert, you don't understand. All this killing…" Maxine stood where she was, and her eyes took on a glassy look.

Alberto advanced on his sister, his fists shaking with anger and his eyes full of dull hate. He grabbed her by the shoulders and shook her like a rag doll. "Dad left, and you never forgave Mother for it. You wanted her to die. You never liked Chloe, you couldn't stand to see me happy! You wanted her killed…MEYRAL'S FATHER! You betrayed everyone that cared about you!"

Alberto swung his right arm and backhanded her with a sickening thud. Her head rocked back and Alberto kicked her in the stomach. Her body flew through the air and she landed near the cliff's edge, leaving a trail of sand and dust behind her.

"You led us here. And then what? You were going to…going to turn us in? We're family, Maxi! Family isn't supposed to betray each other!"

"You're right," she said quietly. "I know that. But I had to do what I thought was right…"

Alberto stomped after her, and she looked up at her brother with tears in her eyes. She made no effort to escape.

Meyral took a few steps forward, but Aldomein stopped him. He looked at her and she shook her head. Sera had one arm outstretched, commanding the soldiers to stand down and let nature take its course.

Alberto dropped to his knees, using them to pin Maxine as he grabbed the front of her tunic. "What the hell, Maxi?" He shook her until the shirt their mother had given her tore at the collar. "How is betraying us the right thing? Explain yourself!" Alberto stopped and slammed his fist into the ground next to her head. "Dammit! Maxine, tell me she's lying. Tell me it's all…all just a big joke. Please!"

Maxine sobbed and turned her head. Alberto froze for a moment, then roared in anger. He smacked his sister across the face, but her eyes never dropped from his. As Maxine opened her mouth, the edge of the cliff crumbled beneath them. She slipped out from under her brother as he rolled onto his side, trying to dodge a fall to his death. Instinctively, he thrust out an arm and grabbed Maxine by her wrist. Alberto lay on his stomach, looking over the edge at his older sister hanging from his arm.

She raised her head and yelled up to her brother, "Bert…I've always loved you…always!"

The cliff around them shook and the small fissures started to spread. Maxine pulled Rubi's dagger out of its sheath at her hip. Some of the rocks beneath Alberto fell away as Maxine plunged the dagger into his arm. Alberto's hand twitched, and in that moment, her hand slipped out from his.

The big man watched as Maxine fell from the cliff. It seemed to take lifetimes for her to reach the bottom, and Alberto watched helplessly as she disappeared beneath the dark waters. The cliff shuddered once more, and Alberto rolled off of the small outcrop as it gave way.

Sera laughed quietly to herself, a sinister light gleaming in her eyes. The soldiers advanced on the two men as soon as their commander lowered her arm. Alberto made no effort to run or fight back. He simply lay on his back in the sand and pulled the dagger from his arm.

Aldomein stepped back, ready to bolt, as the soldiers closed in on them. Meyral whirled the staff around, catching a few soldiers by surprise and knocking them back.

"Fool!" Sera screeched. "You'll continue to fight, even though your cowardly traitor of a father has already fled? You'll continue his fight, knowing that he started this war?"

A few grains of sand began to float and small rocks started to vibrate as the air around Leviathan Pass grew thick with electricity.

"This is your war, bitch!" Meyral shouted. "You attacked us, and you've taken *EVERYTHING!*" He lunged at Sera, but five soldiers wrapped themselves around him.

"Did *Daddy* never tell you what started this all?" Sera asked. "Did he never tell you that he murdered Emperor Erranko's wife, in cold blood, for no better reason than they were vacationing in the wrong spot? Did he never tell you that he bragged about it, even took the bloody sword into the Island Nations to gain some fame? No?" The look on her face was a crude imitation of pity.

Meyral's mouth worked furiously, but no sound came out. "Lies!" he finally managed to scream.

"Lies, you say? Then how could I have gotten this…?" Sera summoned a broadsword out of midair and held it out to Meyral. "Do you recognize it?"

Meyral immediately recognized the heavy, black hilt and the serrated edge. He'd seen it a million times before. "That…that's the sword that hangs above our fireplace. It was passed down—"

"Yes, it's Jaspar's. Now explain to me why I have it. Explain why it has the empress' blood on it!"

"No…no," Meyral muttered without conviction. "You must have taken that when you raided Berrywillow."

"If only that were so, dear boy." Sera shook her head sadly. "The truth is a hard thing to swallow, I know. It's never easy to hear that your father isn't the man you always thought he was." Her face darkened and she looked toward Alberto.

"YOU SON OF A BITCH!" the redhead yelled and leapt at the soldiers flanking him, making sure to land fists in each of their faces and send them flailing over the edge.

Still yelling, he sped toward Meyral in a reddish blur and body slammed him to the ground. In a flash of blue, Alberto and the Nordcross soldiers holding him were launched skyward. Alberto was hurled directly into the cliff overlooking the pass, causing a rockslide that buried the big man and sent large boulders careening across the small strip of road. A few carriages and a group of soldiers were smashed by the falling debris.

Meyral pushed himself off of the ground and tried to dodge the rubble, but he wasn't fast enough. A cluster of large rocks fell around him, and soon he was buried under the wreckage.

He tried to open his eyes, but he couldn't. He tried to scream, but his mouth was full of dirt. He struggled against the enormous weight crushing his body, but all he managed to do was cause the stones to shift slightly. He felt the life being crushed out of him and his mind started to cloud over.

Suddenly his vision exploded in a wave of blue, and he was taken to an unfamiliar forest in the dead of night. He heard rushing water and the unmistakable sounds of a struggle. He saw his hands…

Those hands aren't mine, it's not real!

…close around his father's sword. The gaudily dressed woman in front of him begged for her life, knee deep in water. Her words were lost in the confusion of the battle happening around Meyral, but he knew that whoever was holding that sword wouldn't be swayed. As the blade plunged itself into the blonde woman's body, over and over, Meyral's consciousness faded entirely.

* * *

Aldomein danced around the falling rubble. More than once she had to shove a soldier into the path of a boulder to get herself to safety. When the noise subsided and the dust settled, she slowly backed away from the chaos. Nordcross soldiers ran around in complete disarray. The few who had managed to keep their cool cautiously inspected the fallen debris that covered the boy.

A cracking sound reached her ears and she stopped in her tracks. The pile of rocks exploded upward, sending dust and pebbles all across the pass. Aldomein caught a glimpse of Sera as she dove for cover, and she was disturbed to find the blonde grinning the entire time.

Aldomein watched in awe as Meyral rose out of the newly created crater. A thick, azure aura surrounded him, and his eyes glowed like sapphires set in white marble. The staff seemed to pull him across the road toward Sera. He launched a small blue fireball at her, but she knocked it away with a weak flick of her wrist.

"You fool!" Sera shouted. "You have no idea the power you possess!"

Meyral didn't respond. Instead, he hurled lines of lighting at the Nordcross platoon. Aldomein watched as the battle quickly turned into a bloodbath. Her eyes were glued to Meyral's swift and deadly movements.

The lighting that came from the staff was unlike anything she had ever witnessed. When it struck a person, it cloaked them in a sphere of cobalt light. Their armor melted and flames quickly eradicated what was left of their flesh. The air seemed to be charged with pure power, and she felt fear for the first time in a long while.

Sera's guard whipped Aldomein's face, bringing her back from the edge of fright.

"Now, now, behave," Sera muttered. "My apologies, he's been a bit restless lately. But honestly Aldomein, I have a problem. You still won't join us, and you've done so much for me. I just can't risk you being…free."

With blood pouring down her face, Aldomein flipped backward over and over, avoiding each strike from the assassin. She flipped back one last time, then shot forward and stomped on the end of the chain-whip, ignoring the spike that drove into her heel. The assassin struggled to free his weapon as Aldomein snatched up the emperor. She held the blade of her axe to his neck and stared Sera down.

"Call him off, or your darling emperor loses his head," Aldomein said.

"You wouldn't dare!" Sera hissed.

"Try me. I got my payment. When I walk out of here, you'll never see me again. Let's not make this any messier than we need to."

There was a long, tense moment, and Aldomein was worried that Sera was considering killing them both. Then a blue bolt of lightning streaked by her head and she called off her assassin.

Aldomein backed away as Sera approached the emperor's body. She placed one hand on Erranko's neck and raised her free hand. She muttered something in an archaic language, and some of the blue aura surrounding Meyral was sucked into her hand.

"Kill the bitch!" she shouted to her assassin.

Before Aldomein could close the distance between them, a burst of green flame erupted around Sera and Erranko. A moment later, they were gone.

Aldomein continued to advance. She swung her axe at the assassin, but he knocked her weapon aside with a flick of his whip. As she recovered and tried to pull the axe back to her, he slashed her across the chest, tearing at her flesh and ripping away the top part of her brassiere.

"Lucky shot, asshole," she growled. "It won't happen again."

Drenched in her own blood, Aldomein dove, and in a flash her axe was back in her hands. She swung at the assassin, who barely dodged the attack. He whipped at her face, but she expected it. She ducked down and jabbed him in the gut with the blunt end of her weapon.

The man in black took the hit and turned it into a back flip, somehow still striking out with his whip. Aldomein had to cartwheel a few times to avoid his strikes. She stopped spinning and he stopped flipping, and the two circled each other, waiting for an opening.

The assassin lashed out again and the bounty hunter was able to block the whip with the broad side of her axe. He wrapped the whip around the axe handle and pulled with all his might, but Aldomein didn't budge.

Just like every other man she'd fought, he made the assumption that he was by nature stronger than her. She pulled her axe back with enough force to knock the assassin forward onto his stomach.

He tried to pull himself up, but Aldomein slashed down and chopped his right arm off just above the elbow. She was slightly unnerved that he still hadn't made a sound, but it didn't stop her. He reached toward his hip with his other arm, but his hand found no weapon.

"Looking for this?" she asked as she held up his chain-whip. "I believe I owe you a couple hits."

Using his own weapon against him, she whipped his face a few times, turning his black mask into a bloody, shredded rag. She hit him in the chest twice, then threw the whip onto his broken body. She turned and walked away, but she heard him rise to his feet.

"Not done yet?" she asked as she spun around. In a swift and precise motion, she sliced into his torso and tore him in half. "Good riddance."

An eerie silence settled on her and she looked up. What she found horrified her. The pass was filled with death, and the only person left alive was that kid…and he was walking toward her. She found herself rooted to the spot, despite the approaching whirlwind of chaos. A strange euphoria came over her and she felt an immense burst of adrenaline. A crash behind Meyral distracted the both of them, and Aldomein's sudden angst disappeared.

Alberto lunged out from under the rocks that had covered him, and he headed straight for the kid. Aldomein turned back to Meyral and watched as the blue in his eyes dimmed. In the confusion, the power that had overtaken him somehow stilled. Even so, he raised his staff automatically, ready to end the redhead for good.

* * *

Meyral heard something. He was still trapped between worlds, where sensations meant nothing, but he knew he heard a noise. The empty place reminded him of his visions, where his body had been reduced to nothing more than vapors, only this time it was more complete.

Then he remembered his time with Taryn under the almond tree. He stopped relying on his body and he focused his mind. Soon the noise became clear—it was Alberto yelling. His friend's voice was hoarse and angry, yet there was a deep sorrow in it as well. His voice became so loud that Meyral was sure Alberto was on top of him.

Finally Meyral was back in his own body. He could smell burnt flesh. He could taste the blood in his mouth. He could feel the tenderness in his muscles that told him bruises were already forming all over his body.

He heard Alberto's shouts and he saw his old friend clearly. Alberto was no longer a man overtaken by hatred—instead, Meyral saw the fearful, young face that he had known his whole life. Those eyes were the same emerald gems that cried over his mother's dead body, the same ones that cried over Chloe's grave.

The emotions he felt were enough to quell the unbridled power rising inside of him, and he lowered the staff. Alberto barreled past, oblivious to how close he had truly been to his own death.

With his friend safely behind him, Meyral regained more control of his body. He was suddenly gripped with intense pain, as if his skin had caught fire. His hands twitched uncontrollably and he saw that his right arm, up to his elbow, was already completely raw.

Fear stabbed at his heart, at his mind. His fear intensified when he realized the destruction all around him was his fault. Before he knew it, he'd left his body again and his mind was floating in a river of nothingness.

* * *

Alberto slammed into Aldomein and snatched her up onto his shoulders without stopping. The purple-haired huntress could do little more than stare as Meyral's eyes flashed that terrifying blue once again. Alberto didn't stop, and Aldomein was secretly grateful that he didn't have to watch his friend succumb to madness.

Only a few seconds after his eyes had changed, the staff pulled him into the sky. Meyral lunged left and then right as he fought some unknown force for control, and with each lunge came powerful shockwaves. Aldomein saw the strain on Meyral's face as he tried to pull the staff toward him, but it only took the kid higher into the night.

A wave of power washed over Aldomein, and it sent Alberto flying toward the ground headfirst. Aldomein rolled to a stop, and she could feel the land beneath her vibrating. She looked to Alberto and found his eyes already on her. They both lay bleeding on the ground, helpless and afraid.

Aldomein tried to push herself up from the ground, but something in the air had changed. It was as if she weighed ten times as much as she had only a few minutes before. She managed to raise her head high enough to look at Alberto again. He was lying flat on the ground and screaming, clearly as stuck as she was.

All around them, things started to swirl into the air. Before long, the night sky was crowded with boulders, crushed caravans, mutilated corpses, bits of broken blades, and chunks of melted armor.

The sapphire sent out a pulse of cerulean light that encased Meyral in a thin sphere. With each pulse, the bubble became thicker and thicker, until Aldomein could no longer see the poor kid.

* * *

Meyral felt a tingling sensation. It was the only thing he knew, the only thing he could sense in the realm of emptiness. It was the same sensation he had felt when he watched Kain demolish the Ardänian palace, except this time it was much stronger.

Moons be damned! I'm on the pass...Leviathan Pass. Alberto's in danger! Why can't I do anything?

Understanding crashed over Meyral like a wave. He was about to repeat the same mistake that his great-grandfather had made. He knew that his body was somewhere, instinctively fighting the staff, but he knew he would lose. He tried to focus all of his willpower on Alberto, on the love he felt for his friend. It worked before, and he prayed it would work again.

The fog that blanketed his mind began to lift. Meyral could see Alberto's terrified face and Aldomein silently screaming a few feet away from him. As he continued to focus, his mind cleared and he realized that he was high above the crumbling pass.

* * *

The blue light emanating from Meyral sent an odd sensation throughout Aldomein's body. Suddenly everything stopped and hung in midair for one second before crashing back to the ground. The pulsing light reversed and seemed to absorb all the power it had been letting off. Meyral dropped to the ground, clearly struggling, as the staff tried to pull him back up into the air.

The aura returned, but this time it was transparent. She watched as Meyral struggled to contain the dangerous power. Cobalt flames traveled up his arm and down his body, wrapping around his right side. He screamed in agony as the flames came to life and the staff rejected his attempts to quell its authority. She watched his skin peel back from his arm, and she couldn't bring herself to look away.

With one final burst of determination, the boy slammed the staff into the ground. An explosion rang out, and Aldomein was blinded by a bright light. When the light faded, Meyral was gone. Nothing but a wide patch of hot, glowing glass remained where he had stood only moments before.

The cliff above them rumbled and fell apart, spilling more debris onto the pass. Aldomein dragged a stunned and useless Alberto back as far as she could before the ledge gave way right in front of them. Massive boulders and chunks of rock fell into the sea, taking the busted wagons and dozens of corpses with them.

Alberto turned to Aldomein. He was pale and clearly shaken. They helped each other stand, finally free of the strange, paralyzing force. Alberto stared across the ocean as Aldomein leaned against his broad chest.

Earlier that night, almost sixty souls had occupied the pass. Now there were only two.

Silent tears ran down Alberto's face and dropped into Aldomein's dark purple hair as the two survivors held on to the last remaining traces of their lives.

Don't miss the next book in The Old Kingdom Ardänia
Series,
Shattered Memories!

Take a peek at what's in store…

CHAPTER ONE: SOLITUDE

Lars watched as a man in an old, dirty cloak pulled out another newspaper clipping and stared at it. He'd been at it since the bar had opened. He would pull article after article out of that ratty coat, read each once or twice, then shove them back in frustration.

Have I seen this guy in here before?

Lars dismissed the thought quickly. After getting stuck out in the desert, he'd seen hundreds of caravans come through. It had become difficult to tell who was hitchhiking and who was a veteran merchant. He reached down, grabbed a dirty glass, and began wiping it, lost in his thoughts.

This shitty tent could never pass for a real tavern. I would know! I used to have one of the best in all the Northern Federation. Wood paneling on the walls, a solid mahogany bar stocked with exotic drinks from as far south as anyone's been...even the rugs were Old Kingdom silk! And the chandeliers, oh, how I miss them.

"Barkeep," Lars' old friend slurred, "gimme a pint of your finest."

"Right," he muttered. "I could be selling you watered down piss and you wouldn't know the difference." Lars filled the glass he'd been cleaning and passed it to the drunk.

I guess I still have Karloff. It was his idea to move out here to this hell. Chanteclaire...what a pretty name for such a shitty place. You know, that drunk'll probably outlive me and be the only one at my grave. That kinda gives me chills.

As the bartender reached for another glass and continued to ponder his future, his eyes landed on his only employee. She had long, copper hair that was slung over one shoulder, trailing just above her breasts that threatened to explode out of her top. Her shirt was low in the back, and the ends of a tattoo were just visible between her shoulder blades—Lars knew from experience that it was a very intricate dreamcatcher.

I guess if I'm lucky, Karloff might not be the only one at my grave. I could die happy in Jasmin's arms...

The cloaked man rapped his knuckles on the bar and Lars was pulled from his musings. He poured a double shot of whiskey into the glass he'd been cleaning and slid it down the counter. The man in rags caught it with his left hand.

This guy is quickly replacing Karloff as my best customer. He's already on his second bottle today, and *he paid for three in advance...something Karloff's never done. Hell, if I really wanted to retire, I could just call in that old drunk's debt.*

"Hey, Lars, did ya hear that those Northern ber'crats knew we was gonna be invaded?"

"Karloff, don't be a jackass. They didn't know anything about it."

Karloff let out a hiccup and waved his hand in front of Lars. "Ya really t'ink three men and a woman could lay waste to two cities and all the Gates in one week? C'mon..."

"I heard there was a fourth man," a merchant called out from the nearest table.

"Right," Karloff wagged a finger, "but tha's still only five people."

Lars sighed and grabbed another glass. He knew enough to ignore drunks when they started babbling, especially Karloff and his half-baked conspiracy theories.

"Well, some of the Gates were caught up in the Paper Riots, you know..." a salt trader added as Lars looked back up.

"Don't matter, it was all a ruse." Karloff leaned forward, and Lars could smell the aroma of booze and smoke clinging to the drunk. "We're out in this blasted desert," he pointed around erratically, "in a damn sandstorm 'cause those damn ber'crats hired some damn merc'naries to take care o' them damn Gates!"

"My sister married a guy who kept talkin' about how corrupt he thought the government was," the salt trader said slowly. "It got her killed. Toward the end, they were talking about conspiracies and other crazy ideas...just like you."

"So wha' ya gonna do about it?" Karloff asked with a raised eyebrow.

Lars shook his head irritably. "Karloff, you know I don't tolerate fightin' in my bar. Anyone who has a problem with that can leave now."

The merchant and a couple others from his table stood up and slowly walked outside. He turned as he pulled the flap aside and said, "We'll be waiting for you."

A gust of wind, along with a sheet of fresh sand, blew through the bar as he left. Just before the flap closed, an old man bumped his way past the angry traders and entered.

"Oh yea?" Karloff shouted as he got up and made to follow them.

Lars reached forward, grabbed the back of Karloff's dirty tunic, and pulled him back into his seat. "Sit down," he said gruffly, "and have one on the house."

Karloff looked at him, and Lars could tell he had more to say. He opened his mouth, but instead of ranting, he filled it with beer. Lars scoffed and looked back at the tent flap. The old man still stood at the entrance, slowly looking around the bar.

Another new guy...

The newcomer wore dress pants and his shirt was clean. His plaid vest was red and purple, but his shoes were an awful shade of dark blue. Lars watched the new customer pull out a handkerchief, spit into it, then look inside the used napkin. He replaced it in his pocket and walked toward the bar.

Karloff stirred, but before he could spout out any more rants, the cloaked man rapped on the counter. Lars was more than grateful to have an excuse to walk away from his old friend.

I'd love to sneak a peek at who the hell my new best customer is...

Lars purposely undershot the drink so that the man would have to reach for it, then waited and watched as he stretched out his arm for the glass. The man's entire right hand was covered in thick, blackened scar tissue. Lars had seen some things back at Gate Five, like a man who had somehow survived being burned at the stake...but these scars were different.

Lines of cobalt shone through the torn flesh around his joints and knuckles. The scars on the back of his hand made a design like a swirl, and more fissures disappeared under his sleeve. The deepest of these cuts flashed more of that luminous blue. The scars wove their way along his blackened skin in some kind of pattern, but Lars turned away before he could distinguish it.

The cloaked man noticed Lars' gaze and he let out a slight chuckle. For the first time that day, he raised his glass high enough that he had to lift his chin from his chest. His hood and hair fell back, revealing a horribly scarred face that perfectly matched his hand.

Three burn-like slashes traveled from under his cloak and up the back of his neck. They each took out chunks of greasy hair and parts of his ear as they continued around his temple and up his face. The scars ended just above his right eye.

Lars shuddered and continued to stare.

The eye itself was solid white, with no pupil or iris to speak of. It was ringed by more of that burnt scar tissue, and its eyelid was completely missing. His staring, exposed eyeball made his features seem too large for a normal man's skull.

"…and so, it's really all connected. Leviathan Pass, the Gates, and why us merchants gotta roam the desert now."

"That's brilliant, Karloff…" Lars said in a bit of a daze.

When the bartender managed to steady himself, the man gave a slight scoff and pulled his hood back up. Then he reached out his gnarled hand and knocked on the bar, but the noise it made didn't sound quite right.

His eyes never left the man, and he spilled more booze onto the countertop than into the glass. He finally slid him the double, but the drink stopped short again. Lars groaned and readied himself for another look at the horror before him.

Shit…get a hold of yourself. You've seen worse…

The dirty man grunted and reached out with his right hand, blatantly shaking the sleeve back to give Lars a better look at his arm.

Maybe he's a soldier here to escort the convoys. Nordcross kept promising to send some.

He began to feel a little better.

Hell, I bet he's either undercover or off duty…even so, something about this guy makes me a bit uneasy. And it's not just the scars or his crazy eye.

"Excuse me, barkeep."

Lars happily pulled himself away and addressed the old geezer who'd just entered. "What do you want?" he asked.

"Name's Guillaume. I'm a miller by trade." Guillaume reached out his hand, but Lars didn't take it.

"Miller? Does it look like anything grows around here?"

"No, I guess not…" Guillaume trailed off. After a moment of silence, he added, "May I please have a sherry?"

Lars reached under the bar for a dusty bottle and poured the old-timer a glass. "That'll be two pieces."

"Would you take a small diamond in trade?" the old man asked as he fished a velvet pouch out of his vest.

"We only deal in gold out here," Lars said. "If I started bartering, I'd be up to my ass in goats and salt by the end of the week…so no."

"I get that a lot," Guillaume said with a frown as he pulled two gold coins out of the purse.

Lars bit one to make sure it was real as his new customer rambled on about some swamp, a mine, and how Nordcrossers don't appreciate fine jewels. He ignored most of the monologue and poured the man his sherry.

Guillaume took a sip before glancing around the bar appreciatively. "This is a lovely place," he mused.

"It's just a tent," Lars shot back.

"Well," the old man continued, "the town is quite quaint…"

"No, it isn't! The only reason anyone gives two squirts of piss about this burnt piece of land is the well."

"I guess water would be worth more than gold around here."

There was a long pause, and Lars got the feeling that the old man was thinking hard.

He wouldn't be the first to try to control that well. No quicker way to wind up dead out in the desert. Using free water to dilute booze, then sell it to parched merchants? Now that's *legitimate business.*

Guillaume took a longer drink this time, and the look on his face told Lars that he hadn't been in the desert long enough to forget how sherry should taste. He swallowed hard and set his glass a little farther away. "That's why I'm traveling out to the Western Frontier," he continued. "I hear there's all kinds of work out there, and a man can make himself a fortune if he's smart."

The dirty man slammed his fist on the bar and Lars walked away to pour another drink, thankful to leave the newest yahoo in a long line of yahoos still to come. Lars turned back to Karloff as he filled the glass, but the drunk had already, much to Lars' dismay, slid his way down the bar. He sat next to the cloaked man with his back to Lars.

"See, way I heard it…" Karloff paused with a dazed look on his face until a hiccup brought his mind back into focus. "My uncle, see he's one o' them higher-ups, he said Nordcross offered five times what them terr'ists' bounties were to be split 'tween the ber'crats."

The cloaked man stayed perfectly still and Guillaume mimicked him, both clearly listening to what the drunk had to say.

"Lars, m'boy," another hiccup took him by surprise, "ya mind…uh…wazzit…pourin' me anothurrr drinky poo?" Karloff's eyes were now set in completely opposite directions and the reddish blotches on his cheeks had spread to his entire face.

"Dammit, Karloff, you've had enough! I'm cutting you off before—"

"Lars, 'lax…I'm fine, ya dig?" The drunk mimed punching, but he fell over in the process. "Jess' like that," he said from his spot on the sandy ground.

"You dolt, you're gonna hit one of these support beams, and then the whole damn tent is gonna come down!" Lars shouted.

Guillaume offered Karloff a hand, and with the old man's help, he clumsily climbed his way back to a standing position and took a seat.

"T'anks, mister."

"Don't mention it. You said your uncle is from the North?" Guillaume asked. "I'm from the North too. What's his name? Maybe I knew him."

A greedy twinkle found its way to the old man's eyes, but Karloff didn't notice. He was too busy finishing the abandoned sherry for him. "His name is Irgoth, ya heard of 'im?"

Guillaume only smiled and shook his head.

Karloff nodded stupidly and looked back at the dirty man a few stools away. "The hell's your problem?" Another hiccup found its way out of his mouth. "You ain't said a word. I'm sure you got somethin' to say 'bout those terr'ists and…and all the shady shit…"

The man finished his drink as Karloff left Guillaume and stumbled back down the bar, smoothing out his frazzled mustache as he went. Lars made a motion to stop him, but the drunk waved him off. Karloff's eyes caught the words that the man had been carving into the wood with his fingernails:

Their numbers are few,
And stained in sin.

About the Author

Preston Robison was born and raised in the Central Valley of California. He received his Bachelor's degree in physics from the University of California, Santa Barbara. His previous jobs include small-time acting in L.A., farm work in Lancaster, security in Santa Barbara, and teaching in Bakersfield. For several years he worked at a zoo, where he became inspired to begin writing his first novel. Preston enjoys eighties hair metal, terrible horror movies, and almost any fried food.

Find him on Facebook, Tumblr, and Twitter:

www.facebook.com/prbison
www.prestonrobison.tumblr.com
www.twitter.com/prestonrobison

www.ingramcontent.com/pod-product-compliance
Lightning Source LLC
Chambersburg PA
CBHW072116250626
47159CB00007B/2465